DATE		

GOLDEN
COUNTRY

A Novel

JENNIFER GILMORE

SCRIBNER
New York London Toronto Sydney

SCRIBNER
1230 Avenue of the Americas
New York, NY 10020

SCRIBNER and design are trademarks of Macmillan Library Reference USA, Inc., used under license by Simon & Schuster, the publisher of this work.

For information regarding special discounts for bulk purchases, please contact Simon & Schuster Special Sales at 1-800-456-6798 or business@simonandschuster.com

DESIGNED BY KYOKO WATANABE
Set in Spectrum

Manufactured in the United States of America

1   3   5   7   9   10   8   6   4   2

Library of Congress Cataloging-in-Publication Data
Gilmore, Jennifer.
Golden country : a novel / Jennifer Gilmore.
p. cm.
1. Jewish families—Fiction. 2. Jewish fiction. 3. Domestic fiction. I. Title
PS3607.I4525G55 2006
813'.6—dc22   2005057586

ISBN-13: 978-0-7432-8863-7
ISBN-10: 0-7432-8863-7

For my grandparents:
Charlotte and Sidney, Maurice and Jane

He had listened from such a distance that what he saw was an outline, a caricature, and an abstraction. How different it might seem, if he had been able to see these lives from the inside, looking out.

—*Delmore Schwartz, "America! America!"*

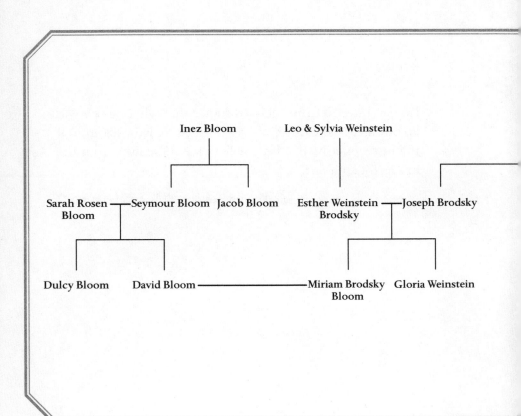

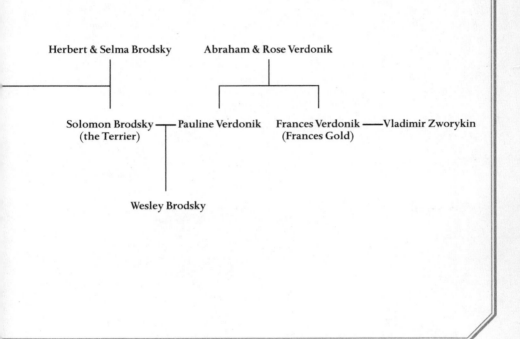

GOLDEN COUNTRY

Irving Berlin! 1957

IT WAS JOSEPH BRODSKY, the one person who had never caused any trouble, who did not want his daughter to marry David Bloom.

"I will not have my grandchildren brought up on filthy money," Joseph told his wife the evening after Miriam had called from New York with the news.

Married! Miriam had screamed so happily into the phone. Instantly Joseph remembered her, a girl in a yellow bathing suit on the dock by Sebago Lake, her hands on her hips. When had her bones grown into a woman's body? He imagined her limbs elongating before his eyes as if he were watching the time-lapse film of a flower blooming, a crystal forming: his daughter growing up and away from him.

Joseph had been readying for sleep before the phone call. Now, sitting on the edge of his bed, he paused a moment before removing his shoes. Then he set upright the milk carton he had taken to putting by the bed so he wouldn't have to get up to urinate so many times during the night. Joseph was beginning to feel the effects of age—the *real* effects, ones that seemed to rise up from that strange place deep within him where his faith was stored—and to refuse the marriage troubled him. He wanted to be sure his daughters were taken care of. But David Bloom? Of all the men on earth. He didn't know the boy well, it was true, but history is history. End of story.

"What are you talking about, Joe?" Esther sat at her vanity slathering her face with cold cream.

"Mob ties." Joseph nodded his head to emphasize the gravity of this statement. He thought of his own brother, the day he left Brooklyn for that gang of thugs and how his mother gave all of Solomon's belongings—his comic books, shirts, his telescope with the broken lens—to Henrietta Szold. For the Hadassah, his mother had said. And that woman had sent the package back—a clean cardboard box tied tightly with twine—without so much as a note.

"How do you know for sure?" Esther asked Joseph.

"I know because I know," he told her.

Only once had Joseph discussed Solomon, and that had been when he'd come home late from a terribly hard day on the long selling road. Frustrated by how little such a long day had yielded, Joseph walked in the door, drank three glasses of peach schnapps, told Esther the story, wept, and then tried unsuccessfully to undo his wife's bra in the kitchen.

"And how's that?" Esther watched in the mirror as her husband dipped his feet into his leather slippers. "For Christ's sake, Joe. Miriam can't be running around that city—single and loose in Manhattan— forever."

If only from the state of her daughter's bitten nails, Joseph knew that Esther was right. He could see that Miriam had anxieties. She'd been neurotic since she was a girl—once they'd had to drag her out of a child's bathtub filled with chemicals. Esther had found her in a ball, coiled as tightly as a pin curl. I'm getting clean, Miriam had said when questioned as to what on earth she had been doing. But what did that mean? My little girl, Joseph had thought when he was confronted with the image of that pink, raw body. And then the image much later, of the girl in New York, a brand-new nose hidden beneath seeping bandages. Her eyes were two bruises on the moon of that blanched, frightened face. This had been the only time Joseph had questioned his wife's intentions.

Miriam might have anxiety, but some of the Brodskys' friends' kids had been true problems. Ethel Cohen's daughter was institutionalized. Drugs, they'd said. Imagine. And Arthur Friedman's boy was a no-good drunk. No matter how Art tried, that boy was always showing up at his doorstep at all hours, inebriated. Joseph knew he had been blessed with two good girls, who had not given them a moment's real worry.

"I just know, Es." Joseph spoke softly, rubbing his head. "Please believe me." His scalp shone brightly, shiny as linoleum, through his thinning hair.

Esther turned away from the mirror to look directly at her husband, one arm hooked over the back of the chair. Her face was a mask of white, but for her eyes, black as ebony buttons, and her pink mouth, drawn up like a change purse. Even like this, like a snowman she looks, thought Joseph, she was a treasure to him.

"Whatever you say," Esther said. "Evidently he's not a gangster anymore. Now the man hangs around with Irving Berlin. Broadway, Joe." Esther paused, uncharacteristically hesitant about what she was about to say. She held her head high as she looked in the mirror. "Do you want your daughter to be one of those girls in that terrible city who gets a reputation as a tramp in her youth and as a lesbian in her old age? And that, mind you, is only if she ages *well*."

"Now come on, Esther," Joseph said. The previous day Esther had read him something about the problem of single girls in the city, from "Dear Maggie," the syndicated etiquette column that his wife and her friends phoned one another over daily. Especially since the war, Esther had read, pointing her chin toward Joseph, as if it had all been his fault. She's your daughter too, Joseph had told her.

Now Joseph turned away from his wife and to the window, the boughs of the evergreen at the side of the yard sagging with last night's snow. Beyond his yard and down the hill was Casco Bay, where last week Joseph had seen a seal at low tide. Looking up the habits of the harbor seal at the Portland library hours after the sighting, he had had to laugh at himself. How on earth did I get here? he had thought happily, knocking a pencil to the side of his head as he read about molting seasons.

Broadway, thought Joseph. Irving Berlin. Esther went down to New York City all the time now to see Miriam and catch a matinee, and Joseph knew this thrilled her. But Joseph, who'd had to be begged by his wife to move so far north, rarely liked to go back to New York. He liked the peace of his new little town, where he walked to the Penny Wise for milk, removing his hat for the neighbors he passed in the street. He liked his walks through the woods, stomping over moss and earth, the pleasant smell of pine, the call of the lighthouse that blinked in the distance through the fog.

The one time Esther had gone with Seymour and Sarah Bloom, she had come home chattering about the house seats and how the Blooms knew the very best places to eat on Broadway. When they came in from the street, a table by a window was waiting just for them, a flickering candle in its center. She made it clear to Joseph that though she didn't want to live anywhere else but Portland, dinner and a show in that beautiful, beckoning city was a perfect evening.

"Not just off zhe Mob," Joseph said. "Off a people like you and me." He slapped his chest. "Good people."

But Irving Berlin! Joseph got up from the bed, and Esther noticed he did so a bit wearily. He looked up to see his wife rub her own throbbing hands—she'd had to get her wedding ring loosened last month just so it could slide over the knuckles of her once-slender fingers—and clutch the bedpost to stand up. Joseph knew he was no longer the handsome and strong man Esther had once walked arm in arm with by the Charles in the late autumn afternoon, scarlet and mustard-colored leaves swish-swishing in the breeze. And he knew his wife had not planned on a man with a mother who spent most of her time on her cracked front stoop dreaming about Poland, a man whose speech would always betray them. And yet, here she was, still with him.

And Esther? She was no longer the slim girl he'd waited for on the stairwell in that boardinghouse in Cambridge, only to walk with her out into the street. Joseph had tried to make her feel that he would always be waiting for her. Slim. That had been before the kids and before the gallbladder had come out; before she couldn't stop with the cream cheese and jelly, with the damn Hershey's. Joseph could see her now, the young girl who left Portland, Maine, for Boston to work at Filene's Basement. The shoes! And the folding folding folding. She complained she would go mad from it and the way the women pushed their way through her just-folded clothes, snapping them open to check for irregularities.

"Irvink Berlin." Joseph leaned down to his wife. "It's true." He kissed her on the forehead, lingering for a moment to feel the mentholated smell of her cold cream traveling up his nostrils and into his sinuses. When he took his mouth from her face, his mouth was a ring of white and Esther's forehead was marked with the impression of his lips.

"Nowhere could you have that happy feeling when you aren't stealing that extra bow," sang Esther, slightly off-key as always.

My Irving Berlin is different, thought Joseph. "From the mountains to the prairies to the ocean," he sang to himself. "My home sweet home." He had been born a million miles away. But this country had been good to him, and though his mother would raise her fist from her new apartment on Riverside Drive and spit on him to hear it, it was true.

"And such a nice family," Esther said of the Blooms. "*Very* intellectual." She wiped the cold cream from her face.

"They *are* nice," Joseph said again. "Western European." He shook his head as he said this, remembering his neighborhood, block upon block of Eastern Europeans, and how they all longed to be from music, and art, from the land where they drank tea out of the most delicate of china cups. He was walking toward the bathroom. That side of Europe, they had the culture, it's true, he thought, one really can't deny it. And Miriam is in love. But the past. The past.

At the threshold of their bedroom, he turned. "It's a good match?" he asked his wife.

"It's a good match, Joe," Esther said, nodding her head slowly.

Joseph blocked the idea of his daughter's future father-in-law at the "right" end of a gun. Perhaps all the rumors of Seymour's involvement with Solomon had not been true, he reasoned. Perhaps Seymour, thanks to his exceptionally good fortune and his high profile on Broadway, was only a victim of bad publicity.

Walking down the hallway to the bathroom, Joseph whistled "God Bless America." Maybe Mr. Berlin will be at the wedding, he thought. What would I say if I were to meet him? Tell him: our lives are parallel fairy tales. Or perhaps I should prepare a rhyming greeting. Joseph had begun to devise a limerick to make Irving Berlin smile when, upon reaching the bathroom, the image of his brother overwhelmed him.

Bangbangbangbang went his heart. Only it wasn't love now, as when he saw Esther laughing for the very first time. Who cared she'd laughed at him as his hat spun away into traffic? This was an age-old grief, and for a moment Joseph thought the pain of it would split him in half. His brother. It was unbearable how he missed Solomon. Solomon, who'd left South Fifth Street and come back with more money than God. Joseph remembered the kids pitching pennies on the cracked sidewalk and a horse-drawn ice wagon knocking by as Solomon walked the block in a purple suit that shone when the smallest crease caught the light. Even from here, Joseph could see the Williamsburg Bridge rising out of the East River, tethering his neighborhood to the world.

Sol came in throwing cash from his enormous wads of bills clasped in silver clips, and their mother screamed and ran from it. Joseph laughed now to remember his mother trying not to step in the horse manure on the street as she ran from Solomon's money. Selma Brodsky had told Joseph that her elder son's dirty money would scald them both, that their skin would burn as if from acid and would shrink back from their bands of muscle, and what, then, would people see? Joseph had wondered then about his mother's insides, saddened, ruled by fear. His insides? Hope.

As a boy, Joseph had followed his older brother down the street, crowded with horses and carts and boys playing stickball, on the way to Mr. Berkowitz's candy store: Wait for me! he'd called out to him. Solly! he'd screamed. And then, just as soon as it had come, the memory was gone again and Joseph was left gripping the cold, clean marble of the counter.

Joseph splashed cold water on his face and looked into the mirror, shaking the image of his mother screeching like a dying animal as she tried to dodge Solomon's money. Destroyed, she'd say in Yiddish. *Mekhule.* That was when Joseph had decided he would work hard for money so clean his mother could wrap a baby—his someday—in the bills he would earn for her. And he had.

"Joe?" Esther screamed from the bedroom. "Are you coming to bed?"

"In a moment," Joseph said, staring into the glass.

CHAPTER 2

Chemistry: Joseph Brodsky,
1925–1938

MIRIAM WAS GETTING MARRIED.

"Finally," Esther said to him when they had resolved it for good. "Thank God. After all, she is already twenty-six years old."

Joseph too was struck by how quickly it had all gone by. How long ago had he and Esther sat holding hands in the taxi rushing to the hospital only to wait and wait for the arrival of their first girl? Nothing had been easy then. 1931. Even to clean was difficult. Back then, Joseph was a door-to-door salesman—he sold soap and cleansers to offices and petrol stations, hospitals and cafeterias, sometimes even to the women in the neighborhoods in between. The housewives would come to the door wiping their hands on their dirty aprons. In the late twenties and early thirties, there was not yet a detergent miscible in both oil and water—cleaning was a multistage process—and so Joseph was forced to carry many bottles, clanking his way from institution to institution with both petroleum solvent and plain old soap.

That was how he'd met Esther. He had moved up to Boston from New York, in part to escape the shadow of his brother, in part to run away from the burden of his father, Herbert Brodsky, who walked from the city over the Williamsburg Bridge, returning each night to a street that Joseph would always remember as filled with weeping. Also dodging shadows, the low, unstable darkness of her mother, Esther had come south to work in Boston after her father, an attorney at the only Jewish law firm in Portland, Maine, had died. One day in 1926, Joseph watched as Esther slammed the door of the taxi and stared up into the sun, her hand shielding her eyes. A red silk scarf covered her head, and, as she craned her neck to look up at the house she was to live in, the scarf slid down to her shoulders, revealing her shining, auburn hair. Joseph ran downstairs to help her with her bags and into her room in the building they would share.

"Thank you," Esther said. Her dark eyes shone as she pressed a coin into Joseph's palm.

"No." He laughed. "I don't vork here. I live here too," he said. "Downstairs."

"Oh." Esther looked at him, confused. She had told her mother this would be a house of women. "Well, thank you for your help then."

Joseph dropped the coin in Esther's hand, the tips of his fingers brushing her palm. Esther smiled at Joseph as she pushed the door shut and left him alone in the hallway.

Years later, when they would go to Coney Island and slip into the gypsy's dark tent, thick with incense, the fortune-teller would grab Esther's hand and smile as she traced her long life line with her dirty fingers. A long life, she'd tell them. A happy life.

Though Esther Weinstein would not so much as speak to him, Joseph took to her immediately. Something about her manner made him feel completely comfortable and yet entirely disarmed. Esther was both familiar and distant, and for this his love filled him up and spilled over. Yet she resisted his overtures. Did she still believe he was the bellhop? he wondered. No matter how Joseph smiled at her on the stairwell of the building, no matter how he waited for her, hat in his hands, outside on the cobblestone street, she refused him.

"Hello, Miss Weinstein." Joseph was careful to pronounce the W that began her name as he'd try to fall into step beside her when she left the building to walk along the Charles. He wanted to reach out and touch her dark hair, gleaming red in the sun.

"Mr. Brodsky," Esther would say, nodding, her eyes fixed on a destination far in front of her.

Why? Joseph wondered if it was how he spoke. From his conversations with Mrs. Steinway, the landlady, Joseph gathered that Esther was well-off. The daughter of an attorney, Mrs. Steinway had said, wagging her finger at Joseph. Recently deceased, she whispered so loudly she may as well have screamed it.

No matter what Joseph said or how he tried to woo her, Esther could not be swayed. Still, he would sometimes catch her watching him from the parlor as he helped Mrs. Steinway bring the groceries in from the cold street, and once he was sure he saw the dark-haired beauty pull the curtains back from the window as he made his way down the street one twilit evening.

Is it me? Joseph wondered, looking closely into the mirror that hung above the bare dresser of his room. How rarely he had truly seen his face. He looked at his long and slender nose, as bumpy as a spine and curved at the widened tip; he ran his hands over his hair, already thinning. Well, Rudolph Valentino I'm not, that's for sure. Joseph leaned in for a closer look and knocked himself right on the nose.

Whatever it was Joseph Brodsky did to make Esther Weinstein relent and marry him would remain a mystery to him. Eventually she had acquiesced to an afternoon of scones and Devonshire cream at the Parker House Hotel. And on some crisp, still mornings, he had caught Esther, and she had let him guide her over the bridge, fog rising off the Charles as boys cut the still water with their oars, crewing up and down the river. Somehow he had charmed her.

Esther's mother taunted her, a crackling voice from a dark bedroom, telling her daughter how she was marrying down, yet Esther managed to ignore it. As did Joseph, who heard Sylvia Weinstein scream, Better you should marry a shoemaker! the day they traveled up to Portland so that he could ask Sylvia for her daughter's hand. Despite this familiar voice of doom that had haunted Esther's childhood, Esther and Joseph were married on May 21, 1927, the day Lindbergh flew across the Atlantic. If only your father could see this! Sylvia screamed out just as soon as Joseph had crushed the glass. Misunderstanding the outburst, the guests looked skyward, into the sun, to see if they could see the *Spirit of St. Louis* fly by.

❧

Three years after they were married, four years of Joseph's many days on the road juggling his bottles and boxes, four years of his returning, his hat knocked sideways on his balding head, four years of being met by Esther's sheer delight in seeing him again, Miriam Weinstein Brodsky was born in Boston.

When Miriam was still in the womb but beginning to rip her mother open like a loaf of hot bread, the doctor said, "There it is! She's crowning!"

Joseph was in the waiting room when he heard the screaming from his wife. The doctors had warned him off being at the hospital, and yet he had wanted to be there. Joseph looked around and then tiptoed to the delivery room, pressing his ear to the door and imagining Esther closing her eyes against the pain. What must she be thinking? He wondered if his wife was experiencing what he'd heard dying was like—all the images of your life flashing before you. Did Esther think of her father walking through town with her, holding her hand as they wove along the harbor? Did she think of Joseph, bowing to her in the stairwell of their building as he told her, Ladies first?

"Oh my God," Esther said, clearly contracting. "I feel a nose!" she said.

Joseph took his ear from the door and inserted his index finger in an attempt to clean his ear from whatever would have made him hear something so strange.

"Okay, push!" the doctor said. "There it is," he said. "A head!"

"Doctor!" Esther pleaded. "What's her *nose* like?"

Surely there is more to see than this, Joseph thought nervously. For a moment he imagined his daughter's body attached not to a head but to an enormous schnoz. He couldn't help himself, and he cracked open the door just to see what was going on. He was met with a view that was the very reason men stay home on days like this. The obstetrician looked up from between Esther Brodsky's legs, also seeming to question the new mother's choice of words and then, thinking he had heard her incorrectly, went back to the labor at hand.

"Doctor!" Esther said again. "Just tell me. Is it very, very big?"

Her head? Her heart? Joseph thought. No, my wife just said *nose*.

After the umbilical was cut, the infant placed in the safety of Esther's arms, and Joseph pulled inside the swinging blue doors, he got his first glimpse at his daughter. My daughter! It was remarkable. He wanted to recall something that would help him be a good father to her, but he could remember only boys, a block packed with angry young men trolling the neighborhood with his brother. I will always protect her, Joseph thought, tilting his head to have a better look at Miriam.

When the nurse left the room and it was just the three of them, the young family together for the first time, Esther turned to Joseph with tears in her eyes. "Look what you did!" she told him.

"Vhat, Esther?" he asked, by now used to his wife's hormones, which he had hoped had managed to slip out of her with the placenta.

Esther pointed at her daughter's face.

She was beautiful. Had anyone ever been so lovely and so small? "A little loaf of bread," Joseph said, reaching his finger for her tiny mouth, which was already gathered into a kiss.

"Her nose!" Esther whispered, as if it were an unspeakable disease. "Look at her nose. I knew it," she screamed. "I knew I should never have married you!"

Though it was true, the nose was not the most delicate feature on his daughter's face, Joseph was stunned by Esther's charge and had a flashing memory of her walking ahead of him on a street filled with long, skinny trees, branches like the fingers of the gnarled women he'd grown up watching. He remembered the smooth cobblestones he'd stumbled over to get nearer to her as she walked away from him.

"Esther," Joseph said, straightening. "Her nose is fine."

"Fine?" she asked him, beginning to cry. "You'll see fine," she said. She pointed to her own face. "Fine like this? Fine like a cabbage?"

Joseph touched his wife's large nose. "Beautiful like this," he said.

Esther swatted his hand away. "And I'd like to see *you* be ripped in half by a nose," she said. "They've had to sew me up from it!"

Joseph rubbed his wife's arm and pulled the impossibly soft swaddling blanket back to see his daughter's beautiful eyes, still midnight blue. Who in his family had blue eyes? Never had he seen it. "I'm sorry, my love," he said, unsure to which girl he was speaking.

"Let me tell you what you've done. I should know. I spent my life with my perfect cousin Tillie, a nose like a rosebud on her valentine of a face. Her life was all the easier for it, I tell you," Esther said. "Everyone loved Tillie."

"And you," Joseph told her. "At least I did."

"All the boys," she said. "It was because of that nose. Well, and the boobs. And the legs that started right about below her boobs." She started to laugh.

Joseph watched his wife's expression cloud over once again.

"Torn in half!" Esther sobbed. "By a nose!" she said, as Joseph placed his lips to his wife's eyes to try to kiss away her tears.

Miriam's nose informed her childhood and Esther's motherhood. Nightly Esther came into her bedroom to measure the growing protrusion in the center of her daughter's face. From Joseph, Miriam had inherited length, and her nose crept slowly and bumpily down her face. But Essie's contribution of girth began between her eyes and ended where the nose flowered into a round bulb. Esther tried to outwit her daughter's nose, challenging its dominance in a manner similar to the Chinese practice of binding girls' feet.

"You will never feel the way I felt," Esther would tell her as she pressed the nose down and drew a piece of tape tightly around her daughter's head. "I promise you, Miriam, you will thank me later."

I don't think so, Miriam thought as she was forced to push up at her nostrils with the tips of her fingers in a series of daily exercises in order to stop the way the nose seemed to continue growing, curling in on itself at the bottom. Now breathe! Esther would tell Miriam. Through your teeth!

Nights when he was not on the road selling, Joseph watched as his wife tried to stop the expansion of his daughter's nose. How was he to explain to his first girl that Esther could not be stopped, that she was driven by childhood? But weren't we all? Really, Joseph reasoned, this was a gift from mother to daughter, and he convinced himself that one day, when she was old enough to understand what it meant to be beautiful in this country, Miriam would appreciate her mother's efforts to reduce the size of her nose, thereby increasing the quality of her life.

Joseph Brodsky's elder daughter's nose had not stopped growing six years later, when Esther gave birth to another girl, Gloria. Either because her nose was smaller than her sister's or because Esther was so stretched from Miriam's nosing her way into the world, this second birth was not as traumatizing. Or perhaps it was because even larger things were causing the Brodskys distress: Joseph's brother was rotting in jail. In Europe, Germany, now allied with Italy, was assisting the Spanish nationalists. And just this month, Buchenwald had opened to house professional criminals.

"Next it's zhe Jews," Joseph told Esther. "I kid you not."

"Don't be silly," Esther said. "Never. Not in a million years."

Joseph snorted.

He spent more and more time on the road, terrified that one day all that was going on in the world would be cause for everything here to be taken. He cried when he read Guernica was destroyed.

"What is it, my darling?" Esther asked him, one breast flapping, loosed from her brassiere, Gloria wrapped up in her arms. She'd been begging her daughter to nurse. Please, Gloria, she'd said, thrusting her nipple at her. Take it already. Just take it, she'd said, shaking her breast at the infant. That was the moment that Miriam peered in to see what was going on with her new sister, this Gloria, who was getting all the attention that had once been hers. Just as Miriam dipped her head over her sister's, she was squirted in the face with her mother's breast milk and ran out of the room, shrieking.

"What's the matter, Joe?" Esther asked her husband.

"An entire city," Joseph said. "Destroyed. What will become of us?"

Despite extra time on the road, Joseph wasn't able to sell much—people were too panicked to buy a thing.

The spring day in 1937 when he went to try to sell next door, to the Silverses' house, was one of the best days and one of the worst days of Joseph Brodsky's life.

It began as a particularly bad day on the road. Some schmuck at Chebra Gemilath Chesed Burial Society had even gone so far as to turn Joseph away at the door. "You think I can afford to clean?" the man had asked him. He had not even been wearing a yarmulke.

"But you must clean up after the dead!" Joseph was horrified.

"These are tough times, mister," he'd said, slamming the door.

Had he been a different man, Joseph might have wedged his foot in and tried to explain that cleaning was a necessity—like food, as important as water, shelter—not at all an extravagance. One must remove the dirt from the graves, he could have told the man. But he was tired tonight. Exhausted.

Joseph knew that the man had been right; these were tough times. When had it been easy? Almost a decade before had been the Panic. No one would buy a thing. Now the war had created such a shortage of soap that the price—four cents a bar—seemed outrageous, even to his most steady clients.

And so, as Joseph got out of the car that night in front of the Roxbury home he had to work so hard to be able to rent, he decided to make one more stop at the neighbors' to try to unload just a little bit of product.

Evening soaked up the street as Joseph headed to the Silverses' house, three doors down from where he and Esther and his two girls lived. When he rang, Mrs. Silvers came to the door, untying her apron.

"Hello, Mrs. Silvers," he said. "Evenink."

"Mr. Brodsky," she said, smiling. "Good evening." She folded her apron in perfect quarters.

Forever plagued by migraines, Esther had sent her daughter over to the Silverses'—For the love of God, Miriam, go to Janie's house already! she'd said from her bedroom, the curtains pulled closed—and Miriam and Janie sat upstairs playing tea until Joseph rang the doorbell.

Mrs. Silvers turned to get Miriam, but seeing Joseph's valises, his hat in his hands, she must have sensed that there was something else on his mind.

"Please come in," she said.

Joseph bowed toward her and picked up his suitcases.

Then, out of the corner of his eye, Joseph saw Miriam leaning over the banister with her friend. He hadn't known she was there or he would not have made the stop.

"I know you are busy." Slowly, Joseph bent to open his suitcase. "I see how you work, me too, Mrs. Silvers, but look what I have here.

Zhese"—he held up some glass bottles to the light—"zhey will save you so much time."

Joseph could see his daughter's disappointed face as he stood to hand Mrs. Silvers the bottles. Why does my daughter look down on me this way? he thought.

Now Mrs. Silvers placed her apron on the stairwell and reached for the bottle he handed her. She slid her glasses down her nose. As she read the embossed, illegible words on the raised glass, Joseph waited, looking around the room.

"Let me show you," he said. "It vorks like a dream, Mrs. Silvers. Really a dream. First zhis, then zhis, and you have yourself a clean kitchen. My own mother uses zhis process." He saw his mother, Selma Brodsky, sweeping the front stoop where he grew up, a useless act. Like desert sand and tumbleweed, the city grime built up again within minutes. It broke his heart to think of his mother's endless sweeping. "Can we try it in zhe kitchen?" Joseph started walking toward the kitchen and out of his daughter's range of vision.

Mrs. Silvers bought a bottle and a jar from Joseph that night, and he knew it was not out of sympathy but because she could see from his demonstration how much she needed those products and how much they would help her with her work, which, when it came right down to it, no one really appreciated. Certainly not Mr. Silvers. She'd told Joseph how he'd come in from outside and stomp through the house in his muddy rubbers. Joseph Brodsky had really conveyed his passion for getting a surface clean.

Joseph pretended he had not seen his daughter, opened the door, and walked out into the night alone. It was late April and the air was a bit brisk, an evening filled with hope. Soon Miriam would be catching fireflies in Franklin Park, just across the street. He remembered last year: he and his daughter capturing the lightning bugs in their cupped hands, the small whisper of those wings, a concession to their palms. Joseph would help Miriam put them in jam jars, the tops pounded with holes for air, and the fireflies would blink like crazy, a halo of light around the jar created out of their fear. It almost made Joseph forget the way he saw his daughter look at him tonight.

She had not run to greet him, and he had seen her looking down at him from her friend's stairwell. He thought of when his daughter was born, how he and Esther took Miriam to see his parents in Brooklyn and Joseph had looked north to see the lights clicking on in the Chrysler Building. That year they opened the Empire State, and he always associated the magnificence of that building with Miriam: the year his daughter was born was the year the tallest building in the world was built. The following year the Empire State would also be filled with light. Maybe I'm in the wrong business, Joseph would think. And he thought that now.

When had he not known Miriam's presence? From infancy there was a smell to her that connected to his very cells. His cells were joined with her cells, and whenever they were near each other, in every room of the house, Joseph could sense his daughter. As she grew into a girl—little worms to fingers, rings of fat to skinny legs: ankles, knees, and thighs—his sense of her also grew. He felt her watching him, and already he knew that gaze was beginning to change. What would it turn into as she grew into a teenager?

Joseph wanted to ask his daughter something: Why you look so ashamed? he wanted to scream up to her. It was the only time in his life he had ever thought of violence. His parents barely spoke English. They were forced out of Russia, and they believed they were going to a place where gold lined the streets, where gold was in the trees, as easy to pick—for anyone!—as apples. Such lies. Nothing is easy, even the simplest of things: this job as a salesman had once been difficult to attain. And with what had Herbert and Selma Brodsky ended up? A tenement in Williamsburg beneath the Elevated. They practically lived under a bridge, like that troll in the Brothers Grimm. His older brother had become a regular thug. I have shelter and a family, he had thought as he knocked at the Silverses' door.

Joseph had not known it could be much better than those days, though he could have done without the sore feet and so much time on the road. How he missed Esther. He only wanted to hear her scream his name in exasperation. He wanted to pull into the driveway and see his daughter playing in the yard with the other children of the neighborhood. Irish, Catholics—even though as a child he had once fought with these brutes, he liked that there were different kinds of people in

Roxbury and that his daughter would not be raised in the narrow manner in which he had been, his mother's face gone vacant over Friday's candles, his father with his leather tefillin wrapped around his bicep, shaking him into prayer. In the old way, his family would not be able to worship together, and often Joseph would think of the idea of Esther and his girls so far away from him on the holiest of days.

There was a set of swings in Franklin Park, and, walking home that evening, Joseph thought of Miriam's little-girl legs reaching out, pumping at the air to carry her upward. This was all he had wanted. You don't know shame. He had looked up the staircase and wanted to slap her.

This, Daddy, this, she had said to him on many evenings as she climbed into his lap. Her tiny fingers pulled his tongue from its red cave. Say it right! she would tell him, and her voice stunned him with its demand and its confidence. And he had thought of Solomon then, how his brother had traded in his Russian accent for the absurd language of American gangsters as soon as he'd left Brooklyn. Who was kidding whom? Joseph wondered.

But by the time he'd gotten two doors down, as he approached his own house, his anger had dissipated. Joseph was thinking only about what was in front of him: Esther's eyes illuminated by candlelight, Gloria's pudgy fingers, a good meal on the table, and Miriam's questioning. She's just a girl, he thought. Perhaps this is the new American way.

That night, while the Brodsky family listened to Baby Snooks on the radio in the living room, Miriam crept downstairs into the basement, where her father spent hours mixing chemicals as he worked to find a cleaner that would work on both oil and water. How much easier to carry one product instead of two. You'll see, he told his daughters as they watched him formulating late into the night. We'll be rich!

Miriam hadn't believed him. She was too young to understand that in America, anyone's fortune could change, too young to know there was a side to her father that was not content to beg. From the basement she could hear the laughter on the show, the grown lady's voice lowered and heightened into a baby's voice as she ran her fingers over the different glass bottles—amber, blue, clear—all corked and lined up perfectly, powders in clear glass jars, slivers of soap in neat piles on the old wooden table. She thought of watching her father from the stairwell that day, his wilting face, all his features collapsed. This, she reasoned, was why fathers went away to work and why their daughters never saw the things they did there. Miriam imagined twilight in their neighborhood, car doors slamming shut, men in hats walking up stairs to their homes, briefcases held tight to their sides.

There were stacks of notebooks, and Miriam opened one to see her father's scrawl, tiny pencil marks of numbers and foreign names. Below the worktable where her father stood each weekend, struggling for a solution that would change their lives, Miriam spotted the bathtub that had been used to bathe her as an infant. She curled her toes at the sight of the bath, her bare feet cold on the cement of the basement floor. Had she ever been so tiny? As Miriam had watched her father that afternoon, she had felt sure she was covered in a film of dirt. She had felt it on her skin, had rubbed her arms with the palms of her hands, run her hands across her face over and over again, brushing off invisible insects.

"Is there something on me?" she'd asked Janie.

Janie had looked closely into her friend's face. She had tilted her head. "I think there is," she'd said. Janie had swiped her finger over Miriam's face as she squeezed her eyes tight.

Now Miriam lifted the tub, which smelled of disinfectant and alcohol and clay, as if nothing could shame it, out from under the table.

Miriam, only six years old, wanted to be an infant again, a loaf of bread in her father's arms, wrapped in a blanket and tickled on the chin by her mother. She did not want a brand-new sister. She did not want her mother to tie back her nose and send her out of the house. Miriam wanted to know what now seemed unbearable: where her father went all day. Uncorking bottles on her father's worktable, she began pouring them into the bath. Crouched down, she spooned out heaps and heaps of powder, combining it with different liquids until the mixture was so thick that she had to add more. Just last week she had made a cake with Esther, and she had mixed in the flour with a wooden spoon. Only this was man's work. This is what it feels like to make something important, Miriam thought, imagining her intent father, his spectacles slid down to the end of his nose, suspenders hanging lifeless at his sides, shirtsleeves rolled up to the elbows. She added and poured until the bath was filled with solution.

Fully clothed, Miriam stepped in. As if it were filled with steaming water, she slowly lowered herself into the vat of chemicals. The fluid surrounded her, swishing over the curved rim and running onto the floor. She noticed how it tapered into a thin line, leaving in its wake a trail of white on the cement. Miriam thought of her father scrubbing another family's floor. Then she curled into a little ball, her body as tight as a fist, and lay down.

●

Miriam awoke to the startling and all too familiar sound of Esther's screaming. "What on *earth*?" Esther placed her hand over her mouth and yelled for her husband. "Joe?" she screamed. "Joe!" Esther yanked Miriam, who had passed out from the fumes, out of the bathtub and rushed her into the workshop bathroom, where she thrust her head under cold water.

Joseph stood breathless at the threshold. "Vhat happened?" He could see Miriam's arms and feet were bright red. "Sugar?" he said. "Vhat happened, sugar?" he asked Miriam.

Miriam looked over at her father, her mouth contorted by her enormous, quivering frown. She shook her head.

"What in the world were you thinking, Miriam?" Esther pulled her daughter's arms up and slipped the shirt from her head. Under the shirt, the flesh was pristine, and Joseph was sure he could see beneath it to the thumping of his daughter's tiny blue heart. Esther wet down the hand towels—nice ones, which Joseph knew she would rather not have ruined—and rubbed Miriam's arms. Her skin looked raw, as if layer upon layer had been peeled away.

Miriam shrugged.

Joseph remembered her looking at him from the stairwell and saw the apology on her skin. He regretted wishing violence on her. "Let's get you into zhe bath, sugar," he said.

Joseph picked up his daughter and held her. He smelled the salt on her face from her tears, and the ammonia and glycerin and alcohol. Her own scent had been scrubbed away, stripped by cleansers, covered over by fragrance, and this terrified him. Had she been trying to escape him so soon?

As Joseph carried her up the stairs, Miriam remembered being lifted by her father from the backseat of the car on the many nights they had driven home from visiting her grandparents in New York, or after a day at Old Orchard Beach. He would pick her up out of the dark, walk her slowly upstairs, and place her head gently on her pillow. From her bed she could see out to the backyard, and, as her father put her down, Miriam always wondered what would be out there for her when she was too big to be lifted. What was in that mysterious black world? Joseph would leave the door just enough ajar so that the hallway light was a bright rectangle into which, if she needed, Miriam could rise and disappear.

Tonight Joseph brought his daughter up two flights of stairs from the basement and into the bathroom. She clung to him, her legs wrapped around his waist, her arms gripping his neck. He had to peel her off to set her into the tub.

As Esther washed Miriam, Joseph went downstairs to check on Gloria. Not a month ago, one of Esther's friends had gone to check on her own daughter and found a snake sleeping in her child's crib. That was an image that neither Joseph nor Esther could shake, and they often found themselves in Gloria's room five, seven times an evening, feeling under her warm blankets for reptiles. Tonight, like every night, she seemed fine, her light hair—sure to darken, Esther warned her husband, as all the hirsute Brodskys were wont to do—spread out on her pillow like a sunflower.

Afterward, Joseph went down to the basement. He wanted a moment alone, to clean up Miriam's mess, to right the thrown-open pages of his notebooks, the uncorked bottles, the powders spread like confectioners' sugar over his workstation. Joseph did not want to think of his daughter scouring herself in a mess of solvents and chemicals. Instead, he focused on what he always focused on: finding a cleanser miscible in both oil and water. It was his mission, a physical mantra, and now he emptied the bath in the chemical sink, and, after a quick look at the previous day's notes, he began to mix. He added from a bottle here, some fragrance there, heaped in more powder. Each time was about to be the time it happened, and Joseph made notations as he went.

He tested the concoction on the schmaltz from last night's dinner. He knocked his pen against his head. He clicked his teeth with his fingernails and then added more soap. He tested it again. And that's when it happened. In that moment, magic: a synthesizing of solvents which in that exact moment became soluble. Joseph could tell—simply to take the cloth and swipe it over the chicken fat dissolved it. It was what is beautiful and knowable about science, and Joseph was sure he could see the particles breaking down, little cleansing bubbles rooting out the grease. He imagined them with tiny scrubbing hands, scouring the soiled fabric. Joseph was positive. He'd found his cleanser.

And he was right.

The day Miriam tried to wash herself away was the day that Joseph Brodsky discovered the first two-in-one cleaning product. He would name it for his wife. He had already thought it out—yes, to name some*one* after a living being, well, this is a horrible curse, but a *thing,* well, Joseph decided he would not be jeopardizing Esther's life were he to call his new product Essoil. Joseph would bring Esther into every home, every synagogue, every hospital. Esther. Esther at work, her particles connecting with grime and overpowering it; Esther ensuring that no surface be left impure.

That night, after both Miriam and Esther were asleep and Joseph had washed up and checked Gloria's crib for snakes a third time, he crawled into his bed, parallel to his wife's. He had met a man on the road years ago who told him: Young man, get off the road before the sand settles permanently in your shoes. What exactly had that meant?

Joseph had met him before the Panic—who could have known how desperate everyone would be to sell something? Anything. How many towns did Joseph have to drive through before coming home to Esther? In winter, his hands cracked; in summer, they sweated. Already he had the hard touch of an old man. Joseph had nodded at the man and thought to himself: Getting off the road is an easy thing to say, yes, but not so easy a thing to do. When he let himself think about it, he could see that perhaps getting off the road was a dream, one that was even more important to him than the dream of his family.

Joseph could not have known what the birth of Essoil would bring him. But he was excited by his creation and couldn't sleep. He got out of bed and tiptoed down the hallway to the study he shared with

Esther. Their two desks faced each other, and often, as Esther paid the household bills and Joseph kept track of his commissions, they would look up and find themselves staring at each other. Try as he might, Joseph could never keep a straight face. The sight of Esther, hair pulled into a net, her long nose nearly connected to the red lips set against her tanned skin, always made him smile. Hello, my love, he'd say to her.

Esther would wave his words away with a flick of her wrist and a roll of her large brown eyes, but one side of her mouth could not help but reveal the smile always there beneath her surface.

Now Joseph took out a slip of writing paper and sat back in his chair. He clicked a fountain pen against his teeth as he thought of what he would like to say to his brother:

April 26, 1937

Solomon,

I will not call you by that name you call your self. It has been many years, Sol. You were my big brother. Remember the way I followed you around on the streets. You could not get rid of me. But now I am a man. Maybe I became a salesman, perhaps you would spit on a man like me but what you did was not right. I think perhaps you have suffered now enough. All these years, I say to myself: I have no brother. I am alone in this world but for the family I have chosen. Sometimes I think I started with the cleaning products to clean up the filth you leave behind you. Even just to think of it gives me a taste of grit in my mouth. And then I remember when we came here, and before even, back in Russia, how you were my hero.

This has become much longer than I had wished. This is just to say you will always be my brother, my older brother. You will always be Solomon to me. Please do not forget who you once were.

Stay well.
Joseph Brodsky

Joseph put down his pen and looked out over Esther's desk to the lighted street. He remembered the day Solomon had come for that neighborhood girl, Pauline, and how he had whisked her away. Joseph had felt terrible for her little sister, Frances, and for the way the whole neighborhood turned on the Verdonik family because their elder girl had run away with a gangster. He could see Frances as a little girl, a short, squat thing, hairy as a monkey. Everywhere he turned she was behind him, and he had wanted to tell her: Go away! You with your dirty sister! But of course he had felt pity for her. It was his brother too; and so Joseph would buy her candies and pat her head when he saw her playing in the street.

He folded the letter to Solomon now and put it in the bottom drawer of his desk. Where would he send it, after all? Rikers? It was ridiculous. He'd read in the *Herald* that the Nazis ordered all works of Marc Chagall to be taken down from German museums, and here his brother was doing time in Rikers. No matter what Esther convinced herself of, Jews were dying. Joseph could see it then, as clear as the streetlamp outside his window: He was at the start of his life. Everything that had happened to him—meeting Esther, the births of his daughters—had made Joseph feel as if his life were beginning just at that moment. It was his way. But Solomon, he knew, always saw his world as if it were on the cusp of ending.

Joseph rubbed his rough, cracked hands together and rose from the chair. He would again go check on Gloria and then head upstairs, slip into Esther's bed, curl up against her, rest his head against her back, feel her heart thumping, pumping blood through and through her. Here, there would be safety. He would lift up her nightgown and wrap himself around her, taking in his wife's skin, the scent of wax, all kinds of flowers. Tonight he would kiss her neck and trace the outline of her breasts and hips, the backs of her thighs with his hands, and tomorrow he would begin the empire that would bear her beloved name.

CHAPTER 3

Prospects: Seymour Bloom,
1925–1937

JOSEPH BRODSKY'S OPPOSITION to the marriage of his daughter and David Bloom was unbeknownst to Seymour Bloom. He couldn't have cared one way or the other who his son was marrying, as long as David was happy. And compared with the kinds of girls—more like bear cats—David had been going with before, Seymour knew he should consider himself lucky he'd ended up with as decent a girl as Miriam Brodsky.

"As I've always told you, son, you must follow your heart," Seymour said to him when David telephoned with the news. He had thought that perhaps David would come uptown, with Miriam, and they would have announced their engagement together, not this casual phoning his father up one evening and just telling him the news, as simple as buying a carton of milk. Marriage was not a simple proposition, after all.

"You've never told me that," David said. He drummed his fingers on the kitchen table and looked outside to the tree-lined street.

How different was the West Village, a place filled with artists, and music, and the smells of an entire world—a whole other country than the Upper East, David thought. Just now he remembered all those nights he had waited in the dark in the kitchen for his father to come home, how he had watched his father as he quietly slipped into the house without seeing his son. He remembered his smell on those nights—of the outside, of petrol—and how so often his pockets were stuffed with bits of rope and rolls of duct tape, items that even as he saw his father remove them from his pockets, David thought were saved for boys.

"That's not true." Seymour cleared his throat. "That's not true at all. I've always told you to pursue all your dreams."

Hadn't he? That had been something Seymour had always meant to tell his son, meant to show him, but, now that he thought about it, perhaps he had not. Had his own life not been evidence? It distressed Seymour that he had neglected to teach his son such a simple tenet. It had taken him an entire life to learn this, a life he had lived in the hope of being able to pass this lesson on to his son. A lifetime, and now it turned out his son might not be the kind of man who would follow his heart. That he had not managed to pass this down, or that his son had not been able to learn this, depressed Seymour.

When he hung up the phone, he thought about the prospect of his son marrying. And he tried for a moment to summon the passion he'd once had for his own wife. When did he have passion for his wife? It was such a sad state of affairs, really. He rarely thought back. What was the point of it? Now, as if he were recalling it for the first time, he remembered the day he'd met Sarah Rosen.

It had been on the Duck Pond in Central Park—Sarah's blades cut the ice in a perfect figure eight as she looked over to her smiling father and crashed head-on into Seymour. Seymour, who had never been skating before, thought the accident had been his fault, and after apologizing profusely, insisted on buying them both hot cocoa.

What wonderful hair, Seymour thought, looking at Sarah's blond, shoulder-length corkscrews escaping beneath her wool cap. Seymour and his little brother had come to New York from Paris with his mother, Inez Bloom, just a decade earlier, in 1915. It was Inez who had always instilled in her son the belief that the first thing to look for in a woman was her hair. She got this theory from experience. Banking on the presumption that when nobody has any cents, still they come for their hairs, she had recently signed a ninety-nine-year lease on a small beauty shop in Brooklyn, right near her apartment, where she lived down the hall from Mae West.

Ultimately it was Sarah's hair, falling in ringlets, that made the handsome Seymour pursue her. He imagined telling his mother of the curls, coiled as if wrapped around an invisible finger, and their light brown sheen—Almost blond, Mama! he would say.

What Seymour, who was just beginning his career in sales— everything from adding machines and encyclopedias to bootlegged liquor—lacked in formal schooling he had managed to make up for in pure physical grace and charm. He was tall and broad, and his dark looks—black hair, olive skin—were in ideal contrast to his WASPy features, from the sweet curve of his nose to his heart-shaped face. Though he was not an educated man, Seymour managed to maintain an air of sophistication.

The erudite Sarah, he remembered now, was always a girl of exaggerated, ill-fitting parts. What she held in stature, which he had thought unusual for any girl, let alone a girl of Sarah's age, she lacked in general prettiness. Hers was an acquired beauty, as one might have said of Bette Davis had one never beheld her on the screen. Sarah looked as if her body had been stretched in an accidental, haphazard fashion. Her neck was swan-long, nearly begging strangulation, and her nose was as long and thin as a swizzle stick.

Seymour would never know why she chose him, though he would marvel at it often—was it to have a single place to put all the blame for everything she'd never have? He often wondered if, when they'd crashed into each other on the ice that day, she hadn't been literally jolted out of her mind.

Although she was an intellectual girl—always with that long nose in the Shakespeare, the Chaucer—Seymour knew it was Sarah's body that reached for him that day. He had felt it as she sat across from him, sipping cocoa after their collision, Seymour's young brother spinning on the ice and waving; he could see her rising in her seat, hovering, her skin buzzing with happiness. When he reached out to touch her hand, a shock passed between them, and he knew that, would he like to have her, Sarah would be his.

Perhaps Seymour did not see then that he picked his wife primarily for her fine hair and the very awkwardness that, for some reason, translated to him not as clumsiness but as a sort of elegance, as if Sarah was above certain learned rules of conduct. The way she threw her head back when she laughed did seem to him to be good breeding, making her appear both young and old at the same time. And soon he would discover that her wit would make them the axis on which many parties spun, so much so that when they turned to leave there was always a general hush, as if the guests simply could not continue on without them.

Seymour and Sarah were married in 1925, just after the posthumous publication of Kafka's *The Trial.* Sarah received a copy from her friend Celia. "Perfect reading for the honeymoon!!" Celia had written on the card. "Have a ducky time!" Sarah used the card as a bookmark, and every time Seymour saw it he cringed.

The morning after the wedding—a Long Island affair, with a reception on the lawn that went well into the evening, swooping beams of light, floor-length dresses stained with newly cut grass and champagne—Sarah Bloom woke up inconsolable.

"What is it, my dear?" Seymour turned to ask her. He could see Signal Hill from their room at the new Montauk Manor, where they had spent their wedding night, a car having whisked them away and driven them almost as far east as the road would take them.

"It's nothing," she told him.

But he wouldn't have it. Why was his wife crying? Last night, while all the guests were milling about eating canapés before dinner, Sarah had been the kind of woman he had never dreamed he would have. Thank you, she told the guests as they made their way down the receiving line to her, Yes, it's true, she agreed with them, smiling, always touching their hands in the exact place they wanted their hands to be touched.

"What is it, my love?" Seymour reached out to touch her hair.

Sarah sighed. "Am I really to spend my life with a man who actually goes door to door selling *things*?"

Seymour rolled away from her, stunned. She hadn't seemed to mind his occupation last night when, high as a kite on champagne, she tore off her wedding dress with abandon and got down on her knees. "Come here, Sy," she'd said, winking, and he'd moved to the edge of the bed and watched her mouth, free from the red lipstick he had never seen her lips without, move toward him, smiling.

That had been here; his legs had dangled over this very bed as she had moved to him, her mouth opening. "What would you *have* me do, Sarah?" he asked her now.

"The thing is"—she put the back of her hand to her head, dramatizing her evident hangover—"what else *can* you do?" She turned onto her stomach, her ear to the pillow. "Nothing, I'm afraid."

"Surely you don't mean nothing, Sarah," he said, but was met by silence.

Seymour hated her then, this woman who had been his wife for less than twenty-four hours and had already turned against him. He knew then and there that he would live his life not to please her but to make sure she never had the opportunity to speak to him this way again.

It would be nearly twenty-five years before Arthur Miller would expose onstage the terrible emptiness of the salesman, but still Sarah did not hesitate to tell Seymour that her life was like that of the wife of a beggar. How could she live as she was accustomed on his small commissions?

And so Sarah soon welcomed the financial support of her father, an act she flaunted to her new husband.

"Do you like my dress?" She'd twirl before him in her brand-new Adrian. The way the crepe de chine was cut and how it joined together again against the grain, at peculiar angles, shooting her body through with light when she moved, had made Sarah have to have the extravagant gown she had seen from the street and tried on just for fun. When Seymour reached out to feel the exquisite fabric, she slapped his hand away. "This wasn't a gift from you, my dear. This was from Daddy."

"My darling"—there was hardly a time when she did not speak down to him—"I cannot go with*out*," she'd say. Dragging him to the opera, to the ballet, to the theater, she'd tell him, "A girl cannot live a life without art!"

Though Seymour's mother had coveted glamour, art had been the last thing on her mind when her children were growing up. Seymour knew his mother wondered why she had even come to this country, especially after dark, when the underworld rose to the surface of their

Brownsville neighborhood and the screams of young men being knifed and the shattering of glass sounded through the streets. There was no way to go out and have any fun.

In Brooklyn, how far had Inez been from her own mother, braiding challah on the rue des Rosiers? Three streets over was the fish market; they could all hear the men's Yiddish screams overlapping when she strolled with the two boys in the afternoons. Yiddish! Inez always told Seymour it was a peasants' language. "I thought this was the new world!" she'd despair to her son. "Might as well just have traveled east in Europe," she'd say.

Basic needs—and later, in his teenage years, money for fancy dresses—were her main preoccupation. We lived *generically,* Seymour would say.

Because Inez did not have the means to provide access to things cultural, she had always debunked them as *homosexual.* In fact, all things that Seymour yearned for but could not have—gold cuff links, for instance, box seats at the opera, a white room filled with natural light—Inez labeled homosexual, so much so that Seymour began to associate the word with wealth and possibility, with things longed for but utterly unattainable.

But Sarah insisted on art, and so it was with her that Seymour went to the theater and lost himself completely for the first time. Each and every time a production ended, the lights coming up, Seymour felt he was waking from a dream. In his daily life, he'd always been aware of his surroundings—the terrible ticking clock, the changing weather, the people passing by on the street. There was no escape from reality. Even while making love to his wife, Seymour did not experience what many of his friends discussed over scotch and cigars and what he had read about occasionally in the magazines he had hidden under his mattress as an adolescent. He had imagined the sensation would be science, a burst of energy and pressure, a subsequent release of reality, as if one were spinning into space for one moment at a fraction of the speed of sound or light. But sex was not so for Seymour. Though he had orgasms, they were nearly clinical in their arrival. The theater—especially musical theater, with its silliness and gaiety—transported him to a time and place that was entirely and deliciously other. Theater was an experience that was closer to *living.*

In a way, going to the theater brought him back to the year he turned fourteen, when he would watch his mother play hostess at the Joint, a Harlem club owned by the cruel Madame Lutille. Somehow in Brownsville, the slum infested by cockroaches and gangsters where Seymour grew up, Inez had managed to go around with what he'd thought surely was the only Jewish boxer in New York but turned out to be one of many tough Jews from Brooklyn, and the two held court there. Joe Crews was on a winning streak, and all the celebrities went to shake his meaty hand. Inez had, in turn, bullied them, using her French as a weapon.

"Non, non!" she'd say, wagging her finger. *"C'est pas comme ça."*

"Bon*jour*," she'd say, stretching out her language.

She always found a way to tell them no. No table by the window. No book of matches. No, I'm so sorry, but there is simply no more caviar. When it was said in French, everyone seemed pleased.

An inveterate pessimist, Inez managed each month to put a little aside to save for her beauty shop, the one she had been eyeing since she came to this country. The rest of the money was spent on fashion—a green tulle gown by Madeleine et Madeleine, a Paul Poiret evening coat.

Despite the recent Volstead Act, which ratified the Eighteenth Amendment, prohibiting the sale of alcohol, the Joint managed, for a while, to thrive.

Over the years at the club, Seymour saw Irving Berlin sip a French 75 as he leaned in to Edna Ferber at the corner table. And when Benny Leonard won the world lightweight boxing championship, Seymour was there as the whole world came to the Joint to celebrate his title.

But that had been almost a decade before Seymour married Sarah. Now he would never be able to take his wife by there and trick her into believing that Inez owned the fabulous place. The Joint had been destroyed by Prohibition and the brain damage Joe Crews received when fighting a Catholic boxer. Inez kept him in the back room, and she would bring him carrots mashed by the cook. Eventually the lack of liquor and the absence of a celebrity boxer to anchor the clientele had forced the place to close, and now the Joint was a boarded-up old storefront in a neighborhood where kids stood on the corners, waiting for someone to give them something to do.

The theater spoke to Seymour the way the Joint had spoken to his mother. But all those evenings of *Sunny* and *No, No, Nanette*—the Cinderella musicals, which Seymour loved because the heroines always started poor and ended rich—were funded by Sarah's father. Each Sunday, Fritz Rosen would come over and ask about his son-in-law's *prospects,* a word Seymour had once loved, as it had meant all things possible, but soon began to despise, as it came to mean everything improbable.

Sarah felt her husband could make up for the deficiency of his education and social class only with money. She did not hesitate to tell him this, and neither did her father, who had insisted that they take a place on Manhattan's Upper East Side—the *least* attractive place he would allow his only daughter to live.

"I am not a girl of the boroughs," Sarah, who had grown up on Long Island, would say.

"Oh, Sarah," Seymour would tell her. "Please." Why hadn't he married one of those nice girls who worked in his mother's shop, on which she had just three years ago signed a ninety-nine-year lease? Seymour had watched the Greek who owned the place turn the corner, headed back to postwar Athens, a place far easier to navigate than Prohibition America. Why, Seymour wondered, hadn't he chosen someone who would be happy with what is, as opposed to what should be and should be and should be?

Seymour had no plans to be a salesman for the rest of his life. With or without Sarah's taunting, he was going to be someone, someone else. He thought of those limos pulling up in front of the Joint, the stars lingering on the sidewalk in their jeweled gowns and cloche hats, waiting to be photographed. That blinding white light of a bulb popping bright. Like Inez, who spent all her money on dresses to impress this clientele, and deceive them into believing that it was she who was running things, Seymour loved the money of the whole affair. He loved the decadence. But most of all, when he sat down and really thought of it, Seymour loved the theatricality—everyone equaled by the accoutrements and the drama of the arrival.

For now, however, Seymour was only a handsome man next to

whom most women wanted to stand, and so Sarah's father supplemented their rent as well as their entertainment, gradually, yet efficiently, emasculating Seymour Bloom.

Seymour knew from the wash of grief he encountered upon his return from a day of trudging around town with cumbersome adding machines that Sarah did not spend her days like other married women. Other married women passed their time with women like themselves. They prepared food for their husbands. And they took care of their children.

Their children. Dulcy, their first child, was born in 1927, the month after *The Jazz Singer* hit the screen. Sarah had gone to see Al Jolson star in the first feature-length film that everyone was talking about, not realizing how uncomfortable she would be after only forty-five minutes. She'd cursed her unborn child for all that it was making her give up as she dragged Seymour out of the theater.

Dulcy was born before the Panic, but by the time their second child, David, was born, in October 1931, the world had truly turned black. Seymour preferred to see it differently. Seymour saw the birth of his first son as the year the George Washington Bridge was finished, hovering like nothing short of a miracle over the Hudson and connecting New York to New Jersey. It was the year the tallest building in the world, the Empire State, opened. Seymour couldn't get over these two feats, progress he'd never believed he'd see in his lifetime. New York was growing even if the rest of the world seemed in danger of falling away.

Sarah Bloom's life, and the world as she had known it, she reasoned, had ended. Sarah had all but given up. She had taken to what she called dancing but what anyone who watched her would call dressing up like a strumpet and drinking in the basement.

Mary, the housekeeper, another basic need paid for by Fritz Rosen, who insisted that one servant was the very least in help any young family needed, told Seymour about the way Sarah stashed Prohibition liquor in the basement and spent most of the day down there, listening to ragtime and crying to beat the band.

"She's a dreamer, Mr. Bloom," Mary told her employer one evening when Sarah had gone up to bed. Mary left out the way Sarah, her red lipstick smeared across her mouth, which gave the effect of having been punched, had told her, "You know, Mary, my mind is dying from neglect." Mary had nodded her head. "I might as well pickle the damn thing." Sarah had laughed. Some days, she leaned in close to Mary, who could smell the whiskey on her breath so strong she had to turn away. "What do you think it would have been like to be born a man?" Sarah had asked.

Mary didn't tell Seymour any of this. "I just thought you should know she doesn't seem content," she said. "And also, I found this." Mary handed Seymour a balled-up piece of paper. "I found this letter on Mrs. Bloom's desk."

"Thank you, Mary," Seymour said, reaching slowly for the letter.

As she turned to leave, he looked down at the crinkled sheet with the kind of dread he thought was saved for ringing strangers' doorbells. Who would it be and would they purchase anything from him? Most often, he knew, they would not. Now Seymour wished that Mary had never told him anything. Perhaps his wife's misery, her unused potential, could have gone unspoken between them for a lifetime. Would that have been so bad? And now whatever was in his hands would be some awful concrete evidence of her unhappiness. He hated letters for this reason. Seymour never wanted to know what anyone felt—it would pass, like everything—but a letter, he reasoned, keeps it there as if it had never left. Love was like that too, he knew. He wished now he had never written Sarah love letters so he would never have proof that once he might have loved her.

Would having once loved her make the present more or less difficult? He couldn't even begin to wonder. Seymour read:

Dear Celia:

Sometimes I get to thinking about how it was on the stage at Smith. Remember playing Rosalind to my Celia? What a swell time that was, Smith. Acting! And I didn't even know it. How silly not to have looked around at all those women so hard at work, studying, and not to have wondered where on earth there would be room in the world for all of us! But Smith was cruel—it made me feel like I could be anything. What a dreadful setup, Seal! Did everyone but me know we'd be coming back to this?

He felt the relief pour out of him. A letter to her friend from college. Well, this is all, Seymour thought. Who didn't want to be young and have the chance to do it all over again? This was nothing. This, Seymour decided, was perfectly normal.

Who saved poor David Bloom from his mother's despair? It was Inez Bloom, who discovered that she could show her grandson the affection she could never bestow on her own children. It was all she could do when she saw David not to cover him with kisses. "Ucch!" she'd exclaim, shaking him. Someone who saw them on the street and didn't know Inez might have thought her angry. "I love you to pieces!" she'd scream.

I want Nana, David would cry at night, and, wishing to please his son and keep him from his wife, a rag doll in silk pajamas in their bed, Seymour, when he had the means to do so, would send David down in a company car to his mother. David would look out across the East River as the car made its way down Second Avenue, to Broadway and onto the Brooklyn Bridge. He loved that bridge, because he knew it brought him to Inez and away from his mother. David would think of her in a terrible heap at the bottom of the stairs as he headed toward the bridge and to his grandmother's.

Brooklyn was safety. In contrast to Seymour, who felt only relief finally to leave Brooklyn and be embraced by the riches of the once untouchable and in-the-distance Manhattan, David looked to the right to see the Statue of Liberty and the little red house of Ellis Island, and felt Brooklyn to be offering its open arms.

Just to sit twirling in a chair at the counter of that pink room, bells jingling as the ladies sauntered in and out of the shop, bags hooked around their elbows, filled him with joy. "Davey Davey!" they'd say, tickling his chin. Some brought him peppermints and cherry licorice, the tips of their long nails brushing his skin as they dropped the candy into his cupped palms. He'd watch them walk away, bobbing in their high heels, and brim over with admiration.

Plain and simple, he loved the smell of the place: the thick heat and the hair spray, the strange mix of dye and shampoo tinged with the faint odor of burning. He loved the polyurethane gloss and the way everything from floor to ceiling seemed to shine. The beauty salon was a theater set to him. It was an escape from life and, at the same time, a whole new life. Watching all the ladies sitting under the bubble hair dryers blowing on their nails as they flipped through magazines and complained about their husbands, David would feel both connected to them and utterly distant from them. It was nothing like the world to which his mother insisted he belonged, and it was this that made him at home within the very brightness of the place, a contrast to the muted colors and dark woods of his parents' Upper East Side brownstone.

After Inez had finally let her evening manager take over, she would take David back to her apartment. Most times she would take a long, foaming bath, to remove the burning smell and replace it with the scent of the lavender bath salts she'd had sent from Paris each and every month since she left for America twenty-two years before. Six-year-old David wandered the hallways as she bathed.

Inez happened to have a very famous neighbor down the hall. When Hollywood's Production Code of 1934 and Joseph Breen had ruined her career of sexual innuendo and double entendres, not to mention her finances, Mae West returned to Brooklyn. One evening as David meandered aimlessly, dragging his hands along the raised wallpaper, she stood at her door watching him in the darkened hallway. David saw the light shining behind her, and she looked beguiling to him, her voluptuous frame silhouetted in the threshold.

"And who's this big boy?" she asked him, shaking her hips.

"I'm David," he said, bringing his hands from the velvet of the walls to his sides. "My grandmother lives there." He pointed to Inez's door.

"Inez Bloom," she said. "Ya don't say." *Swish swish* went the hips. "Mae," she said, one hand patting her hair, the other held out to David.

He went over to shake it, peering around her to get a look inside the apartment.

"Wanna take a look around, sport?" she asked him.

David shrugged. "Sure," he said, and she flattened against the doorjamb to let him pass.

A curious child, David Bloom made his way around Mae West's

rather small apartment, investigating, comparing it with his grand-mother's, which had gold-colored rubber covers on all the doorknobs and opaque plastic runners over the carpets in the hallways. In Inez's bedroom there were doilies and dusty bottles of Chartreuse on her long wooden bureau. But as David, with Mae West following close on his heels, wandered into her bedroom, all he found was an enormous round bed resting on a circular platform. Looking at the bed, David wondered if it spun, and so he stepped up on the platform, as if he were walking onto a stage, to take a closer look. He looked up to see mirrors covering the ceiling. David saw himself in the mirrors, and then he saw himself taken aback by his own reflection. He then saw himself smile and resisted the urge to wave. Feeling all the blood rush to his head, he turned back to face Mae West.

"Why do you have mirrors up there?" he asked. Again he looked up to the ceiling, riveted by the upside-down boy.

Once more she rocked her hips. Her flesh, it seemed to David, *moved.* "Because when I wake up in the morning," she said, "I like to see myself."

David had not heard his grandmother enter the room, but he saw her come into view, tying her robe, her hair dripping wet from her bath. Now she stood next to this woman. In the mirrors, warped in the spaces where the squares of glass fit together, he saw Inez reach back and bring her hand across Mae West's face. At the same time, he heard a loud *slap.* When David turned to look at what was actually happening, Mae West was holding her cheek and Inez Bloom was pointing her finger.

"To a six-year-old boy!" she said. "Save it for the talkies!" Inez reached for David's elbow and pulled him out of the apartment.

As he was being dragged into the dark hallway that smelled of boiled potatoes and chicken fat, David turned to see Mae West laughing, her head ringed with a halo of white curls. She waved good-bye to him, and as he raised his hand to do the same, Inez jerked him out of sight.

Much later, David would read his encounter with Mae West as destiny, a sign that he was being fingered for his own brand of performing. But when he came home late that evening and told his mother about the woman with a head of blond curls who slept on a circular bed with mirrors covering the ceiling, Sarah Bloom slapped him across the face. "Stay away from her!" she screamed.

Stunned, his face stinging with his mother's rare touch, David began to cry. "Why, Mummy?" he asked, both hands cupping his left cheek and backing away. He remembered Mae West laughing at his grandmother's cruel touch and could not understand it.

"You don't know this yet, my darling," Sarah said.

David could see she was trying to still her hysteria and undo the damage she had just caused.

"But your mother was going to be an actress too. In college, I went to Smith College—a very, very good school, not every woman can say she went to Smith—I was the star of every show. Everyone came to see me. Me! And now, now who comes to see me?"

David looked up at her blankly.

"We do, Sarah," Seymour said. "Your family." He had been listening in the hallway. He went to stand by his son, placing a sure hand on his shoulder. My goodness, he thought. All this talk of what she might have been had long ago become unbearable. Smith this, Smith that, the classes, the goddamn queues of boys to the friggin' moon. Her wasted life, it was going to ruin them all.

Sarah looked up to see her husband and son standing across the room together. She paused for a moment, and, for a moment, Seymour and David both saw something soften in her. It passed over her face as if it had come from outside her, and then, as quickly as it had come, it was gone.

"My family," Sarah said, and, laughing nearly maniacally, she threw herself back on the bed. "What a hoot!"

They could not live like this much longer. Seymour knew he had to do something or his children would suffer badly. He leaned down to hold his son's stinging face, as if to erase the impact of his wife's angry hand.

"It's nothing," he told David, pretending to strike his son on the chin. "Let that be the worst sock in the puss you ever get," he said as Mary came to take David and put him to bed.

Seymour watched his son look at him with those huge, searching eyes as the housekeeper took him by the hand and led him to bed.

CHAPTER 4

Reading:
Frances Verdonik, 1925

FRANCES VERDONIK WAS nothing short of shocked when she got the invitation to the Bloom-Brodsky wedding in Portland, Maine. How these two families could be more intertwined, she didn't know, but she had never imagined that David Bloom and Miriam Brodsky would find each other again. As she removed the tissue that hovered above the engraved script on the ivory invitation—fancy, fancy, she thought—Frances had a vague memory that she had introduced them years and years ago, at the World's Fair. What a matchmaker I am, she thought, though they had been only eight years old at the time. That had been a wonderful day, thought Frances.

Poor Joseph. He had worked so hard to stay clean, stay away from the shadow of his older brother, and now this. Though she had heard that Seymour Bloom was no longer involved in the Mob, how he could have gotten out, she had no idea. She had never heard of anyone leaving unscathed. Charlie Kellerman had tried, and his entire family had been killed. Everyone but Charlie, who Frances had heard ran a lettuce stand at a roadside farmers' market upstate. Seymour had certainly been the oddest gangster, with this thing he had for the theater. Who else would be getting crates of illegal liquor from Long Island, or taking another useless canary to his death while talking the whole way about the wonders of Gershwin?

But she would be at the wedding. Of course she would—she and

Joseph had been through everything together. And though she had been married to Vladimir now for twenty-eight years, Frances had been in love with Joseph Brodsky since she was old enough to walk down the street and see him sitting on the stoop beside his mother. It was the kind of love that is also childhood and memory and everything good that comes up and kisses you from the past.

As Joseph sat next to his mother, his head on her squared shoulders, Selma Brodsky looked ahead with a steely gaze. Frances knew the look from wishing that her own mother wore it, that Rose Verdonik would buck up against the neighborhood, which seemed determined to drag her family's name into the ground and bury it there.

Frances never got Joseph Brodsky, she would always reason, because of her older sister, Pauline. Now she was grateful for the way her life turned, but it really had been Pauline who had ruined everything, from the moment her family stepped foot on New York concrete. From the day Rose and Abraham Verdonik came from Russia—in 1912, when Frances was just three years old—every single resource had been poured into her, and what were they rewarded with?

Pauline running off with that no-good thug, Solomon Brodsky.

Frances and Pauline's father, Abraham Verdonik, sold insurance. When there was any extra money—very rarely, as it turned out, because insurance wasn't the first thing on an immigrant's mind—it went toward a dress with puffed sleeves for Pauline, dance lessons for Pauline, satin hair ribbons for Pauline. The whole neighborhood knew that, out of all of them, the one most likely to be a true and blue American was Pauline. It was as if young Frances existed only to smile enviously at her sister.

Unlike the perfectly proportioned Pauline, Frances was wide on the bottom and tapered on top, like a pear. And because she developed hair early in life, before waxing was common, before the days of depilatory cream (this would be invented by a rabbi from Esther's hometown of Portland, Maine, nearly two decades after Frances began to develop her mustache), Frances was forced into a close relationship with tweezers. Two hairs sprouted from her chin, and each week Frances plucked them.

Her sister, Pauline, was the beauty on whom even Franny had pinned all the family's hopes. Placing a stack of books on her sister's head, Frances would stand at one end of the room and coax Pauline toward her. Good, she'd say. Hold your head up higher, she'd say. There! And Pauline would glide in her socks across the room. They practiced the wave with no space between the fingers, and a closed-lip smile, because they were going to win Pauline a scholarship to school via the Miss America contest or be damned. And then Pauline would take Frances everywhere she was going. After all, they had been to Atlantic City and had seen those girls waving as they jerked by on their pathetic little floats. Pauline Verdonik was much more beautiful than any of those girls from Wyoming and Mississippi, and if everybody in Brooklyn didn't know it then, at least Pauline and Frances did.

When she thought about it, Frances believed she could pin it all on Eli Horowitz's bar mitzvah. Solomon Brodsky did not notice Pauline until that day, which was also the day, legend has it, that he met A. R. Rothstein, the notorious bootlegger.

That had been some party. Frances had never seen anything like it—the sturgeon, the herring, the plates of smoked salmon sliced as thin and fine as writing paper. Never had she seen so much food. And the chopped liver molded into the shape of a swan, the neck as smooth and curved as if it had been blown from glass. After the ceremony that had marked Eli's passage into manhood in the eyes of God (but not in the opinion of Frances, who found him doughy and immature), she watched Solomon saunter over to a group of young men, nudging his way into the circle of them.

"Wiseguys!" Frances heard Hester Black, the horrible gossip who made the best rugeleh on South Fifth Street, whisper to her daughter. She saw her neighbor shake her fist in the air as her face reddened.

Frances watched Solomon penetrate that cruel circle as she made her way over to the chopped liver swan. Perhaps she felt the relative equilibrium of her world begin to tip and wobble, because a violence welled up in her that she had never before experienced. She saw Solomon pointing his finger, laughing, and she saw her sister, Pauline, preening in the distance, surrounded by their father's friends. Solomon looked out from the group and, from across the room, settled his gaze on Pauline, whom he appeared to be seeing now for the first time. His cold stare, saved for men, softened on Pauline, as if he were accepting the heat of the sun. This was the very first time Frances saw the difference between herself and her sister, and she discovered that she would never be entitled to such a glance, that no one would look up and be stunned by her. Joseph, who stood with his mother, nodding with three old women from the neighborhood, hardly even cast a glance in Frances's direction. Unlike Pauline, whose lovely surface—a gorgeous, ornate cover—begged opening, Frances was a complicated text that would require careful reading. She knew that she would not be leaving, that she would be stuck watching Hester Black and Charlotte Meyer bitch and moan about the price of herring and potatoes on the front stoop each evening for her whole life, and so she took the silver-plated knife and swiped the chopped liver swan right across the neck.

It was a bloodless beheading, but for one brief moment the swan was alive. And then it seemed like it was dying. Its head, eyes set with pitted black olives, seemed to look over at Franny, a sad plea that asked her *why,* before it fell to the floor, losing its elegant shape. Still the olive-eye looked up at her from its smashed face, and for the first time in a long while Frances felt relief. She resisted the urge to step on its head with her Mary Janes, dress shoes that had once been Pauline's, but her imagination took her to a place where she could squash the face beyond recognition.

Not a week later, Solomon left the neighborhood and, everyone heard, changed his name to Terry the Terrier—bark worse than his bite. He began working for A. R. Rothstein and Maxie Greenberg from Illinois. The ladies all shook their heads, and no one stopped to visit Selma Brodsky anymore. *Why why why?* the women of the neighborhood asked one another, clutching their stomachs as if they were suffering from indigestion. But Frances thought even then that she understood. She had watched the boys of the neighborhood spend their youth on broken sidewalks, owned by those tough Italians and Irish thugs. Solomon was a small, thick man, and Frances knew there was safety in a group, authority in its membership. Who didn't feel bigger when able to part crowds because of a couple of powerful friends? She too would have liked that feeling, to walk into the world inside a gang of people, entirely protected from cruelty. At least, Frances reasoned, she had her sister.

Rumor had it the three men started speedboating liquor across Lake Michigan from Canada into Chicago and Detroit, and ended up with an operation shipping whiskey from England across the Atlantic to the coast of Montauk, an unprotected point in the middle of the sound. And from there they'd bring the cases to shore and ship them off to warehouses in Manhattan. Then off to the nightclubs, which, Frances would soon learn from her sister, saved the best seats in the house for the Terrier and anyone who came with him.

From her window ledge, where Frances used to sit and dangle one leg out into the world, free from the claustrophobic apartment and her mother's incessant cleaning, she would watch Solomon come back to the neighborhood in three-hundred-dollar suits to strut down Lorimer, hands jiggling change in his pockets and smoking a cigar. Young boys peered around the corner just to get a look at him.

Her sister always leaned over Frances, practically knocking her out into the street. "Look at that," Pauline said. "Do you see him? I bet he has an automobile."

Frances shrugged. "Well then, why doesn't he drive it?" she asked.

Pauline looked hard at her sister. "Because the car, which I'm sure has a top that folds down, is for rides in the country. Brooklyn would only get it dirty."

"Really?" Frances asked.

"Of course, Franny." Pauline folded her arms across her chest. "He could have any girl he wanted, you know," she told her sister.

Frances was silent but for the knocking of her shoe against the brownstone. The sound of the thud against the house always made her mother scream that she would scuff her shoes, which in turn made Frances kick harder.

"Anyone," Pauline said. Then she looked Frances in the eye. "But mark my words, it's going to be me."

∞

Not everyone wanted what the Terrier had. It was cheating God to get such riches from stealing. And cheating God, well, not even a gangster could get away with that.

The women who did not necessarily disdain the Terrier, like Rose Verdonik, Frances's mother, felt sorry for him. Poor boys, she'd say to her girls whenever news spread that Solomon had come around. Here's Solomon and his friend from the *whosewutz,* she'd say. Poor boys, she'd say in Yiddish. *Farblondzhet.* They are the lost ones, she'd say, speaking of that horrible space that yawned between the parents who came over and their kids who had no idea from where their parents came.

The way the family, the neighbors, the shopkeepers, made Pauline feel so damn special simply for her curvaceous but slender figure and her lovely doll's face made Pauline feel she had a congenital right to a life better than the one she was living in a two-bedroom walk-up in Williamsburg.

"Franny," Pauline said as she brushed out her hair, "aren't you tired of watching Mommy's sad face? And Daddy at that grimy kitchen table?"

Frances shrugged.

"Well, what do they think anyway? They barely speak any English! My God, Franny, my looks will be gone by the time I get outta here!"

"What about Miss America?" Franny asked her sister. "You'll win that, Paw-Paw. Then we'll be famous!"

"*We'll* be famous?" Pauline shook her head, and Frances would never forget the condescending expression that she had wanted to tear from her sister's face.

"Us," Frances said meekly.

"Silly girl. It will be me. And anyway, you have to have money to win. Money to play and money to win. That's what I need."

"I thought it didn't matter." Frances felt as if she would cry.

"It matters. Believe me," Pauline said. "Money is all that matters."

Solomon came back to strut on South Fifth Street by day, but he also headed back late at night, sneaking around to take out the girl he had watched turn into a woman, the girl he had seen from across the room. And here he was in his flashy suits, with his flashy cash, his flashy driver, this man whose wingtips shone so bright you could see your reflection in them, whom Pauline and Frances had known when he was a young boy playing stickball in the street at twilight. And now he came for Frances's sister, to take her into that city over which they had watched the sun lighten and set their whole lives in America.

Frances would always remember the nights Pauline went out with the Terrier. He would sneak around the side of the brownstone and throw pebbles at the window from the tiny alley late at night. Often Frances would let Pauline, whose indelicate snoring blocked out most noise, stay asleep. Then she would go to the window and, through the ripped screen, look down to little Solomon, all dressed up and shiny, waiting for Pauline to join him out on the town.

"Hi, Sol," Frances would say, throwing up the window in her nightgown. She imagined, as she leaned her hips against the window frame, that she had breasts. The warped wood from the sill dug into her stomach. This is what it would be like to be courted, she thought, breathing in the night air.

"Fran!" Solomon would say, always playing along. He'd take off his trilby and hold it over his heart. "Are you gonna be my girl tonight?"

Frances would giggle. Then he'd be Solomon again, not this horrible gangster who dealt in all things illegal, thumbing his nose at all he'd been brought up on. Franny loved this brief time when Solomon pretended to call up to her, until Pauline, whose snores could not drown out her suitor's loud whispering, ran to the window and pushed Frances out of the way.

After Pauline had powdered her stockings and colored her lips and run out the door to meet the Terrier, Frances would lie awake in bed waiting for her to come home. Frances would lie on her back looking up at the water-stained ceiling and try to imagine her sister walking the downtown streets on the Terrier's arm. This is what it's like to be left behind, Frances thought as she imagined her sister dancing the Charleston. She'd had so little experience outside her street, Frances couldn't really picture a thing. But when Pauline would come home smelling of the world outside their apartment—cigarettes and perfume and rum and night air—Frances would always equate this with the smell of becoming an adult.

❧

No one but Frances had an inkling that Pauline would be leaving. Frances knew of her sister's nights out, her impatience, and too many of her dreams: a mink stole draped over her neck, peacock-plumed hats, a large house surrounded by wooden fencing and supported by columns, in the manner of the South, Pauline would tell her. And in 1925 there was no other way for a Jewish girl from Eastern Europe living in Williamsburg, Brooklyn, to achieve these dreams than through a long white veil, a crushed glass, a clutch of yellow rosebuds.

When Pauline entered the steaming kitchen one stifling summer evening, Rose Verdonik was mopping the floor vigilantly, sweat pouring from her brow; Abraham was wearing his spectacles and reading *The Rise of David Levinsky* to Frances for the third time. He was trying to understand how this Yiddish-speaking man was able to write so well—so *realistically!*—in English when Pauline leaned against the door frame.

She said to her parents, "Don't be angry." She said, "Please don't be angry with me, but I'm going to marry Solomon Brodsky."

Rose dropped her mop, Abraham gasped, and they both looked at their elder daughter, stunned.

"Who?" Abraham said. "What?"

Frances looked down at her feet and wriggled her toes.

Rose resumed scrubbing the floor furiously. "You heard her," she said in Yiddish. "That gangster, with the glitzy clothes and the glitzy life. What kind of a girl . . ." Her voice trailed off.

Frances remembered being dragged by her mother to see her old friend Selma Brodsky—Solomon's mother, shunned by the neighborhood since the day Solomon drove away—when she thought no one was looking. They would sneak down the street, Rose pretending they were heading out for milk and eggs, and then Rose would quickly yank on Frances's wrist and dodge up the stairs to Selma's. The two women would talk about old times, what their lives had been like before something like this—as in *this*—could ever happen, and Frances loved the ease between them, something she rarely saw in her frenetic mother. Which was worse? they'd joke over herring, the Cossacks or summer in Brooklyn?

Joseph was there too, at the bottom of the stairs, wondering just who would be coming over now. He already seemed old to Frances, who occasionally would muster up the courage to go to him and, leaning on the banister, her chin on her hands, ask him about school or the weather or baseball. Joseph would answer factually: I'm studying chemistry, it has been a hot summer, isn't it awful about Babe Ruth's ulcer? But all Frances really wanted to know was what it was like to be him, in his Joseph skin, to have his particular fingers and toes, and to walk in the world as he walked.

Everything goes into this girl, and now she is leaving for a common criminal? "I can't even think about it," Rose mumbled to herself in Yiddish as she continued to mop.

"Mommy," Pauline said, hesitating. "He's not a criminal."

Abraham was silent. He leaned his head to the right and then to the left, removing his wire spectacles. He closed the Cahan novel and watched his wife in her frenzy of cleaning. "Rose, please!" he said. "This won't help." He stood and placed his hand at the small of his wife's back to still her.

But it was Abraham who couldn't think about it. Had Pauline tried to pry apart her father's chest and slice open his slippery heart before she had gone and broken it, she would have found only ghosts inside. The ghosts of his mother and father, the spirit of a sister he had watched being taken. The ghost of his elder daughter was the last he could fit inside that beating organ. Frances knew, she could see it in the way her father's back was sinking before her eyes, that this final haunting bore down on him with its fogged, spiritual weight, and, like his friends who worked on the East Side and walked over the bridge night after night, Abraham could no longer stand up straight. On the night Pauline told the Verdoniks she was leaving, Abraham took to his bed.

The next day, Pauline was gone, already a memory.

Frances remembered the two of them playing marbles on the cracked sidewalk, their father walking out the door with his scratched leather briefcase. She thought of her sister, her tiny, delicate feet in Rose's button boots, shuffling across the room. She remembered Pauline's lovely face just the year before, the two of them perched by the open window, *Rhapsody in Blue* spilling in from a neighbor's radio.

She couldn't think about it either. The way her father had worked and worked, only to have their names sullied by the likes of Solomon Brodsky. How her sister had ended up with a man who went by the name the Terrier, who hung around with that infamous Meyer Lansky, was beyond her. How could this be the same girl who had played stickball with Frances and the boys on their street? That had been before Pauline discovered that she was beautiful. And before Frances discovered that she was not. It was before they knew that they were not like boys, that they would never get for themselves what boys could get. Pauline, with her long, thin arms, had batted the ball, and it rolled between Solomon Brodsky's legs, all the way down the block to Mr. Berkowitz's candy store. Frances ran after it, the protective eye of her older sister behind her as she peered inside the store, its chocolates wrapped in golden foil stacked in the window. That was when she heard the ever-present voice of her mother: Eating outside the house! her mother screamed in Yiddish. The dysentery! she yelled, her hand over her heart. Frances had picked up the ball from the street and turned away from the window to run back toward her sister, toward Joseph, forgetting for a moment the unfamiliar longing to reach for those golden candies, and for just one second to have a look inside.

Frances always reasoned that it was the way the neighborhood and his family turned on Solomon Brodsky that had made him run away with her sister. Why else? Solomon had the money, the high, flashy life, and a gang that protected him from the kike-hating world. But even young Frances knew he had lost the love of his father.

After Pauline left, Frances sat on the stoop each night, watching the men walk across the Williamsburg Bridge, returning to their American shtetls. She watched Herbert Brodsky, a man who had once stood on the top step three doors down watching his boys play marbles. He had screamed at them about America's promise. *Goldene medina,* my boys, he'd told them night after night. "For you," he'd tell Joseph and Solomon, leaning down, his arm hooked to each boy's rigid shoulder, "I promise you a golden country."

All the men seemed to walk burdened by that horrible weight of promises made to their children. Watching Herbert, who seemed even more stooped than before, Frances imagined that somehow it was the children who were meant to lift the heaviness.

Though she never heard him say so, it was obvious that Mr. Brodsky knew *exactly* what his elder son did for a living. Mr. Brodsky used to ruffle Solomon's hair and call him his "little kaddishel." Of course it would be him, the older boy, who would say Kaddish for his father when he died. When Sol made himself into the Terrier, though, and began to wear his hair slicked back and high with pomade, smoke cigars, and run around with all kinds of reckless women, Mr. Brodsky started calling Joseph "kaddishel."

Well, who the heck wants to be on the wrong side of God? Frances wondered. She imagined that when the old ladies averted their watery eyes, when the young mothers swung their children to the opposite hip from where Solomon stood, when his father turned instead to Joseph, Solomon must have gotten scared. Didn't he know that God sees everything?

The Verdonik and Brodsky families had known each other in Russia. In the same village, Selma and Rose had kneaded the challah; their fathers had prayed together, their knees bending as they davened toward the light. And when the Verdoniks fled, when Frances was just three years old, the Brodskys were not long to follow.

In Pauline, perhaps, Solomon could be redeemed. A nice Jewish girl from the neighborhood, before the eyes of God, before the eyes of his all-knowing father.

The night Pauline snuck away with the Terrier, Frances woke up from a terrible dream. In it, she and her sister were alone at Ellis Island, holding hands as the man with his mean mustache stamped their arrival, just as he had thirteen years before, only now they were older girls. In her dream, their parents weren't with them, and the man stamped their papers and told them they would have a new name: "Green," he told them, his meaty hands, fingers with bitten nails and bloody cuticles, gripping the bloodred stamp. "Like money," he said, laughing. And then, suddenly, Pauline was gone, flying into the throng of people, all waiting to cross over into Manhattan. Franny looked behind her in her dream, and she found that all the Russians in queues to the water had turned to skeletons. Their skin was melting from their tiny Russian bones when Frances woke up, calling for her sister.

But Pauline was gone.

Frances got up and took out a piece of writing paper and a pencil and began to write:

Dear Pauline: How could you leave me here alone?

But she stopped herself. Where on earth would she send a letter to her sister now?

News of Pauline's exodus with a mobster and Abraham's condition traveled quickly through the neighborhood. All were startled. Abraham Verdonik had worked hard; he had become a respected man in the community. Besides, the insurance. He held the slips of paper with their lives scratched on them, how much each member of the community was worth to his or her family, sick or dead. All the insurance that man sold, and he hadn't taken a policy out on himself! There were so many things that needed paying for, like Pauline's ribbons, socks fringed with lace, which as she got older turned to stockings, a tortoise-shell compact that she demanded.

Though on the surface it was true he favored her older sister, Frances knew that this was merely the shell of his affection, that somewhere in the lovely, breakable egg of her father's love, the yolk was hers. And Frances's heart had always belonged to her father. While her mother's nervousness had overtaken the family with a constant *sveepink out zhe dirt*, the only phrase she said in English, a ceaseless dusting and mopping and scrubbing as if stopping the housekeeping would somehow keep the blood from pumping to her own thump-thump-thumping heart, Franny's father was a calm man and one inclined toward speaking. This is how he was able to keep up with the insurance business, how he avoided what so many in their neighborhood could not, factory work. He managed to convince people how much they needed insurance to protect their families. Even the concept of insurance was a foreign one: Why pay for a nonexistent malady only to put a hex on the entire family? Frances would come in before bed in the evenings, when the men in the neighborhood sat at the Verdonik kitchen table fingering the edges of the stained oilcloth as Rose looked on, scowling. Her father explained that they were not paying for nothing but investing in everything: Insurance, see? A blessing not a curse. You mustn't let your payments lapse, he told them.

He was a fool not to have been more careful for his own family. But Abraham's carelessness was the result of a profound belief that they—the Verdoniks of Williamsburg—were at the exact beginning of things. "Frances"—he would always try to speak to his daughter in English—"in America, no end in sight. Only zhe beginnings here." Whereas Rose, with her inveterate pessimism, had given up on learning English—Who cares? I'll be gone soon, she'd say in Yiddish—Abraham took up the language of his new world with zeal. And he passed this on to Frances.

Late at night, when talk of business or politics was through, Abraham would sit at the edge of his younger daughter's bed and tell her stories. These were the moments he spoke to her in Yiddish, and these stories always held hidden morals: "Once there was a rabbi, the leader of a village that was bordered by a people who hated them. One day their leader invited him over to work out their differences. He served ham! What did the rabbi do?" The moral was always in English: *"He ate zhe ham!"* Abraham told her. "To save his people he ate zhe ham, you see, my Franny-goil?"

Her father's gravelly voice juxtaposed with the sound of her mother in the kitchen scrubbing the roasting pan with steel wool always brought Frances to a peaceful sleep.

Had it been Frances who had fled the neighborhood with a gangster who promised her diamonds and real estate, Abraham's heart might have fallen through his body on the spot. But it was Pauline who had gone, so he simply took to his bed, and it was Frances, now his only daughter, who sat at her father's bedside. She tried to coax him upright while Rose fluttered around the room, picking up knickknacks and placing them back down again.

"Please, Mama," Frances would implore, grabbing at her arm. "Come sit with us."

But Rose would not give in. She would snap her arm back as if she feared it would be taken, and, were it loosed from its socket, her entire limb left in the incapable hands of her daughter, who would clean up this mess then?

Three months after Pauline left home, after she and the Terrier were married in a civil ceremony at City Hall, attended only by Maxie Greenberg, Waxey Gordon, and Rothstein himself, the couple moved up to Westchester.

What was Westchester like? Frances wondered.

She was desperate to know how her sister was living. Frances knew only this room. And lying alone in bed, Frances still found herself waiting for Pauline to come home from a night out. Not only could she not picture what her sister's life without her was like but there was no evidence of her now, no smell to signal where she had been and that, finally, she was back.

If her parents had known that Frances was going to see her sister one sunny day in May 1925, on the train to Westchester from Grand Central Terminal, who knows what they would have done. Frances did not tell them where she was going, or that she was heading anywhere at all; she simply kissed her oblivious father on his clammy forehead and tapped her frenzied mother, who was cleaning out the cupboards for the third time that week, on the shoulder as she slipped out the door early that morning.

Frances was sixteen years old and had been neither in such a magnificent building as Grand Central Terminal nor on a train. The whole building was flooded with light, and when Frances looked up, she saw the gilded constellations of the zodiac twinkling on the ceilings. Hope, she thought.

How romantic, she thought as her train pulled away from Manhattan. At first it was frightening, and then the sensation of relief came over her. It was the very reverse of the moment they'd arrived, the city gleaming in the distance, the way it looked as if it was rising out of the water. For the first time, it felt to Frances, that a girl could make choices. That perhaps she could—perhaps she could go wherever she'd liked. She could return or she could keep going north and north, to Canada, where she'd heard the moose come and eat right out of your hand. Frances had never seen a moose. Or she could get on a different train, one heading west, the one that she read in the papers the Terrier's mobster friends rode out to try to expand their business into California. In ten days she could be there—in California! Frances watched the trees whip by and imagined Hollywood, a place filled with movie stars, and bright lights, and palm trees, and beyond that city, desert, miles and miles of endless open space. What might that be like?

If Pauline doesn't want to be Miss America, well, maybe it could be me, Frances thought, scratching her chin and looking out the train window. Maybe I could be famous. She had to laugh at herself. Miss America. It will never be me, she thought, looking at her face superimposed over the changing landscape. Never.

When Frances arrived in Westchester, she learned that it looked a lot like ancient Egypt. Terrier, who had an obsession with Egypt—this came from the time he was refused entry into the country—had turned the place in Rye, New York, into an Egyptian lair, complete with golden gates flanked by two replicas of the Sphinx.

"I'll tell you why I built the place, Fran," the Terrier said to his new sister-in-law when he went to meet her at the station in his yellow Duesenberg. "Because if I can't go to Egypt, then Egypt sure as hell can come to me."

When they arrived at the estate, the Terrier opened the door for Frances. She had been so bowled over by the luxurious automobile, the fine leather seats, and the shiny mirrors and handles that she hadn't even noticed their arrival until the Terrier swung out his short little arm. Walking toward the house, the Terrier looked back proudly at his yellow Model A.

"Eighty-seven horsepower, baby," he said to Frances as he turned toward the house. "That's an eight-cylinder engine." The Terrier made the gesture of a gun with his right hand.

"It's nice, Sol," Frances said.

"Nice!" he said, laughing. "Nice, she says."

"Land!" he told her. "*My* land! You know, when we were kids on South Fifth, all I could see out of my window was walls. Walls, walls, walls. My father spent his life looking out onto an airshaft. Like animals we lived. Now look." He took a huge gulp of air. "If my father wasn't so damn moral, he'd be proud," he said. "Don't you think he's proud in his own way, Franny-goil?"

Frances pictured Herbert dragging himself up the stoop as if it didn't matter if he ever went inside his house again. "I think he is," she said.

"And my brother too," he said. "But he won't come up here. Not a chance."

Frances was silent, but she understood Joseph. They had both been left to clean up the messes of their selfish older siblings. She wondered, for a moment, why she had come and if she shouldn't just turn around and head back to Brooklyn. Frances thought of the ceiling at Grand Central, the whole universe painted on a golden ceiling.

They walked through the door and into the foyer. Despite the fountain spewing water out of the mouth of a mummified king and the sand, brought in from the Maine coast, the molding stenciled in golden foil, hieroglyphics circling the room, the room still smelled of new paint.

"You know, in ancient Egypt it was customary to weigh the heart of the dead. If the Jews did that, everyone would one day see how it's a decent enough life I'm leading. And I have a big, good heart." The Terrier thumped his chest. "Don't you think?" Beads of sweat were collecting on his nose and his fleshy cheeks.

"Of course," Frances said. She smiled at the Terrier, remembering him just last year below her window, hat in his hands. How could this be the same man who ghosted through town heading toward evil?

Then Pauline walked into the foyer. She looked like an entirely new girl, stunning with a short, soft, bobbed haircut, dangling diamond earrings just peeking out from beneath her thick, dark hair. She wore a long satin gown, and it was barely eleven o'clock. "Frances," she said quietly. She went to hug her sister tentatively.

All the small things her father had given Pauline to make her look more beautiful now seemed ridiculous. A compact? Rayon stockings? These were tawdry and small and useless to her sister.

Frances hugged Pauline back and felt the way a world already hung between them. She had shared a bed with her sister all her life, and now, pressed to her for the first time in months, her sister's body was the structure of a stranger. When she pulled away, Frances could see her sister's face looked harder, her distinct features chiseled, the face now of a woman.

"Hello," Frances said. "Am *I* invited to the party?" she asked, fingering the heavy salmon-colored cloth of the gown.

Pauline laughed. "Darling," she said, "this is my nightgown."

Frances looked up at the symbols that lined the moldings like a painted trellis. "What does that mean?" she asked.

Pauline scoffed at her. "What difference does it make?" she said.

"It means Home Sweet Home!" the Terrier said. "In ancient Egyptian."

"I don't think it does," said Pauline.

"When you asked the designer, over and over again, that's what he told you," the Terrier said. "'I want to know what it means!' she told him over and over. Now she doesn't believe him. Ridiculous. Home Sweet Home it means. It means Pauline will always be waiting here for me." The Terrier tapped her bottom, which rippled beneath the satin.

Pauline shuffled away, and the Terrier turned to Frances. "You've got to see the library, kid," he said.

King Tutankhamen's tomb had been discovered three years previously, and as much as the Terrier wanted to re-create that feel, also, he told Frances, he wanted his house to have the air of intelligence. He walked through the parlor, which was set up to look like the inside of a tomb but with more light, the Terrier explained, and into an enormous library. It was wooded and dark and calming. Frances went over to the enormous leather seats that were perched along a polished mahogany table.

"You like?" the Terrier asked. "Feel them! Come on, feel them! Soft as a baby's bottom."

Frances ran her hands over the supple leather and looked up at the walls, lined with books.

"Look here, kid, I got the Dickens, the Fielding, the Henry James." The Terrier went around the room reading names from the leather-bound spines. "Proust," he said.

Frances thought of her father with his wire spectacles reading and rereading those old, yellow books at the greasy kitchen table before he took to his bed, and she tried to shake off the extreme weight of that memory.

Pauline sauntered into the room. "But how many have you read, Terry?" she asked her husband. She put her hands on her hips. "Huh?"

The Terrier looked up, squinting, his mouth, which was normally quite large, drawn up into a horrible scowl. "You can't talk to me like that!" he said. "I don't care who you are!" he said. And then he turned back to Frances. "Look here, doll, those are real books with honest-to-God pages."

Pauline rolled her eyes.

Frances nodded and took down a volume of T. S. Eliot, the board thick and crass, covered in new leather, the binding not yet broken. She flipped an edition of Richardson from the shelf and then a Charlotte Brontë, the pages not yet cut. Each book she took down was as brand-new as the one before. "They're beautiful," she said to them both. Again she remembered her father, the days he sat up straight and slammed a book closed to shock Rose into ceasing to clean.

Frances rubbed her arms.

"Cold?" The Terrier asked her.

Frances nodded.

"Let's go back into the desert then!" he said, putting his hand at the small of Frances's back to guide her out of the room and into the sand-filled foyer.

Frances could stay only a few hours, because she had to return before her parents suspected she had gone to see her sister. After lying on Pauline's massive four-poster bed, her legs scissoring the air as Pauline showed her gown after gown, pearl after diamond, fur coat after mink stole, Frances became restless. She began to miss the little flat she shared with her unhappy parents, next to her unhappy neighbors, on an unhappy and yet somehow hopeful street. Anger, the kind that she had experienced when she took down that chopped liver swan only a little over a year ago, came over her. It was not jealousy, Frances was sure of this. Though she would have liked a dress or two, where on earth would she wear it? It was just anger. Anger that her sister had abandoned her for this life. This life with the Terrier, a life of things. Was having things worth giving up everything? Your family? Was having things better than winning the Miss America contest? Better than fame? Even Franny could see her sister was going now for infamy.

Frances strolled the grounds of the estate on her own, walking all the way down to the man-made river, "the Nile," that the Terrier had had put in and maintained with a state-of-the-art irrigation system. After sitting on its rather small bank, Frances went back to the house to get the Terrier to take her to the train, and to say good-bye to her sister.

"I'll drive you back, kid," he said when she found him in the kitchen, eating sturgeon with his fingers, straight out of the waxed deli paper. "Want some?" He held out the package to her.

Franny shook her head and panicked. If she came back with the Ter-rier, the whole neighborhood would know exactly where she'd been. And they'd have some things to say about where she was headed as well. It would make everything worse. The neighbors would become convinced that the Verdoniks were in cahoots with their daughter, that they stood behind every lousy decision she'd made.

"But I *love* the train," Frances said meekly.

The Terrier threw the sturgeon back into the icebox without even folding the paper over the fish. "Nah. You don't. You love the car, doll! I have some business in Brooklyn anyway," he said.

Was he testing her? Did he know that she didn't want to be seen with him? Frances had no idea. She thought of the prospect of not having to pay the train fare back into town. There she went, just like her sister. Frances pulled at her single whisker as she deliberated about what to do.

"Okay," she said. "If it's not too much trouble."

"Off we go!" he said.

Frances wandered the house looking for her sister to say good-bye, and she found her in the library. Pauline stood in her nightgown on the ladder that slid across the walls so one could reach any book one wanted. Pauline must not have heard the soft padding of Frances's entry, because Frances watched her open a book with a grand and vio-lent gesture that sounded like a bone cracking and then replace it on the wall. Frances watched her sister do this with three more books, imagining that each was a bone breaking, resetting, and settling back into its proper place in the skeletal system.

"Pauline," Frances said quietly. "I'm leaving now."

Pauline jerked around at the sound of her sister's voice. Tears ran down her lovely face. "Bye," she said. She handed Frances the book she was holding. It had a hairline fracture along the spine, as delicate as a spider's thread.

"What are you doing?" Frances asked. Had she gone mad, the way everyone said about Mrs. Goldstein, who one day took all her furniture out of her house and lay on her couch on the corner of South Fifth Street until some mothers sent their sons to help her back inside? Perhaps Pauline had been hypnotized, some kind of mobster black magic, which must have been how the Terrier had gotten her up here to begin with.

"If you got the books," she said, "might as well look like you've read them." Pauline shrugged and took the book back from her sister. Frances nodded.

It would finish her father off in earnest to hear such things, Frances thought. Again anger rose in her, and she resisted the impulse to knock her sister off her ladder and rip her face—the mask she wore, those earrings, the straight black hair—just tear this from her face and watch her sister scream.

"Sol? I'm ready to leave!" Frances yelled into the tomb of the living room as she turned to walk away without so much as kissing her sister good-bye.

CHAPTER 5

Electricity:
Joseph Brodsky, 1931

THE FIRST FEW YEARS of their marriage were difficult times for Joe and Esther. Their love was bountiful enough; it was just the money that was on the scarce side, despite his brother's wealth. Joseph wanted nothing that came printed with the Mob's greasy—stains not water soluble—fingers. Sometimes he wondered whether he was not just cleaning up behind his brother. Joseph imagined his life as if it was an actual cloth, swiping through layers of soot and dirt in an attempt to reveal the glorious, shining metal beneath. He knew he had to build his own fortune, in his own manner, in his own time.

Though Joseph liked being his parents' only son, and though he believed in a pure life of good works, at the bottom of it all, it was really Esther and the prospect of children that kept him from going into business with the Terrier.

"Don't even mention his name to me!" Joseph would scream at Esther when she asked if they could just this once take a loan from Solomon.

Even on his most demoralized days, he would not consider it. Joseph raised his voice only when it came to talk of his brother.

"But, Joe," Esther would say softly. "He's your brother!" She'd tear through the silver wrapper of the Hershey's bar with her teeth. Ever since she'd been pregnant, she couldn't get enough of them.

"I don't have a brother!" Joseph would scream back, kneeling to pick up the bits of foil his wife had spit on the floor. "You know, Esther, you're going to get fat!" he'd tell her, rolling the foil into a ball between his fingers.

"I know," she'd say, laughing, taking it from him to throw away. "You'll still love me, right, Joe?" She would go to give him a kiss on the lips but hit his nose instead.

"Correct," said Joseph. "But it's bad for your health, you know, and I'd like to keep you around for a vhile."

How had his life turned out this way? That feeling he had when he came back with nothing. Or he should say, when he came back with everything. Nothing sold. How could this be? Joseph had known salesmen who really lived the high life. His old friend from the neighborhood Bernie Rottenberg—light fixtures, bulbs, he sold—he ate at all the fancy-schmancy places, wined and dined his clients on those huge boats on the Long Island Sound. Perhaps when he decided not to go into business with his brother, Joseph had thought, There is still the possibility for grandeur. As his friend had. Bernie sold light. There was power in looking out at the skyline of a city at twilight and saying, "Let there be light!" It was a little bit like playing God, Joseph thought now. Would that have soothed his mother or worried her?

His mother had always told him: God is in the smallest things. Cleanliness is next to godliness, yes, he'd thought, watching the buildings light up at night, but illuminating the city was sure to be the work of God. He was in the light. God was not in the corked glass bottles and bars of fat and clay Joseph carried with him in his two leather valises.

The Terrier was making more dough racketeering than anyone from South Fifth Street had ever dreamed possible. But at what price, all this money? Joseph had heard from his mother that Mendel Shulz (Ethel's husband, she'd said, incredulous when Joseph had said, Who?) had seen Solomon on Kent Street, by the water, chasing after some poor fellow. Solomon had jumped out of a car with another hoodlum and thrown this poor kid up against a building, punched him in the head and in the stomach, and, when he'd keeled over, Solomon and his buddy had kicked him. Then they hopped in the car and drove off, left that guy just bleeding on the street. "Like an animal!" Selma had said to Joseph, and he had not been sure if she'd meant his brother or his brother's victim.

Joseph didn't ask if that man was still alive. That was the last time Selma Brodsky would discuss her elder son.

He tried not to think about the kind of violence his brother involved himself in, orchestrated even, as he lugged bottles of his own—instead of liquor, it was jars of Procter & Gamble soap flakes, and bars of Ivory—all across southern New England. Though the flakes performed poorly in hard water, leaving a ring in the washing machine, dulling colors, and turning whites gray, Joseph had to find an effective way to convince the industries he sold to, and the homes he stopped in along the way, that Procter & Gamble was the brand to buy.

"The soap that floats!" he'd tell them, holding up a clean, white bar of Ivory. No matter what, he loved the smell of that soap, each and every time he took a sample out for show.

"That's a lovely dress you have on, Mrs., Mrs., what is your name, miss?"

Selling was not his calling. And Joseph knew because of this he would be fired soon. He knew he needed to find something that would make him money. Esther had suggested he start his own dry-cleaning business. Since that lucky man Stoddard had found the petroleum solvent that made dry cleaning a safe profession, Esther was insistent on it.

"You'll be home," she said. "No more nights on the road. We can go to Maine." Esther put her hand over her heart.

She had it all figured out: The dry cleaner was going to be on the corner of Baxter Boulevard and Franklin Street, and that meant that she was going to live just down the block from where Joseph worked, not far from the street where she'd grown up. Though now it's an old folks' home, she'd told Joseph, as if his finding this out would somehow change his plans. Can you believe it? And they expanded the place, built right over where I buried my appendix when I was a little girl. I had it in a glass jar and I buried it and now the old folks' home is built right on top of it.

"Can you imagine?" Esther had said.

Joseph could not imagine one of his wife's internal organs covered by an old-age home, it was true. It gave him the creeps that part of her was already buried. He had to admit, though, that the idea of customers coming to him was appealing. From the moment they walked in the door, a sale completed. Still, he refused. In the end, Joseph felt he could make more money on the road in his Chevrolet, the windshield open, the breeze in his hair, thoughts of all the great things the future would bring clanking around his brain like the bottles on the backseat.

"Maine?" Joseph said. He couldn't imagine what it would be like to live so far north. He had been there only in the summertime, which he had to admit was breathtaking. One evening he and Esther escaped her mother and went to Amato's for Italian sandwiches. Upon seeing the sun setting from a distance, they had pulled onto a dirt road, driving until they reached water.

"Casco Bay," Esther said. It was as if she was now breathing for the first time since she'd left Portland. "Casco Bay."

Joseph watched the sky turning to twilight, a crescent moon rising. It was so beautiful—clean and cold and pure—that Joe promised her then and there that someday he would take her back there to live. "But not now, Esther," he said as he tried to turn the car around to head home to her mother.

Esther became suddenly enraged. "Not now? Why not now!"

"Calm down," Joseph said. Sometimes his wife's rush to anger startled him, but he had always found a way to kid her out of it. Even just placing his hand high on her thigh, heated from her fleeting rage, signaled her to relax a moment and put what had happened into context. Frankly, Joseph could think of a million reasons why not, but strangely what came to mind was a joke his father always told him.

There was a Mr. Cohen, Herbert Brodsky always began, who was trying to run a store in an Irish Catholic neighborhood. He wasn't doing much business—all the Irish Catholics were getting all the customers. So, figuring he had to do something to change things, he went to the judge. Cohen says, "Judge, I want to change my name to Kelly." When the judge asks him why, Mr. Cohen tells him his story and how he feels it will help his business. So the judge allows him to change his name. Not a year later, the fellow comes back and the judge asks him if he wants to change his name again. Mr. Kelly says, "Yes, I do." "You were Cohen, now you're Kelly and now you want to change it again," the judge says to him. "That's right," Kelly says. "Well, what would you like to change it to now?" asks the judge. The fellow tells him he would like his new name to be Flaherty. "And why on earth do you want to change it from Kelly to Flaherty?" asks the judge. "How is that going to help you?" "Here's how," says the fellow. "You know people come in and they ask me my name and I tell them it's Kelly. So the first thing they say to me is, Well, what was it before you changed it?"

The joke used to infuriate Solomon. You think no matter what we're just Jews? he'd scream at his father. No matter what? You've got it all wrong, he'd say, stomping out of the kitchen.

But Joseph always considered this less a joke and more a cautionary tale: See what happens when you try to move away from where you come from? You lose your good name. Just like when we came over. It will be so horrible, you will lose your self twice.

His wife was from here, but Joseph was not. He embraced the diverse Boston neighborhood he now lived in, but he considered Maine a country of sameness. Doing business among strangers. This was what he did now, yes, but he moved around. He was always free to go, and he did not rely on people coming to him. He imagined them all, tall and white and fleshy in their wool caps, and, before they gave him their filthy laundry, they'd take one look at his face and ask him his name.

"Because it's not the time," Joseph said. "You've got to calm down," he told his wife again.

"Calm down?" Esther slammed her hand against her head and looked out the window. "Calm down he says," she said to no one.

Joseph was trying to get the large car out of the small box he had somehow parked in during the excitement of watching the sun go down with his wife. In his frustration, he nearly backed up into the only other vehicle on the street.

"Joe," Esther screamed. "Watch where you're going!"

Joseph took a deep breath. He considered himself a patient man, and yet, right now, his patience was slipping away. He visualized a stream of water swirling down a drain. He was turning around to go back to his mother-in-law's house, where he would be forced to listen to her berate Esther for marrying down. A black life you'll have, Sylvia would tell her daughter, as if he weren't sitting right there, holding Esther's hand. A life of wanting more and more and more, Esther's mother would tell her. That's what you will have.

"Esther, I spend my life in zhis automobile. I know how to drive it," Joseph said. "Will you please just shut up?" he said, avoiding the other vehicle just in the nick of time.

"Huuuh?" Esther sucked in her breath. Her eyes went wide, wild with anger. And then she shut them, crossed her arms, and pointed her chin to the sky.

Joseph tried to turn the car out of the awkward space. He reversed it a little and then jerked it forward. Sweating into the crown of his hat, he turned to look behind him, then down at the gearshift.

He reversed slowly, looking into the rearview mirror. Out of the corner of his eye he could see his wife smirking as she turned around to watch his progress.

Suddenly the back of the car slammed into a tree, and Joseph and Esther were pitched forward.

"Oh my goodness!" Joseph said. He turned to his wife. "Are you okay? That must have been in my blind spot."

"Musta been," Esther said. "I'm fine," she told him.

"Thank goodness," he said, breathing.

"I saw it coming," Esther told him, shrugging her shoulders.

Joseph clenched his jaw and looked straight ahead, his knuckles white as he gripped the steering wheel. "Well, vhy on earth didn't you say something zhen?"

Esther turned to her husband, her arms still crossed over her chest. "I would have, darling, but you told me to shut up."

Joseph stared at her blankly for a moment and then got out of the car—now backed halfway onto the grass—to assess the damage.

Esther leaned out the window as he leaned over the left side of the automobile. "I know you spend your life in cars, Joe, believe me, but I gotta tell you, you've always been a dreadful driver."

Though Joseph had promised Esther he would get her back to Portland one day, he imagined the town in winter, bleak as the North Pole but for the evergreens popping up out of a thick blanket of white, people barely speaking as they passed in the streets, bundled with so much clothing they could hardly wave hello. He imagined a stillness that he wanted to covet for its tranquillity but that he knew would feel closer to death than to calm.

Joseph knew he could make something of his own, just as Stoddard had. This was when he began to work to find a cleaning product that was miscible in both oil and water. Though he was not a businessman, Joseph knew there was an opening in the marketplace, a space like a doorway he was sure he could walk through and fill with his small stature. But it would take work and experimenting and documenting and formulating and mixing, and this was what Joseph set out to do.

Joseph told Esther about Solomon only once, and this admission had been brought on by liquor, something he rarely indulged in. But Esther's asking to take money from his brother made him remember Solomon again. He remembered looking at the night sky through Solomon's telescope. That had been incredible—looking out into the black of what felt like another universe entirely. And then their tiny kitchen, Shabbos at their crooked little table. Though Joseph often thought of his brother, on the surface he remembered him more as the villain he'd edited from a wicked fairy tale that was life growing up in Brooklyn.

How could his brother turn his back on this?

Though Joseph willed himself not to think of it, simply not let it pass into his thoughts, he couldn't help himself. For the first time, he understood his brother. Who knew it would be so hard to get so little in life? Why hadn't his father told him that on the stoop as he told his sons the future was theirs? Why not cut corners? Joseph thought now. Who really sees anyway?

God sees. But also I do, thought Joseph. He remembered his father's spectacles, fogged from the steam of his mother's cooking, four pots boiling on that tiny black stove. It's just knowing, thought Joseph, not seeing.

All those weeks he spent on the road away from Esther, he'd still make time some Friday nights to get down to Brooklyn when he had a very southern route mapped out for him. When he drove over the

Williamsburg Bridge to his parents', it was always the same: he wished he had something to show for himself. And he dreaded the flat view from the bridge, no skyline, as he headed into bleakness. Pulling onto the block, kids playing stickball in the street the way he had so many years before, depressed him. Getting out of his car and looking up to see Frances Verdonik sitting on the stoop—did she ever leave that exact spot?—also depressed him. Was she waiting for her sister to come home? The only way Pauline was coming back was in a coffin, thought Joseph, scolding himself for thinking it at the exact moment the thought came into his head.

What was this girl waiting for? Frances always looked like she was about to burst into tears.

Hello, Frances. Joseph would always tip his hat to her. What else could he do? Sometimes he would bring her a bar of soap tied up with string like a present. For your mommy, okay? he'd say.

Joseph wished that he could be the good son, that he had the means his brother had to give his parents what they deserved. He wanted to sit at his mother's table, her white tablecloth pressed and cleaned from the week before. He wanted to bow his head as he had on so many Friday nights in his youth, recite the brachot, watch his mother fill his plate with tsimes.

But his father's way, the world of that Friday table, that no longer made sense to Joseph. Nothing made sense to him, he realized nights alone on the road, only your thoughts to drive you half mad. He thought of the universe on those nights. He watched the universe in the stars. He listened to it on the radio. The very fact that radio existed, Joseph thought, was more fantasy than God. Mystical, perhaps, occult forces he knew nothing about. Not God. What had happened with his brother, it was not personal. What had happened in Russia, this was not personal either. God is not personal. It is the nature of the universe. It is humans. What's going on here, on South Fifth Street—Pauline's little sister about to weep on the front stoop; his mother, her hands in her lap as she sits at the table covered by that clean tablecloth waiting for her son to come home so she can tell him: my beautiful boy, so good, my only son. This was the image that nearly broke him—here on the open road in the middle of this black night, Esther rubbing lemons on her elbows and knees before bed, that was God.

It didn't make sense to him anymore, this. His father's many rituals. The morning prayer. How could he betray his father and tell him that he didn't want to pray and tefillin anymore? Why, Joseph thought, do I have to wear a prayer shawl to show that I am thinking of God under my underwear? Perhaps he was more like his brother than he'd thought.

Joseph remembered when he and Solomon sat in the living room playing marbles and watching their father put on his phylacteries, those little square boxes he placed on his head and under his left arm. When he began to shake back and forth, rocking and rocking, Solomon turned to Joseph and said, "He's all charged up with electricity! Look! It's making him move!"

Joseph laughed and then stopped himself. He had not wanted his father to hear him.

But visiting his parents as an adult, he felt the same way about it. What is it exactly? Joseph wondered. It seemed artificial to him, external. Wasn't it enough to have God in his heart?

It was not enough. In how many ways could a person be chosen? Chosen, Joseph began to think, was something else, a mark perhaps. Like what happened on his honeymoon. He and Esther had gone to the Laurentian Mountains, just outside Montreal. He had known that there was anti-Semitism in the area and that there were certain policies operating in the hotels. Mostly to avoid embarrassment, Joseph wrote to many hotels and resorts, letting them know he and his wife were Jews and inquiring about their policy regarding this undeniable fact, as they had not wanted their honeymoon ruined by someone telling them they were not wanted. The hotel they finally picked had said nothing about it. They were welcome and they went there, and stayed for an entire week, swimming and playing tennis, walking in the woods, making love before dinner, and listening to the band play each night beneath the stars. They'd played Irving Berlin's "Blue Skies" every evening, and time after time Joseph held Esther close to him and had confused her heartbeat with his own.

The first night had been quite funny, actually. Esther all dressed up in her special wedding lingerie. She had gone to the bathroom down the hall in these ridiculous satin slippers and without a robe, and when she got out of the toilet, she had no idea which was their room. Esther had stopped at nearly every door: "Joseph?" she had whispered, scratching like a cat on the doors along the hallway. "Joe?"

Joseph had heard her when she got two doors down from their room, and he had thought it so funny, he'd almost let Esther come all the way down the corridor to him. But instead he'd opened the door and, hands on his hips, waited for his new wife to turn and come toward the sliver of light.

"Hello, my darling," he'd said, pulling her inside.

"Boy, am I ever glad to see you," she'd said, giggling into his arms.

They had planned to leave on Labor Day, and so the Saturday night before the end of their trip, Joseph went down to pay the bill. Suddenly, in front of him there was a sign that said "Christian clientele only." Joseph had never seen the sign before and, confused, he went back upstairs to ask Esther if she had seen it.

"No, Joe," she said, placing the book she was reading on her chest. "I haven't seen any such sign."

"You're sure?" he asked again.

"Positive," Esther said.

He went down to straighten it out. In the lobby, he asked for the manager. When the man came out of his back office, Joseph told him what had happened.

"You know zhat I'm a Jew, don't you?" Joseph asked.

"Of course I know that," the manager said.

"Well, it seems my vife and I are not velcome here," Joseph said. He pointed to the sign.

The manager reddened. He turned to the desk clerk and yelled, "Take that sign down immediately!"

When Joseph asked why they had the sign in the first place, the manager told him that Jews were welcome in the summer, but there was a new policy that come Labor Day—high season because of the fall foliage and the apple picking—the clientele did not want Jews around. "The sign is down now," the manager said, nodding toward the desk clerk. "It will be fine."

"Zhis does not go on and off like a spigot!" Joseph said.

"I apologize," the manager said. "The sign went up two days early."

Joseph and Esther went to the dance that night, and they danced the way they had on all the other nights. When "Blue Skies" played then, though, Joseph felt something crawl into his throat and attach itself there. As he held Esther, who had drunk quite a bit of champagne, he took in the all-over smell of her, wondering would that lump ever leave him.

At the end of the evening, they returned to the room, and as soon as they'd opened the door, the smell of roses overcame them. Esther squealed and clapped her hands to see that the room was filled with enormous pink roses. They were on the dresser, on the nightstand, on the writing table, as well as thrown across the bed.

"How beautiful!" Esther cried. She twirled around the room. She took a stem and placed it delicately behind her ear. "It's so romantic, Joe!"

"It sure isn't," he said. "Let's pack."

"Come on," Esther said. She placed one rose between her teeth and went pawing at Joseph, her left foot kicking the ground like that of a filly.

"I'm sorry, but ve are leaving tonight!" he said. Still dressed in his evening clothes, Esther nursing a torn lip from the rose stem she had clamped between her teeth without realizing it had thorns, Joseph drove them south into the black night, the Lucky Strike Orchestra coming through on the radio—"While you listen to Weber and Fields, or sit out a dance, we suggest you reach for a Lucky, always kind to your throat. Now we open with 'Dip Your Brush in the Sunshine'"—just as they hit Boston.

Joseph couldn't bring himself to tell his father of this experience. Somehow it was easy, as a kid, to explain the fights he and Solomon got into with the Irish and the Italians who were behind every corner, waiting to attack, waiting to tell the Brodsky brothers, We are better than you. Joseph knew this experience informed the decisions his brother had made that had left a hole in his family where Solomon once had been physically, and also a hole of silence where once there had been stories and memories and talk of the future. So much could never be spoken between these two generations; it was unnatural, thought Joseph, never to say a word about it.

But he knew that this injustice would hurt Herbert as the world always seemed to hurt him, as his elder son had. It was important for Joseph to give his father the gift that his father was so sure he had given him: this country. *Goldene medina!* How could Joseph look his father in the eye and tell him, No, Father, what we have here is a fool's paradise?

Always, leaving his parents' home, it was the same. He had known what his father had *not* wanted for him: don't be a bad boy, don't turn away from your family, don't stand on the corner that way like the bad boys, don't turn your back on God like all bad boys are wont to do. But what had his father wanted him to be?

"But my dreams," Herbert had said when Solomon told him he was leaving. "What about my dreams?" his father had pleaded. "And *my* dreams?" Solomon had screamed at his father. "What about *my* dreams?"

Silence.

Joseph had looked up from his studies at the unusual sound and seen his father's desperate face. Silence is the sound the dashing of my father's dreams makes, Joseph had thought then.

Driving back up to Boston, where his wife—a woman he would live every day unable to believe she had actually chosen him—waited for him to come home, Joseph wondered as he had when he was a boy in his father's loud house: Is this strange silence the sound of the dashing of my own dreams?

CHAPTER 6

Irrevocability:
Seymour Bloom, 1928

SEYMOUR BLOOM WAS MAKING his own sales calls in Westchester, New York, which was how he stumbled into the Terrier's lair. Three years after Frances had stood in the library and watched her sister crack the bindings of each new book, Seymour Bloom stepped through the golden gates, past the oasis with its trickling waterfall and tropical grasses, and, beneath the imported palms and golden moldings, he tried to sell Pauline a set of encyclopedias.

She seemed interested enough. "Knowledge of everything in one place," she said as she peered through the door. "How convenient. That's something my husband will really love." Pauline invited Seymour through the golden doors and into Egypt.

As he stood in the threshold, his back to the closed front doors, Seymour, not realizing he was in the desert, watched Pauline look at him the way one who has been trapped in the desert for a long time looks at a tall, cold glass of water. He sensed her thirst as she slowly led him into the living room.

"What brings you so far up here?" she asked, coyly placing her hair behind her ears.

"I find that people like to read in Westchester," Seymour said. "There are not a lot of people around, and they have the time and also the space to store all the volumes. Books take room," he said, raising his eyebrows. "You sure have lots of room up here."

Pauline nodded. "That is true," she said. "Plenty of room."

She brought Seymour into the parlor and sat him on the velvet chaise. He took out the A volume, the first in the set, and turned the pages to show her the fine paper, the beautiful type, the wealth of information that could be obtained in such a short period of time, such a condensed amount of space. Pauline leaned into him. Looking slyly over at the glossy pages that held so many things—*aardvark, abacus, abalone*—Seymour watched her.

"I like the *destinations.*" Pauline flipped through to Argentina, then Australia. She sighed as she ran her hand over the yellow and green map, her finger tracing the picture of the large continent.

"Never been?" Seymour asked her.

Pauline laughed. "To Australia? I can't say I have." She shook her head. "You?"

"Not exactly," he said.

"But anyway, the Terrier—that's my husband, at least that's what people call him—he never takes me anywhere. 'I like you here, Toots,' he says, 'so I know where you are and what I'm comin' home to.' More like 'so I can shtup my mistress in peace,'" Pauline said.

Seymour sat upright and cleared his throat. The Terrier. He wondered if he was the gangster who kept getting written up in the papers for illegal liquor distribution, who had been linked to all those shootings (including that of the infamous gangster Monkey Mars, who had turned up riddled with bullets in front of the Crossroads Cafe on Ninth Street), but no one had been able to prove a thing.

How many Terriers could there be, and living like this? thought Seymour.

Pauline got up warily, and, as Seymour lined the heavy books up on the glass coffee table, she stood in front of him and leaned in. "Some iced tea?" she asked. She pushed her tits up with the blue-white insides of her arms and placed her hands between her knees.

Seymour could not have known what it had been like for Pauline, a woman so clearly not from these parts, to live up here alone. He could not have known that Pauline, who had by now spent more than enough time in the desert, had been with the Terrier for nearly three years and had only just gotten used to having sex with a man three-quarters of her size, that to compensate for their imperfect fit, the two had grown accustomed to kissing on the stairs, Pauline three steps below, the Terrier bending down, his plump fingers reaching for the heart-shaped ass he'd seen the day Frances beheaded the swan and he had met his future business partners. And Pauline had accepted their way of adapting to the outsides of each other. Dripping in jewels and topped by a feather hat, mother-of-pearl pins poking out from the brim, she actually took it quite well. Seymour had no idea that her favorite way to make love to her husband was naked but for her long chocolate brown mink, one of the three furs the Terrier had purchased for her for their first anniversary. How could Seymour know the way Pauline enjoyed standing in high heels, feet planted firmly on the floor, the silk lining of the mink cold against her skin, the collar tickling her neck and breasts, as the Terrier made love to her while parked on a low stool? Never did she feel more powerful or more loved.

Seymour noticed Pauline's feet first because he had been looking down to avoid looking at her tantalizing breasts. Her feet were small and gorgeous, attached to the slimmest of ankles, which led, in turn, to an extremely fine pair of legs. He willed himself not to think of Sarah's monstrous boats, a steel sledgehammer attached to each of the legs she pulled into bed, one after the other, night after night. In his mind, Seymour climbed the ladder of Pauline's well-built body, entirely unlike the upright coffin of his wife's figure, and landed on the final rung of Pauline's pretty face. Her hair was as fine as black spun silk—Sleeping Beauty, Seymour thought, resisting the urge to reach up and run his fingers through the smooth, dark fibers, the back of his hand along her white, porcelain cheeks.

For a brief and perverse moment, one that he would try to shake away for years, Seymour had an urge to enter her, as if to split her open from top to bottom and wear her like a coat, slide into her skin one arm after the other and become her. And he wondered if this was not why his wife wanted a mink coat so desperately, to have the feeling of slipping into another's pelt and thus becoming someone else.

As Seymour was imagining trying Pauline on, the Terrier walked into the house.

"Pauline Paw-*Paw*?" he screamed from the foyer. "Whose crummy ride is out front, Paw? A Model T?" he said. "Ha ha!"

Now he stood in the archway leading into the parlor, and Seymour glanced at him, a short, thick man, with an angry red face, a collapsed nose, and fleshy, sagging cheeks. Seymour looked hard at the Terrier. What must he be seeing? Seymour thought. Here his wife was, leaning over a man. And if he did say so himself, Seymour was not as squat and squishy as the Terrier. What was this Sleeping Beauty doing with a man like that? Seymour had no idea that it was his very body that would make Pauline's husband, who hated athletes nearly as much as rats and snitches, pull a gun on him.

"Uh, hellooo?" the Terrier said, pointing his gun slightly at Seymour but more at the encyclopedias.

There was a moment of silence as Seymour looked up from the couch, the image of this lovely girl he would have loved to wear just about anywhere already only a memory replaced by violence. He stared straight at the gun and began to laugh. His whole fit body shook, not with the knee-slapping laugh of Pauline and the Terrier's old neighborhood, where the women on their stoops seemed to shake the street, but with a delicate suggestion that seemed in opposition to his large body.

"You don't cares I kill ya?" the Terrier said. "I've seen men shit their trousers when I've held this at them." He walked closer to Seymour, pointing the gun at his head. Seymour felt the irrevocability of the cold steel. "I've seen 'em try and run away too. Or beg me for their life. But never this. You laughin' at me? You think something's funny?"

Seymour wiped his eyes and held out his hand to the Terrier. "No," he said, straightening. "Not laughing at you at all. Hello," he said. "I'm Seymour Bloom," he said. "Your wife was kind enough to invite me in. I have been talking to her about this lovely line of encyclopedias." He saw her legs again, one foot tapping the floor gently as she rocked back and forth, her large, firm breasts shaking with her generous hips.

Pauline, who had not breathed since the gun was drawn, let out a deep breath and began to cough. "Terry," she said. "Really." She shook her head at her husband, trying not to look at Seymour.

The Terrier lowered his gun when he saw the leather books, embossed in gold. "Pretty," he said. With his free hand, he ran his hands over the covers. "Nice. Bloom," he said. "You mean Blume? You in disguise?"

"Not really," Seymour said.

"I see," he said. "You're the quiet type."

Seymour shrugged.

"Seymour," the Terrier said. "You speak Jewish?"

Seymour nodded slowly, eyeing the little man before him, saliva foaming at each side of his mouth. "I do," Seymour said. "I prefer English though."

Now the Terrier began to laugh. He turned to Pauline. "I can just see it, Paw-Paw. Can you see Rothstein's and Greenberg's faces when I show up with this one? Like a goddamn gentile. None of the Sicilians can tell me I'm loadin' 'em down with a bunch of Hebes, can they? But let me tell you something." He looked straight at Seymour. "I never got down on my knees for any Christian. Seymour the Goy! Laughs down the barrel of any gun."

"I dunno, Sol." Pauline shifted her feet. "It's really up to him, isn't it?"

"Seymour the Goy!" the Terrier said again. "Here." He threw the gun at Seymour, who, after a split second of fear, caught it surely and swiftly. "How about we move you into a more profitable line of sales?"

Seymour thought for a moment. What exactly did he have to lose? After all, anything could be a more profitable line of sales. He thought of the photos of gangsters turning up on weedy Long Island beaches. Would that be him? Or would he be powerful, respected, feared, the things he admired about these guys when he read about their exploits in the papers? He pictured Rothstein, elegant in his suits and cuffed sleeves, his gold watches. That could be me, Seymour thought. I could be him.

Seymour scratched his chin. He looked at Pauline, who smiled encouragingly. He thought of his father-in-law. "Prospects?" Fritz Rosen asked him over and over in the same nightmares he lost his teeth in, as he did in so many of his dreams.

For now, it would work, a beginning, finally a beginning. He thought of Sarah, happy in a new fur coat. He thought of the pearls, how they would sit perfectly at the base of her long neck, resting like drops of dew in that dip at the bottom of her throat. Here, he would say to his wife. These are from me! Me!

Seymour thought of going to the theater every night and one day—he let himself think it now for the first time—one day having enough money to put on a Broadway show of his very own. Broadway! His name listed in *Playbill* for everyone to see. For now, it might be okay. Seymour could begin to dream. For now, he had nothing to lose.

The Terrier was already pouring the brandy. He handed the glass to Seymour, who held the snifter high in the air and then took a long, slow sip without saying a word.

CHAPTER 7

Peppermints:
Frances Gold, 1925

FRANCES DID TAKE THAT RIDE home with the Terrier after visiting her sister in Egypt. How could she refuse it? The Terrier had removed the top, and they had driven down to Manhattan in open air.

"Whoopee!" she screamed, so overcome by the wind ripping through her hair and over her face that she didn't have time to worry about showing up on her street with the Terrier until they hit the Bronx River Parkway.

"What?" he asked when Frances tilted her head back to earth and got uncharacteristically quiet.

"I can get out here," she said a few blocks from South Fifth. If only it had been a Sunday, she thought, preparing for the street, the women walking around the corner to the carts on Broadway for black bread, holding hands with their children. "This is fine," said Frances. "Thanks!"

"Don't be silly," the Terrier said. "You ashamed of your brother-in-law, Fran?" he asked.

Women were already coming out onto the stoops, wiping their hands on their housedresses, to watch the Terrier pass in his fancy car. Frances thought, He's showing off. He wants everyone to see his car. Why do I have to be in it? But what she said was, "No, Sol, I'm not ashamed."

"I didn't think so," he said, driving painfully slowly. "Don't want to hit any kids playing in the street!" The Terrier laughed.

"Please don't drop me off in front of my house." Frances began to panic. "It will kill my parents." But they were already turning the corner. "It's not enough you sent my father to his bed," she said suddenly.

The Terrier was silent. "Okay, Fran," he said, stopping the car.

But it was too late. Frances's mother was already running toward her, arms flailing wildly. Before Frances could say a word, before she had walked fifteen feet from the Terrier's car, hitting the trunk with the heel of her hand as she walked away, which the Terrier read as the final signal for him to go, Rose Verdonik had descended on her in a rage.

"What are you doing?" Rose screamed in Yiddish as she delivered blow after blow to Frances's back. "How could you?" she screamed, punching at the air, at Frances's shoulders, until she collapsed into the arms of her daughter in a fit of tears.

"It's okay, Mommy," Frances said, stroking the hair that had sprung loose from her mother's taut bun. "I'm sorry," she said.

Frances watched the Terrier drive away, his yellow car a little spot of sun shining through the grime of the street.

A crowd had gathered around, and, when they saw that Rose had calmed down, the women began to disperse, shaking their heads and leaning in to one another to whisper how the Brodsky boy had taken both those girls to pleasure him upstate.

"I'm not leaving." Frances tried to comfort her mother. "I just wanted to visit Pauline. I missed her," she said, holding back tears.

Perhaps there were reserves of strength in Rose's stomach, in the depth of her gut, or in the wrinkles of her worn heart, because she managed to gather herself up and turn to her daughter with the kind of fury a mother saves only for her children. "I hope you're happy," she hissed at Frances as they walked toward their brownstone and toward Abraham, who waited in bed, with no idea what had happened outside his bedroom. "You will kill your father," Rose said. "Believe me, I will not tell him, but he will know what you have done and soon he will be dead. Then what will we do, Frances? Then what will we do?"

But living on South Fifth Street had not trained Rose in keeping secrets, and she was unable to hide from her husband what her daughter had done. In an act more cruel than even her daughter had suspected her capable of, she let it slip to Abraham—the very moment they walked through the door from the street—about Frances's behavior.

"How could you?" Frances said when her mother came into the kichen.

"What?" she asked her daughter as she opened and closed the cabinets, rearranging her jars of pickles and beets. "All of a sudden, the fault is mine?" she said to her daughter in Yiddish.

Rose had decreed it, and so it was: the very morning after hearing that his younger daughter had trespassed through the house of his elder daughter, a house built of lies and dirt and affronts to God and humanity, Abraham began his descent in earnest. When Frances brought her father his Cream of Wheat, he said to his younger daughter, "Ucch, zhe taste zhis leaves in my moutss. It is zhe taste of zhe copper. Death!" he said. "I'm dyink!"

Jeesum Crow, thought Frances. It can't be true. This is a ruse to teach me a lesson.

She felt her father's forehead: not so much as a flush of fever.

"I tell you, my daughter," he said. "I taste zhe taste of death!"

Frances had no choice but to believe her father, and so she set out to find a way to remove the taste from his mouth, thus removing the possibility of her father's death.

She thought first of stuffed cabbage, Abraham's favorite meal. After three dinners straight, though, Rose tired of both the taste and the toil. She told her daughter, "Look what you've done. I can't make the cabbage day in and day out for this man. This is your fault. You do it. You cook and clean and cook and clean and cook. Or are you trying to kill me as well?" The smell of the boiled leaves was thick throughout the house and was moving into the porous walls, joining the cockroaches.

And still her father tasted death. Frances thought, Perhaps he is only thirsty? She brought him a cup of milk and slipped in some Bayer powder. Though her father refused to take any medicine and was suspicious even of having it in the apartment, Rose loved Bayer (from Europe!), insisting on the aspirin powder for all household emergencies. Frances occasionally saw her mother smiling over the bottle as she tapped the powder into her tea on days when she was not ill. And twice she saw her mother spooning the powder into the wash.

Frances brought the glass to Abraham. Though he gulped down the milk, and though Frances waited for the aspirin to work, her second attempt at curing him was also unsuccessful.

Then she thought of peppermints. Perhaps that flavor, the cool menthol, could wipe away the taste, and thus the prospect, of death.

Two days after Frances came back from visiting her sister in Westchester County, she went to Mr. Berkowitz's for some penny candy. Frances had never bought from him before because of her mother's insistence that the two girls eat only at home. Food outside the home, *from off zhe street,* was always suspect. In fact nothing American—except the flavored seltzer, which for some reason was acceptable—was to be trusted. And candy? Why, it was ludicrous to eat such emptiness, to throw money away on something that doesn't *fill you up in zhe stomachs and make you strrrong,* Rose would say, gathering up her fists, ready to fight.

Many kids hung out on the corner by the candy store, waiting for someone like the Terrier to drive up and give them a chance to make their names. When Frances reached the store, the boys loitering outside taunted her. They scratched their armpits like chimpanzees and screamed insults about her sister. Pauline had once been the buffer between Frances's body and the body of the world, but now there was no beautiful girl to divert attention.

Holding her head down as she walked into the store that first day, Frances looked at the melting fudge through the smudged glass that Mrs. Berkowitz, or sometimes their daughter, rubbed with a towel each hour.

It was a small store, with huge tubs of American-style candies like jelly beans, orange candy corns, and scarlet cherry mash, but also halvah and soggy sesame sticks. Three dull brass spigots with cracked black handles lined the soda fountain, where Mr. Berkowitz mixed Coca-Cola and egg creams. By the register were stacked papers that went back weeks: the *Daily News* and the *Brooklyn Daily Eagle,* and also dated, yellowing newspapers from Europe, which were what the old people stopped in for, no matter how many weeks had passed since the headlines had been news. Across from the counter there were two tables, each with three chairs, and in one of these chairs sat an old woman with a pad of paper, pen, envelopes, and a roll of stamps.

Frances spent some time examining the different sweets. Just the sight of the gummed fruits, crescents of green and orange and yellow dusted with sugar, the long strands of bright red licorice tied up in knots, the sunny butterscotches and caramels, teased her aching taste buds. She longed for an egg cream: for that first mouthful of chocolate, followed by the metallic taste of seltzer that, she thought now, might be the taste her father mistook for death. Frances had not known how much she craved sweetness until her mouth watered at all that was spread out before her.

While she moved through the store, a young man came in and sat across from the old woman.

"What should I say?" he asked in Yiddish, placing a coin on the table. He was a handsome man with large hands that he ran through his thick, dark hair.

The woman responded in a much quicker Yiddish. "I give you the story," she said, "and it costs you more." She nodded her head toward the coin.

He shook his head. "You are a mean woman, Etta," he told her.

She shrugged her shoulders. She wore a kerchief and looked a bit like a gypsy, Frances thought. "Then get someone else to write your letters, Herschel," she said. She laughed—very few teeth.

"Calm down. Calm down," he said. "Just tell my wife that I am saving and I will send for her very soon. Can you tell her that? That I am saving and saving and saving, that all I do is work and think of her arrival with my son."

"Of course," Etta said. "This is America, Herschel. You say what you like, you get what you pay for. I won't write how I seen you walking the streets with Maimie Schmidt, arm in arm, Herschel. What do I care?"

Frances scooped up a handful of Brach's, and, taking a long, thin strand of red licorice along with the peppermints, she paid for the candy. When the man had gone, she went over to the letter writer. Though her Yiddish was a bit rusty—she insisted her parents speak English in the house—the language was still hers. Frances said, "You write letters for money?" In the Verdonik household, money was big conversation.

The woman didn't answer but sealed Herschel's envelope closed and began to copy out a foreign address. She pounded a stamp on the right-hand corner.

Frances sat down on the edge of the chair and scooted up to the table. "Do you write letters?" she asked.

"What does it look like?" the letter writer said.

This was a woman, cruel and efficient, like any number of old women Frances had known. "Better than the factory, huh?" she said. How many of the women in her neighborhood schlepped to Hester Street each morning to work the sewing machines?

The woman looked up at her, annoyed. "What do you know from the factory?" she said. "Who are you anyhow?"

This was the point in any conversation that Frances had begun to dread. Whereas once she would have said "Frances Verdonik" with pride, now everyone seemed to have heard about her sister's marriage to a gangster. "Frances," she said. She looked up at the walls, which were yellowing and cracked, stocked with shelves of gelt, wrapped in a shimmering gold foil. "Frances Golden," she said. But that didn't sound right. Too hesitant, she thought. Not only did Golden say not gold enough but it said not gold *truthfully*. "Frances Gold, I mean," she said. She felt that the name alone made her sparkle, she herself wrapped up in the fancy foil.

The woman scratched her chin. Four long hairs sprouted from it. "I don't know any Golds," she said.

"We write our own letters home," Frances said.

The woman threw up her hands. "Why are you wasting my time then?" She waved Frances aside, and an old woman stepped out from behind.

Frances put her hands on the table and pushed herself up. "Oh," she said. "Sorry."

The woman slid into the chair. "Etta Valensky," she said, "you write to my cousin and tell him how well I'm doing."

"Lie again you mean?" said Etta. "Sure. It's a lovely life you have, Rebecca. What do I care?"

The woman squinted at the letter writer. "Whatever it takes."

Etta nodded.

"And then I want you to write to my son. In California! Tell him to come and visit his mother. Write to him to come in time for the holidays. Only you must do it in English—this boy speaks only English! He's forgotten all the Yiddish!"

Etta shook her head. "Only in Yiddish," she said. "How many times do I have to tell you people? I write the letters only in Yiddish. I speak ten languages—all of them Yiddish!"

Realizing she was staring, Frances turned to walk home and try the peppermints on her father.

As it turned out, Abraham Verdonik had a weakness for peppermint candies. Round and swirled white and red, square and chalky green, even stretched into Christmas-style canes, the peppermint gave Abraham childlike delight. When Frances held out a piece twirled in clear cellophane, he sat up in bed and leaned against propped pillows. And while he sucked at the candy, it was as if Pauline had never left a trail of stunned grief behind her. It was as if Frances had never shown up on the block in that yellow car with the roof removed, a gangster at the wheel. In these moments, Abraham smiled and discussed what he'd read in the *Forward,* or something Franny had read to him previously, which at the time he had greeted with only a pallid silence.

"Zhat Hannah Breineh," he'd say of Yezierska's heroine. *Knock knock* went the hard candy against his teeth. "So ungrateful zhat one. Zhe children move her up zhe town like she's a real lady and she doesn't like it!" Between his sucking and his accent, Abraham was nearly impossible to understand.

But he was talking! Frances hadn't known how much he would love them, how they would cover up the copper taste of death and bring him again to the happy juice of language. She hadn't known that her reinvention had begun right there in Mr. Berkowitz's candy store, or that the seed of an idea had been planted there. She would sell what Etta Valensky could not—English. She would be the one to write to everyone's children. Only she wouldn't charge extra to lie. She wouldn't charge extra to make these parents' lives seem like the *goldene medina* they were sure they were going toward when they packed up for golden—no Gold—America.

Frances set up shop right next to Etta Valensky, who was not at all pleased until she saw the way it enhanced her own business.

"More people will come," said Frances, when they see that they can write to both the past and the future in one sitting.

Etta liked the way the girl put it. Many times mothers had begged her to write to their children and she'd had to turn them away. "As long as I do all the Yiddish, you can have the English," Etta told her.

By the time Frances turned seventeen, lines twisted around the block like Mr. Berkowitz's licorice. And so she continued her education, writing what the old ladies and old men who had lived in the Ukraine and Lithuania and Poland and Russia told her. What she noticed most about these people, as they slowly slid into their chairs and put their heads into their shaking hands, was their fear. They spoke to her with immediacy, as if they had been storing these stories away for safekeeping and only now was it okay to let them loose. Sometimes, as they spoke, their hands moved, like the wings of birds in flight.

The people loved Frances; she had a way of always making her customers feel at ease. She smiled encouragingly, sometimes touching a trembling hand. And as Frances had had her share of trouble, even for such a young girl, people could sense her empathy and they were drawn to her. They had her write to many relatives, but what surprised her was how many letters she wrote to unborn children. These almost always began: *You may not know me and I may be gone by the time you've arrived but there are some things I want to tell you. . . .* It was interesting that, despite the bitter and sarcastic way they spoke, the old people chose to preserve mostly small, good things. They had her write about their mothers who sang them lullabies to sleep, the way a tree threw a shadow on the front of their childhood house. They told her of how a plum tasted, the quality of light in a forest clearing, the indescribable smell of lavender. And it was in the very smallness of these details that Frances knew these stories were true.

The other letters went to adult children who had left Brooklyn. *I know you don't have time for your mother,* these letters usually began. They went on to describe either the decaying physical condition of the person dictating or to express how much their lives had improved since their children had left them to wither away alone. No one told the truth. Those who on paper were bedridden were usually quite well, as Frances saw when they stood up and walked away from her letter-writing station. And those who showed themselves as the very portraits of good health were often racked by fits of coughing, their skin so translucent that she could see the twisting ropes of veins and arteries beneath, like maps of their troubled histories.

All actors, Frances thought. It is our way. And then she thought again: I would like to be an actor. Here I am, she thought, the curtain breaking open. Someone else's story, yes, but here I am to deliver it to you.

While Frances wrote to what was about to be, Etta wrote to what already had been—the relatives waiting to come, the ones too infirm to make the journey, those who would never leave. Though many of the letters were succinct commands—come on this ship, at this time, and bring the marriage certificate—many were great, complex fantasies upholding the ideas that those who had not yet arrived were able to believe. *I have a great house with many dogs,* wrote Moishe Wexler, who lived in the tiny flat above the store. *I eat at all the fancy restaurants, where people serve me on silver trays, and then I go out dancing all night long and only wish it were with you,* wrote the emaciated Lev Cohen.

When the letters were answered, Etta and Frances read them to their recipients. The letters from very far away, Etta's letters, always carried bad news—the death of a father or brother, pogroms, and rumors of a nearby village being razed. But the ones in English—those from within North America's borders—were almost always about happy occasions—brises, namings, bar mitzvahs, plans for travel.

Frances now had access to history. Once she had written someone's story, it seemed that she owned it in some way, that she had in fact experienced it. Can you see me now, Pauline? she'd think, imagining herself high on the hill in the city of Budapest. I am not waiting for you in that airless room, she would think as she walked across the Charles Bridge and into the city of Prague, Tyn Cathedral rising in the distance in her imagination. And so her real life, the life of a pear-shaped girl covered with hair whose beautiful sister had left home for a fairy tale to which Frances would never be invited, whose mother couldn't stop herself from cleaning, and whose father wouldn't get out of bed, began to fall away.

∾

Though Frances never told Abraham and Rose of her newfound career, it was not something she purposefully hid. How could she? Her father had only to walk down the street to see his second daughter seated at a table like a fortune-teller, a line of old-world patrons waiting for her to read their palms and predict their futures, snaking along the block. But Abraham rarely left his bedroom, let alone the apartment. And though Rose went out onto the stoop to sweep away the day's dirt from the steps, she didn't visit with anyone anymore. Even if the neighbors were kind enough not to speak of it, the fate of Pauline was always in their hearts. So Rose stayed away from gossip, which included a few stories about her husband, who had taken to bed with the whole neighborhood's insurance. Had she listened only once, the gossip would have brought Rose news of this strange Gold girl who would translate a story and send it to whomever for two cents, not including postage.

Each evening, Frances slid her money through the slot in the glass jar in the kitchen. Just the *clink clink clink* of the coins made her mother relax a moment on her broom, something like a smile dimly lighting her face. Perhaps she believed the cash was sent to her from Pauline, whom Abraham refused to see or speak to. Rose was in no position to turn down money, and so she never asked.

Sitting in a chair beside her father's bed clutching the peppermints Mrs. Berkowitz gave her for free each day—the least she could do for all the business the young woman brought to the store—Frances had a wealth of stories to tell. Without a book nestled in her lap, without the aid of the tiny lamp on his bedside table, Frances now told her father stories about gypsies and cafés, about trains and travels. And she told them with such authority—she had written them down, after all—that Abraham never questioned her sources. Perhaps he thought it had been he who had told his younger girl these tales, even though they took place in mountains he had never climbed, along rivers he had never crossed, in cities with cafés where he had never even sipped a coffee. If the stories set in Hungary and Lithuania perplexed Abraham, he never revealed it. He simply rested back on his pillows, pleased with himself for his one good offspring. Perhaps for a fleeting moment he thought, I was wrong to put everything into Pauline. Perhaps he thought, A girl who is smart, who can tell a story, she is more helpful to her family, to the world, than a girl with a pretty face riding by on a float. This kind of girl is a waste. She will always be waving good-bye.

Two years after her sister ran off, Frances overheard the whispers on the street that Pauline had given birth to a son, but she did not go see her sister or her new nephew. She remembered their dreams, which had always been Pauline's dreams. Pauline would be the beauty queen. Pauline with the lovely ribbons spilling from her hair. Why was Frances the one who was stout as a teapot and forced to eat limp cabbage and potatoes when her sister was dining in high style? Why did Frances have to work so hard, become someone else, to keep her family going? Franny's resentment had grown large, her anger at being the one left behind building and building until it became its own permanent structure. Soon her anger became a place: it had a roof, and windows, and an enormous wooden door that she could lock and slam shut, put the key in her dress pocket, and walk away.

In the winter of 1928, just as the copper taste in his mouth seemed to have been completely neutralized by peppermints, Abraham Verdonik died in his sleep.

With his body growing cold in their bed, Rose scrubbed the bathroom tiles and all the exposed bathroom surfaces until she could see her own reflection in them. Frances watched her bending down to see her warped face in the gleaming tiles. And so it was Frances who had to make the funeral arrangements.

But Frances also needed a place to put her heartache, and she shocked herself with the way she needed ritual. What had she known from tradition? When she placed the towels on the stoop with a pitcher of water, as Reb Bender had instructed, Rose screamed, "What are you doink?"

"People need to wash off from the grave!" Frances told her. "They can't bring graveyard dirt into our home!" Just the thought of the curse made her shiver.

This idea of dirt also troubled Rose, but still she thumped her forehead. "The Cossacks will get us!" she said in Yiddish. "They'll know!"

Rose had wanted to cremate her husband. "Graves are for zhe livink!" she said. "Zhey are so we may visit. Zhe dead don't come, Frances, zhey're dead!"

Maybe she simply couldn't deal with having yet another place to have to clean. But surely the threat of dust would have kept Frances's mother from cremating her husband. Frances imagined her keeping Abraham in a nice urn on the dresser, her mother opening it, and, like a little genie, Abraham swirling out and granting her the wishes he had never been able to make come true while he was alive.

Frances wouldn't have it. "He was a Jew," she said. "Why must you take that away from him?"

At the burial, Frances stood with her mother, a few folks from the neighborhood, and the rabbi over the grave and watched her sister pull up in a long black car. In her black veil and dark glasses—who did she think she was, Janet Gaynor?—Pauline stumbled across the grass in high heels and bent over Abraham's grave. She did not look at Frances. Is she not going to so much as speak to me? Frances wondered. Was the Terrier in that car? Frances craned her neck to get a better look. Pauline didn't seem to see anyone as she took a handful of dirt from a shovel the rabbi held out to her. With her jeweled fingers, Pauline threw the dirt, her body heaving with what Frances came to believe was merely drama. Then Pauline got into that car and drove away.

Back at the house, Frances prepared the place for the shiva. Surely she's coming to the house to mourn, Frances thought as she pulled out a cinder block for her sister to sit on. Like a love-struck girl, she waited for her sister, and each day she was met with what she now realized she had always been met with: disappointment. Frances remembered all those times she had watched her sister preening, all the times Pauline had taken the largest slice of babka, how she had abandoned Frances for a life of luxury. For things. Money. As she waited for her sister to come and grieve for their father—their father, who had given them life, who had brought them to this country, who had tried to give Pauline what she had wanted but had tried as well to show them the value of learning—Frances mentally threw the key to her house of rage into the East River.

The only thing that quelled her fury was faith. Each evening, after her stint at the candy store, Frances, who had never before set foot in a synagogue, went to minyan, though she knew neither she nor her mourning would be counted. Despite the fact that she was not his son, Franny said Kaddish for her father every night for that year, and every night for a year she lit a candle in memory.

And each night Rose begged her not to do it. "The Cossacks vill get you!" she said. "We come to zhis country to get away from zhis Jewish business, and here you go with zhis prayink all zhe night long, every day?"

But every time Frances watched the flame flicker from the draft that always made its way in through the kitchen window, she was confronted by her father and then by the loss of him.

For many years Frances paid off the burial—she would not have her father buried in Potter's Field, where the poor of the earth met again beneath it. Lucky for her, the funeral director also happened to be in need of a letter writer—he wanted all of Europe to know of his grand success as a mortician in America. A deal was struck between them. He wanted the letters to be written in English so all would know he was a real *American*. And if they had to pay someone else to read the letter for them? So be it.

"An eye for an eye?" the mortician said in Yiddish, winking at Franny. And then: "You don't want to let your father go under without a shining Star of David on the coffin, now do you? And, Frances," he said, "you want it to be bronze, yes?"

In losing the two people closest to her, Frances's already split-apart self began to divide further, a fork in a country road. Slowly, slowly, after the nightly minyan, the stories upon stories, slowly Frances Verdonik veered away from herself and headed into the horizon, toward Franny Gold.

At the end of that year of grief, eighteen-year-old Franny lit a yahrtzeit for her father, put the plaque down on the earth in memoriam, and stood up from placing a stone on the cold marble. She went to the candy store and sat at her station, watching cruel Etta torment her clients. She smiled at her own patrons, keeping her head down low, not knowing that the moment she looked up, the next person in line she smiled at would alter her life forever.

CHAPTER 8

Caught: Seymour Bloom, 1929

AS JOSEPH BRODSKY WAS struggling on the road, and Frances Verdonik was making a name for herself as the Gold Letter Writer, Seymour Bloom was making heaps of money in the Terrier's liquor distributing organization.

Even after having their first child, Dulcy, a pleasant enough girl who Seymour thought would surely divert his wife's melancholy, Sarah still seemed to be slipping away. Slipping away from him and also from herself, he worried on one of the nights Mary came to him with another of many of his wife's unsent letters, this one found crumpled beneath her writing desk.

According to Mary, who spent most of her hours with the Blooms' first child in that brownstone on Seventy-first and East End, Sarah painted her lips strumpet red, grabbed her long cigarette holder, and sneaked down into the basement to *dance.* Just as Seymour had entered his own underworld, Sarah too was spending an inordinate amount in her own place belowground.

Seymour wasn't home much by day, and there were many nights that the Terrier insisted Seymour accompany him out.

"Now, Sy," the Terrier would say, when Seymour paused for an instant. "It's why I brought you in. As polished as Rothstein, you are. They love you! If you only enjoyed yourself, my friend, you could be one of the cheeses."

But there was little Seymour liked about being involved in the Mob aside from the money. Would it be more enjoyable to be higher up, to be the one to *delegate*? Sure, but Seymour didn't see himself in it for life, at least if that choice was still his. Those evenings after playing cards with the boys, all of them scheming to get more money to expand operations, each overtipping the cigarette girls to be remembered as a hero, he'd be anxious to return home only to be met by a closed, dark house. Sarah would already be in their room with the door shut tight. Seymour would make his way up the shadowy stairs, hovering outside the door, deciding whether or not to enter. In pool halls and smoky rooms and clubs and casinos, in all of Manhattan, people sought Seymour out just to shake his hand. He snapped his fingers and the world was his world. And here he was, terrified to enter his own bedroom.

As he hesitated at the door, without fail Seymour would think of Sarah and how she had stretched out her hand to that fortune-teller's on Coney Island, before they were married. They had laughed their way from the boardwalk into this woman's tent, and she had instantly stilled them both with her terrible black gypsy eyes. Your life line is long but it is barely visible, she had told Sarah. This is the worst kind. Who wants to live like that? she had said. Sarah had been unable to look at Seymour, and he had watched her throw her head back and laugh, pooh-poohing her fortune. I am sad for you, the gypsy had said as Sarah ducked out of the tent, pulling Seymour right behind her. He had not known to whom the fortune-teller had been speaking.

Mary had tried to warn Seymour, but he had not wanted to listen. As far as he was concerned, what Sarah did all day and where she was getting her liquor—from his own stash in the basement saved for the times when the ship sailing across the Atlantic would not make it to shore—was only hearsay.

Thank you, Mary, he'd say calmly when she told him she was worried about how Mrs. Bloom was spending her time. That will be all, Mary, he would tell her.

Seymour found out precisely what Sarah had been doing with her time on a brilliant autumn day when the ship hauling liquor from England didn't make it to Long Island. Seymour had made promises; he had orders to fill. One of these orders was going to an Italian restaurant in Murray Hill with a rather mean proprietor named Manny Mannicelli, who hated using the Jews to get his liquor but, because of the strange affinity between the Jews—the brains—and the Italians—the brawn—was forced to use the Greenberg-Terrier-Rothstein operation. That day Manny received several bottles of cut whiskey, shipped directly from the Bloom basement, where Sarah had only days before been kicking up dust as if she were at a country dance on a Saturday night. When Manny Mannicelli served the watered-down spirits to some very special patrons, the shit truly hit the fan.

Seymour was called many names that evening by both the Italians and the Eastern Europeans, and his life was threatened in Italian and Yiddish, mostly for what he would not admit to, which was that he had cut his liquor and had not served one of his best clients the real stuff.

"I did no such thing, Terrier," Seymour said into the receiver, holding his head high in his own defense. "I am sorry to hear that this has happened," he said in the slow and measured way he always spoke. "Yes," he said. "I'll see you tonight." When Seymour hung up the telephone, his fingers lighted on the receiver for a long pause.

Sarah, who had stood in the dark hallway, trembling, listening in on the conversation, crept into the light. "Dearest," she said, which startled Seymour, as he had rarely—had he ever?—heard this groveling tone in his wife's voice. "Perhaps I can clear things up for you."

She told him about her afternoons in the basement. "I like to go down there all dressed up and be alone," she said. She explained the way those crates waited for her, calling when she was merely brushing out her hair, sitting at the vanity. She told her husband how she sipped at the liquor tentatively, all dressed up and strung with long strands of fake pearls, enjoying the burn of the liquor as it traveled through her, as if it left a path of fire in its wake. But what would begin for Sarah in the late morning as the jitterbug would turn by early evening into a wash of silence and grief.

"I pretend." She told her husband not only about what she did but about what she had been meant to do. "I thought I was going to be an actress. I thought I would act on the stage, Seymour!" she said, her lips trembling. "Since school this is what Celia and I told ourselves. That we would be actors."

Seymour listened patiently as his wife recalled her years in college.

"Gosh, I remember the leaves turning, that lovely smell of school starting, girls out in the quad, books pressed to their chests, running off to Latin and the Victorian Novel and Astronomy. And in the evening, the chaos of the dorm, all of us signing out on our way to mixers, Amherst boys downstairs in queues that seemed to reach all the way to the moon. My life was going to be beautiful," Sarah told him. "It was going to contain everything."

Seymour had had enough. Fine, she had wanted to be an actor, and her talent was not exactly being utilized here, in this house, but the bit about the college boys was just plain cruel. Seymour did not have an education, he knew, but his wife had been tricked by hers, it seemed to him. It had made her believe her dreams were possible. For a brief moment, he felt sympathy for her: Why send a girl to school? he thought now. For what? To show her who she'll never have the chance to be? It was criminal really. The Terrier should wave his gun around somewhere about it.

Dreams? Until he'd married Sarah, Seymour had not even had the opportunity to have them, let alone try to make them come true.

But why he had married a woman with so many *thoughts* was beyond him. He had not signed on for all this neurotic business. And though he knew exactly what had transpired—he had known it from the moment he received the call from the Terrier—Seymour wanted to hear it, once and for all. "That's all well and fine, Sarah," he said, "but what does it have to do with what has happened to the liquor?"

"I've been taking small tastes," his wife said. "Little, itty-bitty ones, over time. And I've been topping the bottles off with water. That's all," she said.

Seymour knew she had taken more than delicate sips; he knew that a third of the liquor in some of the bottles had been replaced by water. A little cutting was always expected, but this had been dramatic. Had she done this because she'd been too high to think clearly? he wondered. Or was his wife trying to sabotage him?

"Do you know this could get us killed, Sarah?"

"Well, I'm sorry," she said. "What kind of work do you do that a little water in the liquor can get you murdered? Huh, Seymour?"

He clenched his jaw but was silent.

"This isn't the life I had planned, Seymour," she told him. "You have not given me the life I'd imagined."

He looked at her blankly. "I can see you are very sorry," he said.

"I am sorry," she said.

"Me too," he said, looking out the window to the street, where one of the Terrier's drivers was pulling his town car up in front of the brownstone.

Seymour leaned over the driver's seat. "Where are we headed?" he asked calmly.

The driver looked straight ahead, turning off Seventy-second and onto Park.

If Seymour had been anxious about what a night spent out with the Terrier would hold before this incident, he was filled now with total dread. He sat back and placed his fedora over his face as they made their way through town, to Brooklyn, Seymour was sure. The nights he hadn't been out with the boys, the infamous incidents they all talked about over craps and cigars now turned in Seymour's mind into cautionary tales: Luciano, left for dead on the docks last month waiting for his heroin to come in. Heroin, Seymour thought now. Christ. How had he gotten into this? Luciano had been pistol-whipped, ice-picked, his face cut to hamburger meat. But he survived, Seymour thought. Lived to tell it, which is why we call him Lucky, right? Would he want to survive such a thing? Which would be worse for his daughter, Seymour found himself weighing: to have a damaged father or no father at all? And then there was Joe Bernstein, who'd run the "bottling" company where the liquor the Terrier brought in was really cut, where all the fake labels were manufactured. Bernstein had been hijacked while driving to a vacant warehouse, a prospective new factory, just last year, and still no one had found his body.

Seymour didn't even know what Bernstein had done. Had the Terrier been behind poor Bernstein's disappearance? It would be difficult to imagine otherwise. Everything was connected, as intertwined as family, as ivy, as roses: punch someone in the gut here, over there, across the river, someone else bends over from the pain.

The ride was far shorter than Seymour expected. The driver stopped at Forty-seventh Street, in front of the St. Francis Hotel. The short ride in itself was a good sign, he thought as he made his way slowly through the crowded lobby, downstairs, and into the back room, where he had played craps on countless nights. Seven members were gathered around the craps table, the Terrier facing the door, when Seymour walked in. His heart banging like a succession of gunshots in his chest. And yet Seymour was greeted as if nothing had happened. "Hello, hello, no Broadway show tonight?" they teased. "Make you feel better if we do a little soft shoe for ya?" Mad Marty Mendel said, sticking his leg out from under the table and pulling up an invisible skirt. Seymour laughed uneasily, his eyes darting around the room. He waited for a door to open, and for chopper-wielding henchmen to storm in and take him out in high drama.

But it didn't happen, not when they invited him to sit down, not after the cigars were cut, the cards dealt, the whiskey poured, the chips stacked. Not when the dawn crept in through the tiny basement windows. That's when the Terrier scooted his chair out from under the table and called it a game, gathering up the slips of paper with all the money owed him.

He turned to Seymour. "Goy," he said. "Did you take the booze for yourself? Did you double-cross me?"

"No." Seymour looked around the table, from one man to the next. "I did not," he said. His heart was racing, and he surprised even himself when he heard his own cool voice.

The room was silent but for the sound of Fender Face puffing his cigar.

The Terrier nodded at the sagging faces; they all nodded back at him. "Everyone is entitled to one honest mistake." The Terrier held up a pudgy finger, dirt or blood beneath the nail—which, Seymour couldn't tell. "One."

Seymour shook his head. He waited in the terrible silence that always preceded the sounds he recognized: a knife sliding open, the slow cocking of a gun. Outside a car door slammed. Who else was coming?

"That's that," the Terrier said, brushing his hands together. Then suddenly, he smacked Seymour on the back of his head, hard.

Seymour's ears rang, and he closed his eyes for a moment. He thought of his mother walking out the door in Brownsville into the screaming, violent street; he thought of Sarah rolling back and forth on her silk sheets. Seymour opened his eyes. "Okay then," he said, bowing to the table he'd just lost two thousand dollars on, and, cutting his losses, he turned to go home.

Seymour fixed it with Mannicelli, assuring him that diluting the product was an honest mistake and not something of which he made a practice. He waived the fee and arranged for double the order from everyone else's basement the next day. And the following day, Seymour special-ordered a liquor from southern Switzerland, where the juniper berry was abundant. He decided on gin for Sarah because it was a more feminine drink than those dark bourbons, but also because it was a clear liquid that could be imperceptibly diluted with water. And if he couldn't see it disappear, well then, it hadn't disappeared. If how much she consumed was in direct relation to her unhappiness, then Seymour wished not to see those proportions.

Seymour would never know if the reason Sarah started drinking outside the house was that she had been discovered drinking in it or that, as Dulcy grew older, it got far more difficult to sneak downstairs without the little girl howling her way out of Mary's arms and toward her mother's resistant embrace. Though Seymour had not asked, he had been told by Celia's husband, Ed Wolfsheim, that the two took their martinis at the Plaza in the afternoons. Ed was an attorney who had once represented Rothstein and had made a name for himself by telling the boss to say not a word in his own defense. No one had ever pleaded the Fifth before, and the case had gone straight to the Supreme Court.

Despite his good fortune, Ed, like Seymour, had married an unhappy Smith girl. Though the two men rarely spoke of their wives, once in a while bits and pieces of information filtered through. "I think they go to the Plaza on Wednesdays," Ed told Seymour. "A special room in the basement they've got over there. I don't really give a damn, but what if someone sees them?"

"So what?" Seymour said. "Who would see?" It seemed to him that Sarah spent an inordinate amount of time belowground.

"Sy," Ed said. "You gotta get more savvy, you wanna stay in this business. They get caught drinking in this town, you'll lose your backing. Trust me."

Seymour shook his head in disbelief. This was why he could never be a businessman in earnest. He never saw the glitches that were sure to occur around each bend in this endless road. He foresaw the problems only as they presented themselves. "If you say so," he responded.

"I do," Ed said. "I say so. You're crazy if you don't think the Feds are after the Terrier and Greenberg for anything and everything. Drinking is not legal, remember? This is why you're making so much jack. And this is why I hang around with you, just in case you might need my services."

"So should we have them followed?"

"Followed?"

"Yeah. Scare them up a bit?" Seymour said.

Ed laughed. "Why not?" he said.

Seymour Bloom would never be able to explain to himself why he did not hire someone else to follow his wife. He could even have paid the concierge—who he did not know was already paid by Sarah to guarantee her and her friend anonymity in the secret bar beneath the Plaza Hotel lobby—or one of Rothstein's shotgun riders, even some nobody just dying to pitch one of his brilliant ideas, anyone to tell him when his wife arrived, when she left, and to scare her out of ever doing it again.

Instead, something he didn't recognize in himself—love, revenge, anger, violence, it all felt the same to him now—brought him to the Plaza that following Wednesday, five months after Sarah had almost gotten him killed for siphoning off the bourbon.

When the car dropped him in front of the Plaza Hotel, Seymour crossed Fifty-ninth Street to Central Park. The carriages beckoned him, the horses stomping their feet and snorting, shaking their heads to try to free themselves from their bridles. It was sad, really, how these horses were now used mostly for people's enjoyment. He remembered back in Brooklyn, how the horses pulled carts through the street, carrying ice and dry goods. They pulled the fire wagons. And Jesus, did they crap everywhere. Seymour remembered whole streets devoted to the manure, and the stench of urine on humid days. But the horses were useful then. Now, to work them this way for pure entertainment seemed cruel.

Seymour placed his hands on the ledge and peered over into the park, where women held hands with their children as they walked along the path. Old ladies pulled their tiny dogs around, birds swooped in and out of the trees, and swans glided along the glass surface of the water. It was a tremendous day. The azaleas were blooming, also the cherry trees that bordered the park. Simply gorgeous, Seymour thought, instantly envious of any man who had this woman here, the plain one smiling down into a large blue pram.

Seymour, in his hat and a trench coat, walked out of the bright spring sun and into the Plaza bar around 3:30 and sat in a banquette in the far corner of the room. He caught a glimpse of himself in the mirror above his seat. I look like a gangster, he thought. He had to laugh at himself. I think I am a gangster. Look at me. Seymour remembered his mother bending at the waist to greet the patrons at the Joint, sticking their cash into the massive trap of her brassiere.

Celia was the first of the two women to come in, and Seymour had to note that she looked like a million bucks. Her printed dress hung just below her knees, and Seymour could see her pretty garters barely sticking out from under the hem, her stockings rolled just above the knee. A golden snake—something the Terrier would surely have coveted for his wife—encircled her upper arm.

Celia nodded at the bartender, who, as Seymour had requested, brought her to a seat near the front of the room, her back to Seymour. He brought her a drink right away. As he placed it on the table, she removed her gloves finger by finger, unpinned her hat, and leaned back in the seat.

Sarah came in about ten minutes later, placing her beaded bag on the table as she slid into the banquette next to her friend.

"A martini please, three onions," she said, pointing to her friend's drink and holding up three fingers.

"Lovely day, isn't it?" Celia said.

"Oh, who gives a hoot," said Sarah. "Spring. I can't even bear to walk through the park."

"Why not? I love the park. Especially this time of year. It's like being in Europe!"

"Well, I know. I know I should want to walk through the park and look at all the blooming cherry trees, but lord knows, when I see those mothers bending over enormous prams cooing at their children, it simply makes me ill," Sarah said. "I'm terribly sorry to say it, but it does." She slammed back into the seat with a sigh.

Seymour watched her drink arrive, her bright smile turn to disdain, and her hand wave as she sent it back. "No, this is two onions and I said three," she told the bartender, and he returned with a small dish of pickled onions. She shook her head incredulously at the man and dropped one into her drink.

"I'm sorry, darling. How are *you*?" Sarah said, licking her fingers. She looked as if she would lean in and pet her friend's rosy cheek. It made Seymour a bit sad to see her even a little happy with someone else.

"Well," Celia began. "I'm all right, I suppose. Ed has been busy lately. Extremely." She raised her eyebrows.

Sarah nodded. "Seymour too," she began. "What do you think he's up to?"

"You should know," said Celia.

"Oh, who cares. To tell you the truth, Seal, sometimes I positively hate him. Oh, how I hated him when he was a salesman," Sarah said. "Because he wasn't rich. He had no connections, Seal. I can't tell you how this *limited* me. His mother is a hairdresser. A hairdresser, for Christ's sake! And now, even though he's making so much dough we can't spend it fast enough, I still hate him because, well, he used to be a salesman."

"But, Sarah," Celia said. "Seymour is a divine man. He's so tall and handsome, clean as a piece of chalk," she said.

Seymour glanced in the mirror when he heard this and brushed his hands lightly over his face.

"Chalk?" Sarah asked, leaning down and taking another sip.

"Seymour has edges," her friend said. "Not like Ed. Ed is . . . a blurry little man with a big gold ring." Celia laughed. "And to top it off, he's an attorney. No interest in the arts. None. Just craps and law. Seymour at least loves the theater."

"It's true, he does," Sarah said. "Isn't that strange?" She giggled.

The two women sat quietly for a moment, sipping their drinks.

"You know," said Celia, breaking the silence of their drinking. "I should have married an actor. I had such plans. But my mother made me marry Ed. 'Go to New York and be an actress? Over my dead body,' she told me. I think the gin is getting to me."

"Remember we were both going to be actors?"

Seymour couldn't help rolling his eyes at this. He thought now how easy it was to blame someone else for something you just never did yourself. But what if she had and had failed? After all, who was to say Sarah would have made it past her stupid little college productions, her father clapping from the first row, a dozen roses waiting for her on the chair beside him?

Celia nodded as she sipped her drink, the gin dribbling a little down her chin, which she wiped with the back of her hand. "'Let us sit and mock the good housewife Fortune from her wheel, that her gifts may henceforth be bestowed equally.'" She paused for a moment. "What I have for a husband is more ink than chalk. His brutal effect washed everywhere."

Sarah looked inquisitively at her friend, as if to place this last line somewhere in the Shakespeare. "Well, now Seymour seems to be in liquor," she said. "Liquor!" She held up her drink. "Ain't that just a kick in the pants?"

The two women laughed into each other, and Sarah ordered more drinks with a twirl of her long finger.

"If Seymour was to leave me, where would all my anger go?"

"Hmmmm." Celia nodded.

"What I'm saying is, don't we need one place to put everything we despise? Perhaps I couldn't live without my husband."

"Because he's gorgeous, that's why," Celia said. "And he adores the theater."

Sarah nodded. "Of course I loved that he was so handsome. No one looked like that at Amherst," she said.

Seymour could see immediately that his wife was progressing into a blue mood. Even from where he sat, he could see her eyes cloud and her head tilt with melancholy.

"Cheers?" Sarah said hopefully, holding up her glass.

"Chin chin," Celia offered halfheartedly, meeting Sarah's wobbly martini with her own.

Seymour watched as they drank two more martinis. Their talk

moved to *The Sound and the Fury,* which Sarah thought was positively brilliant, though Celia much preferred *A Farewell to Arms.* Sarah insisted it didn't have to be one or the other, but Celia felt you were either a fan of Hemingway or a fan of Faulkner, not both. Never. When they started talking about Mary Pickford and the Academy Awards, Seymour was sure the conversation would turn back to their dashed dreams. He glanced at his pocket watch, surprised to note it was nearly 6:30. What of Dulcy? Had Sarah completely forgotten she had a child? Did she expect Mary to *raise* Dulcy? What of dinner? Mary did the cooking, yes, but she needed *guidance.* It was true he had told Sarah he would not be home until late evening, but he did not realize that this meant she would not be home either.

That was when he heard Sarah slur loudly. "Celia," she whispered, nearly licking her friend's ear. "Shall we, just once for fun?"

Celia smiled cattily at Sarah and looked up, heavenward, Seymour thought, until he realized the look went aboveground, to the hotel rooms.

"Sarah Bloom, you are very naughty." Celia laughed. She slapped Sarah's hand and then took it, guiding her as she clumsily slid out of the banquette.

"I plead the Fifth!" Sarah squealed, raising her right hand.

The two women laughed.

Seymour watched them stumble out of the bar, two women, one flesh and curve, the other, straight, stretched bone. He sat completely still as they leaned in to each other, making their way to the lobby. He had a strange thought: Perhaps they will fit together well, he thought to himself as he touched the brim of his hat and tied the belt of his dark coat. He cleared his throat and went over to the bartender.

"How much do I owe you?" he asked. Nothing. Seymour had done nothing.

"I should charge a pretty penny for that show." The bartender laughed.

"They come here often?" Seymour asked.

"About once a week. But they never leave together. Not like that anyway."

"Like what?" Seymour looked at him sternly.

The man laughed. "Like nothing," he said, wiping down the bar.

Seymour nodded his head. I am a gangster, he thought to himself. "That's what I thought," he said.

Seymour never discussed with his wife what he had seen transpire that Wednesday at the Plaza. He had seen quite enough, and yet still, two nights later, as he sat in his study looking at receipts, Mary insisted on handing him another balled-up letter.

"I thought you might want to see this," she said.

"Why, Mary? Why would you think I would want to see this?"

The housekeeper shrugged. "I thought you might want to know what your wife was up to is all," she said.

Seymour looked down wearily at the fine, wrinkled paper. "Thank you, Mary," he said.

She stood over him, watching as he peeled open the ball of paper.

"Thank you, Mary," he said again. "That will be all."

As she turned to leave the room, Seymour began to read.

25 April 1929

Dear Celia:

I'm terribly under the weather today, Celia. All I can do is stare out the window. I can see the river—it seems like it's running just beneath me. For some reason I am thinking of East Tremont Street on Long Island, where I grew up in my mother's house. It was crawling with roses. I used to sit on the arm of my father's leather chair as he handed me his spectacles, and I remember their delicate tortoise arms, like tiny, breakable icicles. And today, I'm remembering my mother's parties on the shore, the way the moonlight shone off the water, those swooping beams of light. I never stopped to wonder if Mother had been happy. Do you think she was happy?

Sometimes, downstairs, I take these huge swigs of whiskey from the bottles Seymour has stored down there, for lord knows what. Is it strange to tell you it makes me feel like a man to drink that way? Or maybe it makes me not feel like a man, but for once not feel like a woman. The liquor burns right through, and I imagine it's like light, that this beautiful light is caught in me—and who on earth will ever see it there? Sometimes I think I like to drink as a way of letting that light out into the world.

What I want to say is this: being with you yesterday was a true joy.

Sadly, the great pleasures of my life have been in what is about to happen: the scratch of the Victrola needle at the very moment Joplin is about to play, the day's very first sip, and watching you slide out of your dress. Hello, I wanted to tell you.

Oh, the melancholy of a morning after drinking. It's positively adolescent. I am being silly and so dramatic!

See you soon I hope.

> *Your,*
> *Sarah*

Seymour put down the letter and peeled off his spectacles. He leaned into the upright wooden chair, which sighed under his weight, and rubbed his eyes with his index finger and thumb.

I'm so tired, thought Seymour. He thought of his mother, how easy she had been at the Joint, greeting all the people when they came in. He remembered her in her shop, talking to her clients about Harry Houdini, radio, the outrageous price of butter. She had a public face, it was true. Alone with her sons, the tone was harsh and efficient. She did not smile and touched them only when their hair had grown too long.

The misery, though, this misery was different. He was tired of his wife's misery.

Rising from his chair, Seymour reached to the ceiling, stretching his long arms. He cracked his knuckles, tucked in his shirttails, and rolled down his sleeves. And then he walked across the hall to the bedroom he had shared with his wife, if sometimes tentatively, for just four years.

Sarah was curled up on the left side of the bed. When he got nearer to her, he could see her hands were clutched into fists, like those of a fetus or an old woman filled with rage. "Sarah," he said. He touched her shoulder.

Sarah stirred and looked up at Seymour, who sat down on the very edge of the bed.

"Hi," he said.

She rolled onto her back slowly and looked vacantly at the ceiling, her hands, still clenched, resting on her stomach.

"I was thinking," he said, placing his hand back on her shoulder. "Why don't we have another baby?"

Sarah didn't flinch or say a word.

"Someone for Dulcy to grow up with," he said. "A boy maybe, or even another girl, who knows?" Seymour felt suddenly filled with hope. "That will be part of the wonder of it. Will it be a boy or a girl?"

"No, Seymour," she said, still not moving.

"Come on, Sarah," he said. "It will be good for you. Good for us both," he went on, rubbing her shoulder. "We'll be a family," he said.

Sarah was silent.

"Really," Seymour said. "A family!"

"Uh-uh," Sarah said, shaking her head and looking up, toward the ceiling, through it, beyond it somehow, toward the sky.

CHAPTER 9

Eyes: Frances Gold, 1929

SOME FOLKS FROM SOUTH Fifth Street who had watched Frances Verdonik grow into the neighborhood letter writer said she would have been happy sitting at the shaky table in Mr. Berkowitz's store until long after Etta slid from her chair, clawing her chest as if to prevent her evil heart from ruining her old body. But by most neighborhood accounts, Frances knew, the very instant she saw Vladimir Zworykin in the candy store, that he would be the one to take her away. People said Frances knew from the moment she looked at him that he would make her famous: they said she saw her name in lights in the pupils of Vladimir Zworykin's eyes.

The day after Frances stood from placing a stone on her father's grave, she looked up from her letter-writing station to see him standing above her. Vladimir was from the same village as she. The last time she had seen him she was a three-year-old girl and he a young man off to St. Petersburg, for an education, her father had said, wagging his finger at Frances. Her father. Frances still sighed jaggedly at the thought of him.

Seeing Vladimir made Frances wonder about her village for the first time in many years. She thought by now that the shtetl must surely have fallen into the sea. It was a place she could hardly even consider any longer. She could remember it only by the people leaving. Frances remembered standing at the doorway: Pauline was tying a kerchief at the nape of her neck. Had she turned to smile coyly at Frances?

"Frances," Vladimir said. He paused, scanning her face, as if, Frances imagined, on its surface was written an important text that he had studied long ago, one he had kissed as he closed its pages.

"I've heard you can tell my story."

His voice was deep, and its timbre struck a chord in the pit of Frances's stomach.

"I would like to explain myself to my father," he said.

She felt a rumble that was either hunger or vibration, the resonance of nimble fingers moving over harpsichord strings.

"Does your father speak English?" Frances asked.

"I'm afraid he does not," Vladimir said. "I can write in English myself. Also Russian, you know. But my father, only Yiddish."

Frances looked disappointed as she pointed to Etta. "She's the one you need to talk to."

"That's a pity," Vladimir said, looking over at Etta and shivering. "I was hoping you could tell him that being called to science is perhaps not so different from being called to God."

"I'm sorry, Vladimir," she said. "Etta and I have an agreement. I do the English, she does the Yiddish."

"Perhaps this is a story I could tell you somewhere else then." Vladimir grinned. "Over tea, if you have any interest."

Frances remembered her sister's silhouette the day Pauline had captured Solomon's tentative heart. She remembered Joseph walking away as if he hadn't even seen her. Bolstered by her name, Frances Gold looked up at Vladimir, her face—chin recently plucked—tilted to one side. Her eyes, her finest physical feature, blinked wildly. "Why, Vladimir," she said, "that would be just divine."

"Perfect!" he said as he leaned over to ask her quietly for her address.

Frances thought of her mother meeting Vladimir at the door. Whether Rose was happy to see him or not, it would be a scene Frances could not endure. "Come for me here," she said. "I'll be waiting," she said, smiling up at him.

The following Sunday, Vladimir came to the candy store to pick Frances up and take her out for bialys at Kossar's Bialystoker Kuchen Bakery on Grand Street. Frances had suggested it. It was a place she had gone with her father and Pauline, Abraham between the girls, holding their hands as they walked over the Williamsburg Bridge. Frances felt tea with Vladimir was far too formal. And besides, she loved the pillowy softness of those bialys, the way she was comforted as she watched the baker throw flour wildly about the room.

As they walked over the bridge, Frances thrilled to the largeness of the structure, the immense cables suspended above the roadway, the enormous towers tethering the bridge to the bottom of the East River, to earth. The river caught the warm afternoon light, and the city rose in the distance. Had it looked this way when she crossed with Abraham and Pauline? Frances hadn't noticed then. Even though they were only heading to the Lower East Side, the destination felt like the future, Brooklyn to her back, the past, just as Russia had once been. Frances realized how much the feeling of leaving delighted her as she and Vladimir talked about what he'd been doing since she had watched him put his chin to his chest and head for St. Petersburg.

"I came to New York with nothing," he told her. "Nothing but a proper education," he said.

"And the smarts of a villager." She laughed.

Vladimir looked at her sideways.

But even at nineteen Frances knew that the combination of these two elements nearly always produced a positive reaction. She knew from watching one after the other come over to the neighborhood from the old world that book smarts and a complete disregard of life's practical difficulties nearly guaranteed immigrant success, the young Russian she now walked beside included. Frances smiled at Vladimir and looked up the river toward where the Terrier and her sister were schtupping in furs and making a life together inside a faux tomb. Behind her, the bridges strung parallel, hooking laces of a corset.

Vladimir, who had just begun working at Westinghouse as a researcher, told Frances how he'd become a scientist. "I intended to be a rabbi, like my father, and yet it was science, not God, that kept me up at night, questioning. Questions I could answer, finite answers soothed me in a way that God could not," he said. "The questions of faith can never be truly answered. Does that make sense to you?"

Frances, whose thoughts of God had once given her the comfort that nothing else could, did not say so to Vladimir. He was talking about something different from comfort, she knew, an age-old understanding that Frances realized she herself did not possess. She looked over at Vladimir and smiled, the way she did at the people in the candy store. To each person she nodded her head and encouraged him to tell her all his secrets and lies. They all looked from side to side before they leaned in to tell their stories to Frances.

The warm look seemed to have the same effect on Vladimir. "Normally I don't talk so much," he said. "But with you, Frances, I feel very comfortable. Like I am finally living in my skin." He reached for her hand, and Frances allowed him to take it. She smiled brightly at all the people walking back from Hester Street with their bags of black bread and smoked fish. No one noticed them, so fixated were these pedestrians on getting across the water. No one seemed to be enjoying the journey.

"Tell me more, Vladimir," she said, stroking his forearm with her other hand.

"Well, I must say, and I have never said so out loud, that I felt burdened by my Hebrew studies. When I looked at the world on a, well, a molecular level, I suppose, it elevated me."

Frances nodded encouragingly. Go on, her eyes told him.

"It was for me the way I imagine my father felt when he prayed to God. Kind of how I feel looking at you." Vladimir laughed. "It is amazing. I have never met anyone comfortable in two worlds—the old one and the new. It is a gift, you know," he said.

Frances's heart soared. It was the first time since her father had died that it did not feel caught on something sharp, about to rip open.

"Thank you," she said.

By the time they stepped off the bridge, South Fifth Street behind them, a memory of dusty stoops and smoke and disappointed women looking over to their bowed husbands, Frances had fallen madly in love with Vladimir Zworykin.

And, despite her youth, her hairy chin, and her burgeoning bottom—or perhaps in part because of these things—Vladimir also fell in love with Frances. Every Tuesday and Thursday after work, he came all the way from New Jersey, where he worked, for Frances. He would walk into the candy store and, for a moment, watch her making people feel at ease. "Sid," she'd say in Yiddish, both hands over the man's bony one, "just think for a minute what you'd like to say. We're in no hurry here," she'd tell him, leaning back in her wobbly chair. Vladimir would rest against the counter sipping seltzer, browsing the *Red Gazette* from Moscow, and watch Etta torment her customers as he waited for Frances to walk with him through the neighborhood and back to her stoop. There they talked well into the evening together.

Rose knew exactly what was coming. "You're going to leave me too?" she asked Frances each night after Vladimir left for his flat on Hester Street.

"No, Mama," Frances said, watching her mother scrub the linens until her hands were raw. But Frances knew that one day, if not this day with this man, it would be true.

Four years after Pauline fled her family with the no-good gangster, much to her mother's consternation and terrible bouts of late-night cleaning, young Frances Gold married Vladimir Zworykin on a snowy February day at City Hall. As she said, "I do," clutching the daisies Vladimir had bought from a cart on Hester Street, Frances watched the huge flakes of snow clinging to the leafless tree boughs that scraped against the windows.

So caught up was Frances in marrying Vladimir, she did not realize what a civil ceremony would mean. What, no breaking of the glass? She silently panicked when the brief ceremony was over. How will we know the fragility of all things? How will we know to preserve our marriage and that, like all beautiful breakable things, marriage is an irrevocable act?

And then Frances panicked out loud. "No Ketubah!" she said.

"Frances, we have a wedding license. Who needs a Ketubah? My goodness, do you think I'm going to collect a dowry? This is the twentieth century. All we need to be is legal," her new husband said.

Frances was silent but not in agreement. She remembered her parents' Ketubah, hidden away in the back of a closet, the one place her mother never seemed to clean. It was written in Aramaic, and it had these beautiful, detailed paper cuttings in blue and green. "Well, how could we not stand beneath a chuppa!" She grabbed Vladimir's arm. Frances was not a girl who'd had the luxury to spend her childhood dreaming of her wedding, and so she had not known until it had come and gone—so quickly!—what she might have liked it to have been.

"Our life together will be without a solid foundation!" Her nails dug into Vladimir's wool peacoat.

Vladimir kissed his new wife, and she kept her eyes open, watching as the snowflakes clung to his black eyelashes. "To that, I believe I have a solution," he told her. He took Frances's hand and guided her away from City Hall.

"Where are we going?" she asked him, the two of them trudging through snow, Frances still grasping her bouquet, the red ribbon that held the daisies together a slash of vibrant color in the white day.

Vladimir was silent, and Frances let him take her, looking back at the hushed city as they stepped onto the walkway of the Brooklyn Bridge. They walked without speaking, snow falling lightly around them, gathering in slow, quiet heaps. When they got to the center of the bridge, Vladimir stopped.

"Look, my dear!" He gazed up, blinking away snowflakes.

Frances bent her head back. The way her neck stretched her chin toward the sky, and the view of the overwhelming awnings of the bridge, the massive structure climbing into the heavens, the falling snow, made her giggle.

Vladimir kissed her eyelashes, laced with snow. "A beautiful structure," he said. "See? The perfect foundation!"

She threw her arms around her new husband. "Not exactly a chuppa climbing with roses," she said. "But it will do." Frances walked to the edge of the bridge and threw her bouquet into the East River.

"To science!" she screamed, laughing.

The flowers arced against the gray sky, the red ribbon trailing behind. "For the fishes," Frances said, returning to her husband's side, the two walking hand in hand down the incline and back toward Brooklyn to tell her mother their news.

Frances never went back to the candy store, not even to kiss Mr. Berkowitz once on each cheek and tell him, Thank you. Here is where I decided I would be a star. You will hear of me one day.

Frances left her mother's house for Vladimir's four-story walk-up on Hester Street. In Manhattan! she told herself, when she tried to kiss her mother good-bye before she turned away. Rose stopped the scrub-

bing she had begun as soon as Frances told her of the marriage long
enough to admonish her in Yiddish: "You are heading backward, my
daughter, to the old world."

The Lower East Side was once the sole neighborhood in the city
Frances had ever been to, and though most people from her neighborhood despised it—the noise and the stink, the only place to get some
space to oneself on the rooftops between the sheets pinned to the wash
lines—Frances always felt closer to something there. Until she'd gone
to Grand Central Terminal on her way to visit Pauline, this was what
the city was to her. Carts lining Hester Street at the Khazar market—
barrel pickles, herring, fruits, and also men's work pants and shoes.
Women pointing to chickens, squawking in cages, and the butcher
slaughtering them right there, blood running into the street.

But there was also the Forward Building on East Broadway, a testa-
ment to thought. And the Garden Cafeteria, where all the intellectuals met to exchange ideas. These were the cultural places that had
made her father proud. And somehow Frances felt being in Manhattan
brought her far closer to glamour and fame and fortune than the
brownstone in the shtetl of South Fifth.

Vladimir did not need to be prompted to ask Rose to come live with
them. She laughed at him and adamantly refused. "I am not," Rose had
screamed at Frances and Vladimir in Yiddish, "put on this earth to be
your maid!"

Frances shook her head at her mother.

Instead of Rose living with them, Frances went back to South Fifth
Street to pay the rent each month and help her mother with the
household chores. It made Frances sad to pin the wash to the line—
clothes for only one, her mother's undergarments, the discolored
crotches, fluttering in the breeze.

No matter how often she came back to sit by the window and listen
to her mother's ceaseless complaining—now I am alone, all I did for
you people and everyone has left me, left me alone, soon I will be forced
to take in a boarder!—Frances avoided the candy store. All those stories
felt burdensome to her, as if, now that she finally had her own story,
those of her neighbors had become less important. Walking down the
block, toward her mother's flat, where she had grown up and watched
her sister lean in to the mirror and paint her lips, adjust her hat just so

before heading out into the night, where she had watched her father, her hero, fall, Frances would run into her old clients. Sometimes they would smile at each other as they passed on the crowded street, though often the people turned away from Frances, in part from the anger of being abandoned, in part from the shame of having told her too much. Once Betty Shapiro grabbed Frances's arm on the street. "Where have you gone?" she asked. "Who will pass this on?" she said in Yiddish. Frances tried to ignore Betty's gnarled finger that pointed at her heart.

"Someone will come." Frances smiled at Betty.

But really, Frances knew the neighborhood was already changing, and those stories would sit inside Betty Shapiro and all the others, unless they found a different way to tell them. The future was silence, a lip of snow blanketing these streets. And also the future: Frances willed herself not to think of the letters of warning left on the kitchen table that Vladimir received almost weekly now from his school friends, those intellectuals scattered all over Europe like seeds dropped from the mouths of birds, that told how it could turn out to be as bleak as the past.

Meanwhile, Vladimir continued working at Westinghouse, coming home from the office often well past midnight.

"But what are you doing there?" Frances would ask, raising her head from the pillow, her eyes rimmed with red from the exhaustion of trying to stay awake for her new husband. The flat smelled of fried eggs and boiled potatoes.

Sometimes he would make his way through the nest of her tangled hair and settle into a kiss.

"Is it some kind of secret?" she'd ask him as he climbed into bed and brought her close to him.

"No," he said. "Just complicated."

On one of these nights, Vladimir arrived home to an especially inconsolable Frances.

"I'm all alone here!" she sobbed when he returned after 1:00 A.M. The day before, her mother had put doubt in Frances. I've never heard of working so late into the night. You believe such nonsense? You are crazy! Rose said. *Meshuge* to believe this. When Frances screamed at her husband, she heard her mother's voice, as if it had been this voice that had spoken, not her own, and she brought her hand to her mouth, as if to put the sentence back.

"I promise it will be worth it," Vladimir told her, removing his coat and hat.

Frances held her tongue and did not speak the litany of accusations she had been thinking of the entire evening. A mistress! Already! Gambling! Oh, my God, the Mob has gotten to him! Had these also been her mother's thoughts? "I don't believe you," she said tentatively.

"Okay," Vladimir said. "Here it is. I am re-creating the human eye." He traced his thumb over her eyelid as she held her head back languidly.

Frances snapped her head up and looked at him sideways. "Is that code for something? And does it involve a woman?"

"No one but you," he said, stripping to his underwear and climbing into bed next to her. "There is a tube, a picture tube, and it imitates the condition under which the human eye functions." Vladimir put his large, dry hands on Frances's hip. "It can visually record anything."

"Anything?" Frances smiled, her head on her elbow.

"Anything," he said. "You are my muse." He pulled her close.

"What, now you're a poet?" Frances climbed on top of her husband and leaned back.

"You little beast!" He grabbed her hips with both hands, and she rocked on top of him. Vladimir reached up to touch Frances's face, her neck, and her breasts. "I can see through you, my beast," he said, moving his hand across her chest and resting it over her heart. Once Vladimir had worked researching the X-ray, and Frances now imagined herself, a set of stark white bones on black paper, two-dimensional. She crinkled when you shook her. Frances imagined herself discovered.

Here I am, she wanted to tell him, puffing out her chest as if this would give her a third dimension, and get her husband to look closer, not to her heart even but to her soul.

"If only I could bottle up this light that you are, put it in a box," he said. With a hand on each breast, Vladimir twisted Frances's nipples. The sensation shot through her, a straight and exacting line of pleasure from her chest to her crotch, everything now connected.

"In every American home." He laughed. "A little box of you. We'd be rich!"

In that moment, Frances didn't care when her husband came home as long as he got there. She couldn't care less that he was owned by a huge corporation and that all his hard work, all those nights he came back to the flat, his body a tight coil held together by a tiny, wound filament, were really gifts to someone else. Frances remembered coming home to her mother and putting her coins in that glass jar. *Clink clink clink.* Frances thought she would live her entire life just to hear that miraculous stilling of the straw broom on wooden floorboards.

She thought of the time Vladimir had taken her to the theater, how they had sat in those red velvet seats at the St. James, the curtain about to break open. In that moment when the houselights dimmed, she had turned to him and said, One day that's gonna be me. When the conductor had tapped his stick and the orchestra wound down its tuning, beginning the overture, she had taken her husband's hand in hers and said, One day. Then Hollywood, she'd thought. California! Palm trees and the Pacific Ocean. She'd thought of herself wading in the sea, a huge hat on her head that she had to hold on to so as not to lose it in the wind.

That night Frances made love to her husband, watching him move beneath her as he explained himself to her. She knew she could never be apart from Vladimir and his lovely, holy science. She knew he could make her a star. In every American home, she thought. I believe, I believe. She leaned down to kiss his face, his shoulders, his taut neck, her love for him then as strong and fortified and necessary as the towering awnings that supported the Brooklyn Bridge.

Vladimir was not lying—he would re-create the human eye, and in so doing would control what the eye would see. In 1929, the year that Frances and Vladimir stood on the Brooklyn Bridge, Frances throwing her snow-dusted bouquet into the East River, Vladimir invented the Iconoscope, the television camera.

But the Kinescope, Vladimir's second invention, is the device that, through a directed beam of electrons, translates the pictures it receives into images on the screen. Some say meeting Frances was Vladimir's destiny, Frances his complete and total inspiration. Would he ever have discovered the Kinescope without Frances Gold? Never.

The electron beam in the Kinescope strikes the back of a phosphor coating, and, for a split second, that charge glows. As Vladimir worked into the night, what he imagined was translating his wife's very energy and placing it into a confined space where it could be saved and played whenever he liked. I want to capture you, he'd tell Frances. Her warmth, her way with the old neighborhood and the folks of the new world, inspired Vladimir to find a way to bring her into every American home.

The Kinescope was going to be huge, but either Westinghouse, which soon made Vladimir director of research, could not see this, or perhaps, like so many other major corporations, it was, in the end, not big enough to back it alone. It needed investors. And, despite her husband's wishes to keep what he was doing under wraps, here was where Frances thought she might be able to help him in return.

As enraged as she was at Pauline, for leaving, yes, for abandoning her for a life of *things,* for not sitting shiva for their father—*their father!*—Frances had managed to keep positive feelings for her old friend Solomon. She still remembered him the way he was before he became the Terrier, how he would come back to the neighborhood and bring her chocolate-covered cherries. Solomon had given Frances the first pair of shoes that had not been her sister's hand-me-downs: Mary Janes. The day he brought them, the patent leather shoes refracting light, hooked to the ends of his plump fingers, Franny had done the two-step on her front stoop and imagined she was a beautiful girl at the Ziegfeld, dancing with Eddie Cantor. And riding home with him in his breezer the day she had visited them in Westchester County. Frances was not ashamed to say that it was the first time she had ever felt the wind in her hair.

She could not sustain her anger at Solomon the way she could not help but remain angry at her sister. She did not debate if it was wrong for her to tell Solomon what her husband did each night. Vladimir needed the money to make his invention come to life. And she with it. Before the Kinescope, before Vladimir, she had been merely the vehicle to anyone else's voice.

Besides, Frances rationalized, Solomon and Joseph had also known Vladimir and his family.

"From Russia, Sol!" she told him, bending in to whisper when she entered Egypt for the second time in her life. "He's just like your brother." The thought of Joseph pleased Frances, and she stood up for effect. "Now where's this nephew of mine?" she asked. She hadn't ever seen him, and he was already two years old. This was part of why she had gone all the way up to Egypt to see Solomon on Pauline's shopping day, he assured Frances, who had been opposed to meeting him where he currently held court, at the Knickerbocker Hotel on Forty-second Street.

"He's around somewhere," Solomon said of his son. Then he scoffed at Frances. "My brother? No: my brothers are the boys I met here, in New York, the ones who schlammy the maggots who have wronged me, the boys who, just when I look at 'em funny, do what I tell 'em."

"Come on, Sol." Frances tried to joke her brother-in-law out of what she willed herself to think was only a bad mood.

"No, Frances, my brothers are not pathetic salesmen traveling New England peddling their pathetic little wares. They are the opposite of this, the opposite of our fathers."

"Vladimir is doing something exceptional," she told Solomon, flushed from the thought of her husband being brilliant, as brilliant as her unrecognized father had been. Her nephew came running into the room, as if from nowhere, and Frances pulled him up onto her lap. "Look at you!" she said. "Hullo, Wesley!" Frances leaned down to rub her considerable nose with his growing one. "I'm Auntie Frances."

Wesley looked like a miniature version of Solomon, down to the hooked nose and fleshy cheeks, which shocked Frances. She thought her sister would surely have tired of Sol and moved on to some West-chester dish, someone who could take care of her when the Terrier was off doing whatever it was the Terrier did when he left, oftentimes for days. Rumor was the Mob was expanding upstate and into the Mid-west—the Mafia was not just a New York City problem anymore—and Frances imagined the Terrier barking and humping his way through little towns and coffee shops across America. She thought perhaps Wes-ley was from the seed of another man, but there was no mistaking this baby as anyone's but the Terrier's.

Wesley grabbed at her nose. "Ouch!" Frances peeled his little fingers out of her nostrils. "He's making a picture tube!" she said to Solomon, rubbing her nose. "Honest to God."

Solomon imagined one of his son's drawings mounted on construction paper and rolled up tight, but he didn't let on. "A who?" he said.

"A picture tube—it's gonna put images on a little screen!" she said. "Pictures and sound at the same time!" she said.

"Really?" The Terrier tilted his head.

Frances punched him in the stomach with the arm that was not holding Wesley.

"Ooof," he said, deflecting her.

She had to laugh. How, she thought, can a man kill countless other men and still be hurt by a woman's touch?

"What?" he said, rubbing his stomach. "What!"

"What are ya going to do, put a number out on me? You know, Sol, it wouldn't hurt you to do something honest." Frances sat back, becoming serious. "You've got a kid now." She folded her arms and looked down at Wesley, propped up next to her on the couch like a tiny man. "Let me tell you, you could invest in worse things," she said. "Believe you me."

"You need money, Franny-goil? You just tell me." Solomon was already getting up to go to one of his many stashes of ready cash.

"Stupid man!" she said. "You never heard to invest? Just sell sell sell, shoot shoot shoot? Listen to me. You should put your money in this. For him." She pointed to Wesley. "It's gonna make you more than any of this stuff." She waved her arm around the gilded room. "And then you can walk away."

Frances could read her old friend, and she watched the thoughts flicker over his face. She knew from that face exactly what Solomon was thinking. He was thinking that he could not walk away, not only because the bosses wouldn't let him now but because he could never live the life of a straight man. Nine to five, not for him. Even those boys in racketeering, offices in the factories, the ones Frances had read were in "garments," boys with their own secretaries—not for him. Maybe, she thought now, some folks just have the criminal in their bones.

That face! thought Frances. A nose bashed in from God knows what, those sad, drooping eyes, more spaniel, she noted, than terrier.

She sighed. "Don't you have dreams, Solomon?"

He tilted his head as if he'd never considered such a question. "I do," he said. "No, I did," he said. "My dreams, if that's what you wanna call 'em, they've all come true already. I mean, I'd like more territory, I'd like to off the competition, but, basically, look at all I got." For what seemed like the fifteenth time, the Terrier swung his arm around the room.

"That's sad," Frances said. She wondered what it would be like to be done yearning for something more. "Me, I'm dreaming all the time. Dreaming for Vladimir, also for myself. Dreaming I can be an actress."

"A who?"

"I want to be an actress," Frances said. "On the stage. That all right with you?"

"Fine with me," Solomon said. "What do I care? Pauline said she'd heard you were in the writing business! What happened to that?"

Frances's ears reddened at the thought of her sister hearing news of her. How had she known? To whom had she been speaking? "Yeah, well, now I wanna be an actress, okay?"

"Sure," Solomon said.

"Thank you." Frances shook her head. "Listen to me, Solomon Brodsky." Her wide bottom settled deeper into the velvet sofa. She took Wesley's little hand in hers and began to tell Solomon the real reason she had come. "So not for you? Fine. Do me a favor. Tell your brother," she said.

She would have done it herself, but she knew Joseph didn't have the money. It was heartbreaking to think of him all the nights on the road, bent over the trunk of his car, pulling out those old, scratched-up valises. Or dragging them on the train. She saw his face and imagined it was falling toward the street. Even though Joseph had been married for years, it still hurt her to think of him arm in arm with another girl, someone fancy and from New England, she'd heard. How long since she'd seen Joseph? An image of a young boy carrying a very large yellow dish to the baker for his mother rose into her consciousness. What are you doing, Joe? she'd asked him, always following. He never shooed her away, like so many of the boys in the neighborhood. Our stove is too small, he'd told her, balancing the heavy pottery dish with one hand as he pressed a nickel in Frances's clammy hand. Do you want to come with me to Mr. Stretsky's? he'd said. You can give him the nickel so we can use his oven.

Frances smiled to herself at the thought of that little boy. She couldn't believe how fast the years had flown by, but at least, she thought now, at least Joseph was in love, like she was.

"Be sure you tell him," Frances said, rising from the couch. She leaned down and patted Wesley's backside.

How she wanted Joseph to have what he wanted, which she knew in part had to do with making his mother happy in all the ways the Terrier had not. Frances remembered Selma Brodsky walking the neighborhood in a daze when Solomon left, and how Joseph always brought her home, his hand at the small of her back, guiding her. If Frances could not be in his dreams, she knew she could at least help make some of those dreams come true.

"You're serious?" the Terrier said. "Not a chance, Fran. I haven't spoken to him in years. He won't talk to me. I sent him a wedding gift, you know. A set of Baccarat tumblers, beeaaut-ee-ful, straight from France. You know that damn package was sent back without so much as a note?" He shook his head.

"Hey!" Frances said. "That's what you sent me! What am I gonna do with four glasses from France?"

The Terrier smiled sheepishly. "Listen, toots, I don't need my brother and his big fat morality. Between him and my father, how am I going to get through the day? Why don't *you* tell him?" he said.

Frances had learned drama from Summer Lebrau, who always looked away as she told a story, her eyes filling with clouds. I want them to know my life was *elegant,* she would tell Franny. Now Frances looked at her brother-in-law and revealed to him a face she had practiced on many occasions alone in her room, the click-clicking of her father's peppermints and labored breathing emanating from the room next door.

"I just can't call him," she told Solomon. She thought of her new husband. Vladimir was the right one, the right investment, the one who would set the world on fire. She loved him. And the thought of making love to him made her shiver. So why, why? why! was she still broken over Joseph? She could not ask Vladimir for the scientific explanation, though she knew there had to be one, some chemical reason that she would never stop wanting Joseph Brodsky. Her blood craved his blood. She could taste it, and still the thought of him made her mouth water.

Frances stood up to increase the drama of the moment. "I must leave, Sol," she said.

Just then Pauline walked into the foyer. "Hulloooo?" Her voice echoed through the house.

Frances froze as she watched her sister enter the living room. Just seeing her in this ridiculous house, all her packages and hatboxes knocking against one another, enraged Frances. I am a closed door, she thought. I will not let this person through.

The Terrier fidgeted, as if the thought of these two women running into each other under his own roof terrified him. He stood up. "Okay then, Fran," he said.

"Oh!" Pauline forced a smile. "Frances. What are you doing here?" She set down all her bags and boxes. Pauline looked stunning in her blue cloche hat and georgette dress, tied with a midnight blue sash. Pauline shone, scrubbed cleaner than Rose's wooden floors. Wesley ran to his mother, and she scooped him up in her thin arms, jangling with bangle bracelets.

"Hullo!" she said to Wesley, covering the boy with kisses. He laughed and wiped his face.

Frances looked around as if to place a faraway sound. "Did you hear something?" she asked Solomon.

He groaned. "Come on, Fran," he said. "Let me take you to the train."

Frances ignored him. "You listen to me now. Vladimir will be doing an expo of sorts in town next month." She looked at Solomon and took her wrap from the maid, who had miraculously appeared, holding it out for Frances to climb into.

Pauline put Wesley down and then tried to stand in front of her sister. "Frances," she said. "I'm sorry. I know you don't understand, but I couldn't—"

"There will be a demonstration," Frances said to Solomon, who looked around nervously. "Think about what I've said," she told him. "I'll be waiting outside," she told him, furious that she could not make the dramatic exit the scene called for.

Frances managed to look kindly at Wesley while nearly knocking her sister over as she marched out. She could hear Solomon calling after her.

"An actress, huh? I'll be right out," he said.

"A who?" Frances heard her sister ask.

"An actress!" the Terrier said. "Franny wants to be in pictures!"

When Frances stepped outside the door, she took in massive gulps of breath and leaned against the house. I said the stage, she thought. Then she thought of her father's funeral, of waiting for her sister to walk in and keep her company in her grief. Frances would never forget that moment, night filling up that stinking, grieving room, when she realized Pauline would not be coming. It was the first time she had understood she'd lost her sister. She realized that day she was to walk the world alone.

But that isn't what happened, Frances thought now. I have a companion in my loneliness, she thought.

She could hear her sister's voice. "Well, don't just sit there, Sol. Get up off your fat arse and take her to the train, why don't you!"

"What was that all about anyway?" Pauline said again when her husband didn't answer.

Frances could hear the loud sound of her sister's heels clicking against the marble floor. Peering in through the window, she watched as Solomon walked toward the foyer and her sister went to the bar to pour herself some of the Terrier's illegal liquor. She watched her sister toss back her drink, her long chandelier earrings tilting, poised to slice open her perfect cheeks.

CHAPTER 10

Currency, Investing, 1929

FRANCES WAS THE ONE who called to tell her old neighbor about her husband's about-to-be invention. Maybe the years of travel, and the struggle to make enough to keep that Yankee wife of his in the style, had changed him. Maybe now he would listen to her and take some money from his brother to make an easier life for himself up there.

Frances took a deep breath and lifted the receiver. "Operator," she said. "Long distance, please. Joseph Brodsky, Roxbury, M-A."

Long distance, she thought, as she waited on the line for the operator to place the call. Here I am calling long distance to reach someone who once lived only next door. She remembered his face, always a little sad as he gathered himself up to walk into his parents' house. After Joseph left, he was sure to check and see if Frances was on her stoop, and he always had a nice word for her when he visited. It touched her to think of him then, fingers on the brim of his hat and leaning his head in her direction. Frances's heart would always stop for sad men.

What was Joseph doing today? she wondered. Each day she had seen him leave and come home, but now it was years since she had spoken to him.

"Hello?" she heard on the line when the connection was made. Joseph sounded startled.

"Joe," she said. "It's me." Frances was silent. Me, she thought. She saw herself as a girl running away from the neighborhood bullies.

Monkey! they screamed. Not her, she thought. Me. "Frances," she said.

"Vhat happened?" he asked. Why would she be calling him? Was anyone left from the village? Had they all been sent to Siberia? Did Brooklyn finally fall into the sea?

Frances laughed. This call was not cheap, and so she got quickly to her point. "Everything's fine, Joe," she said. "But I have this idea for you," she began and then told him about her husband's invention and what it could mean if he invested in it.

"Vhaat?" he said. "You call me on zhe long distance for zhis malarkey?" Money she wants? Joseph was amazed. All this time has passed and she calls for money? Black Tuesday had made things even worse for Joseph. No one wanted to buy from him anymore, and Procter & Gamble was cutting back on the entire sales force. Sending all those men, tiny ants, to march across New England was prohibitively expensive, and you didn't have to be a rocket scientist to know that Joseph wasn't going to be the last one standing. Esther was still convinced that opening the dry cleaner was the answer, but Joseph had come to despise the idea. Then he remembered his wife's story about her appendix, buried there beneath her childhood home, and the thought of childhood made him soften toward his old friend. "Where you zhink I have this money to give you, Frances?" he asked her.

Frances hesitated. "It's not for me, Joe," she said. "It's for you. You have to trust me. This will make you rich."

Rich, thought Joseph. How? He was already thinking of trying to save enough money to buy real estate in Florida, the state where the sun always shines, where all the money is. Joseph had pictured oranges growing as large and heavy as planets, the noon light catching the sea as distinctly as silver knives turning. He imagined that the moment he stepped over the line from Georgia, the street would be lined with money. It wasn't so different from how he had imagined all of America when he was coming over, only he hadn't known then what U.S. currency looked like and instead had pictured the streets sparkling with huge chunks of yellow gold. Real estate would get him off the road. That old man had dandruff snowing on the shoulders of his ill-fitting blue suit. But Joseph could never get that kind of cash together. Not now. "Rich," he said. "What makes you think I vant to be rich anyway, Fran?"

"You want to be comfortable, no?" she said. "For your future children, no?"

Joseph thought of children. He saw blank faces on little bundled-up bodies running toward him in the snow. Were these Maine children? "Of course," he said.

"You could always ask Solomon," she said quietly. "I know for a fact he would give you the cash interest free."

"Interest free? Zhis is vhat you sink is zhe problem, Fran? Do not even mention his name to me!" Joseph said.

Frances had never heard him raise his voice. Never. She sniffed loudly.

"He's dead to me," Joseph said softly. "Dead."

"Joe," she'd said. "Come on, he's your—"

"Gone already," Joseph told Frances. He remembered Solomon hanging around on the corner, waiting for some wiseguy to come by and ask him for a favor. Scram! he'd order Joseph when he came out of the candy store. "End of conversation," Joseph told her. "But, Frances," he said, "it's lovely to hear your voice."

On the other end of the line, all the way in New York, Frances quietly set down the receiver. She knew Vladimir would find his money. She knew he would be unhappy to hear she had called to try to get money for him. And yet, Frances had done it for Joseph. She had! Poor Joe. If only he would listen, she thought. Life could be so much easier if only he would listen.

Who was the one who listened and who actually had money now to invest? Seymour Bloom.

"Something big is happening tonight, my friend," the Terrier told him the day after Frances had shown up in Westchester. "Don't say I never did anything for ya," he said.

Seymour's heart filled with dread at the phone ringing this time of evening. What horrible thing would he have to do? Some of the boys got used to it, he knew, but Seymour never got blasé about roughing someone up, even a young punk who was trying to move in on the territory. No matter what the nature, these calls to get Seymour to play cards uptown caused him trepidation. The idea of sitting across from those terrible faces, each a broken palm, knife marks as long and deep as life lines, the talk of all the plans and deeds to come, rumors of who had betrayed whom, who was about to, it was all so foreboding.

"Not tonight, Terry, please," Seymour said. "I have plans to take Sarah to a show tonight."

"A show."

"Yes, Terrier. *Fifty Million Frenchmen.*"

"Are you pulling my leg?"

"No, Terrier. This is the show we're planning to see."

"You and your big fat ideas," the Terrier said. "You and your *culture.* Relax, Mrs. Grundy. I want to talk to you about the pictures."

"The pictures?" Seymour asked.

"Sure, Seymour. Just about the pictures."

When the Terrier explained what he could of Vladimir's invention and this demonstration at the New Amsterdam Theater, what Seymour saw immediately was what he had spent his life trying to find: a way out. Would it be possible to tell the Terrier, No, I mean it, not tonight, not ever, thanks for the memories, but let me out of my deal with the devil. Seymour had been careful. But he knew how it was with those guys. He knew they told you, Okay, buddy, go to your little shack in the woods, go to your nice little life in the country. And they let you sit there for a week, thinking that you had made it. That you had cheated God in some way, maybe, that out of all the men placed on this earth, this one, this schlemiel with a brain as sorry and crackable as a goose egg, was going to get away. Such mean, false hope. That's when the boys came for you. Seymour knew because he arranged it. They pulled up just to say hello, hey, putz, how's it going out here in the shack in the woods, your wife making jam in there and pickling radishes, how sweet, come on, let's go for a ride. And still, sometimes they didn't know, or they pretended it was just an old friend come for some fresh air to catch up. As if any of those guys were friends. And yet, Seymour knew there was loyalty, only it never seemed to be to one another. Even the widows, the ones he had kids from the neighborhood drop fifty bucks a week to. Some of the women ripped it up in their faces, it was true, but some kept that money, lived on it their whole lives. Those were real gangsters' wives, thought Seymour. Women who could watch their husbands murdered and take the money from their killers, invite them in for dinner every Monday following.

Just the way he had laughed in the face of that gun the Terrier had pointed at him the year before, Seymour decided now he would laugh in the face of his destiny. What did he care? Sometimes, he reasoned, a man has two fates, two fortunes. The one he stumbles into and the one he has to work to find. He is destined for both. Who cares if they're mutually exclusive? And so in November 1929, Seymour Bloom walked down Broadway to Forty-second Street to the New Amsterdam Theater to see if this Kinescope was the golden path out he had hoped it would be.

As Seymour walked into Times Square, he was thinking not about what he was about to see—Broadway! the future!—but about what it would bring him. What would it be like, he wondered, not to be beholden to the Terrier, who was beholden to Greenberg, who in turn answered to Rothstein? What would it be like for Seymour to look at his father-in-law and for once not feel shame about all he was not providing, or shame about the manner in which he was providing it? What if something happened and the Terrier just sent Seymour's family to live upstate? He could see it now, Sarah in some country cottage, poured like spilt gin over a wooden table. It made him laugh for a moment, the thought of his wife in the middle of a pastoral setting, peeling potatoes. He saw his future children running around without clothes on, their feet as dirty as gypsies'. How much worse could it be?

When Seymour arrived at the theater, he walked straight up to the stage to Vladimir Zworykin, director of research for the brand-new RCA, a division of Westinghouse, and introduced himself. "Seymour Bloom," he said, reaching out his hand. "The Terrier sent me." He shook the inventor's trembling hand.

Seymour felt Vladimir's fear and for a moment was confused by it. Then he realized exactly what this man was thinking: Oh my God oh my God oh my God, was what he was thinking. All this work, all my education, all my studying, my faith in God, it's all come to this? He'd seen it half a million times, and Seymour chuckled a little to himself as he thought of Vladimir, wondering now if it had been his wife who had sent him. No. Seymour knew this man would not believe it had been his wife, not his wife, the very same girl he'd mounted last night? How could that be?

Seymour knew it was cruel, but he did enjoy watching Vladimir shift his feet, clear his throat, and look around, perhaps to see if the two Westinghouse execs were in the theater. Seymour knew how it worked for a man like Vladimir—those men practically owned his internal organs, his blood and muscle, his entire insides. David Sarnoff could easily have sent for one of Terry the Terrier's minions to get rid of Vladimir for good. This power to make men question their entire existence just by my presence will be hard to lose, he thought.

Seymour gave in. He touched Vladimir lightly on the arm. "Not to worry," he said. "I've come to see this invention of yours," he said. "It sounds so exciting. Image and sound at the same time. I want to help," he said.

Vladimir took a step back, and his entire body seemed to sigh with relief. His mouth quivered into a smile. He nodded. "Well then, I have something to show you."

He led Seymour to the back of the stage. There Vladimir uncovered the receiver, and, without too much fanfare, he turned it on.

A pinpoint of light on the black screen blew quickly into an image of a dark-haired woman waving to the camera.

"My wife," Vladimir said, breathing.

Seymour nodded, knowing what Vladimir had to be feeling, which was that his wife was a good good girl, how could he ever have thought she would hurt him?

She looked like a good girl. And she looked pretty in an old-world sort of way, her white skin a bright contrast to her dark hair and eyes.

"Frances," Vladimir said. "This is Frances."

Seymour shook his head and then stopped, watching this woman wave to him. The image was grainy, but he could make out her hand slowly waving. At him. Hello, America, she said, earnest and self-mocking at the same time. Hello!

Seymour's heart crashed. Here was his childhood in Brooklyn, his young adulthood in his mother's beauty shop, the girl at reception knocking her pencil to her head, a calendar spread out in front of her filled with her unintelligible scribble. He could smell that shop still, and hear the women's screams as Inez tore at their scalps, and he could smell the present, the stench of alcohol all day, those dropped bottles on the Long Island shore from a sloppy delivery, and then the night smell of his wife, gin often spilt in their bed. Nights he would have to peel her off the floor. Here was his past, but on the screen this man's wife was all of a sudden the future, some Jewish girl from Russia, beckoning him away from memory, waving hello.

It was fairly unbearable his life, and yet, the money. The money. His mother with her hair salon and his little brother, Jacob, on his way to college. College. It had once been an impossibility. And his father-in-law always pointing at him with a mean, knowing finger. He'd always reminded Seymour of the old photographs he'd seen of Abraham Lincoln. Seymour could not give up what he had without something. Something like this.

"Wow!" he said to Vladimir. "Very complicated. Very scientific. But at the same time very beautiful, as art is beautiful."

Vladimir seemed pleased with this assessment. "Thank you," he said. "I think of it as art as well. Shall I tell you how it works?"

"Of course." Seymour scratched his chin. "Please."

"Well, it's quite simple, really. A camera is focused on an image through a lens and onto an array of photoelectric cells that coat the end of a tube." Vladimir opened his receiver to show Seymour the inside. "The electrical image found by the cells is scanned line by line by an electron beam and transmitted to the cathode ray tube here." He pointed at the tube.

Seymour had gained interest and lost interest at the exact same time. "I see!" he said. How he had tired of sitting before the radio looking sideways at his wife's disappointed face. Surely all men felt this way. But were all women disappointed? Seymour believed right then that they were, that perhaps Vladimir science could explain it. Disappointment, he reasoned, was a female gene, part of their chemical makeup. And if this were so, all men would pay to the gills to welcome this dark-haired, thankful, and smiling girl into their living rooms. "Okay, Vladimir," he said. "Where do I go to invest in our future?"

Seymour Bloom became one of the primary Westinghouse backers. And were it not for the fact that all that beautiful science was to be used for military applications, Seymour could have had his television, woman after woman smiling into each and every American living room, in a matter of months. But the immediate returns, along with the money he had made already, were enough that, as the Panic spread its inky tentacles across America, Seymour could get out of the Mob. He had been careful. For one, the cops loved him for the very reason the Terrier had brought him in in the first place—they could talk to him. And getting paid by Seymour was easier on them than getting paid by someone they couldn't talk to. Seymour had managed to make only a few enemies—he had dealt with the shipping of goods exactly as he was told to. He had been on time and prepared for every task he was told to perform.

And because the Terrier had brought him in, the other boys let the Terrier handle what they came to call the "goyisha situation," which was how they referred to Seymour in moments when he missed vital meetings because he just had to go to the opening of *Funny Face*. It wasn't that they didn't trust him—Seymour was known for his honesty—they simply did not understand him. Men admired Seymour for his quiet strength, a trait regarded as a weakness in his own home. Everyone liked and relied on Seymour, and though he could have risen quickly in the ranks thanks to his Protestant good looks and his highfalutin' airs, could have become the heir to Rothstein himself, he was for these very reasons a threat to the higher-ups and, for these reasons as well, a safe man to let go.

"You're lucky as hell, Sy, no one's gonna take you for a ride," the Terrier had told him. "Least I don't think so."

Seymour pushed out of his head all the scenarios, the calls that could be made, the car stolen, the plates changed, and Seymour to be picked up and driven to his death. He knew he could be found and buried in a marsh way out in Canarsie.

After they threw him back like a bad fish, as the Terrier would always put it, Seymour waited for science to reward him for all his troubles. Night after night he went to the theater. Each evening was connected to the one before, the years before, those nights he had sat next to his wife in the dark and for the first time been transported to another place and time, a place where all he had to do was sit back and enjoy the show. While Seymour waited for Vladimir Zworykin to make him even richer, Joseph was still driving in the dark, making his way through cities and towns, opening and closing doors, begging people to buy. Both men were searching out the destiny neither had yet been fortunate enough to stumble upon.

CHAPTER 11

The Joint: 1931

SEYMOUR WAS WRONG. Destiny is destiny. Either one stumbles upon it or it is completely elusive. Joseph, whose routes were mapped out for him each week by a Procter & Gamble dispatcher, had not yet found his; Frances was polishing the fruits of her own; and Seymour was lucky enough to stumble over his destiny twice.

Seymour had the perfect opportunity to realize his dreams when, after seeing *Of Thee I Sing* at the Music Box, he sat at a back table at Sardi's, wishing he had become an actor. He thought of all the girls lined up onstage in bathing suits at Atlantic City, typical birds waiting to be chosen. Couldn't he have been the presidential candidate in that show, picking the nicest one? If not in life, thought Seymour, then certainly in theater. In many ways Seymour knew he had acted his whole life, yet he had never received applause for a single performance. Who was waiting in the reeds to clap their hands together for Seymour Bloom's role as the Broadway-loving mobster? The Terrier? Hardly. Seymour always knew there was part of Terry the Terrier that wanted to see him slip and fall.

At Sardi's, a stranger took a seat in the empty chair across the table. "Seymour Bloom?" he said.

Seymour shut his eyes. Please, he thought. Not here. The Terrier *would* do it here, at Sardi's. Poetic justice, as it were. In front of everyone. There was Louise Brooks, right there. Was this astonishing beauty going to see him die? Not now, thought Seymour. So many things to do. He opened his eyes to get a look at the man he was sure would do him in when he realized, there was no way this was the one. This one had seen better days in his faded suit, which was at least a size too large. His hair, what there was of it, was in complete disarray, and the man needed a decent shave. Even the Terrier had more class than to off him like this.

"You probably don't remember me," he said. "I'm Caleb Candor. The writer?" The man held out a bony hand, and Seymour took it grudgingly. "I used to hang out at the Joint. With your mother and Joe. Joe Crews. I remember you when you were a teenager," Caleb told him. "Now"—Caleb Candor put both hands out in front of him, palms up—"now I see you're all grown up."

"Why, thank you." Seymour bowed his head toward the stranger. The Joint. Seymour thought of it often, the way his mother ran to meet the clientele at the door, her dresses billowing out behind her, revealing that she was glamorous yet necessary. Nights Seymour came with his mother to work, she watched out the window for the fancy cars to pull up. As the driver got out and opened the door for a film star or a theater actress, Inez would motion Seymour over and point. Look, Seymole, she'd say. There's Minta Durfee!

Seymour always looked over her shoulder to see who was about to come inside.

"Of course I remember you," he said, though he couldn't place this man. He didn't know any writers. Or if he did, he did not know they were writers.

What Seymour remembered in the moment this man took a seat across from him was really Madame Lutille, the cruel old French lady who owned the Joint. She sat in the back room going over her receipts and cursing America and the women of the Christian Temperance Union. Seymour's mother pretended the place was hers, and she greeted the guests as if it was her home, the leather banquettes and long wooden bar part of her own living room, when in truth it all belonged to Madame Lutille. That she hired Inez, as far as Seymour could tell, was the Frenchwoman's single act of kindness in the world. But the arrangement had its advantages: Inez was a fellow Parisienne, which meant Madame Lutille could shout out commands in her native tongue without stopping to use lowly American idioms. More important, Inez was neither too pretty nor too thin; no one famous would fall in love with her. She was not terribly tasteful in her appearance, and she was trying to get out of the factory to save some money. Madame Lutille was happy to have Inez pretend she owned the establishment because it made her work harder, which meant Madame Lutille could do less without the worry of paying Inez a competitive wage. It also brought Joe Crews around most every night, and this was a man—a boxer on a winning streak!—who so many people wanted to see.

Madame Lutille didn't know what Seymour knew, which was that Inez was just waiting for Joe Crews to make enough money to buy the place out from under the old bitch.

Seymour smiled. "Madame Lutille. Remember Madame Lutille?"

"Vaguely," Caleb Candor said. "She didn't come out front too often," he said.

The one distinct memory that emerged out of the hot sticky soup of Seymour's youth was of that woman. One night he had gone looking in the back rooms for Joe Crews. What he needed from Joe he couldn't now recall, though Seymour would always remember the way Joe made him feel as if he had a father, a strong man, who would protect him in the world. A boxer. Seymour was constantly amazed at what Joe did—he *fought* for a living. And, even after his accident—which left him unable to fight, yes, but also, it seemed to Seymour, left him unable to think, or to remember words and how to close his mouth when eating—Seymour always looked up to Joe Crews. He was powerful, and Seymour had not known personally many powerful men. When Seymour was fifteen and wandering around the back of the establishment looking for Joe, he'd stumbled upon Madame Lutille counting her money. Her fat legs were spread before her, and her horrible, nearly blue tongue slithered from her black mouth. She licked her thumb and then separated each bill before slamming it down on the table, where money was stacked in huge piles. Seymour sucked in his breath at the sight of her. Madame Lutille looked at him with a steely gaze: You want my money, little boy, don't you? her look seemed to say. And he *had* wanted her money, he had wanted to run in and swipe a stack of bills; yet at the same time that money was repulsive to him. How many hands, how many dirty fingers had handled those bills before they had gotten into Madame Lutille's clutches?

"What can I do for you, Caleb?" Seymour asked, shaking the image away.

"I hear that you love the theater," Caleb said. "And I have a little something you might be interested in." He took out a large manila envelope, as frayed as his lapels. He unwound the red string that clasped it closed and took out a sheaf of papers, which he then handed to Seymour.

Seymour took the manuscript. Each page was yellowing along the edges and seemed to have been dipped in water many years before.

"My libretto," Caleb said. "*The Joint.* I wrote this when the place closed down. Kind of an homage."

Seymour grinned. "You don't say." He leafed through the papers, nearly every one ringed with coffee. "Does this thing have music?" he asked.

"It does!" Caleb said.

"Let me take a look then," he said. "Tell me where to get ahold of you."

Caleb looked down at the tablecloth. "I'll be here," he said, now looking up sheepishly at Seymour. "You can always just find me here."

Seymour gave Caleb Candor fifty dollars for his script and in return received the right to do to it whatever he needed. Caleb had seemed more than pleased with the arrangement, though he did ask for a steak dinner to celebrate. He wrote it ten years ago, he told Seymour. But there was plenty more where that one came from, he said. All you need to do is ask, he told him, shoving tenderloin into his mouth. He took a huge gulp of Chianti and wiped the corners of his mouth. Seymour couldn't tell if it was wine or blood from the rare meat that left an imprint on the white napkin when Caleb Candor so crassly set it down on the table.

"This is going to be a show to end all shows!" Seymour said, looking away from the spectacle of the writer's eating.

It would be nothing like those shows he'd sat through with his wife in the beginning of their marriage, thought Seymour. Though he enjoyed musicals, he thought those from the twenties were such fluff and frosting, without virtue. Not for him. He thought of *Show Boat,* which broke every tradition of theater. It was an epic. He remembered watching that show and feeling both euphoria at the genius he was witnessing and the utterly deflated sensation that always comes from watching the genius of someone else. For the first time there were real themes: racism, miscegenation, a sad marriage. And the success. It seemed to be making way for a different sort of theater.

"Caleb," said Seymour, "in this terribly *depressing* time, we will not drive theatergoers away, but we will embrace them with drama, music, dance. This was what the theater was meant to be: absolutely everything."

"Sounds good to me," said Caleb. "But people want to have fun. I know I do," he said, tapping his glass and gesturing for the waiter to bring more wine.

Seymour's first mistake was letting Nat Allen have a go at the libretto. Or maybe his first mistake was hiring Nat Allen, a former Ziegfeld Follies director, as his director. But Nat had come to Seymour via the Terrier, as so many things had. How could Seymour resist the opportunity for Broadway? He won a turn at the Majestic in a card game. You can have it starting in October, the Terrier winked. The place was just two blocks north of the Knickerbocker Hotel, the Terrier's "office," from where, Seymour knew, he could keep tabs on everything.

The Terrier told him, "Don't say I never did you any favors, Goy." He bit his soggy cigar.

So many favors, it was impossible to turn them all down. "Since when did I become your charity project?" Seymour asked.

"You're forgetting all my charitable contributions to Israel, aren't you?" the Terrier said. "Why does everyone forget that?" The Terrier closed his eyes and breathed, in and out.

"I haven't forgotten that," Seymour said. Not only had the Terrier sent money but he'd sent carloads of arms for the military as well. "You are a generous man."

"Well, I like a good musical too, ya know," he said. "You've made my life so glamorous. You can't blame me for feeling amorous," he'd sing, which Seymour always took to be a warning.

Nat Allen thought that his musical—he corrected himself, *Seymour's* first musical—should be about real people, the real story of Inez, Seymour's hardworking mama, and her rise to grand hostess, the toast of New York City.

"It's a hard time. People want to see something fun also," Seymour said, recalling Caleb Candor's simple advice.

"Precisely," Nat told him. "And let those *immigrants* go to the pictures for their fluff!" Promptly, he eliminated the dancing waiters and the overflowing glasses of champagne. "You think this is vaudeville, Seymour?" he chided. "Come on. You do what you do, let me do what I do."

He did have a point, Seymour thought, as he let him get rid of Inez's gorgeous dresses and her famous clientele. He let Nat Allen strip the play of his mother's fairy tale to the story of a girl from Western Europe who came to America with dreams that would go forever unfulfilled.

When it came time to cast his musical, Seymour couldn't help but remember the lovely girl who had transformed from a pinprick of light into a full-blown image on a television screen, the one he had seen months ago, beckoning him to the future. He wanted to capture this— this feeling—of the past and the future in one glance.

No stars. Only real people, Seymour decided right then. *The Joint* will mark the talent, the talent will not mark the show. The pretty, dark-haired girl should play the lead! Seymour thought. It will be brilliant.

Then Seymour made his second mistake, which would turn out to be one of the biggest mistakes of his life: he thought of his wife. Sarah should read for the role, he thought. Though this thought and the subsequent and impulsive way he followed through on it could be viewed as the lovely, selfless act of a husband trying to grant his wife her dream, there were many who came to think that even giving Sarah the opportunity was more the horrid and selfish act of a husband who was trying to dash that dream for good.

Either way, Seymour brought Sarah in the next day to audition.

Never would he forget turning to see his wife walk into the theater in that powder blue gown. She was tall and slim, built like a rectangle, and she walked down the aisle slowly and deliberately. As he watched her walk up to the stage, her head held high, Seymour realized he had enlisted his wife to play his mother.

And he realized in that single moment that there was no good alter-

native to this now inescapable situation. How could he win? His wife
got the part? It was horrible. She was to play his mother. His *mother*. She
didn't get the part? Well, they might as well both take the gas pipe then.

"Hello," Sarah said in a voice as deep as Tallulah Bankhead's. She
slithered across the stage, her chin held high, her long nose reaching
to the ceiling. She turned to look out into the empty theater.

Onstage Seymour's wife was a photograph: inaccessible and grand
and one-dimensional. He looked at Nat Allen. Which disaster would it
be? he wondered. Yes or no.

"This is a fabulous canary!" Nat said. "But can the canary sing?" he
screamed up to Sarah on the stage.

"Why yes, she can," Sarah said slowly. She walked over to the piano,
thumped the lid three times, and began to sing. "Falling in love again,
never wanted to . . ."

Had Seymour ever heard his wife sing? He looked up at Sarah,
amazed by her, and all the reasons he had chosen her to be his wife
became clear to him. She was incredible! His, and yet she was a thousand miles away.

Seymour was grateful he could give her this chance. Perhaps this
would keep her out of speakeasies and out of Celia's bloomers. He
hoped it would. He hoped Nat's answer was yes.

"What am I to do, I can't help it."

"Fabulous, little canary," Nat screamed when she was done. "Thank
you."

As if she had done this every day of her life, Sarah glided back across
the stage and, lifting the hem of her dress so as not to fall, stepped carefully down the stairs. She nodded at Nat, smiled and winked at Seymour, and then left the theater.

"She's perfect," Nat said. "The Roaring Twenties and the Depression
rolled up into one."

"Wonderful," Seymour said. But his goodwill had already begun to
fade, and something he couldn't name started to nag at him. Was that
his conscience pulling at him, the same tug he felt when he arranged
for the plates on the car to be changed, the keys left in the toilet of some
candy store on South Fifth Street in Brooklyn? It was unnameable now,
as it had been then, but Seymour knew that no matter what, as bad
news always does, somehow it would announce itself.

The Terrier named at least two of Seymour's fears when Nat called to tell him they had a lead for the production. He slammed into the theater from the Knickerbocker, red-faced and, again, with the gun.

"What is it?" Seymour had said flatly to him. "Put down the gun, Terrier," he said.

"Your wife?" the Terrier screamed. "*Yours?* Mine's the beauty queen," he said. He did not put away the gun but waved it vaguely in Seymour's direction. "Don't tell me you haven't noticed."

"She is beautiful," Seymour said carefully, remembering the first time he'd laid eyes on Pauline. For a moment, he felt that he owed everything—the mess, the fear, the violence, but also the cash, the glamour, even this here musical—to that endless pair of legs. "But she is not an actress."

"I know that, Seymour," Terrier said. "Don't you think I know an actress when I see one? But her sister sure as hell is. Frances Gold is who should play this part."

Seymour tried to negotiate what to do with his face. After all, he too had thought first of Frances. But now, it simply could not be. Now his wife would be playing his mother, and, unless he wanted to end his marriage once and for all, this was what he had to do. Besides, this was his musical. His. "This is mine, Terrier," he said.

"Pardonnez-moi?" the Terrier said, bracing.

"Look, this wasn't just my decision. You wanted Nat to direct, Nat is directing. You wanted it at the Majestic, and what do you know, here we are at the Majestic, conveniently located two blocks from your office. Anyway, Nat agrees. It was he who cast Sarah, not I." Luciano on the dock, his face shredded. Seymour remembered the craps game the night Sarah's folly with the gangster liquor had been discovered. The energy it had taken to appear calm while inside his heart was racing, that had cost him more than anything, he realized now. The acute knowledge of being one thing on the outside, a whole other entity to himself and himself alone on the inside, had never left him. He carried this duality with him now in all his dealings, both in and out of his house.

"Not I?" the Terrier quipped.

"Yes, 'Not I.'"

"*Moi?*" the Terrier asked.

"*Pas moi,*" said Seymour, smiling, his heart filled with rage.

Humming his way out of the theater, the Terrier seemed somewhat appeased. But, as Seymour knew well, one could never tell. Though he had stood up for his wife, just as he had when she'd watered down the liquor and nearly gotten them killed, Seymour couldn't be sure. Could he have thought of the means to get Sarah out of the production without destroying her completely, he would have. And were there a way to have taken back his first kind thought of pleasing his wife and making her whole again, he would have done that in a heartbeat.

"Great news!" Seymour told his wife that evening, pushing aside his growing dread to place both hands on her cold cheeks. "You got the part!" He did not mention, were she to take it, their lives could be in jeopardy.

"That's wonderful, dear," she replied, as calmly as one who had been headlining Broadway shows all her life.

That was all? That was it? He had thought he would be rewarded at least a little for what he had given her. As far as he was concerned, it beat the fur coat she had to have last winter, and she could show a little excitement, for Christ's sake. She could throw her arms around him and be happy for one goddamn minute.

He thought of Sarah holding her gloves in her right hand and leaning in to Celia, heading upstairs. For once she had seemed so easy in her skin. What did they do up there? Seymour wondered, both repulsed and aroused by the thought of Sarah unclipping Celia's stockings and reaching out to touch her.

When Seymour had broken out a bottle of the 1928 Salon champagne and was pouring Sarah her second glass, however, she began to let her happiness show.

"I'm a tiny bubble, rising to the surface of the world," she told her husband, raising her glass. "Pop!" she said ebulliently. "How I love you, Seymour," she said, leaning in and kissing him sloppily on the lips.

Well, that's a bit better, he thought, pouring himself another glass. Worth being killed over, I can't say.

How long had it been since they had made love with true abandon? Seymour could not remember. Had they ever? He couldn't recall, but tonight Sarah mounted her husband in the marble foyer.

"Broadway," she said, unbuttoning her dress.

Seymour had always had a weakness for her small, perky breasts. "You will be a star," he told her, reaching for them with both hands. In that moment he wanted nothing more than for his wife to be what she had always wanted to be. And if she were a star, and he the producer, what a fine couple they would make.

It was as if, Seymour realized, each was allowing the other's dreams to come true at the exact same time, and this rare and beautiful moment was reflected in their lovemaking. By the time they had reached the bedroom, the stairs too had been a platform for their mutual appreciation. When Seymour finally fell into bed, exhausted, he felt that he had his wife back, which was exactly what he had wanted when he'd called Sarah up two days before and told her, "Put on your dancing shoes, my dear, and come down here for the biggest audition of your life!"

If Sarah had not gotten the good news about winning—or having been won—the lead, perhaps she would not have drunk so much champagne, which always made her wild and reckless. And without the champagne, she would not have made love to her husband so many times and in so many ghastly ways. Most likely, she would not have made love to her husband at all. And if she had not had sex with him three times, once upright against the banister, wood as smooth as bone, perhaps she would have spent the next nine months looking forward to her name in lights and in all the papers.

But instead, what happened was this: two months after Seymour moved against his wife, her head pounding the spiraling stairs, he sat in the doctor's consulting room next to her and watched her gasp and cover her mouth upon hearing the news. The yet-to-be-named David Bloom, tiny as a pebble, lay in her womb, waiting for a big entrance of his own.

The doctor couldn't have been more pleased with his diagnosis—this was, after all, a time for rebuilding a population depleted by war.

He patted Sarah, who now sat up straight in her chair, on the back and
chuckled across the room at Seymour. "Congratulations!" he told
them. "Let's cross our fingers for a boy," he said before tossing her
folder into the hanging file on the back of the door and walking out of
the room.

"You'll have to postpone the show!" Sarah said as soon as the doctor left. Her nails clicked manically against the wooden arm of the
chair.

Seymour's whole body sighed. It was over. Every emotion, he had
foolishly let himself forget, has an equal and opposite emotion. "I can't
postpone it, Sarah," he said. "Do you know who got me this space? It's
not an indefinite time frame we're working within here."

Sarah clenched her fists. "I should say so," she said. "Who were those
fat men with those horrible scarred faces hanging around the lobby
anyway? Don't most people try their productions out in St. Louis or
San Diego before hitting New York City? Why don't you do that?"

Sarah was turning red. Seymour closed his eyes. His wife hadn't
minded who showed up for rehearsals before, that was for sure.

"What is wrong with you anyway, Seymour! Speed up the production then. Yes! Speed it up! Let's just do it right now!" Sarah jumped up
from the chair and went toward the door. "Right now. I'm ready!"

"Relax, Sarah." Seymour stood up slowly. He felt old. As if he had
been replaying this scene for too many years.

"You stupid salesman," she said and began to cry. "I don't even
know which is worse! Never to know because I never had the chance
or to have had the chance and have failed." Sarah's body shook with
grief. "Well, now I'll never know! Everyone always told me I had real
star quality."

Seymour moved to embrace his wife, but she would have none of
it. Her palm circled her belly lightly. "What's in there anyway?" she
asked, her hand clenching into a tight fist.

"Our baby," Seymour said. "It's a miracle." He put his large hand on
her shoulder, but she pushed it away.

Seymour shook his head. Only two months ago his wife had been
filled with regret, stuffed so full of dashed dreams and cravings for all
the things she would never have, he'd thought she would explode. He
had known this, and he had tried to alter it. And he had changed her,

changed her inside, Seymour had thought. Her very chemical makeup. He had filled her with all the lovely things that women were made of: soft, sweet-smelling stuff, good, pure things. Now what was she filled with exactly? The thought terrified him.

Sarah took her mink from the coatrack, and Seymour helped her into it. "I could hide it, you know," she said, straightening. "Look." She stood, straight as a pin, her coat flapping open as if it were her own skin and she were an animal, skinned alive. She shook her head and took her alligator purse, which had been dangling beneath her coat.

Seymour considered it for a moment. But Sarah was not a curvy woman—with Dulcy she had shown after only three months. It wouldn't be long now. And the sickness. Sarah would never be the kind of woman who got through her pregnancy unscathed. Vomiting all morning. And Sarah was so sensitive to being nauseated, she could not brush her teeth for her entire pregnancy. Just the smell of the peppermint, the way it seemed to be covering up something terrible, made her retch.

Seymour and Sarah Bloom left the doctor's office, her head hung low and, for a brief moment, against Seymour's chest, clutching the gold chain of her bag, which knocked against him. *Bump, bump,* he felt as he hailed the taxi home from St. Vincent's, a heartbeat. The Blooms sat together in silence watching the city change as the taxi headed up Seventh Avenue. As if to punish them both, the cabbie went along Forty-fourth Street, past the Majestic, where the production—Seymour's production—would open in eight months, then east, through Times Square. It was twilight, those lights just switching on, and actors milled about, smoking in alleys, readying to go onstage for the night.

"It's so terribly unfair," Sarah said quietly.

"It's simply unfair timing," Seymour said. "Only the timing is unfair. Really, Sarah, we are quite lucky."

"You know, when I was at Smith, there was this girl, Liza something or other, I can't remember. She got pregnant her freshman year and crossed over into New Hampshire to have it done with once and for all. By a country doctor."

"Sarah!" Seymour said. "Please. We wanted another child. We want someone else for Dulcy to be with. How can you even think it?"

"How far exactly *is* New Hampshire?" she asked.

"I cannot have this conversation with you," Seymour said. "There is a limit," he said.

Sarah nodded as she looked out the window. "Even for me there is a limit," she said. "Limited."

When they arrived at Seventy-second Street, Seymour paid the taxi and helped Sarah out of the cab, up the front stairs, and into their bedroom. Still in her mink coat and clinging to her purse, she collapsed on the bed. She turned on her side and curled into a ball, her long body now a question mark. What, it seemed to be asking—herself or Seymour—did you really expect?

Sarah Bloom lay that way for the rest of the night. She lay like that through the next day and the next, though Seymour was able to get her out of her coat and into her silk pajamas when he came upstairs later that evening, carrying a wobbly glass of hot milk that Mary had heated for her, but that Sarah refused. And this was how Sarah Bloom stayed, curled on the left side of her bed, until, seven months later, David Bloom broke his mother open and fought his way into the world.

Seymour never told Sarah that perhaps it was all for the best she had been forced out of the production. He didn't have the nerve to tell her that the Terrier had shown up periodically over the last two months, waving his gun and demanding his sister-in-law at least have a go at the part. "I thought I told you Frances," he'd say. "Frances! Are you fucking deaf?"

Seymour had managed the situation by remaining calm. "I hear you, Terrier," he would say gravely. Inside, he'd been filled with hysteria. What am I doing? he had wondered. How am I going to make it out of this alive? "I'm listening," he'd told the Terrier.

When it became clear that Sarah could not play the part of Inez Bloom, Seymour decided to do what his heart had told him to—and what the Terrier's gun insisted on—in the first place. He phoned Vladimir Zworykin to see if his wife would be interested in the theater.

Vladimir had to laugh. "Would my wife be interested? I imagine so. Why don't you ask her yourself?"

Vladimir had always been short with Seymour, and it still irked Seymour that he did not have the power to make the man see his control. He had grown used to a different dynamic with other men.

Seymour thanked the scientist for the home number he gave him. "And how's my television going, Vladimir?" he asked.

"Your television."

"Yes," Seymour said. "How's it going?"

"These things take time, you know," Vladimir said. "Why don't you give Frances a ring?" he asked him, and hung up the phone.

When Seymour called Frances Gold to see if she would like to come for an audition for his first production, he told her how he had seen her on television.

"You were lovely," he said. "I think you will be perfect for this part."

Frances tried to still her heart—could he hear that frantic beating over the phone? The theater! Hollywood! An endless horizon, palm trees blowing in the breeze. "You thought I was lovely?" she asked Seymour. Because seeing herself on the screen was the first time she had felt beautiful on the outside. Capturing her moving made all the difference, she thought. Unlike the still photographs, in which every pore and hair on Frances's face was evident, here, her personality could come through. Her knowing smile, her laughing eyes, her hair, which, when you looked closely enough, did have a natural sheen. She loved herself on what would become the television, and she was glad Seymour could appreciate her too.

"I did," he said. "Are you interested in the theater?"

"I am," she said. "Extremely interested. What exactly did you have in mind?"

When Frances showed up for her audition, Nat Allen was stunned. This was not the beautiful young girl the Terrier had been screaming over. This was not the lovely beam of light Seymour had promised him for his lead.

Nat grabbed Seymour by the wrist and pulled him to a dark corner of the theater. "You promised me a beauty!" he hissed.

"Well, she looks a lot like Inez," Seymour said. She did seem far less ethereal in person, it was true. But, truth be told, she looked a lot more like his mother than Sarah had.

"Look," said Nat. "The hourglass on this one is missing at least half a day. Instead of big tits, we have a big ass to contend with. And what of those delicate blond curls? She's got a veritable bird's nest up there."

As Nat berated Seymour for his choice, Frances felt disappointment of her own. When she'd pushed her way into the theater and saw the stage, empty, naked, unlighted, strewn with seltzer bottles and balled-up tissues, she had been taken aback. Frances had never seen a stage without its set, the lighting, the actors stomping back and forth, holding hands and taking their collective bow. And this director, he was a hostile one.

Nat and Seymour came back to their seats in the front row. Nat cleared his throat.

Drawing on her experience at the candy store, where she had sensed what each person needed from her and responded in kind, Frances waddled to center stage, leaned over, and shook Nat's hand aggressively. "Don't look so glum." She laughed, sensing his disappointment. "A dance comes with this walk too."

Nat relaxed and laughed. "Pleasure to meet you, Frances," he said.

Nat was furious at the time that Seymour had made him waste on this girl, but, as he would later tell the producer, she somehow got softer on the eyes. It was as if the more she talked, the more one's perception of her, the very eyes with which he watched her, drenched her in soft, flattering light. As soon as Frances read, he told Seymour, he knew she would have an ability to connect with an audience.

"Can you sing, Frances?" he screamed up to her.

"I can!" she said. She tapped her foot and looked over at the piano, as if it would just begin to play her a tune.

"I was blue, just as blue as I could be, ev'ry day was a cloudy day for me." Frances sang as if her very life depended on that song, and she smiled broadly, shaking her voluminous bottom and lightly snapping her fingers.

It is certainly hard not to be taken with her, thought Seymour. He looked over at Nat, who was inadvertently smiling back up at Frances.

"Oh, it doesn't even matter," Nat said. "It's what the Terrier wants anyway."

The next day Frances Gold was cast as Inez.

Seven months later, in the autumn of 1931, the Terrier was made head of the bootleggers in New York. It was right after Japan invaded Manchuria, and Seymour would always associate these two events, despite the massive difference in global implications. It was just that, everywhere on earth, someone small was being overtaken. As Japan planned to colonize East Asia, so began the Terrier's work in narcotics, establishing a ring that expanded his empire across the nation.

Two weeks after the Manchurian Incident, *The Joint* was set to open.

"A little early if you ask me," Seymour told Nat.

"Agreed, agreed, but we said October, and here it is, October."

"What's the hurry?" said Seymour.

"Why don't you ask the Terrier?" Nat said. "He seems to be on a tighter schedule. And we can't postpone now! Do you know how that will look to the press? We'll get reamed!"

"It's better to be prepared than to rush a show into opening," Seymour said with as much authority as he could muster.

Nat laughed. "Seymour," he said. "Sometimes you just gotta sit back and take it like a man."

On October 6, two days before *The Joint* previewed, Sarah Bloom gave birth to David Bloom. She had sobbed so hard throughout the labor that the nurses had to slap her three times to make her breathe. She was so inconsolable that David had to be taken away by the nurses, who were worried Sarah's breast milk would never come in because of her excessive grief.

She insisted on drawing the blinds and lying in the dark.

"Poor woman!" they all said to one another at the nurses' station outside her dark window. "Why is *she* complaining?" one asked.

"Dumb Doras," Sarah said to her husband. "Nitwits."

Seymour could see the sliver of light beneath the door. He could hear them chewing like cows, eating their cream cheese sandwiches and sipping coffee from the Horn & Hardart Automat.

"Sarah," he said, reaching for her hand and trying to catch a glimpse of his watch at the same time. Curtain was at eight o'clock, he reminded himself nearly each minute. "They'll hear you." As he did with most women, Seymour had a way with the nurses, who had swooned over him when he had come to meet his wife after the delivery. He had laughed and smiled at them, knowing this would guarantee they took good care of his son.

His son. Seymour thought of David Bloom's red, crooked little face. It had been a fairly easy birth, but still the newborn's head had been slightly misshapen, though the doctor had assured Seymour this was temporary.

Sarah curled into a ball and wept. All Seymour could think of was the curtain opening with a swish and those nurses feeding his newborn son with a bottle on the floor below.

Seymour arrived at the Majestic just as the houselights went down. It was probably for the best that he missed the scene outside, theatergoers, actors, producers, and lawyers milling about. He would one day be able to predict with uncanny accuracy the outcome of any show by the crowd gathered on the street on opening night, but for his first show, who knew? And who knew if one of Greenberg's yes-men, mad as hell that Seymour could just walk away from all they'd been doing in town—walk away from the money, the nightclubs, the girls, but also walk away from the hard part, the worry, the violence, and now all this business with drugs—who knew if he wouldn't come by this very night and do Seymour in? He'd heard just last week that Benny Longman, a two-bit pickpocket who had been out three months, who wanted to become an honest-to-goodness family man, was brought to a house in the country where three street punks threw acid at his face and hands. Seymour couldn't imagine the pain of one's flesh being eaten by chemicals and then, of course, the mark of that day branded on one's skin forever.

He knew the Terrier certainly wouldn't protect him. Or protect his children.

As Seymour slid into his seat between his brother and Inez, his anxiety slipped away and he was filled with nothing but pride. He was proud of his show, and he was proud to be the father of a son.

Inez Bloom slapped her son on the knee. "How's my grandson?" she asked him as the orchestra began its tuning. She squeezed both his cheeks, hard.

Pride. It was not a feeling he recognized—so much of his life had been ruled by shame. Feeling proud was a hell of a lot better, Seymour thought as the conductor tapped his stand. That delicate little stick! This sure is the life, he thought.

And then the show began: Frances entered in an enormous feather hat. She looked sideways at the audience, shook her hips, and in a thick, French-Russian accent said, "Well, I sure could use a drink."

The audience was already in stitches.

Seymour swiveled in his seat. Laughter? He hadn't anticipated this. This was supposed to be drama.

"What is this?" Inez hissed to her son.

"I'm not sure," he said. His pride was beginning to fade.

"That," said Inez, "is not me."

Frances began belting out a cheerful tune about loving America.

"Everyone's a star at the Joint's glorious bar," she sang, her cheeks puffed as if with chocolates. She greeted all the clientele and posed with them for the camera. There were flashbulbs popping, gossip columnists typing, and affairs and intrigues among the tables. Frances negotiated them all, as the story wove back and forth from the present of the Joint to the past of her childhood. Flashbacks to Paris were at stage right, where a young Inez pranced around the Eiffel Tower, a satchel of books dangling from her arm. Romping through the Champ-de-Mars, she sang a charm song about what it would be like to go to America and walk on the shining streets.

But things changed in the second act. Here Frances made her entrance alone again, her housedress torn and her fading expression forlorn.

"Woe is me, it's already nine," she sang. "I confess, I confess, the Joint is not mine!" she sang.

Frances, who had taken a few lessons from her hero, Fanny Brice, looked overly despondent. She turned to the audience, her mouth practically hitting the floor, her large eyes drooping.

At stage right, the young Inez made crepes, handing them to a queue of men waiting outside the Moulin Rouge. They watched her as she poured the batter, laughing because she was not one of the spectacular girls inside.

The audience laughed again.

Everyone was laughing at his mother, and Seymour's heart, soaring when he had walked into the theater, now banged hard and heavy in his chest.

Then Frances, as Inez, begged Madame Lutille for a job as a sous-chef. Frances played up the despair, begging and then placing the back of her hand to her forehead and throwing her head back in mock misery.

Again, laughter. The audience was whooping.

"I bring you to this country and you make me a stock of laughing?" Inez clutched Seymour's arm.

Seymour shook his head. "No, Mama," he said. He felt her nails, filed to points, digging into his skin. For a brief moment, he wondered what his mother had been like then, dusting the crepes with sugar and seeing the men disappear into the Moulin Rouge to watch beautiful women dance.

Seymour was brought back to the here and now quickly and surely. He watched in horror as his mother, overcome with the rage and humiliation of this moment and, Seymour could tell, the humiliation of her life, stood up. She wagged her finger toward the stage. "Horse-feathers!" she screamed—to Frances—in flawless English.

The actors stopped their singing and held their hands to their foreheads like sailors on the bows of boats squinting into the light. Frances peered out into the audience, hands on her hips. She pointed at Inez, who was stomping out of the theater. The actress shrugged her shoulders and, as the spotlight trailed Inez's departure from the Majestic, the audience was again in hysterics.

It was a shame that wasn't the opening night and the performance the press would see. But the audience loved it—they cheered as Inez left the building. And when the curtain closed and then opened again, the crowd stood and called out Frances's name, whistling as she folded herself in half for her bow. Looking out into the audience, she caught herself searching for her sister. Perhaps, Frances thought, Pauline would come to see her here. Perhaps she would realize that, though Frances was not the pretty one, she too was tapped for greatness. Why, Frances thought, at the greatest moments of my life, do I always think of Pauline?

෭

Knowing it did not go as he'd always imagined it would, the way it did in all of his dreams, Seymour declined all postshow invitations, even to the cast party. He did not want to stand around eating canapés with Frances Gold, and he did not want to see Caleb Candor. He did not want to rub elbows with the Terrier's minions, who were sure to be milling around, casing the place. Besides, Seymour had to go to the house to get ready for his first night with his son, who was expected home from the hospital the next day. On his way backstage to congratulate the cast—he had resolved to not so much as shake Frances's hand—he ran into Vladimir, also on the way to his wife.

Seymour wagged his finger. "Your wife!" he said.

Vladimir shook his head, and, for a fleeting moment, Seymour sensed in him the same fear he'd felt when Seymour had met him at the New Amsterdam Theater. "I know," Vladimir said. "She played it all for laughs. I had thought she would be a little more . . . Tolstoy."

Seymour couldn't wrap his head around it. The rehearsals had been different. Had it been the audience that changed the performance? Had Frances tricked him?

"But she has a gift. Did you see the audience? Everyone responded to her. My wife," Vladimir said, shaking his head. "She will be terrific for the shortwave," he said. "Just you wait, Seymour!"

"I'm waiting," Seymour said. "And waiting."

"Perhaps you're right," Seymour said when Vladimir did not respond.

"A great show, my friend." Vladimir put his heavy hand on Seymour's broad shoulder. "Congratulations to you."

Seymour continued on to the cast, where he wished everyone well, slapped Nat on the back, nodded in Frances's direction.

When she came over to speak with him, Seymour, nearly three heads taller, looked down at her and scolded his leading lady.

"Like *Show Boat*," he told her over and over. "*Show Boat*. That is the tone of it, and if you don't like it, well, go get a part in someone else's show."

Frances's mouth quivered, her eyes filling with tears, and Seymour willed any of the consequences of speaking so harshly to the lead of the show away. So, the Terrier came for him. Better to be dead than to have his musical become a comedy that humiliated his mother. Better to be shot in the eye than to go home to the despair of his wife.

He headed out into the evening. Taking a long, deep breath, Seymour looked up at the black sky and began to walk uptown. Perhaps he had been wrong about musicals, he thought, passing the theaters just letting out, people in their hats and furs milling on the sidewalks. Theater was just like the movies after all. This is America, the theater and the cinema told America. Buster Keaton; Clark Gable? Here is the Wild West. Here is the Dust Bowl. Here is the beautiful girl. But it wasn't real. It troubled him now, the way the audience had laughed and laughed at his mother's accent. Was Frances Gold playing it for laughs, or was the laughter something sinister, something he would once have been able to fix with a simple phone call to the right man?

He would no longer be able to call in the right man. A shame, thought Seymour, remembering what it had been like to wield power in the world. This, he thought, would remain broken.

No one can say if *The Joint* could have been a hit had Seymour not gone and scolded poor Frances, ensuring that, the next night and the few that followed, she played the part for what it was: a dramatic musical. Whatever might have been, *The Joint,* and Frances, never recovered from the way Seymour had forced them both to be something they were not. The press panned the show as "false," the characters as "one-dimensional," the story as "banal." Frances Gold, the stage name she would always use, was called "laughable in a dramatic role." *The Joint* closed after only eight shows, and Seymour, who had put up all the capital, promptly lost it all. Inez could not sense the separation between herself and her character, and, until the day she died, she was furious about the injustice done to her in *that horrible play.* The only reason Inez forgave her elder son was that he was the connection to her new, first grandson. For her grandson, for David, she would rise above it.

But after the first preview, Seymour did not yet know what the critics would say. He did not know that no one would buy tickets once the critics said it or that the production hinged on people buying tickets based on what those critics would say. It had not gone the way he'd dreamed, but there still was the potential for greatness. Seymour was heading home, and tomorrow his new son would be there with him. Turning south for just a moment, he could see the Empire State glowing. See how high? Twelve hundred forty-five feet, he'd read in the papers, and open to the public. He shook his head—it was really unbelievable. He would take his new son there and tell him: You can do anything. See, see what they've done? See what they've built? Together they would look past the new George Washington Bridge. How wide. This city, Seymour thought. How could he ever live elsewhere? His mother had brought him here on a boat to Ellis Island, and he had shamed her. He had been a bad son. Did this make him a bad man?

The lighted buildings surrounded him, their visceral brilliance quickly a memory as Seymour continued uptown. Life and theater? he thought. The same thing. Only the theater was supposed to be much more fun.

CHAPTER 12

Fleeing: 1934

FRANCES DID NOT RECOVER quickly from her not-so-stellar reviews. Devastated that her first show had closed after less than two weeks, she went back to Brooklyn to help her mother with her washing. She scrubbed Rose's undergarments and linens and hung them on the line. As her mother's bloomers billowed in the wind on those few cool spring days, Frances took stock of her old neighborhood, how much the young people had changed in the short two years since she had been gone. The younger brothers of the boys who had once taunted Frances thought the Terrier was a hero. Like Solomon when he was a kid, standing on the corner by Mr. Berkowitz's store waiting for an opportunity, these boys, Frances reasoned, were all looking for anything to take them away from the hunched, weeping Jews. That sadness had stayed the same on South Fifth Street. Gangsters countered that sadness and fear: being taken, Cossacks chopping off their heads, the haunting feeling in their mothers' stomachs of the danger of a world of hate moving closer and closer still. How those young boys hated weakness! Frances could see it in their greased-up hair and their scowling, freckled faces. They hated their fathers' lectures, their mothers' bending toward candles, toward sorrow, toward a memory their sons did not want to touch. It was always mourning. Those boys started smoking and making catcalls on the corners. They looked different, it was true, like little wiseguys, Frances thought as she passed by carrying smoked fish wrapped in butcher paper under her arm. Those boys, she determined, had begun to have hope.

And then, two years after *The Joint* opened and closed, two years after David Bloom and Miriam Brodsky were born, Tom Dewey, assistant district attorney of New York City, who had been secretly tracing everything the Terrier did out of the Knickerbocker Hotel on Forty-second Street, took Terry the Terrier to court.

But Tom Dewey was not the only one who wanted the Terrier to fall.

In the end it was Brooklyn who betrayed Solomon Brodsky, just as he had turned his back on Brooklyn. Plenty of the gangsters starting up, the ones who were not cowed by the cross looks from old ladies or from the young mothers who shifted their babies to the opposite hip when they saw those heavies turning down their streets, the ones who weren't so desperate for love, went back to the old neighborhood and walked around. They jiggled their pocket change and showed off their watches and gold rings, they bent down to smile and cluck at the babies. They talked to those angry, freckled boys and became their role models.

But the Terrier got big enough never to have to go back to a place where he was no longer wanted. Why suffer? he would say to Frances when she berated him for staying away. They hate me? Well then, I hate them. I have enough hate without going to greet it on that horrible street.

On December 5, 1933, the Twenty-first Amendment pulled back the Eighteenth, legalizing liquor and rendering the Terrier instantly obsolete. Who needed him or his booze now? And when his power was gone, a couple of Brooklyn small-timers to whom the Terrier had denied access to Rothstein sent Tom Dewey some papers that showed he hadn't paid his taxes in full since 1926. By August, Tom Dewey had more than he needed to go up to Egypt and bring the Terrier downtown in handcuffs. Solomon Brodsky—a.k.a. the Terrier—was the very first Jewish mobster to go down.

Frances decided not only would she go to the trial but she would bring Joseph Brodsky with her.

"This is not a question," Frances said the second time she called Joseph long distance in five years. "This is a demand."

Joseph was silent upon hearing the news. See? he thought. God sees everything. The world is coming undone, and my brother is the criminal here. Was Solomon aware of what was going on back in Europe? There a man was consolidating his power so as to take over the world. This man was setting up camps for killing. He was setting fire to the place of government. And Solomon was torturing some poor man to death beneath the brothels and candy stores of this city that had taken them in and saved them.

Joseph thought of his father turning in his newly dug grave, turning because of his son, and over what was to come. This was the golden promise? Never here, Herbert would have told him. Nothing will happen in America, this is the golden country. Joseph had gone back to say Kaddish for his father, but he realized then, The man is already dead. Can he see me here crying over his grave? Can he see me here with this fistful of dirt? It had taken him weeks to get the sound of the dirt and stones hitting wood out of his head.

"You're crazy," he said to Frances. "I'm not goink. To a trial? It's beyond crazy." For the first time Joseph was happy his father was not alive to bear witness to this; he simply felt sad for his mother, enduring more humiliation alone.

"It's only for taxes," Frances said. "They'll only be talking about the money."

Joseph laughed. "That's vhat you think. They're gonna bring up everything, believe me," he said. "I don't even vant to know it." Joseph was thankful that his brother had remained so much of a mystery to him. He read the papers, yes, but he did not know what going to narcotics or expanding the operation out west had really entailed.

"You know this may be the last time you see your brother," Frances said.

Joseph meant to laugh—ha! ha!—but instead he snorted. "The last time I saw my brother, Frances, was vhen he left my father's house to go be a criminal. I believe he had a gun in his belt vhen I watched him through the door. Zhis man? He is not my brother."

"Then you should come and watch him be punished. It doesn't matter. You should be there. For your father's sake."

Joseph was silent. "You brink up my father? He would not have gone near zhis trial. Belief me."

"You only have one chance, Joseph Brodsky. He is your only brother."

"It is true. My only brother. I zhink I will sit zhis one out too," Joseph said. "But, Frances, it's always nice to hear your voice."

Frances sat up front on October 20, the day Solomon Brodsky's trial began. As she climbed the steps of the courthouse, she remembered walking up these same steps holding Vladimir's hand and a fistful of daisies. Today was a gorgeous autumn day, the brown, red, and yellow leaves swirling around her feet as she made her way into the massive building.

Frances sat in the aisle seat of the third row and watched Pauline enter the room. She wore a hat the size of a small planet. For a moment Frances imagined she was watching her sister being married, and here she was, slowly walking down the aisle. Had Pauline been the bride, Frances would have gasped at her sister's beauty. But they had not attended each other's weddings, small and unceremonious as they were, and Pauline walked not like a bride but like the shamed wife of a criminal. She looked as if she was terribly ill or prematurely aged, and Frances refused to catch her eye. Instead she turned to see who else had come to watch the Terrier fall.

Frances recognized so many people from the neighborhood, including the many men who had sat discussing business and politics, drinking Turkish coffee with her father in the kitchen until dawn broke over the city. She and Rose used to clear the cups and saucers, sneaking peeks at each man's fortune in the settled coffee grounds. Were these men here to gloat over the Terrier's demise, to prove to themselves that selling brassieres and fixing the soles of shoes, unrolling reams of cloth, cutting swatches of taffeta and raw silk, was the purer work, the moral work? So what it doesn't give you a glitzy life, at least you are working for your children so that their lives might be better, at least, at the very least, you are on the right side of God. Or were they there to pay their respects to Herbert Brodsky's son, who came over from Russia and got lost, as lost as they feared their own children would be, as lost as they were when they looked in the mirror and wondered who they had become.

The mobsters, Frances had read in the papers, had been warned off coming. Rumor had it Greenberg forbade it, and there was a car outside making sure no one from inside entered the courthouse. There was no Greenberg, no Rothstein, no Kid Kugel. Somehow Frances had expected those worn, cruel faces to be there, and she wasn't sure if they were protecting Solomon from their association with him or protecting themselves from an association with him.

As she watched the neighborhood file in, Frances saw Joseph slip into the courtroom. She had not seen him since before she'd married Vladimir, and his face revealed each minute of every day of those years. Joseph had gone from a boy to a man, and his features were already sinking. Frances had a strange urge to touch his face, to somehow fill his collapsing features with air.

She could see Joseph in the middle of the back row, still standing, his hat clasped in his lap, his head bent forward, as if he were at shul. His lips moved, but she wasn't sure if he was making a sound.

Yeetgadal v' yeetkadash sh'mey rabbah, Joseph said. *B'almah dee v'rah kheer'utey* . . .

The Terrier was brought out in cuffs, and he sat next to his attorney, Ed Wolfsheim, stripped of all his dazzling accoutrements, looking straight ahead at the judge.

v' yamleekh malkhutei,b'chahyeykhohn, uv' yohmeykhohn, Joseph continued his Kaddish. As if the Terrier had heard, which he could not possibly have, so softly was Joseph speaking, he turned around in his seat, searching for a sound or a smell he seemed to recognize. But he couldn't have seen Joseph, so far back was he, hidden in the crowded courtroom.

Frances had said it would be only the money, but Tom Dewey had done his homework. He had interviewed over a thousand witnesses, reviewed two hundred bank accounts, traced the toll slips of more than one hundred thousand phone calls. He presented information on the washhouses for liquor barrels, drops for the delivery and concealment of liquor, a vehicle repair garage, an Egyptian lair in Rye, several hotel suites, and sixty Mack trucks. Dewey asserted that the Terrier, who had claimed a net income of $8,100 in 1930, had an unreported net income of $1,026,000 for that year. Where, the assistant DA asked, his mustache twitching, did the extra million and eighteen go?

After five days, 131 witnesses, and over nine hundred exhibits, Dewey rested his case. It was now up to the Terrier to prove how, with such a meager income, he had acquired so many assets.

Under the advice of his counsel, the only thing Solomon told the jury was, I plead the Fifth.

He's saying nothing? thought Frances. She had never heard of such a thing.

His brother was defying everything they'd been taught yet again, thought Joseph. Here is a man—a Jew!—and he doesn't talk? Only fights with his hands. Joseph said Kaddish for his brother each day of the five-day trial. Five days of not selling, someone else traveling the roads he traveled, someone else begging on the streets on which he begged.

It was the verdict that stopped Joseph's obsessive prayer, his praying for the dead, as if this final judgment was what finally brought Solomon Brodsky back to life.

Nineteen years, the judge said, pounding that mean gavel, and Joseph sat back, his elbows on his knees.

What he remembered was before any of this: playing stickball in the street with his big brother, the sun going down somewhere far away, the eely twilight creeping across the neighborhood, a signal for them to head back home. Joseph though of Saturdays, how they had held hands walking together to shul, their parents close behind them. Joseph had not enjoyed synagogue, though. He was embarrassed to say so, but he hated to be separated from his mother. As she walked away to pray in the upper section, Joseph would be left with his father and brother. We are men, Joseph thought. Men are different, they see the world differently. He had looked to his brother to show him what this meant. Solomon stood when he should stand, but he wore his yarmulke down over his right eye, so that he looked like a pirate. He pretended to read the prayer book, not right to left but upside down. Their father tried to still Solomon, but he couldn't. And Solomon would always set out to prove that their father was a powerless man. Even as a boy, Joseph felt shul was a place to be serious, and when Solomon would not listen to their father, it hurt Joseph, as he imagined it hurt God. It was as if Solomon was born without respect.

And look at what all of Solomon's power had done. Joseph sneaked a glance at his brother, a short, stout man in a blue suit, seated next to his lawyer, whose only defense for his client was not to utter a word.

Didn't say a *word*. How could that ever help you unless every word you had to say, anything you uttered, would prove you guilty?

Nineteen years.

Frances watched the Terrier, who was suddenly transformed back into the man his parents had intended him to be: Solomon Brodsky. Solomon, a man like anyone else—not old, not young, not slim, not pretty, not tall—looked at the floor. Pauline sat straight as a coffin, avoiding her husband's eyes.

How could her sister have been so stupid? thought Frances. Gave everything up for what? A couple of mink coats, a seven-carat ring, and a mansion so far away from home. Her family's good name. Pauline did not look up once, not even to watch her husband be taken away in handcuffs. Now what would become of her? Frances had heard stories. When a Mob husband was killed, the killers often looked after the widows, made sure they had the money they needed, made sure their kids were safe. But what would happen now that the Terrier had simply been put in prison? None of his gang had been sent to jail before, and Frances wondered if her sister would be killed because of it. Somehow she expected one day soon to get news of her in the East River, a photo in the *Daily News* of a fashionable woman washed up somewhere in Astoria, still wearing her big hat.

Frances tried to smile at Solomon as he walked by, but if he saw, he made no sign of it.

When the verdict reached Brooklyn, those cruel young boys destined to find their own way in the Mob world, who couldn't wait to watch the Terrier go down, were heartbroken. They had always thought that the gangsters would fight back and that, finally, finally the Jews would win.

Joseph refused to pay his respects with Pauline, who sat shiva up in Westchester.

"Shiva." Joseph shook his head when Frances told him where she was going. "That is disgusting. The man's not dead, after all."

"Didn't I see you there saying Kaddish, Joe?" Frances asked him.

"I was saying the mourner's prayer," he said. "I was mourning."

"That's what one does at the shiva," Frances said, though she did see his point. Even so, she decided that out of respect for Solomon, who had actually been her friend, and who was dead to the world now, she would carry a kugel upstate.

Frances made her way up to Egypt alone, without Joseph or her husband, who had refused to be a part of any of it. She watched her sister, who had not so much as lifted a finger to help when their father passed, prepare the house for the shiva. Pauline covered the mirrors and lit the candles. She put out the herring salad, the smoked salmon and bialys, the silver coffee and creamer.

"Should we call a rabbi?" Frances asked.

"A rabbi? Why would he come? Do you know who my husband was?"

"The rabbis had a certain use for your husband and his friends when they needed them," Frances said. "Anyway, he's still alive, you know."

"Not to me he's not." Pauline set out a bowl of nuts.

"Why? Because he can't buy you another fur coat?" Frances asked.

"Whatever you say, that man is dead to me."

"How can you say that? You think anyone believes you didn't know what he was doing all day?"

"Think what you want," Pauline said.

"I already do," said Frances.

Frances remembered mourning for her father. How could Pauline not have sat with them?

"Just who do you think will be coming to this anyway?" Frances asked her sister.

"I don't care," Pauline said. "Anyone who wants to know how I feel about it. Anyone who might want me dead and might think I'm still connected to him. So if you don't like it, you can go ahead and leave."

Frances nodded. Her sister believed she was going to be killed. Was this a shiva for herself? "I think I will," Frances said, appalled at just about everything her sister had said and done for the past eight years. "Good-bye then."

Pauline looked over at Frances and stood still for a moment.

Even with the makeup, all the jewels, her bobbed hair, Frances could see her sister for the first time since she'd left South Fifth Street. She is a scared little girl in a costume, thought Frances. And, in turn, Pauline seemed to be seeing Frances for the first time since she'd gone, looking at her with the fierce and tender love of an older sister. "Bye, Frances," she said.

As quickly as it had come, her look passed, and Pauline returned to bringing out the silver to place in the empty parlor, which was still decorated like an Egyptian tomb.

Frances walked past Pauline and onto the pebbled walkway, past the palm trees and the sphinxes; she pushed open the golden gate with the flat of her hand, thinking of the bars that Solomon would be behind that evening. Though she couldn't be sure of it, Frances thought she might not ever see Pauline again. She could never have imagined it, all those nights Pauline had folded back the bedcovers and told her, Come here, don't be afraid. Cold January nights, the coal always running out, the two of them, pressed against each other for warmth. Had anyone told Frances that she would one day walk away from her sister forever without looking once behind her, she would have thought they were out of their minds.

Seven days after the Terrier's trial, Pauline Brodsky and her son vanished. Into thin air, the *Post* reported. Many women left New York and changed their names to avoid gangster ties, the *Post* said. They became Donovan or Dickens and disappeared into the straight world. Perhaps this was what Mrs. Terrier had done. *"Has the Terrier's Bitch Fled the Kennel?"* the headline read.

For days the papers reported how repossession men were stripping the house of everything: the furniture, the fine china, the cars and tennis rackets. The papers ran photos of many of these items—fine Chinese vases, silver tea services, solid gold statuettes.

"Would you look at this?" Frances said over breakfast one morning with her husband. She stood up from her chair and went to Vladimir, seated across from her. She punched the paper open for him. "Just look!"

"I see it, Frances," he said, delicately tapping his spoon at his soft-boiled egg.

She had to laugh at the idea, more her fantasy, of all of Solomon's possessions—a pharaoh's riches—being taken away to be buried with him. "I really should go up there."

Vladimir lopped off the tip of his egg, and Frances gasped. It was as if he had chopped off the top of her thumb. Bits of yolk dribbled down the shell and the silver egg holder, then slowly began to pool in the little saucer she had brought him moments before with such care.

"Absolutely not," he said. "It's a crime scene. Do you realize this? It's the scene of a crime."

Frances looked over at her husband. He had a permanent red welt on his nose from working so late in his spectacles, and she looked at it now as he put down his spoon and rubbed his eyes. "Come on. It's not really a crime scene. I just want to know what's happened to everything. There might be some of my mother's stuff, you know."

And just what were they doing with all those books? Frances wondered. She remembered Solomon's pride in his library. Yes, he loved all his possessions, but he had been particularly proud of having so many books.

"No, I won't allow it, I'm sorry," Vladimir said wearily. "Enough is enough, Frances."

Frances felt like she would cry. "But I must go up there!" she shrieked.

The more hysterical she became, the calmer her husband got. "Nope," he said.

Frances stormed out of the kitchen and into the bedroom, where she threw herself on the bed. She considered defying Vladimir as she had her parents when Pauline had gotten married.

Frances could hear the tinkling of Vladimir's spoon as he resumed eating as serenely as he'd been before she'd stomped out of the kitchen. She could hear him turning the pages of the paper in a slow and measured fashion, and this infuriated her.

She wished she was back at her parents' flat on South Fifth, listening to her mother's cleaning, her father's ceaseless talking, as she waited for Pauline to crawl into bed with her. Where had her sister gone?

For one moment Frances thought not of what Pauline had stolen from her but of the small moments of kindness that had passed between them when they were girls. Her earliest memory was one of the first times they'd slept in this country and how, when her excitement had turned to a heightened anxiety, she had crawled into bed with Pauline, slipped beneath the covers, and curled up next to her. Pauline had lifted her arm and let Frances place her head on her chest. Frances remembered crying and crying that night, for no reason she could name even now, but for a general sadness for a lost past, an anticipation of a difficult future, inexorable change, and Pauline had pulled her close and let her sister drench her nightshirt with tears. That night Pauline had been her hero.

Frances got up. She went to her vanity and sat down, looked herself in the eyes. She raised her chin and cast her eyes downward just a bit, her head tilted to the side. Her father appeared in her eyes. Frances could see Abraham, trying to get out of bed, and at the same time she *was* him, her look now identical to his, the eyes attempting to be strong but instead only pleading. In her mouth, which tugged downward at the sides, Frances saw her mother's loneliness. She pulled her wild hair back from her face. Everywhere she turned, she still saw her sister.

Frances thought now of the first night of *The Joint,* before the critics came, the night the costume girl had pinned back that beautiful, fading dress. Frances had twirled before her, and the girl, pins in her mouth, had been hidden beneath her skirts. The night Frances had closed her eyes and lifted her face to the makeup girl, who brushed powder gently over her cheeks and drew a mole above her lip. Frances had wished her sister could have seen her at that very moment, when people bustled around her, preparing her for stardom. Once it had been Frances who had bent over her sister, filling her lips in with colored stain, and that night it was she whom someone dressed and colored, she who was about to take center stage. What now? she thought.

Frances imagined her sister walking through the door, right now. Here I am, she would tell Frances. I've been gone, but now I'm back. It's the two of us again, as it used to be. Perhaps she would be gliding toward her in her stocking feet, a stack of books on her head. Remember Miss America? Pauline would say. Remember Mommy's roast chicken?

Frances turned away from the mirror and toward the doorway.

"Pauline," she said. Frances shook her hair free and placed her hands on her wide hips. "Pauline," she said, "do you recognize me?"

CHAPTER 13

Iconography of Hope:
Joseph and Seymour, 1939

THE DAY JOSEPH DISCOVERED Essoil, he had no idea how huge, and how necessary, his two-in-one cleaning product would become. To start with, Essoil the all-purpose cleaner was used in many different industries. The dry-cleaning industry, which, despite Stoddard's pure and odorless solvent, still required two steps to clean garments fully—they were cleaned once in the solvent, then rewashed to remove all insoluble oil, such as perspiration—was the first to jump onboard. This new one-step process cut work time in half, which also cut the cost in half. Essoil was soon snapped up by commercial laundries, hospitals, schools, and prisons. The very institutions that had once turned Joseph away while he was on the road were now begging him for his product. The Depression only fueled the need for Essoil, as it saved so much money and time. After Rikers put in an enormous bulk order, not a day went by that Joseph didn't think how he was cleaning his brother from a distance and that perhaps from this distance he could purify him.

The way it seemed to go with Joseph Brodsky, however, was never the way it went with the rest of the world. In the twenties, while everyone was having the time of their lives, Joseph was working his pants off to no end. Closing out the thirties? It had never been such a wonderful time for Joseph and Esther. Only two months ago they had bought a house in Brookline on Pleasant Street. Esther wanted a plush, cream-colored carpet, and a living room with an Art Deco, Oriental touch.

She paged through countless shelter magazines and pointed out her favorite designed rooms to Joseph. Gorgeous! he'd say, always deferential to his wife's fine, modern taste. Vhatever you like, Esther, he'd say. Joseph admired his wife for having married him when he was only a salesman, a Jew from Russia by way of Brooklyn, when her father had been a well-respected lawyer in Portland. He admired her for her belief in him, and, now that he could do so, he would give her anything she liked.

The rest of the world, Joseph knew, was not so fortunate. People who had once eaten in high style were stealing mustard and sugar for dinner from the Automats. But worse, if you asked Joseph, was what was happening in Germany. Esther could not deny it anymore; the Night of Broken Glass was a concrete event. It had been in the papers. There was no escaping the looting, the broken shop windows, the shattered synagogues and defamed Jewish cemeteries.

And what of all the German Jews who disappeared the next day? "Where did they go?" Joseph asked.

"On vacation," Esther said over the family dinner. "To the moon. What do I know where they went?"

"The moon?" Miriam said. "You can't go to the moon."

"You're right, sweetie." Esther cut meat into small pieces for Gloria. "I was only joking."

"I know it is impossible to comprehend. But how can you think zhis is funny?" Joseph asked.

"I certainly don't think it's funny," Esther said. "Not one bit. But I have to believe it was only one event." She served Joseph a hefty piece of brisket. "How could this all be true? I have to believe it was a single night and that the mentality of the crowd took over. Otherwise, how am I to just go on?"

"You are an idiot if you zhink zhis," Joseph said.

Esther looked up from ladling carrots. Miriam and Gloria giggled, covering their mouths with their hands.

"Zhink zhis!" Miriam said.

"Stop that," Esther told her daughter. "Right now."

"I'm sorry, Esther, but don't be a fool. And let me tell you. Our children vill be next." Joseph looked sternly over at the two girls, who quickly stopped laughing.

"That's enough, Joe," Esther said, her eyes filling with tears. "Daddy is just tired," she told her daughters, gravy spilling onto the plastic tablecloth as she tried to spoon some over Miriam's beef with a trembling hand.

Next thing Joseph knew, the Bunds were rallying in Madison Square Garden. And, for the first time since Solomon went to prison, Joseph wished his brother was back on the streets. When news of the broken bones and skulls of all those wretched Nazi sympathizers hit the papers, Joseph knew it hadn't been the work of rabbis. It was the only time Joseph Brodsky cheered for the gangsters, grateful that the Jews had for once stood up for themselves.

Esther had sworn off the news altogether. All she read in the papers was "Dear Maggie," the new syndicated advice column. But she had to pass the op-ed pages to get to it, and not a week after the Night of Broken Glass she came across a reprinted *Times* editorial opposing the partition of Palestine and suggesting instead that the Jews should resettle in Africa.

"Africa?" she said, after reading the piece aloud to Joseph. She unpinned her hair and shook it free. "What on earth is that supposed to mean?"

"I don't believe it," Joseph said, tearing the paper from his wife's hands.

Esther placed her hair behind her ears, waiting for her husband to tell her she had misread.

"See?" he said, punching at the page. "See?"

And yet Joseph was prospering. It was all he could do to scramble a company together and start pumping out enough Essoil to fill the enormous demand. Essoil had become such a phenomenon in one short year that Joseph was invited to bring his invention to the World's Fair. He received a letter hand-signed by Grover Whalen himself: *In our effort to promote clean lines and pure forms,* Mr. Whalen, president of the Fair Corporation, wrote, *we would like commercial products such as yours to be demonstrated at the Fair. In the hopes that this new mechanized world we inhabit will be a fit and clean place to live in, we think that the designing of a social structure should merge with the design of daily use.*

That the World's Fair was going to be huge was not up for debate. It was going to change each and every visitor's life forever. Joseph prepared his booth and began to hire employees who would be able to be there over the next few months, not hard given the staggering unemployment. People were willing to work for ketchup sandwiches. And Joseph was finally making enough money to do whatever he pleased.

It was a vision of the future—our future, Joseph thought as he began to prepare for the fair. It had been six years since he had said Kaddish for his father. Each night he had come home early from a day on the road for minyan, a yahrtzeit burning for Herbert Brodsky, that suffering man who had watched his elder son turn bad and then go to prison for something far less terrible than the crimes he'd committed. What kind of a lesson was that? America was the promise. *Goldene medina*, his father would say. America was going to offer his sons their young boy dreams, but he could not recognize that America does not give anything. What it offered for these Brooklyn boys was only what they wrested away from it. And then Joseph said Kaddish for his brother, who as far as he knew was rotting away in prison, with fourteen more years left of his sentence.

The fairgrounds were empty but for the other exhibitors, the construction workers with nails in their teeth tending to last-minute fixups, electricians tapping microphones, the actors rehearsing their lines. The actress who was to be a housewife against the dishwasher—clean as many dishes as she could during one dishwasher cycle—came by the Essoil booth to see if Joseph needed any extra hands while she wasn't doing a show. And the man set to do his show with Westinghouse's Moto-Man, the first robot, stopped in to see if he could have some Essoil to polish him before his exhibition. We've been cleaning him with Essoil and he loves it! the man said. Joseph laughed and gave him a free bottle.

It was incredible to Joseph, this veritable city that had risen from the ash of Flushing Meadows and had turned into the ease, speed, and purity of the future. Here he stood at the stark white Trylon, so incredibly tall, over seven hundred feet, he'd read. Taller than the Washington Monument, and inside was the longest elevator in the world, he'd heard. The future, Joseph thought, is limitless. This fair was the future, a true symbol to the world. And it was a symbol for him as well, the way the world had opened up for him, changed toward him. Now people called him sir. They took his calls immediately. Once again, Joseph realized what Solomon had wanted.

Gimme the herring, gimme the money, the sturgeon, a little schmear here, no please, never thank you. His brother had wanted power and money (and deli), yes, but he'd also wanted to feel like he was part of this country, feel that he was not like their father had been, crossing the Williamsburg Bridge each day for work, a mile and a half to come home to an American shtetl, a little village that screamed and wept, Etta Valensky smirking in that dirty candy store, bringing the community horrible news from the old country. Solomon had had dreams. How had Joseph had none? He wondered this now, passing the Perisphere, a massive, blindingly white sphere connected to the Trylon by a giant ramp.

Everything is for the future, thought Joseph as he made his way on the pastel pink road across the grounds, past the Transportation Zone, where he'd heard the Futurama, an enormous model of American cities to come, could be viewed from moving chairs with individual loudspeakers. He'd read about the highways planned, where drivers could turn on and off roads at a speed of up to fifty miles an hour. Joseph couldn't believe it possible—had he still been a salesman on the road, certainly his commissions would have improved.

Now men were securing the switchback lines for the tremendous crowds expected. Heading toward the Food Zone, Joseph passed Continental Baking Company, a building dotted with colored spots, like the packaging on a loaf of Wonder, this new aerated bread that stayed fresh for days, weeks even. And the Borden Company, the Dairy World of Tomorrow, where inside 150 cows were now being washed and readied for their mechanical milkings. How his mother would hate that. Joseph laughed. Making robots of our food. What goes into your stomachs, she'd say, appalled. And yet, this was science, thought Joseph. Here it was, clean and shiny, gleaming.

My children will inherit this. He could see the Glass Center, a building made of windows and glass bricks, built, he knew, by the same architects who built the Empire State Building, where he'd heard the governor and his board members conceived and planned the entire fair. He never got over the Empire State. How had they done it? Never in his wildest dreams could he have imagined it. What would Bernie-who-sold-light think now? Perhaps it was a golden world after all.

Solomon had ruined everything, Joseph thought, just as he turned to see the public health building, with its statues of the American icons Paul Bunyan, Johnny Appleseed, Efficiency and Benevolence incarnate. Bowing his head in acknowledgment of these American virtues, Joseph thought of the tarnish Solomon had left in his wake. How could his brother have forsaken these qualities? Joseph kept walking, the whole fair before him, inviting him to partake. It was the first time he had felt part of something. He passed board games, card games, a device that measured the thickness of hair, passed a gas mask.

The gas mask? It chilled Joseph through and through. His mother, were she to come to the fair, a thought she never even entertained, would have zeroed in on that one. How wrong his mother was not to have come. All our parents were wrong, thought Joseph; they never left their little street. They had no vision of the future. Everyone had been so scared. He too had been scared, growing up scrawny and taught to fight not with his fists but with words, words in a neighborhood where language meant nothing. Joseph was grateful he had gone north and found Esther waiting outside that building in Cambridge, her red silk scarf tied beneath her chin.

His mother, Selma, the inveterate pessimist, uptown on Riverside Drive. Are you happy, Ma? Joseph had asked her as he settled her in just a few months ago. He had bought her a place before he bought one for his own family. Joseph had been so proud to get her out of Brooklyn and to bring her up to that five-room apartment on the top floor, a place filled with light and high ceilings, views of the cliffs of New Jersey.

"Now I'm all alone, what do I need all this space for?" she'd asked him, running her index finger over the kitchen counter.

He shook his head to think of how Solomon could have moved her out of Brooklyn in a heartbeat, but that she wouldn't speak to her son, wouldn't take his blood money, feared him so that, even with Solomon in prison, she still wouldn't talk of him. They will kill me, his own mother. With pleasure, she had said to Joseph in Yiddish. *Mekhaye.*

Happy? she said to her son in English that day, which made Joseph search for the Yiddish translation and wonder if there was no word for it in his mother's language. Turned out she was miserable. She complained that no one wanted to talk to her. No one wanted to haggle over the price of meat. She'd brought her friend Ruth uptown for some company. Isn't this grand? Selma had said, thankful to have someone to eat with standing up in the kitchen. She'd thrown Ruth an old rag, and the two had eaten herring off a chipped china plate. Just like the old days, Ruthie! she'd said. She had been thrilled when she told Joseph. Until she heard the terrible rumors started on South Fifth Street about how Selma was so stingy she would not even share her good fortune with her oldest of friends.

Selma had refused her son's invitation to bring her to the fair. But it's just over the river, Joseph had said. All those people? Selma had screamed. Over my dead body, she'd said, shaking her head.

He thought of taking his mother to the amusement side of the fair, at Coney Island. He laughed to think of her on the Cyclone, her hair on end, slack skin gone taut as she sped down the enormous dip. Not likely, Joseph thought. One can never win. No matter what, it is a problem, he thought as he wove his way over to the Essoil display. "Try the Miracle!" his banner said in large green letters. Blue and amethyst glass bottles of the cleanser, catching and refracting light, lined the back of the booth like prizes at a country fair. Tomorrow there would be a line of beautiful women, drawing Essoil-soaked cloths over plates blackened with soot and grease. At the exact same time, Joseph himself had directed them. Like the synchronized swimmers! he'd said. And two strapping young men dressed as ship captains would be on a life-sized boat, a model of the double bows of the marine transportation building, cleaning the entire deck until it gleamed.

Joseph had to smile at the marvel of it all. Only two years ago, he would have been reading about the World's Fair in the papers. Esther! He would have screamed up from his reading chair. Look at this!

But Esther was more interested in "Dear Maggie."

Joseph found the column troubling. Very troubling. Even though he railed against the new feature, telling his wife how preposterous it was that women would ask such personal advice from a complete stranger, he did sneak a peek once. He remembered the letter well, because he had been utterly appalled: *Dear Maggie,* an S from Manhattan had written. *Once I was an actress, but now the only role in my future is Manhattan mother. Not a very challenging role—cheers in the morning, a quick visit in the afternoon, and always, when home in the evening, a long kiss good night. I hate myself for thinking it, but I can't bear the infant smells of them, their baby crap, their terrible suffering, the cries and cries all through the night.* My goodness, thought Joseph. It made him extremely uncomfortable to watch Esther seated at the table in that cheery yellow kitchen, poring over another woman's misery. Or was her misery the same? '

Joseph knew how close he'd come to only reading about the World's Fair in the papers. But he was actually here, invited by the governor himself. So focused was Joseph on finding his booth among those of the hundreds of other products and technologies that were being set up that day, he did not see his old friend Vladimir, who, in the Westinghouse Pavilion, as big as a small village, was hunched over his notes. Vladimir stood up and pushed back his glasses just as Joseph passed by, rubbing his rough, chapped hands together, as if for warmth.

Also defying the world gloom, the lucky Seymour Bloom was making his way toward Vladimir. By the time Tom Dewey had come along, like Hugo's Javert, cleaning the streets of all those vicious men, including the Terrier, Seymour had been out of Mob life for nearly four years. Though those guys had protected him, there was no way a Broadway musical producer could be part of a gang. The whole squad laughed at him, everyone but Chuckles, the sad fatso from the Lower East Side who secretly phoned Seymour up for house seats for nearly every show. Got anything for tonight? Chuckles would ask. Seymour always felt it was a demand.

The Joint had cashed him out for a bit, and it had certainly weakened his relationship with the Terrier. It was probably for the best they'd put him away before he could get Seymour back for so much bad judgment. And, even though Seymour had lost a lot of cash on *The Joint*, it had helped him wedge his foot in the door of many productions on the Great White Way, as he invested in other shows. The rest went into the Kinescope, which was about to pay him back in spades.

He passed the airplane, set up so anyone could sit in the cockpit and have a (grounded) go at being a pilot. David would love this, Seymour thought. Seymour hated to think of the eight-year-old son he rarely saw; the thought filled him with the kind of guilt that could be assuaged only by what he told himself: that he was doing all of this, *this,* he thought, mentally waving his hand over the entire grounds of the fair, so his son could inherit something wonderful. Inherit all the things he had not. Don't we work so our children won't have to? thought Seymour. Even now, Seymour knew his work was more complicated than the simple immigrants' mantra: Work! Work! Work! For our children, so they can buy land, so they can have a better life. Seymour was forced to put out of his head the evenings he'd come home to see his wife passed out on the bed, David playing quietly next to her, singing softly to himself. *"Frère Jacques, Frère Jacques, dormez-vous?"* He put out of his head the time he'd come in from the theater, past midnight, and David had come to him with empty bottles of gin. These were under my bed, he'd said, one bottle in each little hand. Seymour had snatched the bottles brutally from his boy's hands, and the hopeful look on David's face had turned into a terrible frown, his lower lip quivering. Did he work for his children, or did he work to get away from his children's sadness? Seymour thought how, tomorrow, he would bring David here. He would bring him to see the Futurama everyone was buzzing about, and he would get David one of the little blue pins that said: "I have seen the future!" which were being handed out to every Futurama goer. He would take David to watch the waves of his own voice registering in light on a machine. And he would keep his son there until evening, when the entire fair would be streaming with magic and light, thought Seymour as he headed toward the Westinghouse Pavilion.

Seymour found Vladimir, hunched over his television. "Good morning, Vladimir," he said.

The scientist nodded, not even looking up from his machine. "Can you believe they're selling these for one hundred and ninety-nine dollars? Who on earth could buy something for such money?" He examined the contraption, flipping the Kinescope light on and off, watching the beam, and readying it for tomorrow's demonstration. "I think it's all a bit embarrassing."

"Everything's got to sell for something," Seymour said. "And besides, it's worth it."

It had been almost ten years since the first time he had seen the Kinescope image of Vladimir's wife. The war. The war. Every last effort went to military applications and it all got slowed down. Business should be business, Seymour thought irrationally. Frances smiling into the camera versus the Frances he had helped to cast in his play; Frances, who'd turned his beautiful drama into a catty comedy. Seymour couldn't help but shake his head and sigh over the whole thing. We live, we learn, he thought now. His mother standing up and screaming at Frances in the middle of the theater. It was all so ludicrous, really.

"Everything?" said Vladimir. "Really?"

"So, Vladimir," Seymour asked, ignoring the philosophical question, "what will you be showing to the world tomorrow? Who will be the first person to be on television?"

"That, my friend, is a surprise. Tomorrow you come back, and tomorrow you will see what the world will see."

"Can't I get a little peek?" Seymour asked teasingly. "After all, you couldn't have done it without me."

"No?" Vladimir said, clearly trying to check his annoyance. "I think, Seymour, you need me a little bit more than I need you."

Seymour shook his head and jiggled his pocket change aggressively. "Fair enough," he said. "I'll come tomorrow then." He laughed. "Tomorrow you can show me." Even though Vladimir was being fairly friendly, Seymour had not been spoken to in this way since he'd sold encyclopedias in Westchester: I don't think so, the wives had said, looking him up and down, and smiling as they slowly closed the door. Sorry. Had it been more than money after all? Now Seymour's power was different—it was not almighty. He could no longer play God. Playing God, Seymour thought as he walked away from the pavilion. Was that what I was doing? His own grandmother crossed a rainy Parisian street toward him in his imagination. She held his hand and brought him across the Marais into the synagogue, the sound of the shofar, an ancient cry he could not shake. How had his mother, her nights in the clubs, her sulking artist friends, the men dangling off her like mink stoles, how had Inez shirked the piety of her own mother? Inez, he knew, had paved the way for him to be who he'd become. His mother, who now took his money greedily, stuffing it into her enormous brassiere for safekeeping, always waiting for more. And Seymour remembered the terrified faces he'd looked into as he nudged one man after another into each of those stolen sedans. Half the time he didn't even know what they'd done. He hadn't killed them, it was true, but he'd certainly got them there in time for the killing.

Seymour wondered if the rest of his life would be his punishment, God's will. His wife: Was it illness that made her deteriorate, her mental health a spiral whose twisting, turning path he could no longer follow? Where did she go? Sometimes Seymour would shake Sarah, gather her up from the bed and shake her like hell, just to see a change on her frozen face, intensity in her eyes again. There were moments when he caught a glimpse of her, her eyes shining for brief intervals with the wit he had once loved. He remembered Sarah on that casting call, floating across the stage, head tilted back, a perfect, grand, stretched silhouette. The way she *forgot.* This is a teapot, Sarah, he'd screamed at her when she'd pointed to the thing, unable to name it just the week before. A teapot, goddamn it! To make the bloody tea.

Seymour knew it was not healthy for his children. And *The Joint,* was that punishment for a life of crime? Now he thought of Vladimir testing, writing, looking up at him with that pointed chin, his mouth gathered in concentration. Would this fail too? Would Seymour now, as he went on, infect all the lives he touched with the cruelty of his lawlessness?

The next day thousands lined up to watch the first public demonstration of television. This was the billing, though a decade before, at the New Amsterdam, had actually been the first. Reading the guidebook of events—twenty-five cents!—Joseph had seen this television listed. It was accompanied by a great deal of fanfare from RCA, and, holding the program, Joseph remembered his conversation with Frances over a decade before. No! No! No! he'd told her. How could you ask me for money? he'd thought. Could this have been what she had been speaking about?

Joseph brought Miriam from the hotel to see the historic event. Esther remained with the younger Gloria back at the hotel, the Carlyle.

"Now we can stay wherever we like, Joe. It must be the Carlyle! It just must be." Esther had told Joseph time and again of her fond memories of going to New York alone with her father for the weekend. After a long trial, Leo Weinstein would reward his daughter for the time he had spent away from her. They would take the Flying Yankee or drive the nine hours from Portland to Boston and then get on the train at South Station and pass through the city. Esther said when they entered New York, her father always reached for her hand.

The Carlyle was fine with Joseph. What did he care? He could afford it now, and it gave him pleasure to fulfill Esther's every desire, allow her to relive every good memory. Whatever you like, my dear, he'd said, and, after writing to make sure that Jews were allowed, which he found they were in most places in New York City, he had booked the rooms himself. And so they stayed at the Carlyle, and the clerks could not have been kinder to him and his children.

As Joseph and Miriam approached the Westinghouse Pavilion, which, he told his daughter, we would see is shaped like a radio tube if only we could view it from above, Seymour led his son, David, to the demonstration. Dulcy was away at prep school, and Seymour brought David as he had promised himself he would. If Sarah didn't want to come, so be it. Seymour had invited her as well, but she had pooh-poohed the idea. It wasn't so much the act of coming but the idea of television that really got her goat. At least films are on a grand scale! she'd said. For Sarah, acting was the theater, plain and simple.

"Oh, just try it out," said Seymour. "And there's so much else to see!"

"No," Sarah replied. "That whole fair seems like a bunch of fascist hooey to me anyway. And seventy-five cents! Fascist is what it is."

She threw the newspaper in his direction, opened to page 6, where that column, "Dear Maggie," ran. His wife had so little passion these days that anything which interested her made him take notice. Often Seymour would sneak up behind Sarah, the afternoon paper spread before her on her desk, as she wrote letters to Maggie, this woman from the papers. Did she think this stranger would finally give her the advice she had always coveted?

"Can't you just *enjoy* anything?" Seymour asked, smoothing out the paper on his lap. He caught some of a letter: *Everywhere I feel so nervous. This anxiety is pressing down on me. I am nervous for my daughters. Also for myself. Sometimes I miss my father so much it is unbearable, even after all these years,* wrote an E, Roxbury, Boston. *I am embarrassed by this, by how I still ache for him, as if I were still a girl.* Seymour flicked the paper aside—so much *neurosis,* he thought. What were these women *becoming*? Perhaps it was all Freud's fault, just as the Germans said, thought Seymour as he shut the door so David wouldn't hear their argument.

"Apparently not," Sarah said, snatching the paper from him. The sleeves of her robe whooshed past him, a flash of silk. "Go have your little fascistic fun without me," she said.

A huge crowd had assembled by ten o'clock, but people weren't allowed in until eleven thirty. Set in the lobby, in front of a Stuart Davis mural with huge renditions of technological innovations, illuminated by natural light filtered through a glass wall, was a Lucite cabinet—new from DuPont!—with a television set inside. The Lucite was used to show a transparent version of the typical cabinet (TRK 12) where a television would be perched, so that the viewers could see inside and watch the device functioning. The press would later dub it the "Phantom Televiser," but to Vladimir it was quite the opposite. The Lucite made the television seem even more physical, and Vladimir told Frances that very morning how he often thought of himself as a doctor looking into a body to see the way it ticked and breathed. Watching it function made his apparatus seem human. My love for this television is greater than I had thought possible, he told his wife.

At the stroke of noon, when the lobby was filled to capacity, David Sarnoff gave a long speech introducing what the crowd was about to see. Miriam stuck her fingers in her mouth, waiting for the lecture to end. Goot? her father teased.

Finally Vladimir turned on the television set. And on clicked Judy Garland, whose movie *The Wizard of Oz* was just now out in theaters. It was a clip of Garland alone on a stool in the studio singing "Over the Rainbow," the signal sent by the RCA's mobile television car to the transmitter at the Empire State and rebroadcast.

Most of the crowd had never seen television before, though nearly everyone had seen the movie. And who at the fair did not believe they had finally reached Oz? The crowd clapped wildly for television, for the living room of the future, for the new Lucite, which was as transparent as glass or water, for Dorothy, that girl adventurer so sad on that stool alone in the studio, and for technology that would take them all over the rainbow. As Frances watched, beaming with pride, she felt just like Dorothy, that girl from the old world looking for a path on the golden streets of the new.

Joseph was amazed. It was the same surge of overwhelming feeling he'd had when they had switched on the Empire State Building, nearly a decade before. He squeezed his daughter's shoulders and thought of the day she was born. Unimaginable, he had thought then, just as he thought now.

Joseph looked down at his daughter. "Vell?" he said. "Sure is something, huh?" He wished she'd sung an Irving Berlin song: "Blue Skies," perhaps. "Always."

Miriam continued sucking on the tips of her fingers. She had seen *The Wizard of Oz* just two weeks before and had been so terrified of the Wicked Witch that Esther had had to leave the theater with her. Her mother had led her up the aisle, and on the way out into the violent sunlight Esther had yelled at the young ticket taker, pointing a finger in his face. This is not for children, she had screamed. Miriam had felt embarrassed because it *was* for children, she knew, but not for one as terrified as she was. Now Miriam waited for the image of that horrible hook-nosed woman to come on the screen and reach her green hands out to strangle her.

Though he had no regrets about not becoming involved with the project, Joseph's mind was turning and turning: See how they love it! He watched the crowd, everyone looking straight at this Lucite box. Could a thing and not a person be a star? he wondered. Essoil should be on television! thought Joseph, picturing his little bottle of cleanser perched on a stool, taking a bow. Whatever it was in there, it didn't matter, people would watch it. What would it record? All the madness in Europe? Will we all sit in our living rooms and watch such horrors? Joseph shook the thought away. Even Esther agreed, nothing good was to come from over there. Over there, Joseph repeated to himself. Not here, on this side of the rainbow, not by this tremendous pot of gold.

Not a hundred yards away, Seymour was beside himself. "Isn't it terrific?" He leaned down to David, who was more mesmerized by Judy

Garland's voice than by the sight of her. It reminded him of his mother. "And the dreams that you dare to dream . . ." David was wondering about his own dreams. He thought of his mother at the top of the stairs, singing and dancing, calling down to him: "And I seem to find the happiness I seek, when we're out together dancing cheek to cheek." Those were wonderful times, and he thought he might like to do what his mother had wanted to do. Could he be an actor? He remembered the way his mother had slapped him when he'd told her of his encounter with Mae West. Suddenly this dream seemed both viable and dangerous.

David didn't want to tell his father that what had really captivated him was the time capsule they had passed on the way in. While Seymour chatted with one of his colleagues, David had watched as two women added fountain pens, alphabet blocks, and an alarm clock to the gunmetal capsule on display.

Miriam too had been mesmerized by the time capsule and the board next to it, which displayed the contents to be buried beneath the fair for the next five thousand years. She looked at the Lilly Dache hat, the Woolworth's clip, the swatches of cotton, rayon, and asbestos. She had wanted a hat like that, but Esther had warned Miriam that her nose was far too big for hats. Not with that nose, you don't, Esther had told her, wagging her finger.

The time capsule was to be opened in 6939. Miriam could not begin to fathom how far away that was. Would she be married by then? To whom? Or perhaps, as she had already grown to fear at her eight years of age, she would be somewhere in the dark, alone.

Frances ran up to Joseph. "Joooooe!" she screamed. She grabbed his arm. "And hello, you!" She bent down to Miriam. "I told you, Joe, isn't it grand?" she said, straightening.

Joseph shook his head. "You ver right, Fran. Truly. It's amazing."

Frances wagged her finger. "Shoulda coulda woulda!"

"Perhaps." Joseph nodded his head. "Perhaps, but only God knows." He looked up at the sky.

"Any news of Solomon?" Frances asked, immediately realizing her mistake.

Joseph grimaced and brought his fingers to his lips. He looked at Frances sternly, while pointing at Miriam. "Pardon me?" he said.

Just then Frances felt a tap on her shoulder. "Oh, Seymour!" she said. "How *are* you?"

"Terrific!" he practically screamed. "Isn't this fantastic?" he said, breathing heavily. Seymour was elated. It was just like watching your own production receive a thundering standing ovation.

Frances smiled. She hadn't seen Seymour in quite a while but knew that he had begun producing some shows and that he'd had a hand in *The Boys from Syracuse* last year. What was the point in holding a grudge? Vladimir couldn't stand him, she knew—that man and his *entitlement,* he'd say—but perhaps Seymour would give her another chance.

In front of them, hoards of people milled around, each one trying to get closer to the new machine.

"Hello, little mister." Frances leaned down to David.

David looked at the ground. There had been so many things they'd put in the time capsule: a Holy Bible, a dollar in change.

"Joseph Brodsky, this is Seymour Bloom." Frances turned the two men toward each other. "Joseph is Solomon's brother," she said hesitantly.

Seymour looked at Joseph and then looked blankly at Frances.

"The Terrier," she said directly to him, as softly as she could speak, which was not too softly, given the bustling crowd and her very nature.

Joseph lifted his chin and placed his hands squarely on Miriam's shoulders.

"Joseph invented Essoil—just over there." Frances pointed toward the Transportation Zone and Ford's Road of Tomorrow, with its spiral ramps, a future superhighway, which seemed a huge distance away.

"Fantastic!" Seymour said. "I had no idea the Terrier had a brother who was an inventor!"

Joseph nodded. He supposed he was.

"Essoil. Amazing. That stuff is amazing. Our housekeeper insists on it. And now, she has so much less work to do, I'm considering cutting her pay!"

Joseph smiled.

"And Seymour has backed Vladi's television for a decade," she said. "I told you, Joseph. It would pay off."

"Ve'll see," Joseph said. "Won't ve?"

"Nothing to worry about on that end," Seymour said. He took

David's hand. "This is my son, David. And you are?" He looked down at Miriam.

Miriam stepped behind her father. He brought her out from behind his leg. "Zhis is my elder daughter, Miriam," he said.

Miriam looked at David and smiled sideways. She remembered the pack of Camels attached to the plywood behind the capsule that displayed the dry goods placed inside. What would she put in a time capsule? She thought of Essoil. She'd like to put that into the capsule so everyone would know what her father had made. She had been proud of him because Esther had been proud. Aspirin. Aspirin tablets were important so people would know how to get rid of those headaches that always plagued her mother.

David smiled back at her, also preoccupied with the time capsule. He had watched them add apple seeds, and he had wondered what if they just grow and grow, pushing their way out before it's time to dig it up? He would put in seeds as well—he liked the possibility of them. Roses. Watermelon. He'd put in lavender oil from his grandmother's bathroom, and the Hair Net she sprayed on all her clients until their hair stood on its own.

"Nice to meet you," Miriam said. Joseph was already pulling her away, much to Frances's consternation.

"Joe!" she said. "Do you remember Vladimir from back home? Don't you want to see him? After all these years?"

"Not now," Joseph said. Just how that man Bloom knew Solomon, he didn't want to know. "He's busy, and I have to get back to zhe booth."

"Yes, Frances." Seymour had such a mix of love and anger toward this woman, he never knew how to speak to her or just what to do with his face when he did. "We should go as well. I'll see Vladimir when it's less crowded. Please congratulate him for me. I will be sending you both a case of champagne!"

She hit him on the shoulder. "Not necessary, Seymour," Frances said. She knew Vladimir would take one sip, and, already swooning, he would tell her he was too high to drink another drop. "Bye, David!" Frances waved to him, already headed out of the lobby with his father.

She went back to find her husband in the midst of the chaos. She could see him from across the lobby, alone, staring out the window.

Getting to the front of the throng of fascinated people proved quite difficult, so Frances was forced to watch Vladimir daydream his big day away from a distance. She knew he was thinking about Albert Einstein, who had given a speech earlier that day, in the rain. Vladimir had been weighing whether science and art weren't more connected than science and faith.

As Frances tried to nudge her way toward her brilliant husband, Miriam and David separated, both with small hands slipped into their fathers'. No one knew then that, in the end, not enough people would attend the fair, and that, when it had been open less than half a year, war would break out in Europe. The billing would no longer be the World of Tomorrow; it would become Freedom and Liberty. The Russia House would become vacant until new fair organizers replaced it with American shows. The amusement aspect of the fair would be expanded—more mermaids underwater, their breasts sprung from their suits, more fat ladies fighting, lines of gorgeous girls walking the boardwalk at Coney Island—to appeal to the people who had not attended, believing the fair too high-minded.

The World of Tomorrow was upon them, and people needed fun. No one had documented Miriam and David's encounter—there was no photograph snapped with the brand-new color film, no footage shot. No pin that marked it: "I have seen the future!" Neither Miriam nor David would remember the first time they met. Both of their fathers held their children's hands on opposite sides of the perfect, shining Perisphere filled with a desperate hope and overwhelmed by what the unknown future was to bring.

CHAPTER 14

Taken: David Bloom and Miriam Brodsky, 1945

WHEN HE WAS OLD ENOUGH to learn just who Mae West actually was, David Bloom read his encounter with her in his grandmother's apartment building as a sign of his destiny. As he grew up, especially after his father used the money from television to reinvest in Broadway and could get house seats to almost any production in town, David spent most of his free time at the theater. Nothing thrilled him more than seeing for himself the mechanisms creating a production—the lighting, the costumes, the makeup, the sets, the women leaning in to one another, waiting for their turns onstage. It was like being *inside* the television, as if he were the very electron beam magnetically deflecting and striking the back of the phosphor coating inside the Kinescope. It was in the chaos of backstage, just at the moment before the performer went on—the greatest moment of potential and possibility—that David Bloom was exactly who he was meant to be. And he knew this *then*—at eight and at ten and at twelve—that here was the place where his heart both stopped and started.

When he followed his sister to prep school at twelve, the first thing he did was take up with the Drama Department. Though he had inherited from his father a large, athletic frame that made him seem older than his years, the better roles were reserved for the older students, which left David to play bit parts. This didn't faze him, though, as simply to remain in the presence of actors was enough. Just to have been involved—to paint the luxury liner for the *Anything Goes* set his first year, or to have tied Hannah Brown's (and at the same time Sherry Longfellow's!) bonnet in *Easter Parade* was more than enough for him.

In the tenth grade, David finally got his dream role. He was to play Nathan Detroit in *Guys and Dolls,* a show that he had seen eight times when it played that year on Broadway in the Forty-sixth Street Theater. How he studied for that part. He practiced shuffling cards, throwing dice, and stacking chips—he studied himself in the mirror for the paradox of disaffection and warmth that was the center of his Nathan Detroit. When he made faces in the mirror, adjusting his eyeglasses—David was nearly blind by fifteen—placing his leg up on a chair, and leaning his elbow on his knee, his fingers propping up his chin, he would think, I could be this person. I could be *cool.*

But he ached for the love of his mother. The nights he came in from Brooklyn to find her passed out in the parlor, on the couch beneath the potted palm, were torture to him, and he longed for some means to make his way through the watery ocean that was his mother drunk and the thick fog that was her hungover. There were moments when David and his mother were quite close. No one had more fun than they did as they made their way through the brownstone walking like Charlie Chaplin or reciting Shakespeare, he on top of the winding staircase, she below, looking up to her son.

David never understood his mother's disgust for the theater. There had been a time, his father had told him, when she had gone to the theater each week. She had known who all the stars were and had kept *Playbills* in her closet, stacked as high as her boxes of special-ordered shoes. But now, each time Seymour left for an opening night, she laughed at him. Go off to your silly shows, she told him. The theater, she would often scream after him, is for homosexuals.

David thought his good news would be a gift to his mother: He thought he had found something she had lost.

"Guess what, Mum?" he called from the hallway of his dormitory. "I was just cast as the lead in *Guys and Dolls!* The lead!" David announced.

There was that sound again: silence. Was she reading the paper?

"Did you hear me? The lead!" David said again.

"No, David," she said. "The theater is for fruits. You don't want an actor's life, my dear. And besides, I want grandchildren!"

"What?" David asked. Hadn't it been she who'd put on the record and belted out "Oklahoma!"? He remembered her, jumping on the couch and singing to him and Dulcy: "I'm just a girl who can't say no, I'm in a terrible fix." She was tall and proud then as she jumped off the couch and ran over to pinch the cheeks of her adoring children, who were in that moment thrilled to have a mother like her. Even though the theater had been his father's livelihood, the seed of that love came from his mother. "What?" he said again.

"I won't have it," Sarah said. "You spend entirely too much time with *drama.* You had enough of that in New York. You are missing *opportunities.* Now be a man, son. Go out for football or swimming."

"But I'm to be Nathan Detroit, Mother," he said.

"No, dear," she said. "You're not. I'll have you pulled from school," she said. "I will." If Sarah was shocked by how easy it was to be so firm with her son, she did not let on. "Swimming is good for a boy. You're very athletic, David. Go be a swimmer. I can see it now," she told him, "the star of the sea."

David pictured a mermaid. He was speechless—this was the first time he saw his dreams slipping from his grasp. No longer could he picture himself holding Adelaide's hand, the beautiful senior Ella Markson's hand, in his. He no longer ran to the front of the stage to bow, the other, lesser players behind them. Perhaps he would have taken a bow alone, the sound of applause, the scattering of roses all for *him. Whoosh,* his mother had instantly dashed these fantasies.

This is what sets humans apart from the beasts we really are: the need for love and the stupid things we'll do to get it. David assented, though he did bargain his mother down and took a bit part as one of the nameless gamblers in a pin-striped suit, an anonymous sinner in the mission, pretending to be saved. Still, he was able to prop up his leg and lean in on his elbow when playing craps. But no lines to speak of. No private bow. He didn't have to attend many rehearsals, which gave him time to go out for swimming as his mother had wished, and the following year David was made captain of the team.

That was it for the acting. David no longer had time to spend in the prop room, marking off the items on the hanging clipboard as he gathered them in his arms. No more hours behind the sets, watching the painters on the top rungs of ladders, clouds emerging from beneath their horsehair brushes. No more rehearsal time, legs dangling from the stage as the actors waited for the director to open the door to the auditorium and emerge from the square of light. It had been a place where David had been as much a part of the scenery as he was at his grandmother's beauty salon, a rush of cold air blowing his hair from his face when any lady from the neighborhood came inside.

Just that single conversation with his mother and David was no longer an actor. He would return to the theater as a businessman, working with his father each day. Seymour had bought four Broadway theaters and was producing shows in all of them, or leasing them out to other producers if he wasn't fortunate enough to have a show of his own.

"It will be only the Blooms and the Shuberts running all of Broadway," he told David, knowing, after all, that there was no getting rid of the Shuberts. "The Broadway Blooms," he said.

David would do what Seymour did: Seymour had an office on Forty-fourth and Broadway, and each day he drove into town in his Maybach. After handing the keys to the valet, he'd hop the elevator to the fifteenth floor, to an office where everyone greeted him with good cheer. "Good morning, sir!" they all sang. One of the girls always took his hat and coat. And each day Seymour breathed a deep, appreciative breath and carried on, a little stunned by his incredible good fortune, always grateful. He'd think of his mother, coming home from the hair salon, her hands burning with dye. It pleased Seymour that Inez had seen her son make money, and that now, though she would never set foot in the theater after the humiliation she had endured during the opening night of *The Joint,* his mother could see him make a name for himself. A name, Seymour often told himself, was invaluable.

Priceless, he'd tell his son.

But Sarah claimed that Seymour had become a landlord: just leasing his spaces to the real artists. What did producing have to do with theater anyway? David had to agree. He was in favor of selling the buildings. After all, there were far more dependable ways to make a buck than in show business.

But David had no idea how hard Seymour had worked or just what he had done to lay claim to those theaters, or why, as unreliable as the theater was for business, it was what got Seymour out of bed in the morning. David had no idea, because his father had never told him that, really, their dreams were as linked as David's and Sarah's. No, Seymour had not wanted to be an actor; he had wanted to be in the audience. Every moment of his life he had wanted to spend looking up at the stage, to be brought to laughter, to tears, to unfettered joy. Seymour had never passed on to his son that it was okay—wonderful even—to be a spectator.

Had Sarah stripped that idea of experience from David? Made him believe that he had to *be* the lead, not be *moved* by him, and then prevented him from playing him altogether? Opening nights, watching the actors join hands and move forward, gesturing to the orchestra, standing until the curtain swooped closed around them, David never ceased to wonder at what he could have been had he not been so desperate for his mother's approval. He would never enjoy a show, so unyielding were his thoughts of all the roles that had been wrested away from him as he watched men with far less talent playing nightly on the stage that bore his father's good name.

Unlike David's, Miriam Brodsky's childhood was informed less by what she wanted than by what she, or more her mother, did not want. What Esther did not want had become enormous. The last straw came the day the *Globe* arrived at the house for a photo shoot to accompany a piece on Joseph, the man behind the Essoil phenomenon. When sipping her tea after dinner, Esther opened the evening newspaper and flipped to the photograph of her beautiful family. Upon seeing it, she screamed so loudly both Joseph and Miriam came running.

"Look!" she said, pointing to the grainy image. "All I can see is Miriam's nose!"

Miriam gasped and brought both hands to her face.

"Esther!" Joseph said. "Now come on."

"Enough is enough," Esther said, peeling Miriam's hands from her face. "We can't fight this fight alone anymore. We're going to New York City."

∾

And so in February of 1945, Esther did what so many good Jewish mothers did and do, which was to take her daughter to New York City to see a certified plastic surgeon and have the torture be done with already. But secretly. Esther made arrangements for them to stay at the Carlyle for her daughter's convalescence, or until the bandages came off. In case something turns out wrong and we have to go back in, Esther told her daughter, making it sound as if Miriam was an undercooked roast.

The night before they were to leave for Manhattan, Miriam Brodsky dreamt of hats. Her mother had always told her that her present profile did not allow for such accessories, as, no matter how floppy or large the brim, no matter how high or pushed back the crown, all that seemed to emerge from beneath the felt or straw or fur was that irrepressible nose. In her dream she stood in Bergdorf's before a full-length mirror as the saleslady passed her hat upon hat, smiling approvingly as young Miriam placed one after another on her head. Each looked more fetching than the one before. Even when a rubber bathing cap was handed over and she tucked her hair inside it, she looked grand, as graceful and exquisite as the Hollywood starlets who pranced around the pools of Beverly Hills.

On the train to Pennsylvania Station, Miriam looked out the window as the scenery flew by and imagined her own landscape changing. She looked over at her mother, who stared straight ahead, hands folded in her lap. Her mother's profile, Miriam noted, was really quite lovely. Esther possessed a timeless beauty, her dark eyes flanked by the beginning not of a big nose but of a strong one, a feature rendering her face both anachronistic and timeless. As she watched her mother, Miriam began to panic that this quality would now be wrested from her own face. Yes, she would be able to wear any hat she wished, but would her face become a generic face? Would it be *her* face? When she and her sister, Gloria, walked along the dock at camp, would people know they were leaves from the same tree? When Joseph took her to Old Orchard Beach, would others know she held the hand of her father? And, like last summer, when she had grown too old to hold her father's hand and had pulled away from him, stuffing her hand into the pocket of her skirt, would others know, as he had to have known, that this was a daughter who had outgrown her father's touch? It's

okay, sugar, he had said as they walked on the boardwalk, past the Ferris wheel, past the house of mirrors, the funnel cake and oyster stands.
Miriam had pretended not to hear him.

She looked away from her mother now and back out the window.
Watching the trees zip by, she picked at a string coming loose on the
stitching of her handbag and brought the other hand to her nose.
Miriam pretended to rub the cartilage as if it itched. Its fleshiness dis-
gusted her, and she pushed the flesh down so that the tip of her nose
touched her upper lip, forming a tentative frown. No, Miriam thought.
It must go, she resolved, and, as if reading her mind and acknowledg-
ing that her decision was the right one, at that very moment the train
went underground.

The Brodsky women headed straight to the Carlyle. Miriam remembered their stay nearly six years before, when they had come for the
World's Fair. But this was no celebration. This time she and Esther
would stay for the two weeks it took for Miriam to recover from the
mad way the doctor broke her nose only to have the chance to mend
it again. Beneath her eyes was such a wash of blues and grays and pur-
ples, she would find herself more astonished by these bruises than worried for the healing occurring beneath the bandages. Miriam peered
sadly out her window onto Madison Avenue, longing to look into the
department store windows, to walk on the cold city streets, to dine in
the cafés, stroll in the park, gaze at the Rembrandts at the Met. But she
would not be humiliated.

"But this is why we *came* here," Esther said, clearly intolerant of her
daughter's embarrassment. "Who the heck do *you* know in New York?"

"I know Nana Selma," she said.

"Well, we're not going to see Nana Selma," said Esther. "Can you
imagine?" Esther laughed and set her voice an octave higher: "She's
getting a new *what*? Heymish! she'd call me. My granddaughter has a
fine nose, just like her father's!"

Miriam flopped down on the couch, ignoring Esther. "I can't," she
said. "I just can't go out there like this!" It was not only her appearance
that shook her confidence—Miriam had been told never to touch the
bandages. Even the slightest knock on the nose could ruin everything.

Imagine it as a gestation period, like when you have a baby, the surgeon had said. Miriam had been embarrassed and could not look directly at him. Now, simply pulling a sweater over her head, she feared for the pressure of the light wool on the bridge of her brand-new nose.

They agreed that going to the movies would be fine. *State Fair* was playing at the Paris, and Miriam knew she could jump out of a cab and into the darkened theater and feel at ease. And it was just by the Plaza, too! How Miriam longed to go inside for tea and look out at the carriages waiting by the park, the dapple gray horses stomping their hooves.

Getting ready to go to the cinema, Miriam was very careful to pull her light green angora sweater gently over her head. It was at that strange point in getting dressed, when she felt that she was both appearing and disappearing at the same time, that Esther called to her.

"Miri!" her mother sang. "Did you bring any perfume? I left my No. 5 at home."

Hearing her mother, Miriam turned her head and, in so doing, did the absolutely unthinkable, the very thing she had lain on her back at night in bed aching to avoid, which was knock herself *anywhere near* the nose. In her turning toward Esther, not only did the sweater press down on her nose, but she also knocked herself on the bedpost, right in the three-thousand-dollar center of her face.

"Oh my God!" Miriam struggled to get her sweater either on or off. But because, in the panic of the situation, she had not decided which way she would rather it go, one arm moved up, the other down, creating more strain on the already broken—and now perhaps *re*broken!— nose. "Oh my God!" she screamed again.

Esther hurried out of the bathroom. "Are there mice?" she asked. "Miriam!" Esther jumped back. "What are you *doing*? Why, you'll bend the thing entirely out of shape!" she said.

Miriam didn't know if her mother was referring to the new sweater set, which had been a present from her father, or if she meant her new nose, which she supposed was more her mother's gift.

Esther went to Miriam and gently pulled the sweater over her daughter's head to reveal her hysterical face.

Miriam pointed at her nose. "I hit it," she said when she could speak, afraid even to bend her head, as if the very force of gravity would make whatever was left of her nose slide down and fall off. "On the bedpost," she sobbed.

Miriam could see her mother was trying to remain calm. She took a deep breath and ran her hands over the sweater, smoothing out any wrinkles. "How hard?" Esther asked.

Miriam had gained a little control over her weeping. Really she was weeping for the whole goddamn thing, for having been given a nose in need of fixing to begin with, one that she had to have *broken,* of all things. And the pain of that breaking, and being cooped up here, her mother coming in from the street with all these beautiful packages and not a thing for her. Why, you got a new nose, Esther said when Miriam pouted. I should think that would be enough for any girl.

"I hit it hard," Miriam said and began to cry again.

Even though it was nearly dinnertime, Esther went to call the surgeon. And even though he was at the Century Club, he told her he would have a look immediately.

"I don't like the sound of this *at all,*" Esther said.

When the doctor met them at the hospital, he whisked the Brodsky women into an examining room. As he stepped back from undoing the bandages, Miriam watched for her mother's expression. The doctor and Esther sighed heavily with what seemed to Miriam to be relief.

"It's fine." The doctor stroked Miriam's shoulder. "Just fine," he said. This calmed her, and she closed her eyes, imagining the sophistication of the chignon she would soon wear at the nape of her neck.

"Would you like to see it?" he asked.

"Yes," Miriam said, her eyes still closed.

"Remember what I told you about gestation? The one thing about taking it so soon from its cocoon of bandages," said the doctor, "is that it's just a wee bit premature." He handed her a mirror.

Miriam was shocked at her reflection. Or more at what was lacking in that image. She had expected all the bruising to be gone, all the glue from the tape miraculously scraped from her face, the puffiness between her eyes reduced. But this was not the case, and, with all that mess, Miriam could not find her nose at all. She furrowed her brow.

"But where *is* it?" She had her hands on her face as she leaned into the doctor. She took in a deep breath, but she couldn't smell a thing.

The doctor went behind his young patient and looked with her into the handheld mirror. "See?" he said. His face rose behind hers. He pointed to two dark spots above the mouth on his own face. Miriam had mistaken what was on her own face for moles or, worse, pimples. Closing her mouth and taking another breath just to make sure, she realized that though she couldn't smell a thing, these were in fact her nostrils.

"Oh!" She nodded.

"As I said"—the doctor turned toward Esther Brodsky—"it was a little premature—a preemie we call it—but it should grow a little bit more unless the blow completely stunted it."

Esther nodded thoughtfully, her finger to the side of her own nose. Again Miriam looked at her mother's face for guidance. "Either way," Esther said. "We love it."

Miriam nodded again and placed the tips of her fingers on her face as gently as she could. She inhaled, but still, no smell.

"Careful!" the doctor and Esther said at the same time. They turned to each other and smiled.

But Miriam was searching with her hands for her nose. She felt a tiny bone running down the center and, at the end, a minute dollop of flesh, as if placed there as garnish. "Thank you," she said and pushed herself off the examining table.

"Yes, thank you, Doctor," Esther said, taking her daughter's hand.

The day of their return home, Miriam was lying on her bed, hands behind her head, daydreaming, when she overheard her mother on the phone with their neighbor Peggy Sanders.

"We had a terrible scare, Peg!" Esther cradled the phone between her shoulder and her neck and moved around the kitchen. "It was quite a crash. Miri hit the back of the front seat, hard."

There was a silence as the woman on the other end of the receiver spoke.

"No," Esther said. "Why, yes, we did take the train to Manhattan. It was in a taxicab. It was just terrible. Why, they should simply be out-lawed."

Miriam wandered into the hallway, her sandals dragging along the shag carpet. She stopped and leaned her head against the wall, running her fingertips along it. Remembering the smell of her mother's house, a combination of flowers and Essoil and cold weather, she sniffed again and nearly burst into tears when what registered was only emptiness. Did losing her nose mean losing her memory? Miriam brushed her nose ever so lightly and tried to imagine the way it would have in fact felt to have her neck whipped back and her head thrown forward when the taxi stopped just short of hitting the car in front of them.

As the doctor had anticipated, the nose would continue to grow, though it did maintain a slightly premature state. It was almost as it must have looked when she had been developing in her mother's womb, before the protrusion had grown enough to knock Esther in the vagina in the first place. But from that day forward it would be only Miriam's eyes and ears that could bring her back to the mixing of bleach and soap and ammonia that worked together to make her father rich. Her mother's smell of lipstick and roses would be lost to her. And with it, taste. No longer would she be able to savor her mother's scalloped potatoes and beef stew, the cotton candy she sneaked with her father on the boardwalk at Old Orchard. Although sometimes she would forget, and, upon entering a bakery, or walking through a field after rain, Miriam would take a huge whiff. Each time it was the same. She would be able to feel the texture of warm bread and remember the flavor of yeast and rye and butter, feel the wet grass between her wriggling toes, but Miriam would never be able to smell again.

CHAPTER 15

Star Quality: Essoil, 1946

WHO KNEW THAT, HOWEVER indirectly, Miriam Brodsky's father and David Bloom's father, so philosophically different, would end up doing business together? As it turned out, Joseph unwittingly teamed up with the ex-mobster Seymour Bloom. Joseph and Seymour would benefit so much from each other, they might as well have been partners.

As Joseph had watched Vladimir's demonstration at the World's Fair, almost a decade before, he'd had a vision: What if Essoil, not Judy Garland, sang its way into each American heart and every American living room? What better way to appeal to the individual? Joseph had thought, as he'd stood with Miriam that day. It would be just like sell-ing door-to-door, only now it would be over the shortwave. All the people who owned televisions would have to listen to his pitch. What choice did they have? Joseph would be right there in the living room with them, and no one would be able to slam the door and leave him holding his two scratched-up cases outside in the cold. No one could tell him, These are tough times, mister. Good-bye.

In April 1946, Joseph Brodsky sat in his Boston office, high above the Essoil plant. He looked over his eight-year-old company, the fac-tory downstairs, the secretaries out front, the accountants, the sales force, the reps coming in out of the cold spring air from their stops at institutions along the burgeoning highways. The world had changed, but what really amazed Joseph was the manner in which it was still changing.

Now he wanted to do something different for his advertising campaign. The one in the national magazines had been a little dull, if you asked him. If not dull then run-of-the-mill: a woman happily shopping for not just one but two bottles of Essoil; a skipper on the bow of his boat extolling the virtues of using Essoil to clean decks. The point was to show just how multipurpose his product could be, it was true, but Joseph hated the inert quality of these ads.

He had tried to be innovative, placing his advertisements right above the ever-popular "Dear Maggie." Just that morning, a box above the column—a tombstone ad, the booker had called it—had appeared with a photo of the bottle and a cartoon woman in an apron singing: "It's so easy when you use Essoil!" He had tried to focus on this, and not the letter below, which he had found disturbing the way he had found the whole column disturbing: *Dear Maggie,* the letter had begun, from M in Massachusetts. *I wish that I were beautiful. What is beautiful anyway? Who should I ask? And who do you think would tell me?*

How terrible, Joseph thought now, watching all the scurrying below. Girls growing up with no sense of confidence.

The radio campaign, though more dynamic, could not, of course, actually show the astounding results of cleaning with Essoil. He could have included testimonial after testimonial—these tended to work best with radio—but seeing the all-purpose detergent clean was really the point, was it not?

Besides, soon no one would need a radio at all—everyone was buying a television. Joseph could see his own reflection in the pane of smoked glass that looked over what anyone would call an empire. For a brief moment, he saw himself on a television screen. He knew he could not be the one to stand up and speak for the very product he'd invented. "Clean up this voild!" he'd say. One couldn't say such a thing now: the mess had grown far too large. Clean up the Nazi criminals? With Essoil! Joseph laughed, mocking himself. I don't think so. But he didn't trust the United Nations to do it either. Those men could not suffer enough. Clean up the mess at Hiroshima? At Nagasaki? Of course it was all impossible. He had heard people's skin melted from their bones. The suffering: it overwhelmed him. What would his father think now? Joseph wondered. Would he still believe that here was the golden country, to which one thousand Jews sailed from Germany with hope, this place whose leader claimed their entry permits were invalid and sent them back?

Joseph shook his head and watched the aging man in the reflection shake his head back at him. Who *was* that? "Clean up this kitchen." That was viable. And he could say it, if he concentrated, without an accent. Joseph knew that he was getting older and that, at the end of the day, he would be only what he had always been: a salesman from Russia. He was going to go on the television and tell housewives to buy from him? He didn't need the advertising agency he'd hired—with an unheard-of budget of over $50,000—to tell him that he couldn't even pronounce *housewife* properly. *Housevife,* he'd say, every damn time.

But he didn't want some Veronica Lake, either, though the way her career had been going, Joseph might have had a chance of approaching her. Barbara Stanwyck would be nice, a family matriarch from Brooklyn. But she was too much her own star, and he wanted the spokeswoman for Essoil to be someone real, someone who looked as if she might actually use the product herself. Joseph wanted a recognizable face but not one that went with another place or product.

Someone like Frances Gold, as Frances still insisted on calling herself, thought Joseph. Even after she married Vladimir, she had kept Gold. For my stage name, she'd said, though Joseph hadn't heard a whole lot about her acting career. A stage name. Joseph laughed to himself just thinking about it. Though he never said it, perhaps for fear of giving himself away, a stage name always reminded him of coming over. The way the officers at Ellis Island looked at you and stamped your name as they saw fit. He could never forget those stern faces, the black uniforms. Had they been black? He would think of those men often, their cruel mustaches twitching like European fascists'. Brodsky had been relatively effortless to say and therefore an easy name to keep. A stage name. It seemed to Joseph to be a way of passing oneself off as someone else. The Terrier. Who was he kidding? Had he not been acting? I'm a tough guy, a wiseguy, you move a muscle, I'll kill ya. To speak that way is a choice; it's an act. What had Solomon been thinking when he watched himself run around like that? And his wife? What did that Pauline think as she passed herself off as a rich matron from Westchester? Where on earth had she disappeared to? In a way, Joseph thought, it was criminal, a sin against God to try to be something that one simply was not.

But then again, he thought, passing oneself off as someone else is an actor's job, is it not? Joseph laughed again to himself. Well, if that were the case, the theater would be a stage filled with immigrants, no actors, no dancers. He imagined the show they would put on: those plucked from Russia or Poland, as he had been, the Germans, the dark Italians, the Irish, all standing in a row, attempting to pass themselves off as family, say, a cast of American characters. Or was it the other way around, perhaps? And people lived their lives like actors. His whole old neighborhood, an ensemble. Life and theater, he thought, the same thing. All of us just standing on this stage of golden streets trying to pass ourselves off as if we belonged.

Joseph thought of Irving Berlin. He loved to think of Irving Berlin, this man who could have been his brother for the way their lives paralleled each other. More so than his own brother. Mr. Berlin couldn't even speak English until he was twelve years old. First the pogroms, then the Lower East Side. Then the "God Bless America," then the "White Christmas." How had he done it? The man was American music, no question. Joseph wondered just who was an outsider and who, exactly, was on the inside. How could anyone tell the difference?

Language, he thought.

And then the thought was gone. He remembered his daughter's return from New York the year before, her nose practically lopped off her beautiful face. Joseph had tried to conceal his astonishment and quell the memory of all the times he had wiped her runny nose, the many moments he had brought his own nose to hers and wriggled them together. Like Eskimos, he had said to Miriam, and she had squealed with delight.

The night Esther and Miriam came home from New York City was one of the few times Joseph had looked at his wife as if she were a stranger.

"How do you like it, Joe?" She brushed Miriam's hair back and shoved their daughter forward to show her husband, as if she were asking him whether he would like to keep her.

"It?" he said. "You." He bent down and kissed Miriam's head. "You're gorgeous," he told her.

Miriam went crying into her bedroom, and Joseph looked up at Esther, a question on his face. He was guilty too, he knew. How could

this not be a crime against God? But who had committed it? He had let
Esther do whatever made her happy; this had always pleased him.
Fine, the stone deck; sure, the Art Deco chandelier; of course, change
the entire heating system in the house so as to keep the rugs a seam-
less blanket, an unbroken expanse that somehow would have been
destroyed by oil heat.

"Estha, vhat have you done?" he asked over the muffled sound of his
daughter's crying. Why was she crying? Was she in pain? Did she miss
who she had been only days previously?

Esther glared at her husband, flaring her considerable nostrils.
"What, you're my mother?"

"Your mother!"

"My mother!" she said. "With the criticism here, the criticism there.
Perhaps you married down! she'd always tell me. Well, I think maybe I
did!" she exclaimed, crossing her arms so hard over her stomach she let
out a small gasp.

"Esther." Joseph was cut to the quick. "Can't I say a word?"

"Maybe it's like my mother said. Because my father died so young,
I have no self-esteem. That's what Maggie says. She says low self-esteem
is a serious problem for today's women."

"Who?"

"Maggie! Dear Maggie!"

Joseph looked at his wife. "This has nothing to do with you and your
self-esteem."

Esther breathed heavily. "I know," she said. As quickly as her rage
had come, it had gone. "The truth is, all the girls are doing it," she told
Joseph. "Miriam will thank us later. She will, Joe, I promise. No one
walks around with a nose like that anymore. It's completely out of
fashion."

"Okay," he said. "Okay, Esther." Perhaps, he thought then, it was
his own selfishness. Perhaps he was forcing Miriam to stay young, trying to will her to remain a little girl he would always be able to recognize. If this was what all the girls were doing, this was the new fashion,
then who was he to stop it?

Joseph remembered his daughters as little girls, and then he remembered Solomon. It was strange the way his brother's memory wounded
him, not the one of the Terrier as a grown man, his ruined face a mug

shot in the papers, his name in all the headlines, but the memory of
Solomon as a boy, the two of them playing marbles on the broken front
stoop. These recollections always pained him. In a similar way, memories of his elder daughter wounded him. It ripped him open to remember raking leaves with Miriam. He'd made huge piles—colors he had
never seen until he moved to New England—for her to jump in. Go
on, he'd say. Jump! Still he could see her elated face as she leapt into the
air and then always, always, his fear as she disappeared, sinking into the
pile, lost to him for just an instant, but lost nonetheless. There had been
so many Boston winters spent making snow angels in the backyard, the
two of them lying parallel, their arms swishing up and down. But those
imprints of father and daughter in flight were already evidence of a
moment lost to him. With his elder daughter, Joseph's sentimentality
had always overwhelmed him. And now, with Miriam nearly fifteen
years old, those early memories stopped him the way his brother's had,
the way loss always would. Watching a daughter grow up, he supposed,
was more about grief than joy.

Again he caught his reflection, a face in the window that looked out
over the factory floor beneath him, where each worker was attending
to his individual task. Joseph tried to focus on his own image. He was
nearly bald now. And yet, this was what he'd always looked like, perhaps with a little more hair, and what he would look like, surely, with
a little—perhaps a lot—less hair, until he died.

What if things were just as they were, instead of what we thought
they should be? What if he found a woman whom America could look
in the face and *see*? That would be the woman to showcase Essoil. Joseph
thought again of Frances, whose photograph he had seen in the *Times*,
a review she had sent to him from back when she starred in that musical nearly fifteen years ago. There had been something timeless about
the photograph—her dark hair and eyes set against the white, white
skin. Joseph had not gone to see Frances in that play, despite the personal invitation she had sent. For some reason he had hidden the invitation from Esther, though now he was not sure why. Perhaps he hid
it because his wife would certainly have wanted to go down to New
York to see the musical. That was what he had convinced himself at the
time, that Esther would have begged and pleaded. Broadway! she
would have exclaimed, her head turned to the left as she clipped an

earring to her right ear. What a fabulous treat. Perhaps Joseph had not wanted to let her down, because they hadn't had the money to take such a trip then. But now, he had to admit, he had also hidden it from Esther so she would not question him. Who is this? Why? she would have asked. Why don't you want to see this old friend Frances?

He couldn't, that was why. Solomon was attached to that musical, however distantly, and, though Joseph wanted to let go of it, let go of what his brother had become, he was not ready to do so then. That had been 1931—Solomon had been expanding his entire empire, eating fried eggs and corned beef hash as he planned with his gang in rural diners all over the country. It was no longer just New York, and soon, Joseph knew, people in Boston and in Maine would know who his brother was and exactly what he did. Who could have known that Joseph would follow him, that Essoil would now be found in every diner's broom closet?

When Joseph finally phoned Frances, he willed himself not to think of the time she had called him about investing in television and the terrible way he had raised his voice to her. He was now calling her with a plan he was sure would help her acting career, or at least get her back on television. She had been right, Joseph had to realize now. But so what? He'd done things his way, and it certainly could have turned out worse.

"Frances?" He rang her at home from his office in Boston. "It's Joseph Brodsky," he said.

Still her heart skipped to hear his voice. "I know it's you, Joseph." Frances shook her head and set the paper down on the couch as she stood up to pull the curtains back from the window. She looked out onto the midtown street where she and Vladimir had moved after the fair.

"How are you, Franny-goil?" he asked.

"Not a girl so much anymore, Joe," she said. She could see her reflection in the glass, hovering above the people waiting at cross lights and rushing down the avenue. Frances had turned thirty-seven last month. Vladimir had rented out the Rainbow Room and thrown an enormous bash. It had been so unlike her husband. Guests had danced until dawn, as they say, and Frances remembered looking down at Rockefeller Center on that spring night and seeing what had been the skating rink empty, an unmarked palm. At dawn the city had looked like she imagined it would have in 1909, when her parents were still in Russia and she was a tiny fist in her mother's distressed belly. Had Pauline stood on her tiptoes to talk to her mother's growing stomach? Or was this an American conceit? Frances didn't know the difference anymore.

That morning after the champagne, the canapés, the noisemakers, the four-tiered cake, she thought to herself that just this party was more than she had ever wished for. She remembered her mother buzzing around the house cleaning, her father discussing politics with friends in the kitchen, Pauline showing off to herself in the mirror. Back then, Frances and her sister never even knew this part of the city existed—who got all the way to Forty-eighth Street from Williamsburg, Brooklyn? Back then, this glorious Rockefeller Center was only a ditch. Amazing that so much can blossom out of nothing. She thought of this city emerging from the ground, and then she remembered the way her father had been returned to it.

"Not a girl at all," Frances said to Joseph rather sadly. Now she thought that perhaps it was not love, as in romantic love, that made her heart beat so wildly at the sound of Joseph's voice but the fact that he was her only conduit to the past. Unlike Joseph, Frances liked to open the locked gates of her childhood. She welcomed the way, when she entered a deli on Second Avenue, she was instantly home again.

"I suppose not," Joseph said. But he could not help seeing Frances as the girl looking out the window, waiting for her sister to come home.

She was still looking out the window, but now it was at the other buildings—at an apartment five flights below in a building across the way; the curtains blowing back in the breeze, and a woman crying into her hands at the kitchen table. Such a huge, lonely city. Perhaps, Frances thought, she was waiting for someone to come back.

Waiting. Frances would always be waiting, she thought. But for what? Her big break?

Let's face it, thought Frances, *The Joint* was not the vehicle I had hoped it would be. And then, thanks to Vladimir, she hardly needed to work at all, though she had been in several off-Broadway productions, and she lent her voice to plenty of radio stories. But Vladimir would never let her move to California. And that was where she'd have to go in order to have a career in the movies. California. Sometimes Frances went mad for dreaming of that place. Los Angeles. Hollywood. It was practically a shtetl out there the way the Jews kept moving west and west, always wanting more from this enormous country than it was ever ready to hand over. Some nights, as Vladimir climbed on top of her, she would mouth the word just to have it in the air: Hollywood. Hollywood. But try as she might to keep Hollywood in their Manhattan apartment, Frances could not help but move with her husband, always cut off from her fantasies of California by the reality of being beneath Vladimir, a different fantasy she could not help but respond to.

Or maybe Frances was waiting for something else. Maybe it was the children that, despite their tireless efforts, she and Vladimir could never conceive.

"To what do I owe this pleasure?" she asked her old friend. The last time she had seen Joseph Brodsky had been at the World's Fair, the day her husband had shown the world his television.

"Vell," Joseph said. "I'll get to zhe point then. I have a proposition for you, one that vill be difficult for you to turn down, I think."

"Really," she said, breathing.

"Truly," Joseph said.

Two months later, Frances put her Hollywood dreams on hold as she closed her eyes to the makeup girl and stepped in front of bright, white lights, gripping a bottle of Essoil in her clammy hands.

In many ways, becoming the face of Essoil was a dream come true for Frances. She was back on television, the way she had been at the New Amsterdam in 1929, when Vladimir had merely flicked a switch and she had bloomed onto the screen, waving to the world the way she and Pauline had always thought Pauline would wave. That was her favorite image of herself—no facial hair or moles to speak of, no panning down to her still-burgeoning thighs, only the contrast of her white skin and her dark features. Television captured her, completely. Her dark eyes catching the light, her personality wrapped up in a box, waiting for anyone to turn the switch, to untie a ribbon and reveal her.

Working again was nice, though Vladimir increasingly opposed it.

Frances didn't think it was her acting that bothered him. Actually, her husband seemed to like to see her recognized on the street, or at dinner, a photographer crowding them and their guests at El Morocco, the flash and snap of the blinding light.

It was the advertising.

"I worked so hard for *this*? This is not science, these advertisements. My father, he is turning and turning," Vladimir would tell her. He told her he couldn't bear to watch her anymore. "Selling another man's wares," he said. "Frances. We don't need the money, you know. It's all a bit preposterous."

All those nights she pictured her husband working well into the daylight hours, the sun rising over the city, the spread of pink and blue and orange outlining each new building and bringing it into the third dimension. Did he think, For what have I worked? Did he think of his father when he saw Frances smiling at him in between programs, her hand a table for Joseph Brodsky's growing empire? Frances knew that once Vladimir had thought a life of science, with its research and experimentation, its hours and hours of solitary study, paralleled a religious life. He had not counted on marrying a salesperson, which was in fact, Frances thought now, what she had become. Please, she'd say into the camera. Buy this! From me.

Television had been her husband's baby. He had conceived it and nurtured it and watched it grow. Into what?

Aside from the tension Essoil brought into life with her husband, Frances loved being close to Joseph again. It was an all-over love, one that was charged with the familiarity of each knowing exactly where the other came from. Frances imagined Joseph's old stoop, his mother's unshakable trance, a look that glazed past Frances and at the kids playing stickball on the street, until the sun went down, the cicadas screaming, mothers calling out to their children finally to come home.

At first, Esther wasn't mad for the idea of Frances doing the commercials. "You might as well have me up there then," she told Joseph suspiciously.

Esther had been making dinner when Joseph came into the kitchen to show his wife a photograph of Frances.

"Hmmm," she said. "Wouldn't people rather have a nice leggy blonde with big boobs?" she asked. "This one doesn't look so different than I do."

"Did you ever zhink, my dear," Joseph said, rubbing his eyes with one hand and holding the photo in the other, "that I chose her precisely *because* she looks like you?"

Esther put her finger to the side of her nose. "I can see this," she said. "I see what you mean."

"And, Estha," Joseph said, rubbing his head, "did I not name the entire company after you? For you. I should zhink you vould want to be sure that I sold the product in the best way I could. Zhis is the face of a woman we can all trust. Your face." He reached out and pinched his wife's cheek.

She hit his hand away.

"I should zhink, my love, that you would trust me by now to make Essoil even bigger than it already is."

Esther put her arms around his neck, pulling him toward her and crushing the photograph of Frances. "I'm an idiot," she told him, smiling. "A real schnook," she said.

Joseph threw the photograph aside and leaned back from his wife's embrace to look at her. He pressed her against the counter and kissed her.

"Joe!" Esther tried to push him away. She looked toward the dining room, where beyond, in their bedroom, the girls were watching television.

"Vhat?" he whispered, moving closer. He could hear the girls' laughter. He lifted up her housedress and slid his hand beneath her underwear.

"Joe," she whispered into his ear as he slid two callused fingers inside her. He moved them in and out of her—in the kitchen! Where the girls could appear at any moment!—and she came suddenly, with a gasp he assumed was from the pure shock of his brazen behavior.

As Esther smoothed down her dress and cleared her throat and moved toward the roast, on the counter by the sink, ready to be ringed with quartered apples and onions, she turned to Joseph, who was smiling at her with a sly grin, and said, "I think this Frances is a great idea."

Joseph nodded. "I told you," he said, smiling.

From then on Esther never voiced a problem with having Frances Gold as the spokesperson for Essoil. And nearly every time Frances came on the television, at least when Esther was not busy with the girls or preoccupied with making lists of all the things she had to do, Joseph received a breathless call, his wife on the line, wondering just when he would be coming home.

"Women of the future will clean the moon with Essoil!"

Miriam sat with her little sister in her parents' bedroom watching television, leaning on her elbows, her chin in her hands, feet kicking in the air. Miriam cocked her head at the television, watching Frances, an old friend of her father's, holding his invention on a flattened palm. Behind Frances, a dark backdrop pasted with stars, the moon, hung above her, caught on an invisible string. Miriam, nearly fifteen, looked down at her nine-year-old sister. Women of the future. All Miriam had access to was a past: the family myth of the night her father invented Essoil, when Miriam, as Esther put it, nearly killed herself with the stuff. But you helped, Joseph always told her. Without you, sugar, where would we be?

There was the not-so-distant past, when she and her mother had taken the train to New York. She rubbed her nose as she watched television. In many ways, as she'd stared at the skyline rising before them on their way into the underpass before Pennsylvania Station, Miriam had felt that *this,* this out there, was the future. Still at night when she was too terrified to sleep, she thought of driving toward that skyline, into the city. The Emerald City, she'd thought. Dorothy. It eased her fears of being old and alone in a dark apartment, television her only communication with the world.

"Mama?" On some nights, after waking with a start from a terrible dream, Miriam would pad into her parents' room, at that tender hour when she turned from a teenager back into a child. "What if I don't have anyone when I'm older? What if I'm in an apartment all by myself?" Miriam had become terrified, yet intrigued, by apartments. They seemed to be both where those who could not afford houses lived and also home to chic, single women who tossed on their pearls, grabbed their blue umbrellas, and ran out the doors to greet their lives.

Esther, her voice tired, cracking from the Winstons she smoked on the toilet in the morning while doing her crosswords, didn't lift her head. "You won't be alone, Miriam."

Joseph stirred beside her, and he knew she was trying not to sound exhausted, even though his wife had something the next day. She had become treasurer at the temple, and there was always lots of work to be done for fund-raisers and meetings. Lack of sleep, Joseph knew all too well, triggered her migraines. "You'll have boyfriends, sweetie. And Daddy and I will be here, even if you don't live with us anymore. Also Gloria will be all grown up then. Maybe you'll live near each other. Wouldn't that be nice?"

The thought of growing up filled Miriam with utter grief as she imagined a life without her parents. Would she have boyfriends? She saw herself hunched over a book. She saw herself studying and walking dreamily through rainy streets with a book under her arm. But she could not see herself at a mixer, curtsying toward a boy who would be hers. She did not see herself as she knew her mother saw her.

Joseph, half asleep next to Esther, was also momentarily jarred by what his wife had told their daughter. Because, after all, they wouldn't be there forever, would they? Who, he wondered morbidly, would go first? He hoped it would be him, because he knew that Esther could live without him. She had all her things: her teas and her committees. She had her town, where soon, he had promised, they would move. What did Joseph have? He had a house of bottles filled with liquid to clean floors.

Watching television with her sister, Miriam wondered: Who was alone in a city like that? What kind of a person? Was *she* that kind of person? Miriam rubbed her nose again, a habit she never gave up, and watched Frances smiling on television. "Women of the future will clean the moon."

Though Miriam was a thinker, she was not a dreamer. But what if she'd let herself *want?* What would her wants be? She did want to be married, to spend her life with a companion. And yet she knew this was not truly a dream of her future. Esther had always told her that her new face—well, her new nose, which gave her a new face—opened up so many possibilities for her.

The future. *Clean the moon.* Now she walked to school with her friends; they went to fairs and baseball games. Summers they spent on the lake in Maine, waterskiing, eating lobster, and munching on candy cigarettes and lipstick. Perhaps here, here was where she would like always to be, but was that a dream?

"What are you thinking about, Gloria?" Miriam said, leaning into her sister. She always wanted to be nicer to her sister. Just last week she had been supposed to take Gloria to the spring festival at school. Gloria was sick with the flu, so Joseph had gone with Miriam. In an attempt to be kind, she'd gotten two red balloons, one for her, one for her sister. Over the course of the afternoon, Miriam had accidentally let go of one of the balloons, and she and Joseph had watched it rise away above the throng of people busy winning goldfish and stuffed bears. There goes Gloria's balloon! Miriam, who had not even cared to have a balloon, had said to her father. He had looked down at her in disbelief. How do you know that one was Gloria's? he'd asked her. Miriam had answered, Didn't you see it? There it is! And they had both turned to watch the balloon, a tiny dot still rising into the sky.

Gloria looked up at Miriam. "I'm thinking that there is Frances, but also, Frances was on the phone earlier. And she's also in New York. How can she be in all these places at one time?" Gloria asked.

"She's really only in one place," Miriam said. "She's really just wherever she is—this was taped earlier, and she called from wherever she just was."

Gloria nodded, but Miriam could tell that she hadn't given a good explanation. What would she be good at? she wondered. Miriam hoped that, like Frances, like her father, she would be so good at something, whatever it was, that she could one day effortlessly say this thing she had become was exactly what she had always dreamed she'd be.

Two hundred miles south of the Brodskys, in New York City's Upper East Side, David Bloom, home from prep school for the Thanksgiving holiday and waiting for Seymour's company car to come take him to Brooklyn, heard a scream from his mother's bedroom. When he ran in to see what the matter was, David saw Sarah was throwing silk pillows at the television, which was playing an advertisement with that short, squat lady he had met at the World's Fair. The sleeves of Sarah's robe, embroidered with green dragonflies, were twisting like black ribbons caught in the wind.

Women of the future! The woman in the advertisement beamed. Now the lady from the World's Fair held out her hand to the invisible audience. *The moon!*

Mary arrived just as Sarah screeched again. After Sarah was done with the pillows, she began throwing pens and paperweights at the television until the housekeeper had to hold her down.

"Please, Mrs. Bloom," Mary told her employer. "Not in front of the boy."

Sarah kicked and flailed.

"You have to stop." But Sarah's rigid body would not give way to Mary's strong touch.

David watched his mother's fiery rant turn slowly to quiet sobbing as she held Sarah, her head in Mary's lap. She stroked her damp, blond hair. "There, there," Mary said.

"Are you all right, Mum?" David went and peered over at his mother.

She nodded from the generous pillow of Mary's lap. "Yes, dear," she said.

"Can I get you anything from downstairs?" he asked her. "A sandwich or something?"

"Is your voice turning?" Sarah asked him sharply.

David looked at his mother blankly. "Turning?"

Sarah began to cry again, softly, like a little girl. "We're all getting older, aren't we, Mary?" She wrenched her arm away from the housekeeper and sat up. "Women of the future . . . how ridiculous. You don't know how lucky you are to be a boy, David," she said.

Sarah looked as if she were struggling to remember something.

"Everything okay?" Mary asked.

"I was just thinking of my mother," Sarah said. "And then I was thinking about our house, on Long Island, but now I can't remember the name of the street. I lived on that street for sixteen years and I can't remember the name! What was the name of the bloody street?" For the second time in the last half hour, she threw herself back onto the bed and began to weep.

"I don't know," Mary said. "You'll remember it soon."

"David, darling, what was the name of the street?"

"I don't know either," he said.

"Think!" Sarah said. She looked her son in the eye. "I'm losing my mind," she said calmly. "Don't let me lose my mind, David."

"I'm hungry," he said. He did not know how to answer his mother.

"Do you promise?" Sarah asked.

"*Okay,*" David said. "Do you want a sandwich?"

"A sandwich? No, David," she said. "A sandwich. Women of the future eat sandwiches?"

Possibly, David thought. Why wouldn't they? He turned to head downstairs, leaving Sarah in Mary's lap. He was tiring of his mother's theatrics. What was so awful about the present? His mother, he knew, was a woman filled with regret. David opened the icebox and took out roast beef and pastrami, Swiss and provolone, Jersey tomatoes, lettuce, French mustard. He slapped down a piece of rye bread and piled the sandwich high. To the moon! David laughed, topping the sandwich with another piece of bread. He thought of his grandmother waiting for him in that pink shop, the sound of hair dryers drowning out the roar of the highway. That shop was what she had wanted, more than anything. While his mother cried upstairs, David Bloom ate the sandwich in under five minutes, wiped his hands of crumbs, and went outside on the silent stoop to wait for the car to bring him to Brooklyn.

Not twenty blocks away from the now calmed Sarah Bloom, Frances Gold had the television on in the living room while she read the paper. She read "Dear Maggie," which was becoming truly horrid, if you asked Frances. All those intimate letters that this Maggie had once responded to with empathy were turning into issues of etiquette. Just last week, when a woman's letter had reached a fevered pitch about feeling like a terrible mother, Dear Maggie had ended her response: *A truly well-mannered woman exerts her good manners most upon her husband and children, and a gracious nature through daily example is, of course, the finest influence for good that there is in the world.* It seemed that she—and just who was this woman anyhow?—was going to help all the troubled women of the world act appropriately.

Well, there were certainly enough new aids—refrigerators, Westinghouse washing machines with punch card controls, electric dryers—to help with domestic life nowadays. How much easier would her own mother's life have been had these luxuries been around—not that they could have afforded them—when Frances was young? And perhaps, thought Frances, being outwardly acceptable, her house and children sparkly and clean, a woman can be more inwardly acceptable. To herself, thought Frances. Acceptable to herself. She thought of Etta, narrowing her eyes at the men whose letters she wrote to all the people in the old country. Etta did not alter her letters: she wrote whatever polished stories and lies she was told to and sent them to the families back home. Dear Maggie's job was to respond to her writers, to offer them hope and, by proxy, to offer hope to an entire readership. She seemed to be saying that acceptable acts of outward expression would change an unstable or unhappy inner life, if only her simple guidelines were correctly followed. Who was more of a liar, Frances couldn't say.

Today's column was a response to a poor woman who had written that she felt ugly and untouchable. Maggie wrote: *Why not try wearing gloves! Gloves are worn during the cocktail hour, and at least the right glove is removed entirely while dining, then worn again for the remainder of the evening.*

Phooey! thought Frances, about to revise her generous opinion and hurl the paper across the room, when she heard her own voice on the television.

Who *is* that? She looked up from the paper and watched herself looking out at herself. *Women of the future will clean the moon!* Is that what I look like? Frances thought, still holding the paper. *With Essoil!*

Frances sighed. She was no different. Not only in what she was saying but how she said it. In an advertisement. If you buy this, you will feel better. She'd had such different plans: theater and maybe, maybe, if only she'd let herself think it, the movies. Frances willed herself not to remember her turn on Seymour's stage. How is it, she thought, that what we want just gets pushed back and pushed back until here we are, approaching forty. Every night, still, she couldn't help herself: "Vladi, I want to be in the movies. Let's move to Hollywood and live in the canyons with an enormous blue pool in our own backyard. Vladi, let's move to Los Angeles and live by the beach. Let's take the train out and watch the world fly by as we go west. I want to be in pictures! Vladi, are you listening?"

"I want to go!" she'd say. "It will get me off of TV," she teased.

But there was no leaving New York City for Vladimir. His focus was on the here and now, on further developing his Kinescope. Who was disappointing whom? Frances wondered now as she watched herself smile into the living room. Could she give this up? she wondered, give up the way that wherever she went women recognized her? Don't I know you from somewhere? they'd ask, tilting their heads, pushing their glasses down their noses, and leaning in for a closer look. What's your maiden name? Frances always nearly laughed. What was it about being on television that made people think they knew you from somewhere long ago and far away? I don't think so, she would say. No, I'm afraid not, she'd tell them.

Essoil advertisements spurred other product advertisements, which in turn spurred even more, which created an entire industry. There was no mistaking Joseph's achievement in both the Essoil campaign and the world of advertising. Journalists lined up at his home and at the factory to talk to him. Janie Silvers, who had bought those bottles from him nine years before, told *Television Magazine,* "Joseph Brodsky never gave up. He deserves all his good fortune because he never stopped trying."

Joseph began to consider moving to Maine and making Esther's dream come true.

When Miriam entered college, over six million bottles of Essoil were sold each year. And by the time she graduated, in 1952, one would have been hard-pressed to find an American home that did not have a bottle nestled in the broom closet between mop and pail, quietly waiting for the opportunity to clean up each and every American mess.

CHAPTER 16

Charmed: Miriam and David, 1948–1957

IF IT HADN'T BEEN FOR Miriam's childhood friend Betsy Randolph, Miriam and David may never have met again. Betsy lived in the house next to Miriam's parents' summer home at Sebago Lake in Maine. On the other side of the Brodsky house was Mrs. Gifford, a deaf lady with a turned-over canoe on her front porch, who gave the girls a magnet in the shape of a horseshoe that separated the different kinds of sand. Sebago Lake was ringed by special purple sand, nearly black, and by July, Miriam and Betsy had filled countless jam jars with it. Along with the empty yahrtzeits Esther filled with tiny, broken seashells, the jars of layered sand lined the sills of the kitchen and the screened-in front porch.

When Betsy, two years older than Miriam, went off to Smith, Miriam insisted she would never follow her there. Not in a million years, thought Miriam. Another four years of Betsy Randolph: Betsy, who always got the catcalls as the two girls walked to the country store for candy lipstick and sugar cigarettes. Betsy, with her little white shorts and halter top, her long, stringy hair highlighted white from the sun. Her bare, tanned feet, toenails with chipped pink polish. Joseph would never have let either of his daughters go without shoes in the street. The dirt, he'd cry, holding his heart, as if bits of dried mud and granules of sand were actually cracking open his chest. The filth.

Miriam had always known she would go to college at one of the Seven Sisters—it was how she was raised, along with ballroom dancing instruction and never cutting her hair above her shoulders—Esther had insisted on it. But when it came time to look at colleges, Miriam could not decide between Smith and Wellesley. She felt that Wellesley had the lovelier campus, but it was awfully close to home. As much as she loved Boston—the different neighborhoods: Italian, Jewish, Irish, Black; the walk over the Charles into Cambridge—she thought it far better to get out from under her mother for a spell. Live independently, she said to the mirror, holding her head up high and looking down at herself looking down.

But it would be better to be near her mother, thought Miriam, than to remain beneath Betsy Randolph. And so it was decided: Wellesley it would be. When Betsy invited her for a weekend at Smith during their winter carnival to get high and just let loose, Miriam decided she would go simply for the fun of it.

Betsy had been pinned—by Ben Belmont, a senior—and so, that weekend in Northampton, they went to a Sigma Chi party.

"I can't believe you'll be graduating!" Betsy screamed, hugging Dulcy Bloom, also raised to be a Smith girl, when she sauntered up to her at the punch bowl. Betsy placed her arms around the girl's neck, her eyes flashing first with approval and then with envy she could not conceal. And it was Dulcy, Miriam noted, who pulled away first from their embrace, introducing her little brother, David Bloom, a freshman at Amherst.

Betsy pumped David's hand. Miriam peered out from behind her friend and waited for her introduction. When she saw it was not forthcoming, Miriam poked her friend in the side.

"Oh," Betsy said, still beaming at Dulcy. "Miriam." Betsy held her hand out limply toward Miriam and waved it for a moment toward the Bloom siblings. "Dulcy is a good friend of Ben's. And this is David. Aren't you a swimmer?" she asked him.

David Bloom was obviously troubled by this introduction. "Yes," he said. "I suppose I am."

So humble, thought Miriam. And then she pictured this boy before her in goggles and swim trunks, cutting the blue water with his strong arms, pulling himself up out of the pool and dripping water onto the cement. At that moment, Miriam ached for the scent of chlorine, and she wished she could smell it now on David Bloom. She sniffed up against him.

"Hi," he said just to Miriam, as if they were two children among adults, just as they had been nearly a decade ago at the World's Fair. Though he had no awareness of that moment, David had noticed Miriam when she first entered the room, how, with her hair pulled back in a chignon, her cheekbones looked like they would leap from her face. He could tell, even with it pulled back so severely, that her hair beamed with good health. "I really love your hairdo." He reached up to bring a strand that had miraculously sprung loose out of her eyes.

Miriam's heart: *bang bang bang bang bang.* Could he hear it? "Thank you." She looked down. He looked just like Orson Welles. Just like him. "You look a bit like Orson Welles," she said. "But I imagine people say that all the time."

"No," he said. "I've never been told that before." Flashes of light burst into David's eyes. Orson Welles, the genius. At seventeen, he already saw himself becoming terribly unlike the man he thought he would be. Perhaps this was the girl who could see through his athletic exterior to the very core of him—okay, he might as well say it, to his *heart.*

They stayed near each other the entire evening, watching as the older students flitted and preened, smoked cigarettes and got drunk. And when Betsy came by to retrieve Miriam as if she were a package waiting to be exchanged at the post office for a slip of pink paper, David kissed Miriam's cheek, lingering there long enough to tell her that, had they been alone, his lips would have searched for her mouth.

That night sealed it for Miriam, and the following autumn it was at Northampton, not Wellesley, where Miriam arrived, bringing with her many expectations. Along with her educational hopes—if it was not a hunger for learning Miriam possessed, it was certainly a desire to be learned—was an expectation of the affection of a swimmer named David Bloom.

And yet, by the time autumn came, David Bloom had already taken up with another girl, Asher Brook. And when she arrived at Smith,

Miriam had been so caught up in the moment—the clubs, the teas, the dieting, the girls, the mixers—she had forgotten the past intensity of her own feelings. By the time things with Asher had petered out—or rather, by the time Asher had fled to New York City to become an actress with a set of Inez Bloom's sherry glasses—and David was single, he ran into Miriam on the Smith campus in another's embrace. A Harvard man, he recalled having heard from one of her dorm mates. His sister had told David she was the heiress to the Essoil fortune. And just as Dulcy had said it—*Essoil*—David had imagined an empty room with billowing curtains, shining with purity. He could smell the fresh, sanitized scent of pine, and it made him remember his grandmother's beauty shop, the way light caught the surface of everything and gleamed. It had gotten so that, when David so much as caught a glimpse of Miriam, he felt as if he were inhaling freshness itself, along with the best parts of his childhood spent with his grandmother. He would look at her and see cleanliness, white, white sheets, a diffuse morning light.

In her four years of college, Miriam managed to develop interests besides boys and pretty hats. She studied Spanish literature and Spanish linguistics. Struggling over conjugation, and attempting to translate such foreign texts always made Miriam think of her father and his ceaseless efforts not only to learn English better but to sound more American. Miriam knew she could never sound Spanish, which may be why when she graduated, she decided she wanted to go not to Spain but to Costa Rica. To the forest, she'd said. Monkeys. She imagined them swinging on branches high above her head. She imagined parrots. Miriam lived there for half a year teaching English, and it was there that she met Enrique Lopez.

Had it been the foreignness that attracted her to Enrique? Simply to hear her name uttered in the throes of passion on a Spanish-speaking tongue? Or was it the way he stunned her with his knowledge of biology: That's a colibri, he'd said at Lake Caño Negro. He had shown her around a foreign land, and she adored him for it. In Costa Rica, she attempted to twist her tongue away from her lisping Castilian Spanish, and as she moved more and more toward her South American Spanish, she thought of staying. But the sad eyes of her father asking her why would always bring her back home. And so Miriam thought about taking Enrique with her, though she knew that, were she to set up house with him in some New England town or city, his accent would annoy her. All that was so natural to him in South America—from the way he dressed to the manner in which he twirled his fingers—would be out of place.

Miriam and Enrique had been together nearly the whole time she had lived in Costa Rica. Here is a lemur, he had said. Here is a long-tailed monkey. Once she had been so overwhelmed by him—his difference and at the same time his *sameness* to her—that she had thrown her arms around him out there in the middle of that muggy forest beneath a sky of wet green leaves. And though she dated many boys upon her return to the States, the way she and Enrique had fallen to the ground, groping each other like wildlife, would give her cause to shiver, and she always imagined ending up in the arms of her Costa Rican lover.

David Bloom had his share of girlfriends after Asher Brook. Esmé Perez was a dark Venezuelan actress with a proclivity toward slamming him over the head with her purse when she'd had more than three drinks. David had once been delighted by Esmé's negative effect on his family. At first, when the two were at parties uptown or slumming in Spanish Harlem, David wouldn't want to make the long trip downtown to his little place on Jane Street, where there were never any clean sheets and no one was there to serve them breakfast each morning. And so he would slip into his parents' East Side brownstone and sneak his girl-friend into his childhood bedroom. The two of them would slide into his twin bed, the sheets drawn tightly across their bodies as if they were two frogs pinned to a resin-filled dissection tray.

Very little cheered David more than the expression on Sarah Bloom's face when he and Esmé came down for breakfast, David in his boyhood terry robe, the sleeves to his elbows. Always barefoot, Esmé would come down in one of his dress shirts, her burgundy nipples pressed against the light shirt cloth that reached just below her underwear.

Sarah feigned disaffection with her son's brazen behavior. "Good morning, dear," she said and flicked open the *Times,* then brought the fresh-squeezed orange juice to her lips with a trembling hand. "What will you have for breakfast?" she asked, never looking at him. "And you, dear?" she said in the vague direction of Esmé.

Esmé extended her long legs and wiggled her scarlet-painted toes at David's feet. She brought her long arms high over her head, the tails of David's shirt rising above her panties, their stark whiteness somehow more obscene than black would have been against her skin. "For breakfast?" She stretched and yawned. "Let's see." She stood up and went to stand behind David's chair.

That was when Sarah looked up from "Dear Maggie." "Yes, for breakfast," she said flatly.

Esmé leaned over David and put her arms around his neck. He felt her breasts, cushioning the base of his skull, and he wondered whether her cleavage was visible to his mother. "A bit of sausage?" She giggled into David's thick hair, and he chuckled.

"Mary, darling," Sarah said, "would you please serve my son's whore some sausage?"

And then, turning to Esmé and David, she said, "I'm assuming you'll take eggs with your pork?"

Enrique Lopez, Miriam was sad to admit, had not been the one for her. This became all too clear when, on his way to New York, where he was interviewing for a job at the World Bank, Enrique briefly visited with Miriam's parents in their new house in Maine. The previous year they had bought a large ranch-style house above Baxter Boulevard that looked out over Casco Bay.

Before Enrique had arrived, Esther took her daughter aside and said, "I hope you have not let this man, well, I hope he has not been *inside* you," she said. "Because that won't do at all. First of all, you realize he isn't Jewish."

"I realize this," Miriam said, sticking her ring finger in her mouth.

Esther rubbed her temples.

Joseph stood in front of the open fridge eating from a carton of Brigham's chocolate ribbon. "Essie, *please!*" he said.

"What?" she screamed to her husband, in the kitchen. "You wouldn't catch a South *American* girl just hopping in the sack with any boy. Those Catholics don't *do* that. That's why he's going with an American. Americans have reputations." Esther collapsed onto the living room couch—the palest pink chintz—and brought her hand to her head. "Miriam," she said. "Fetch me an aspirin before you kill me, will you, dear?"

Ultimately, Miriam would always listen to her mother. In fact, Miriam had not had intercourse with Enrique, though she was bewildered by the separation of this act from the many others that the two had performed together. For hours they would lie around touching, kissing, licking, *feeling*. Enrique too seemed confused about these boundaries, and that night, sneaking into her bedroom while Joseph and Esther were asleep in their twin beds, he tried to make his confusion felt. He did this with such brute force that Miriam pushed him out of the bed, and a rather chaotic scuffle ensued, ending with one of Esther's prized Hummel figurines—the country doctor with his stethoscope—getting broken to bits.

"Huh!" Miriam was aghast. The altercation ended with the young couple on their hands and knees, for neither love nor sex but only to pick up the shards of porcelain.

Miriam demanded her boyfriend's departure, and he left the house in the middle of the night without so much as a word of good-bye to her parents.

The next morning Esther inquired after the man and Miriam made an excuse about a late-night phone call, a sick mother, an emergency at the office—one too many things to go wrong at once, if you asked Joseph, who sat down at the breakfast table across from his daughter and his wife. Miriam's face was still red and swollen from a night of crying. Even her nose seemed to have puffed up, for once making its presence known, as if to honor her grief.

Esther put her hand over her daughter's, and Miriam noticed her aging hands. Looking up at her mother, she saw it in her face as well, how the skin now hung more loosely, wrinkles beginning to blaze a system of trails across her cheeks. Mommy, she wanted to say. She wanted to reach out to her. Instead, Miriam thought how she herself was not getting younger. What if Enrique *had* been the one and she hadn't even noticed? Had she let the right man slip away? And at that moment she remembered David Bloom, a large boy from the swim team, walking away from her. Would she always look at men from this perspective? she wondered, beginning to cry again.

"Such a shame. Enrique was such a nice boy," Esther said. "Your father and I were talking, just now, about how much we liked him. What did you do, Miriam? Must you drive *everyone* away?"

Esmé Perez helped David triumph, if temporarily, in the silent war waged between mother and son for the unprecedented resentment each held toward the other. They had so clearly robbed each other of happiness. But David Bloom's affairs of the heart had consequences similar to Miriam's.

However swell Esmé was on his arm at a party's beginning, by its end—they always stayed too damn long at these affairs, forgetting both how much they had drunk and how severely what they drank affected them—she was a dreadful sight. There was the hissing and the crying, the mascara running down the face, and then the snakeskin bag that without fail made its way over David's head at least once. Ultimately, he got sick to death of being beaten by his girlfriend. His own physical injury outweighed the psychic misery he knew his girlfriend caused his mother.

So one day David marched into Esmé's rehearsal to tell her he was leaving. After making sure she was not holding a hard or heavy object, he simply said, "We're through, baby. Through." His right hand cut the air, and he waited—a little hopefully, as he had not lost his penchant for the dramatic—for the scene to break open.

What followed stunned David: Esmé began to laugh. In fact, she hooted and cackled, slapping her leg as she wiped at her eyes. This was a reaction for which he had not rehearsed, so he looked around to see the other actors bemusedly watching the scene.

Head held high, David walked out of the theater, that terrible girl's laughter behind him until he opened the door and headed into the lobby and then out into the daylight of the street, the heavy outer door clicking closed behind him.

Miriam Brodsky and David Bloom were privately mulling over their dashed affairs when, in 1956, they crashed into each other on the corner of Forty-second and Broadway, one of the busiest intersections in the country. David, now a theater producer like his father, was coming from a lunch meeting with other producers who were talking about talking to more producers to get more producers to produce *Gypsy*. Miriam, who had become a translator for the UN, was getting tickets to *My Fair Lady* because her mother would be driving down this weekend. You don't go to the theater enough, Miri, Esther had said. But Miriam knew this was more an excuse for her to take the trip to Manhattan to see her daughter. "Why don't the boys you date ever take you to a nice show?" Esther had asked after telling Miriam that everyone— everyone!—was talking about Rex Harrison, and Esther could not wait to see this production that had all of Portland buzzing.

Why they were both walking backward—later Miriam would say she heard a large bang that had made her look skyward, but David would always maintain that someone had passed out behind him and screamed as she crumpled to the ground—is still unknown, but they backed right into each other. They snapped around, coming face-to-face on a street corner in Manhattan.

"Miriam Brodsky?"

She was dressed in a red suit with a matching red hat, and she looked sensational. He checked for a wedding ring and found her hands to be concealed by black kid gloves. David wondered at that moment why they hadn't ended up dating in college, because he had really enjoyed her that one evening. Simply the way Miriam gestured had delighted him, and the self-conscious way she held her drink and her cigarette he found terribly chic.

Miriam held the top of her hat and looked up at David. *David Bloom,* she thought. *David Bloom.* And once again: *bang bang bang bang.* She had to laugh at herself. He was not going to dupe her again, no sir. Since then he had long faded into only an idea: this boy who had made her change her mind about college and had taken her from her mother's clutches.

"David Bloom," she said, shaking his hand.

They smiled at each other, oblivious to the pedestrian traffic around them.

"Move it!" someone screamed as he passed by. David put his hand at the small of Miriam's back and guided her to the curb.

☙

Sixteen candlelit dinners, seven Broadway shows, four walks in Central
Park, one hundred and eighteen turns around around the rink at Rockefeller Center, one visit to the Met, two breakfasts, a brunch at the Plaza,
a total of ninety days after they ran into each other on Forty-second and
Broadway, one night at the Shubert (*not* his father's theater, he'd made
sure of it) during the intermission of *Bells Are Ringing,* David got down
on his knees and asked Miriam Brodsky to be his forever. By the time
the lights had flashed on and off, and the audience members were heading back to their seats for the second act, Miriam had told him yes.

   Despite the dirty money on David's side and the family of peasants
on Miriam's, their union appeared to be a perfect match. No one—not
Joseph, not Seymour, not Frances Gold—told them how they had met
nearly two decades earlier on the grounds of the World's Fair and that,
for better or for worse, their families were as stitched together as an
American quilt.

Not a year later, in the summer of 1957, the year Seymour's play *Separate
Tables* won the Tony for Best Actress, *Bells Are Ringing* cleaning up the rest,
Miriam Brodsky and David Bloom were married in Portland, Maine.

   But that makes it sound easy. It was not.

   "Mother," Miriam said into the phone, the day after she had called
to tell her parents the good news. Already the planning had begun.
Esther insisted on having it in Portland.

   "It's *my* wedding!" Esther said.

   "But it's *my* wedding," said Miriam.

   "My mother had hers when I married Joseph, and now I'm going to
have mine," Esther said. "In Portland."

   Miriam could just see it, her urbane friends, David's erudite family,
all riding up to the sticks for her wedding. She'd worked so hard to
become a New Yorker, with her empty fridge and her little brooches
and never a dinner before eight, and now her mother was practically
dragging her to Nova Scotia.

   "Maine is where we're from," Esther said.

   "I'm from Boston," Miriam said.

   "I married your father in Portland, and now you're going to marry
David there as well. It's part of our tradition."

Joseph heard her and shook his head at the horrible memory of Esther's mother shouting orders at his future wife just moments before the ceremony. Stand up straight, for God's sake, Sylvia had said. Don't touch anything. Your gloves. Your gloves! And after the wedding, Joseph now recalled, his mother-in-law had gone to bed and hadn't risen until he and Esther came back from their honeymoon in the mountains outside Montreal. And when they'd returned, glowing from sun, sex, and mountain air, the first thing Sylvia said was: The flowers were nearly dead. How could you have dead flowers at your wedding? Too bad for you both, now you'll have a black life.

Well, it hadn't been a black life, Joseph thought as he went over to Esther, who was still on the phone with their daughter.

"No, Miriam," she said. "Absolutely not."

Joseph had to laugh to himself; the only thing he had heard Esther utter during the whole conversation was no. He was about to interrupt her for one moment, perhaps remove her from her state of contrariness, but he let it pass. Joseph would only get in the middle, and that, he knew from experience, had disastrous consequences.

"'Dear Maggie' says it's where the mother of the bride wants it. And she says there absolutely must be three layers of linens. Three, do you hear me? I just went out and bought *Dear Maggie's Guide to the Perfect Day* this morning. It's tremendously helpful, Miriam. Would you like me to send you a copy?"

"No, thank you," she said. Miriam sat in the living room of her Murray Hill apartment and watched her roommate watering the spider plant by the window. Her roommate was humming, which always annoyed Miriam. She would tell her, please stop, but she continued on and on, as if she didn't know she was doing it. Soon I will be living with my *husband,* thought Miriam. David Bloom, she thought, trying not to giggle, remembering the boy in college who had pulled that strand of wayward hair from her face. "But, Mother," she said. "And . . ."

It was useless. Miriam flicked open the paper, and there was "Dear Maggie" on page 4: *When moving to a new community, always be sure to bring letters of introduction. When the letters are given to the most prominent citizens, you will have an already made position. . . .*

How dated, thought Miriam. She remembered coming home from New York with her mother from getting her nose fixed and how she had cried and cried and then written "Dear Maggie" about the nature of a girl's beauty. How ridiculous. This anonymous person giving us advice? This stranger's guidelines are informing my wedding.

Her mother prattled on. "Chicken, never, never fish. We must have chicken. The fish is never fresh enough, even here in Maine. You just never know. The club does a wonderful chicken Italienne. I also love the cordon bleu. We'll have to do a tasting. When will you be coming for a *tasting*? Their stuffed pea pods are marvelous. Remember, we must invite the Cohens, but let's just pray they don't bring that son of theirs. A *drug addict* I hear. Did you know that, Miriam? Did you ever? Are you listening?"

"Yes, Mother," Miriam said. She thought she could make out her roommate humming "La Marseillaise." It was driving her bananas.

"Does that sound good to you, then, Miriam?" Esther asked. "Because, my darling, I want you to have the wedding of your dreams. It's your wedding, you know. This is your big day."

After the ceremony at the new temple, where, standing beneath the flowering chuppa, David Bloom successfully crushed the glass, whose meaning—virility? the frailty of relationships? the irrevocability of marriage?—he could only speculate upon, both sides of the family went to the Portland Country Club for dinner and dancing.

The three grandmothers—Seymour's mother, Inez Bloom; Esther's mother, Sylvia Weinstein; and Joseph's mother, Selma Brodsky—stood around the buffet. Inez hovered over the caviar, lemon, and onion, and David knew she was trying to make sure the women didn't gobble it all up and leave none for the other guests. Inez was very sensitive to the people there—and, David was happy to note, they did have some fine guests. The man who invented television and his wife, the woman in all those commercials for Essoil. Betty Comden. Vincent Sardi, Jr. Agnes Moorehead. And Inez had invited Mae West.

She pulled David aside.

"Just look at her!" she said, offering up the chopped liver and pickle as she watched Miss West, surrounded by three old men. "Like a *leetle whore*. I won't speak to her!" she told David, who had several other things on his mind. "I won't!"

David looked over to see Mae West, one hand gripping a glass of champagne, the other moving animatedly, her huge breasts bouncing, her large thighs dimpled with cellulite and careening beneath her satin dress as she moved.

"I don't care *who* she is," she hissed at David. "It's insulting! One needs a structured fabric—organza or taffeta—at her age."

"You're nuts," David said. He remembered the first time he had met Mae West, the way she had rocked her hips. Her body was threatening and inviting at the same time, and these two antithetical emotions had merged in David, creating a reaction in him that he now thought of as chemical.

"Is that so?" Inez said. "Nuts? I'll tell you who's nuts, mister. Just look who you're marrying! *A Pole!*" she said, leaning in. "You could have had anyone. Anyone!"

"Stop it," David said. "Please," he said. He rubbed his temples. "Anyway, the Brodskys are from Russia." All the pressure of the planning was culminating in the terrible pressure of the actual day. Plus, David was supposed to toast his wife. It's what you do, Seymour had said. And now he was getting a bit of stage fright.

That Mae West had set him up. He had thought it would be that thrilling with all the girls he would encounter. There had been quite a few, and now, would he be giving them up? David saw all the women he had had then as a long chain of carbons, each beautiful, voluptuous, and interchangeable, only he had never once seen a woman shake her body that way again. His wife was built more like his mother—when Miriam rocked her hips she seemed to be mocking David and not herself.

Inez raised her nose. "Where the Brodskys hail from? Believe me, it once was Poland," she said. "Anyway, so be it," she said. Inez patted him on the cheek, though it felt, looked, and sounded more like three successive slaps. "At least you didn't marry into the theater." She looked both ways. "Not like your father." Inez shook her head and turned back to the buffet so Selma Brodsky would not be left alone with the caviar. "Have you ever seen a villager alone with a dish of beluga? Not pretty. Anyway, Davey, thank God you didn't marry an actress," she said to her grandson and returned to the buffet to protect it from the peasants.

Esther milled around the room, greeting the guests, who gushed over the flowers, the food, even the lighting, which had been placed strategically to eliminate all shadows. Now she munched on smoked salmon and capers, and explained to Joseph about the one thing that had gone seriously wrong.

"I still can't get over that they weren't married by Rabbi Skye. He married us! It's part of our tradition, don't you think?"

"Vell," Joseph said. "It was a beautiful ceremony, Esther. I don't know so much from tradition. You're starting to sound like your mother."

"I am not, Joe," she said. "So what he wasn't the temple rabbi any longer?" she continued. "Does this place remember just how big our checks are each August? And I am the secretary, you know. How could they insist on Rabbi Bernstein? Miriam has no history with him, none at all. It all makes me just a little sad is all." Esther stood up straight. "Otherwise, it was just perfect." She popped a cucumber and cream cheese coin into her mouth. "Don't just stand there, Joe, we need to go mingle with our guests!"

As his wife said this, Joseph looked across the room and saw that Irving Berlin had just arrived. Here! Joseph watched him pat Seymour on the back. Why, it was just like looking in the mirror, though Berlin was at least a decade older. Do lives lived parallel make you look the same? thought Joseph. Or does what we look like inform our parallel lives?

He broke away from Esther and introduced himself, holding out his hand.

"A lovely girl," Mr. Berlin said, smiling in Miriam's direction. "I'm so sorry to have missed the ceremony. We got up here terribly late. We've rented a house in Bar Harbor for the week. Such a happy coincidence. Seymour is a good friend."

Joseph smiled, his heart soaring. "I'm Joseph Brodsky," he said. "Father of zhe bride," he said. He couldn't deviate from his plan, even though he had an idea that Mr. Berlin was aware of who he was.

"She's just charming." He smiled sympathetically. "I've known David for quite a while. They make a beautiful couple."

"Father of zhe bride! A-rah-tah-tah." Joseph did a quick two-step and socked Mr. Berlin on the back. "How's that for a musical?"

Irving Berlin laughed. He looked down at his shoes.

"You vant it?" Joseph asked. "Go ahead. Please take it. It's yours," he said.

Irving Berlin smiled. "How much you want for it?" he asked. He took out his wallet and pretended to pull out a twenty.

Joseph threw back his head and laughed. "A gift!" he said, pushing away the money with both hands. Twenty bucks. For a title. How many bottles of cleanser would he have once had to sell to make twenty dollars? Still he thought of it in terms of product sold. It was a joke now— his company sold millions upon millions of bottles of Essoil a year. Joseph was thankful for this and for Irving Berlin, who stood before him now, at his elder daughter's wedding. "For you," he said, with his best salesman voice, one he had used for years and years, a pleading he no longer needed. "For you, free," he said.

"Why, thank you," Mr. Berlin said, saluting Joseph and then bowing. "It's a pleasure to be here." He turned to make his way into the crowd.

Joseph watched Frances Gold running after Mr. Berlin, her husband in tow. "Excuse me!" he could hear her scream. "Mr. Berlin!" Joseph had to laugh. He hoped she'd catch him.

"You can't catch a man with a gun!" Esther screamed behind them. Then she looked side to side as she clamped her hand over her mouth in disbelief that she had actually said it out loud.

When the meal was finished, the tinkling of silverware fading as people began to think of dancing, David Bloom readied himself to make his toast. He had planned this for weeks now, how he would rise from the table and recite his ode to his new wife for all the guests.

Just as he stood, holding up his champagne glass high in the air, he heard the sound of his mother's voice make its way through the microphone.

"How *could* he?" the voice said.

David looked from side to side. Where was she? He looked up at the ceiling. At first he thought he was dreaming, as he had on many occasions he'd rather have forgotten.

Perhaps *I* am the only one hearing this, David thought. He squeezed his eyes tight as he had when he was a boy, hiding in the school yard, believing if he could see no one, then no one could see him. As when he watched his mother crying, pacing her enormous bedroom, her silk robe billowing out behind her as she manically recited Shakespeare.

"Better he should marry a gentile than a Polish Jew!" the voice said now.

Opening his eyes, David looked out to see the astounded faces of all the guests as his mother, oblivious to her audience, whispered in his father's ear, and directly into the mike.

Seymour sat up straight and, though no one could see this because of the linen—Esther had gotten her three layers—that draped over the table and skimmed the floor, he kicked Sarah in the shin, hard.

"Ouch!" Sarah screamed, again into the microphone.

In this very moment, David realized that Sarah Bloom was unconquerable. David recognized his mother would always win the public war that had been waged for so many years between them.

How many years? thought Seymour. How many years of this?

Joseph was furious. Why, it was as if she were calling his family a bunch of filthy kikes. He stood up and scanned the room, smiling despite himself at table 3, where Irving Berlin sat, his arm hooked behind the chair of a woman, his wife, Joseph paused to assume. He saw Frances look down at her plate, elbows on the table, hands over her ears.

Then Joseph looked down the long head table at the woman who had caused the grave affront. And he spotted Seymour Bloom, seated next to her.

"You dirty mobster! You gangster!" Joseph screamed. His finger pointed straight at his new in-laws.

Seymour had had quite enough himself. If David loved this woman, fine, but that she was related to the Terrier, he could never really get over it. Was his son trying to spite him? For the first time in his life, Seymour lost control.

He stood and pointed back at Joseph. "It was *your* brother who sucked me into that business in the first place!" he screamed.

Sarah threw her head back, finishing her drink. "Mob?" she said, her hand mockingly poised at her breast. "Where?"

Esther dropped a fork and leaned down to retrieve it. Joseph saw her disappear and wished he could crawl under the table with her, just the two of them again, alone beneath a linen-covered bell jar. Two fireflies, he thought, remembering Miriam handing him a jar to punch air holes in. He imagined him and Esther cross-legged beneath the table, speaking to each other silently, through a code of blinking lights.

A collective hush fell over the club, a communal sucking in of breath.

Joseph looked away from his wife and her dropped flatware, and trembled with rage. This was his daughter's wedding. Had he not worked his whole life to give her this day? He looked over at Miriam now, her face a pricked balloon, its artificially tiny features deflated. Let's set them free, she had said, when the fireflies had stopped their flashing. I think they're dying, Miriam had said, and they had unscrewed the lid and set the insects free. Even Joseph had been shocked by how slowly they had crawled out of the jar before realizing they could fly. Had he not gone door-to-door for fifteen years so that he would never have to see his daughter look this way? He would be calm, Joseph told himself.

Esther slowly climbed back up to her seat, polishing the fork with her napkin.

I will remain calm for my daughter, Joseph thought, lifting his head toward the band.

But it was David Bloom who really saved the day by doing the only thing he knew to do, which was to rise above it, as if the wedding party table were a stage. He pulled out his chair and stood on it, holding up his glass.

"To my beautiful wife," he said. He looked over at Miriam with adoration. "The woman who completes me." That would be it. He would not get to recite his monologue, not tonight anyway.

Miriam looked decorously down at her plate. It's like it never happened, she thought, as the band began to play—*You must remember this. A kiss is still a kiss.* Esther had insisted on "As Time Goes By," and Miriam had demurred because sometimes her mother was right; after all, it was a beautiful song.

Climbing down from his perch, the groom bowed to his new bride, and she stood to take his hand. David twirled her around the room, and, as they danced, Miriam slowly rose above the dance floor, her legs kicking out from beneath her. She was as light as air, and David's fingers reached up to touch the tips of his bride's. For one tiny moment, not even Inez could take her eyes from the couple as they circled the room, defying gravity. Soon other couples followed suit, and the entire country club was a swoop of hemlines, a flash of white gloves and yellow boutonnieres, a rush of gentle wind.

Joseph had forgotten all about Irving Berlin. In this moment, he could see only his daughter. "Just like helium," he said, leaning in to his wife.

Esther picked up a chocolate truffle, one of a plate that had been placed on the table on bone china rimmed with gold, and popped it into her mouth. She smiled toward the couple, cocoa stuck in her teeth. "Weightless," she said, reaching for another.

How long would she be aboveground that way? thought Joseph. He remembered the fireflies flying into the night, blinking now, he knew, with happiness. No, with relief. How long before Miriam flew up and away from him? Joseph had thought then. He thought it now. He turned away from the couple, resisting the urge to tell his daughter, good-bye.

CHAPTER 17

Honeymoons, 1957

THE NEWLYWEDS WERE scheduled for a honeymoon in the Greek Islands, and Sarah and Seymour Bloom had arranged to stay with Esther and Joseph Brodsky at Sebago Lake. To get to know one another, Esther had said when she phoned Sarah up to invite them. Joseph had watched her, the phone in the crook of her neck as she shined the dining room table. After all, we're to be family, Esther had said, looking happily at the dirt on the cloth.

Miriam had spent nearly every summer at the lake, walking along the country road, past the mailboxes, large as dollhouses, to the little red house where she could buy candy cigarettes and lipstick. And then, as she grew older, she'd go into Naples for soft serve with the Johnson boy. One time a young male friend of hers from Boston had come up, and the two had gotten so drunk on Singapore slings that Miriam had gotten the car stuck in a ditch on the way out of town. And her father had come for her. He had not scolded her at all as they watched the tow truck pull the Oldsmobile out of the dirt while the young man leaned over a bush to vomit.

That wasn't so long ago, Joseph thought as he helped Esther place the lavender shell-shaped soaps in dishes, smooth as sea glass, in the bath and potpourri in her Lenox cut-crystal bowls on the bureau in the bedroom for their new in-laws. He knew that his wife had taken great pains to make the Blooms feel at home and that she had even given a key to their neighbor so she could place freshly cut flowers in the Steuben vases, arranged strategically around the small—but quaint—guest cottage.

This, however, had all been done before the wedding.

"What will you *do*?" Miriam said to her mother. She stood in front of the mirror, removing the pins that had held her veil in place. "Perhaps David and I shouldn't go," she said, not meaning a single word of it.

"Don't be a lunatic," Esther said.

Miriam laughed, though she knew her mother wasn't kidding. "Don't worry, Mom," she said.

Esther stood behind her daughter, peering over her shoulder. Miriam watched her mother looking at them both in the glass, and wondered whether her mother recognized herself. Once, in one of Esther's infrequent moments of vulnerability, she had told Miriam how sometimes she looked in the mirror and startled herself. Looking at her now, Miriam wondered if she had ever seen this woman who had gone a bit fleshy at the cheeks, where intricate spiderwebs of blood vessels exploded right below her skin. Her mother held her head up and to the side. What am I, a frog? she had once asked Miriam when she found a new sagging at her throat and neck.

Now Esther placed her chin on Miriam's shoulder. "You know, I never had any doubts that I married the right man," she said. "I have been incredibly lucky."

Miriam took her eyes away from the glass and looked at her mother, startled by her honesty.

"I hope you always feel that way. I hope you have a lovely life together, Miriam, like we have, but I pray that you know it as well, while it's happening." Esther reached out and placed her daughter's hair behind her ears. She sniffled.

Miriam closed her eyes and held out her face to her mother.

"In any case." Esther shook herself back. "You must go on your honeymoon," she said. "We'll all be just fine."

"You're sure?" Miriam asked. She put both hands on her mother's shoulders.

That's when she saw Joseph, lingering at the threshold, kicking at a piece of loose wood. "Daddy," she said. She turned and went to her father and felt a wash of grief—or was it happiness?—shake her heart. Was growing older not being able to discern the difference between the two? By the time she reached him, tears rolled down both his cheeks.

Joseph bent down to look at the piece of loose wood. I need to nail this down, he thought. Someone will surely get a splinter or worse, the gangrene! In this way he avoided remembering his daughter, who, when she was an infant, he had tried so frantically to protect that anyone who wanted even to have a look at her had to wear a surgical mask. He did not think of the little girl smiling into his new camera from the top of the staircase, or the one on roller skates falling into a patch of grass, or the young lady pushing back the living room curtains waiting for the arrival of her date, or the woman who turned her back on him to board a plane for South America.

He could not help but remember her at the lake, however, where so many of his good memories took place. Stored in here, he thought to himself, wanting to thump his chest and to break open the cage of his confining ribs to set that delicate organ free for just one moment. To just once not feel its beating and crashing against those fragile bones. He remembered watching his elder daughter separate sand on the beach below the house with a magnet. Black and purple and stone. All summer long Miriam had lined the porch with empty yahrtzeit candles filled with layered sand. Now where did I leave those nails? he thought, standing upright to face this woman who was miraculously his daughter.

"Don't cry, sugar," he said to Miriam, but he was wiping the corners of his own eyes.

A few days after their honeymoon began—after the horror of getting to Santorini, and then recovering from the jet lag, why, it was just about time to turn around and go home—Miriam lay in David's arms. The blue shutters swung open, knocking against the bright white stucco of the quaint hotel. As sweet Aegean air wafted over them, the couple was finally able to relax for a moment. Miriam pulled at the hair on David's tanned arms and, for the first time since they'd arrived in Greece, thought for a moment about the days leading up to the wedding.

"The Days of Horror" David had called them as they were taking place.

Miriam had disagreed. "I don't see the horror," she'd said. "After all, it's my mother who's doing everything."

David had laughed at this, and Miriam had shrugged it off.

Now she looked up at the wooden cross pinned to the white, white wall and tried to remember the best part of the wedding. Most of the girls she knew from school told her that their weddings had been the happiest days of their lives. So much of her young life had been spent listening to such hyperbole. Over those dreadful teas and at the evening mixers in college, friends told Miriam how thrilling their proms and cotillions had been, how much they were gripped by their studies. Most recently, her friend Edith had extolled the wonders of childbirth to Miriam over the telephone, to the point that Miriam was positively green with envy, not so much for the prospect of children but for the very act of giving birth. Miriam knew to question, and yet, whenever any of her friends spoke about her wedding, they did so with a genuine love for the day, and Miriam couldn't help but believe them. Some girls, she was momentarily reassured to hear, didn't remember their big days, though that was soon explained away by the dreamlike state they had been in at the time. These girls wanted to do it all over again, so that the best days of their lives would not be entirely lost to them.

Had Miriam loved her wedding?

Lying with David now, smelling the sea air and listening to the hotelier scream at an American who was checking in after what Miriam knew had to have been an excruciating journey, she thought that not only had she not loved her wedding but she hadn't even liked it. Who were half those people? Shouldn't she at least have been able to recognize them if they were coming to her wedding? Were she to pass them on the street tomorrow, would they know her?

She too had been a stranger, she knew. To these anonymous guests, yes, but also to herself. A stranger to myself, she thought now. Just as she had felt looking in the mirror in that doctor's office all those years ago. But where's my nose? she had thought. And beneath this thought was that singular and paralyzing fear: And where am I? At the wedding, Miriam had smiled and curtsied and bowed her head demurely. A stranger *here* myself, she corrected herself, remembering Kurt Weill's *One Touch of Venus,* which David had berated her for not knowing was a Broadway musical because she had seen only the movie. But inside? Inside grew a ball of rage as tight as a fist. She remembered being a teenager on her mother's bed watching Essoil commercials. "Women of the future!" Frances Gold had said so brightly. Well, here it is, she'd thought as David rose to toast her after his mother had humiliated her in front of everyone. My future is upon me, and *this is it.*

All Miriam could remember about her wedding was a terrible sadness that night. David had not carried her over the threshold into the hotel room, and what shocked her was that she had not wanted him to. All she could hear was her mother the next day, asking if it had happened. This was the only reason she had cared.

David had gone straight into the bathroom, and Miriam had taken off her own wedding dress, laying it over the back of the wooden chair. It had looked like a deflated doll there, waiting for someone to breathe life into it. Miriam had climbed into bed and pretended she was asleep when David came out of the bathroom in his underwear. She had heard the sad sound of his glasses hitting the wood ever so slightly as he set them down on the night table.

And what on earth had passed between her parents and David's? Miriam couldn't get the cruel slur of her new mother-in-law's voice out of her mind.

She sat up in bed, and David's arm flopped on her lap.

"David," she said. She brought her legs up to her chest, put her arms around them, and laid her head on the table of her knees.

"Hmmm." After a day spent lying on the red beach and swimming in the blue, blue sea, a late lunch at the taverna covered in vines and cut deep into the cliffs, homemade barrel wine, and, despite the waiters' warnings—It will make you crazy, crazy!—three ouzos, David was well on his way to a late-afternoon sleep.

Looking at her husband, his thick hair still short from Esther's insistence that he cut it for the wedding, Miriam thought of her father, the way he had stood up and screamed like that, pointing a mean finger at her new father-in-law. Miriam had never seen him so furious. "I want to talk about the wedding," she said.

For a brief and horrifying second, David, slowly stirring awake, thought the wedding was still to come. For an instant, he was being badgered about the rabbi, pestered over the sauce for the chicken, queried as to what their wedding flower should be, begged over and over to help his fiancée, who was rendered utterly unable to make even the smallest decision.

"Daffodils," he said sleepily.

Miriam lifted her head up and patted his neck. "No, sweetie, we chose daisies, remember?"

David sat up and, after a moment, registered the hotel room, the stark white walls, the marble floors, and the wooden bureau dotted with small black holes, the work of termites.

"What, Miriam? I thought we came here to forget all that."

"Huuh!" she gasped. "You don't go on a honeymoon to forget your wedding, David." She was deeply hurt. Deeply. It seemed their wedding had not been the best day of her husband's life either.

"What I mean is we spent so much time on the bloody wedding before it happened, I'd actually like to take the time to just enjoy being married."

He did have a point. And this calmed Miriam for a moment, until she remembered why she'd brought the wedding up in the first place. "That's true," she said. "But I just keep turning over that horrible moment when your mother called me a Polish peasant. And then when my father went completely berserk. I've never seen him like that."

"My mother is crazy, Miriam." David rolled toward her. "You know that. Believe me, that's the nicest thing she's called anyone I've ever dated."

"Okay," Miriam said, cutting him off before he went into all the women he had brought home to Sarah. The actresses. The fabulousness. The charm. She'd heard more than enough about that. "But what did he mean, my father?" Miriam asked. "That your father was a gangster? Is that an insult of some kind? Does it mean something in Jewish?"

David sat up and looked at his wife in disbelief. "It means your father was accusing mine of being a gangster, Miriam."

"Oh." She sat up and brushed her hair behind her ears. "I thought it might be some kind of expression from Russia. Well, *was* he a gangster?" She rubbed her nose.

In truth, David didn't know how to answer the question. Gangster. What did it mean really? He remembered late nights when he sneaked downstairs and sat at the kitchen table in the dark waiting for his father to come home. Was he coming in from the theater those nights? Perhaps he was waiting for his father to come in and lift him up, embrace him, carry him upstairs, and put him to bed.

"I'm not sure," David said. "I'm not sure about your uncle either," he said, in an effort to inform Miriam that he wasn't the only one who had a family riddled with thugs.

Solomon. Miriam remembered her father screaming at Esther if she ever so much as said his name: Don't mention his name to me. Joseph would hold his hands in the air as if to stop the sound from traveling past them.

It was one of the few times she'd heard her father raise his voice. And yet Miriam and her sister had grown up believing that their uncle had died, "In the war," Esther once told them, reaching for her daughters' hands. In this manner, Miriam and Gloria had learned to understand the war: it was a fleeting touch, a brief facial expression that looked strangely conspiratorial, a silence moving slowly through a crowded room.

What war? Miriam thought now as she looked at her new husband in disbelief. The Spanish Civil War? "Fascinating," she said. "Jewish gangsters." She had to admit, she liked the idea of them.

For some reason, the thought of his father filled with violence made David think of *West Side Story,* which he knew was opening in a few weeks. David couldn't wait. How much longer could they be so far away from what was going on? What was happening in the world, anyway? Entire wars could be waged right now and it seemed they would not know it. It was pleasant to drink wine on the cliffs and watch the sun burst upon the sea, to feel as if they had reached the edge of the world. It hadn't felt like they would falter and fall off; instead he felt comfort that they had come here together. David had enjoyed it, but now, frankly, it made him nervous.

He rose out of bed slowly. Did they have the *Evening News* here? He was dying for a little reassurance from Doug Edwards.

"Sweetie," he said, pulling on his trousers. "I'm going to go downstairs and see if there's any news on."

"On?" she said. Miriam had tried to get a *Herald Tribune* all day.

"I remember there was a television in the back room downstairs. Maybe they'll just let me have a peek." David had spent little of his life without a television in close proximity.

"It's in *Greek,*" Miriam said. It pained her that this was a language she could neither speak nor understand. At the market in town, she'd spo-

ken English with an accent she herself could not place, as if this would
make her pass for Greek.

David buttoned his shirt and shoved his tanned feet into the leather
sandals he had bought in Athens. You look like a Greek god, Miriam
had said as he stopped at the first of the rows of booths beneath the
Parthenon. That had sealed the deal, and the more the leather had
worn down to fit the shapes of his feet, the more comfortable he had
felt in the sandals.

"I just want to see, okay?" he said. Why did she have to argue with
everything? He'd imagined his wife conforming to his will, as his sandals did to his feet.

Downstairs, David rang the bell at the desk, and a man came out of the
back room, smoking a cigarette.

David pointed to the room where he could hear the sound of
canned laughter. "May I see?" he screamed, as if this would make the
man understand him.

The manager nodded his head, pursing his lips. "Why not?" he said.

David walked behind the counter, and for a brief and, he realized,
silly moment, he felt the way he had when his father brought him
backstage. Even though he dreaded meeting the cast each evening, he
adored going where regular citizens were not allowed. He enjoyed
watching what was behind the scenes, the process, as it were, and it
always made him enjoy the finished product so much more.

Here, there were no actors smoking, no girls rolling down stockings one leg at a time, to behold. Amid the stale smoke and old couches
there was a television, and David went over to it to try to find the news.
There were only three stations, and Miriam was right, everything was
in Greek, even the one playing *I Love Lucy*. Lucille Ball screaming in
Greek as her lips moved to English made him slightly anxious. There
was absolutely no recognition. He turned the dial anyway, clicking
through the three channels, and then, as if a valentine sent from America, Frances Gold came on the set.

She held a gleaming bottle of Essoil, and though she mouthed
English, the television spat Greek at him. Did they use Essoil here?
David looked around the room for evidence of its work. He took a deep

breath, expecting the clean, fresh smell of his father-in-law: only stale smoke. David looked back at Frances's smiling face. Jesus fucking Christ, David thought, as he watched her smile into the camera, into this back room in this hotel in Santorini. I *am* a part of the world.

The Brodskys and the Blooms had not canceled their time together.

"Jeesum Crow," Esther said to Joseph as they had watched the young couple get into their blue Renault, the shaving-creamed "Just Married" already sliding down the rear window. Tin cans scraped the asphalt behind them as they pulled away. "Can you believe they're still coming, Joe?" Esther put her hand to the side of her head. "I just can't believe the nerve of that woman."

"It will be fine, Es."

Joseph ran his hand over his wife's back. He had plans to ignore the whole incident.

"Pssh," she said. "Says you."

The first day at the house, the two couples kept largely to themselves. But on the second morning Esther succumbed to what she told Joseph—told, or warned?—was her good breeding and walked over the pine needles to the guest cottage.

Joseph could hear her rapping three times on the red door. "Hello, hello!" she said.

He got up from the table and peered out the kitchen window just as Sarah—or at least a woman who resembled Sarah—appeared at the door of the cottage. He could see she wore a sheet wrapped around her body and a sleep mask pushed up onto her head.

Even from the main house, Joseph could hear the gasp that escaped Esther upon seeing Sarah. "*Good* morning!" She tried to recover brightly.

Sarah rubbed her head. "What time is it?" she asked.

"Nearly ten o'clock!" Esther said. "Well, I was hoping you two would come up to the house for brunch," she went on. "And then Joe and I thought we'd go out on the *MiriGlo,* the four of us."

"The who?" Sarah said.

Esther laughed. "The *MiriGlo!* Our little motorboat. Named for the children: *Miri* for Miriam, *Glo* for Gloria! Do you water-ski?"

"She does," said Seymour, who had just come up from the lake, a towel hooked around his neck.

"Do I *what*?" Sarah said.

"Water-ski," said Seymour. Could Esther see inside, where clothes were strewn in every corner and the air was so stagnant one could have sliced it up and served it for breakfast? Seymour hoped not.

Sarah snapped the silk mask from her head, holding it by the elastic band with the tips of her fingers. "Yes. Yes," she said. "Actually, I used to be quite good," she told her hostess.

"Well, great," Esther said. "Fabulous! Why don't you get ready and come up to the house? We'll have a bite to eat and then head off!"

So that there would be as little discussion as possible about the scene between his wife and Sarah Bloom, Joseph rushed back to the table and opened the *Maine Times*. He liked the *Maine Times*—it always made him feel that he was a part of the region. The news of people organizing to protest a wire fence, an announcement of the arrival of a new business in town: it made him feel as if he were once again part of a village.

"What?" Esther said, slamming the screen door.

Joseph looked up from the paper.

"Maybe she just isn't a *morning* person," she said. "Lord help me if you were right about this." Esther took two tomatoes down from the windowsill. "I mean, how many years of analysis am I going to need to know that not everything you say is right?"

"I don't know vhat you are talking about." Esther smelled like the deep, fresh scent of evergreens. It made Joseph think of Miriam and Gloria, and how they would come back from outside, their bare feet covered in tar. He loved those evergreens. "Are ve going skiing?" he asked, pushing up his glasses.

Esther got out a serrated knife, placed the roundest, reddest beefsteak on the wooden cutting board, and began to slice. She looked out the kitchen window. "Joe, look!" she said.

Joseph stood to look out and saw Sarah Bloom in front of the guesthouse on her hands and knees.

"My Lord! What on earth is that woman *doing*?" Esther gripped the tomato so tightly Joseph thought it would burst.

She stormed out the screen door. The door slapped closed three times, and then Joseph, hesitating, followed his wife.

"Everything all right?" Esther called out to Sarah from the patio.

Joseph could see she was still holding the knife, and she waved it in Sarah's direction. Sarah was in the flower beds in a long, silk nightgown.

As Esther walked toward her, Sarah bolted upright, her back still turned. Poor thing, thought Joseph as he approached. But then he remembered Sarah's display—had it been only a day and a half ago?—at the wedding. Slowly Sarah turned to face her new in-laws. Her look had a vacancy to it that seemed to startle Esther out of her anger. "I only wanted some flowers," Sarah said.

Esther put her hands on her hips. "Were there not *enough* in the cottage?" she asked her.

Joseph laid his palm on his wife's arm to stop her. Clearly Sarah was not well. "Ve can get you more," he said. "Zhey are beautiful, no?"

"Of course they are," Seymour said. "And there are more than enough. Thank you." He placed a hand on Esther's shoulder.

"Good," she said. "I'm fixing a light brunch now, and I was just telling Sarah you must come up to the house for a bite and then we'll go skiing."

"Zhe vater is fantastic," said Joseph, looking out to the lake.

"Sounds grand," Seymour said. "We'll be up in just a bit."

This seemed to calm Esther the way only a man could calm her, and as she pushed her way back to the house, Joseph turned to see Seymour helping his wife to her feet. He took the snapdragons she had torn out by their roots from her hands and tried to pat them back into the earth.

Joseph followed Esther into the kitchen and watched her place the knife on the cutting board and open the refrigerator. She took out the smoked salmon he had bought in Portland from Merrill's and the jar of capers. She took out two lemons and a large Vidalia onion, holding them all in her arms as if she were about to juggle, and placed them on the counter. With her palms down, her fingers curled over the linoleum edge, arms outstretched, she breathed.

"Should I even bother with the kugel?" she asked.

"Vhy wouldn't you?" Joseph said.

Esther shrugged. "What do I care?" She took the Pyrex dish of noodles, sour cream, and its cornflake topping out of the fridge, and slammed it on the counter.

"So are ve going skiing, Es?" For the second time Joseph peered around his paper. "Should I get zhe boat ready with skis?"

Esther turned to look at her husband. And he looked at her. What was she thinking? Joseph knew he let in only what he wanted of the world. But Esther seemed just then the opposite of him: nothing ever got out. He imagined his wife, each pore of her a passageway leading directly inside. Once a word or a snatch of dialogue made it through, it fastened to something else in that sea of water and blood. Perhaps, Joseph reasoned, her craziness was these accessed bits of phrases that knocked against the walls of her stomach.

"My stomach hurts," said Esther.

"I know," he said.

"Who are you, God? We'll be ready to go in about an hour. Get the goddamn boat ready by then, okay?"

Only then did Joseph look at his wife's face. "What's zhe matter, Es? Vant me to run out to the stand for some more tomatoes?"

She looked at her husband and shook her head. "No, Joe." She turned the tomato she'd been slicing, the one that bore her fingerprints on its side, and began to cut again. "We've got enough until tomorrow."

"Good," Joseph said. "Good."

"Pull yourself together." Seymour moved in close behind Sarah, whispering in her ear as she stood in front of the guesthouse.

He held his wife's wrist, guiding her up the little steps and into the cottage. But just then its smallness and the odor of dirty clothes and smoke and breath that permeated the dark room that he had been so embarrassed by in front of Esther, were not on his mind.

Still holding her arm behind her back, Seymour pushed Sarah face-down onto the bed. It had been years since he had been genuinely attracted to his wife. Making love to Sarah had once been the erasure he craved, but now he needed to lose himself from her as well. Usually he got himself excited, Sarah on her side, head propped on her elbow, watching him with a mocking gaze.

Yet the pathetic image of his wife on her knees in the moist soil, the way the silk of her nightgown fell over her ass, a shimmering moon sinking into the bed of flowers, the dirt he saw underneath her finger-nails when he grabbed her arm—it all got to him now. In this position his wife revealed a neediness she rarely showed, though he knew she felt it often.

On the bed, he pushed up her nightgown. The silkiness of the fab-ric over his hands and fingers made him harder, and he saw that his wife was not wearing underwear. He slipped inside her easily then, and she pressed against him, drawing him closer. He pushed her into the bed with more force and lay flush against her, the convexity of his own body resting perfectly in the slight concave contours of hers. He reached for her hair and pulled it. She moaned, and so he tugged it harder, as if it were this act that made the sound produced by his wife— a sound he had not heard for ages in this context.

Sarah stopped. "Wait," she said. He stopped moving and kissed her neck. She smelled of sweat and the previous evening's alcohol. Sarah shifted beneath the weight of him, and Seymour started to move as well, but something had been inexorably altered. They were out of sync, and his hipbone now seemed misplaced, that small shift enough to knock them totally off-kilter. He had no idea where to place his hips, and they jabbed into her. As he tried to kiss her neck, she pulled away slightly, which made him put his weight on his arms and begin to move quickly—in and out—in an effort to put them both out of their sud-den misery.

Sarah now lay there like the rag doll she turned into by twilight. And Seymour hated her, this lovely and smart girl who had become a lush of an old woman before his eyes. Just to see her flesh moving sick-ened him. And he could tell that Sarah met his hatred halfway. While she waited for him to finish, their reciprocal emotions coupled in midair.

He moved off her and onto his back. When she rolled away from him, he could see the dirt marks on her knees—two smiles—out of the corner of his eye. For one brief moment a fear came over Seymour as he remembered her in the dirt that way: What is happening to her? he had thought.

She patted his shoulder. "Oh, Seymour," she said.

He was shocked at her affectionate tone. It was not right between them. It simply was not right, and this thought went through both of their heads at exactly the same moment, so that when they looked each other in the eye, they converged in a mournful and apologetic embrace.

Over an hour after Esther had invited them to the house, Seymour and Sarah were dressed, their bathing trunks beneath Bermudas and oxfords. They traipsed up to the main house for brunch.

"How quaint!" Sarah said when they entered the spacious wooden living room, strewn with oval, multicolored braided rugs.

Esther smiled against her guest. "Why, thank you," she said. "Quaint is exactly what my father was going for when he bought the place. We Mainers just adore quaint," she said.

Seymour and Joseph nodded to each other, an informal acceptance of the fact that they would be represented by their wives. Esther guided them toward the dining room table.

"I thought we'd eat," she said. "So we can get to skiing."

Esther brought out the platters of nova and onion and tomato, the bagels, the cream cheese and butter and jelly. She brought out her kugel, cut into squares, browned perfectly on top and placed on her mother's Limoges platter.

"Hmmm! The salmon!" Sarah exclaimed once they'd all begun eating. "Though these aren't New York bagels, to be sure, the lox are to die for."

"Actually, it's nova." Esther smiled at Sarah. "Lox are very salted, you know." Her hand fluttered over her chest. "Bad for the heart," she said.

Sarah shrugged.

Seymour said, "These noodles are delicious, Esther!"

To which Joseph said, "Noodles? It's kugel! You never had a kugel? Esther's is the best in the whole U.S. of A.!"

Esther swatted his words away.

By the time they all had eaten the first half of their bagels and were into their second cups of coffee, there was a silence.

"It will be a great day to ski," Esther said. She pointed outside. "Look how still the water is."

Everyone nodded. The white noon light glinted off the lake. The sound of water rippling over the rocks at the shore came in through the open windows.

"Reminds me," Esther said. "Sarah, do you need a bathing cap?"

"You know, I *do,*" Sarah said. "I didn't bring my silk pillowcase, and the water will make a mess of my hair for sure."

Seymour sighed. Sarah was trying to be nice, and she had been grateful for the gesture, he could tell. She had been terrible, screaming at the wedding that way. In truth, Miriam Brodsky was one of the only civilized girls their son had ever brought around. A bunch of whores they'd all been. Little bitches looking for money or a role in one of Seymour's productions.

"Thank you, Esther," she said. "For everything. You've really been so kind."

Esther nodded to Sarah, smiling genuinely.

Joseph knew that was exactly what Esther needed to hear. A little graciousness. He knew these women would never be friends, and he wouldn't be friends with Seymour Bloom, but for the children, well, they could make an effort.

Joseph said, "Oh, ve have everything here at camp! Zhe skis, zhe life jackets, the preservers. Don't you vorry."

Joseph saw how Sarah cringed when he spoke. Was it his accent? Joseph brought his hand to cover his mouth.

Sarah set down her bagel and looked at Joe and Esther. "You know," she said, "I feel just terrible about what happened at the wedding."

Esther nodded. "Of course," she answered hesitantly, waiting for Sarah to continue.

But she did not continue. Instead, she picked up her bagel and resumed eating.

Even Seymour could tell the mood had quickly turned.

This was an apology? thought Joseph. They would endure these hateful people for their daughter, but that was it. He watched Esther heap on more cream cheese. With that came the strawberry jelly. He stopped himself from sliding the condiments tray away from her reach.

Joseph and Seymour looked at each other. Should we be apologizing too? they both wondered. But who first? Joseph had simply been reacting at the wedding, and Seymour had responded in kind. It was as if they both decided no at the same time. Seymour squeezed lemon over his salmon, and Joseph dug into his kugel. Truly the best in America, he thought as he chewed the cream and sugar, the crunchy top, all of it distracting him from the problems with his new in-laws as it warmed him through and through.

It turned out to be a magnificent day for skiing. Joseph knew that Esther didn't much like skiing, but she did it for him. He had come to adore the sport. Simply to place one toe in the cold water exhilarated him. And driving a motorboat? The boat was not fancy—just a simple sixteen-horsepower, not so great for wear—but there was little that gave him such pleasure.

Her bathing cap flopping with orange and pink flowers, Esther screamed at her husband as she held the end of the taut line. "Slow down, Joe!" Wildly she made the thumbs-down signal, the universal sign for slow. "For God's sake, slow down!" she screamed at him. But she was laughing as she moved rather easily in and out of the wake, her tiny tanned legs sticking out of her turquoise bathing suit, which encased her rather large, rounded stomach. Even as Joseph sped up, shaking his fist in the air, it was clear that they were both enjoying themselves.

Only Seymour didn't want to ski. "I just never have," he told Joseph. "And I can't say I'm too upset about it."

"Now's as good a time as any to start," Joseph told him. It was usually he who opted out of things. Football. Baseball. Who cared? He liked the tennis, but that was it. Here was this man who had probably killed people, and he was scared to ski.

"I don't think so," Seymour said. He shrugged. The thought of these people seeing him fumble and fall was unbearable to him.

So reserved he is, thought Joseph. He couldn't picture Seymour trafficking in liquor or meeting shysters in dark alleys, as he knew his brother had done. Joseph wondered how it was he had ended up surrounded by gangsters. He looked over at Seymour Bloom dressed sharply in his golf jacket and Bermuda shorts, and then he looked down at himself, in swimming trunks and an open Cuban shirt, also his jellies. What made a man make his decisions? thought Joseph. As simple a decision as what to wear. And then as complicated as who to be. Was it a man's wife? wondered Joseph. Because, when it came down to it, it was Esther who had made him resist so much as using his brother's capital to invest in anything. Just to look at her face, and also those of their children, made him want to do right in the world. Had Sarah *wanted* Seymour to do wrong, or had she simply turned her back to it?

And then he wondered what it would be like to live with a woman like Sarah. She really was very beautiful in her own way. Such marvelous skin, and her hair had a brilliant sheen to it. And bright? God, was she bright, with her allusions to Shakespeare here, her Smith this and Smith that, her "This is what I think of civil rights." Opinions, this one had. But, even aside from the dramatics at the wedding, there was something very off-putting about the woman. Frightening even.

"Would you like to drive then?" Joseph asked.

"It's okay." Seymour sat, entirely self-contained, hands in his lap, futzing with his gold watch. Sarah pulled off her navy cotton sweater, and Esther helped her into a life preserver as if it were a coat.

"Come on," Joseph said to Seymour.

Seymour couldn't have known what a gift this was, Joseph letting someone else drive the *MiriGlo*. It was not a big boat, to be sure, but very little gave Joseph the thrill of pulling the gas lever to feel the boat cease and then speed off, watching the hull cut the lake, beads of water flying out to either side of them and hanging there suspended in the sunlight for a moment. He thought of teaching Miriam and Gloria how to drive the boat, and how each Fourth of July they'd go out into the center of the lake. His daughters lying on the deck and the fireworks blooming above them. And then the lull, the darkness but for the moonlight sweeping over the rippling water, the still boats, the strained expectation of beauty, and then the lights again, breaking into flowers across the sky.

"Oh, all right," Seymour said. "Why not?" He shrugged.

Though he had never been at the helm of a boat, it was much easier than driving a car, and after a brief lesson—this is first gear, this is second—Seymour was ready. Sarah had climbed down the ladder and was bobbing in the water, her two skis pointed in the air.

"Wait a minute." She laughed. "Who's driving?"

Esther turned around. She was so brown, and her eyes flashed black in the sun. Seymour noted that she was a very pretty girl, in a sweet manner he had always liked. He could tell that Esther Brodsky laughed a lot. He realized just then, hearing the faraway tinkle of his wife's laugh rising from the water, that Sarah rarely lit up that way. Esther turned back to Sarah, and, raising her eyebrows, she yelled, "Your husband!"

Seymour thought Esther lovely, and so at ease with herself.

Sarah hesitated, her smile fading just a bit before she gave Esther the thumbs-up.

"Okay," Esther screamed toward Seymour.

And off they went, Seymour jerking the boat for a moment and then going steady and picking up speed, Sarah rising shakily, the rope tensing.

"Hooray!" Esther said as she watched Sarah getting her bearings. "See? It's like riding a bike," she shouted into the wind.

Seymour seemed enraptured. He shook his head and felt the air traveling through his hair. He sped up, shifting the boat into third gear, and decided right then that he would get a convertible. How grand would it be to drive into Times Square this way? Then he realized what the problem had been his whole life: why, it had only been the traffic! Had there been no traffic, he always would have felt this free.

"Everything all right?" Esther called out to Sarah, whose knees seemed to be buckling a bit as she attempted to stay within the boat's wake. Her upper body was thrust forward awkwardly.

Sarah signaled for Seymour to slow down.

"Slow down," Esther called back to Seymour.

He didn't seem to notice, so entranced was he with *driving*. Joseph tapped him on the shoulder. "Seymour," he said. "You should probably go a leetle easier on zhe gas."

Now Seymour looked up from the panel, with its compass and speedometer, and into the rearview to see his wife faltering. She was making the thumbs-down signal and then quickly grabbing the rope so as not to lose her balance.

"Slow down!" Esther said, standing.

But there was no slowing Seymour, and he watched, not caring what his face revealed, as Sarah tried to steady herself. Then he watched her let go of the rope. And as they pulled away from her, the bar of the ski rope ticking the water behind them, she dropped peacefully into the water.

"Here," Joseph said, nudging the much larger Seymour. "Let me go around to pick her up."

Slowly, Seymour let out the gas, and the boat slowed. "I can do it," he said. He nodded, assuring his host that he would do it properly, like a gentleman.

Esther slowly pulled in the rope, winding it around her arm and in between her thumb and forefinger, as if it were a lasso. Seymour turned the boat around to retrieve Sarah. As they pulled up alongside her, Joseph leaned down to grab her hand.

"You all right?" he asked her.

"I'm fine," she said.

Joseph could tell that for a brief moment she had been someone else, maybe herself a long time ago, or maybe someone she had always wished she could be. Now she was back to herself.

"Just fine," she said, and, taking Joseph's hand, she pulled herself back onboard. Dripping water, she removed the life jacket. She undid the strap of the blue bathing cap, and, pulling against the rubber, she shook her light hair free. She let Esther place a towel around her bare shoulders. But, Joseph noted, Sarah could not look at her husband. He imagined her as a fragile vase about to be broken to bits.

Seymour looked out across the water to the other side of the lake, where the Brodskys' house stood on a hill of rocks above the shore. A whole other town existed over there. Brushing his hands through his wind-tangled hair, he could see her again, his wife dropping the line and descending. In that drawn-out instant, he pictured the very moment he had met Sarah on the Duck Pond in Central Park, she all rosy and bundled up against the weather. As he pictured her gradually sinking into the water, he remembered crashing into her on the ice, how he had clumsily turned around and watched her slip and fall.

CHAPTER 18

Thanksgiving:
Brodsky, Verdonik, Bloom, 1960

MIRIAM WAS STILL FRECKLED from the honeymoon, and David had managed to hang on to two bottles of ouzo purchased from the Athens duty free, when the newlyweds bought a brownstone with access to a large outdoor space on 105th and Central Park West.

"Are you sure we want to be so far uptown?" Miriam asked nervously.

"But you didn't like the place in the West Village," David, who had fallen in love with a brownstone on Horatio Street, said. "You found it seedy down there, which is ridiculous."

"Well, isn't there something in between?" she asked.

"No, Miriam," he said. Did everything have to be a compromise? "I don't want to live in midtown."

Miriam sighed.

"What about Brooklyn?" David was cheered to think of it.

"Absolutely *not,*" she said. She thought of all her father's terrible stories, the way he had worked so hard to get his mother out as soon as possible.

"There are parts of Brooklyn that are wonderful," he said. "Brooklyn Heights has a view of the whole city."

"There is a stigma to Brooklyn," Miriam said. "No."

"Then the Upper West Side it is," David said, resisting the urge to tell his wife she had never even been to Brooklyn. "I want some room to breathe. I want a garden," he said.

It was also near the park, and Miriam imagined the two of them taking walks every Saturday morning, arm in arm as they aged together. She remembered looking into his eyes beneath the chuppa. And she thought of the night in the hotel, before they'd left for Athens, and how she had shivered, her shoulder to the windowpane, thinking how scared she'd been to be alone as a child. Now she remembered the bare branches of the yet-to-bloom trees outside the window, terrible claws, swaying in the wind. Miriam had had nightmares that she would go to sleep each night alone. "You're right, David. By the park sounds perfect," she said, kissing him on the nose.

The young couple's parents, and grandparents for that matter, had worked hard enough. Miriam and David Bloom now lived in art. There was little in the brownstone that did not stem from the theater, be it the sheet music stacked along the piano no one ever so much as thought to play or the signed, framed posters of *The Music Man* and *The King and I* and *Guys and Dolls* that lined the walls.

David Bloom began to garden his small patch of land. Why, I could live on a goddamn kibbutz! he thought, digging the trowel into the earth. As he planted tomatoes, he thought about how his mother would loathe this idea and smiled.

As David guided climbing roses over wooden trellises and pruned their hoary thorns, he was reminded of the way his grandmother had braided her clients' hair. The year before, Inez had sublet that beauty shop to two Hasidic girls—they were wearing wigs, what did they know from cutting hair? she'd said.

As her husband gardened, Miriam worried her way into language. The more she read, the more books took over the bedroom, proliferating like David's plants. They were piled on the floor next to the couple's bed and beneath it, stacked on the veneer top of her bureau. But Miriam's books were all French or Spanish titles, from far-flung places such as Algeria and Morocco and Chad, the nearest coming from Paris or Barcelona. I must maintain my languages, she would tell herself, checking dictionaries for words she could just kick herself for forgetting. Each year she took an evaluation, and, though she would always receive the highest rating, it was never quite good enough. Miriam was always going for Native Speaker.

In this way, Miriam and David divided their kingdom. But when David came in from his garden with bunches of flowers clutched in his fists, dirt up and down his arms, his brown shoulders sprayed with freckles, Miriam was almost always led away from her foreign lands. Just to see her half-naked husband smelling of sweat and earth, clutching blossoms like a boy, stirred her in a manner that his getting into bed and turning toward her never had. When David came in from the garden, it almost always led to a session of rutting and romping.

As months went by, David became even more preoccupied with his garden, and he watched in horror as leaf miners, mites, nematodes ate their way through his most carefully tended tomatoes. He was dismayed to find that fungus had developed on the fuzzy green tips of his flowering beans.

"I just wish I could garden all day long," he would tell Miriam. "I wish I could protect it," he'd say, all the time knowing he had to go to work. David was not obsessed with the theater any longer—if he couldn't be in the shows, then he could care less where the theater was headed or if he would be a part of it at all. He had become a businessman, but one without a competitive edge. So what, the Shuberts took over Broadway? They could have the whole White Way as far as David was concerned. They could have the fucking world. Needless to say, this attitude did not sit well with Seymour, and father and son would go days in the office without even the exchange of pleasantries.

The prospect of his garden's devastation caused David much anxiety. Just the threat of one more ruined root, another deteriorated daffodil, drove him to start experimenting. In the basement, he worked in the enormous washroom sink to find a product that both prevented rot and removed whatever havoc had already been wreaked.

They came in powders and waxes and aerosol sprays, in liquids and solids, in crystals; clear and white and yellow and blue. All weekend long David worked, applying chemicals to his seeds and cuttings and petals and bulbs and stamens and stems and roots. He wrote up his findings in a composition notebook, a black-and-white marbleized affair like the one Joseph had used so many years before. Miriam watched her husband as she had once watched her father, his hair thick and wild, his glasses crooked as if he'd just been socked in the face, as he held beakers up to the dim light.

As it turned out, Essoil, something David had painted on his tomatoes one morning as a joke, was the most efficacious in keeping them completely free from worms and all kinds of molds. Like Joseph, David liked things clean and shiny. When he got right down to it, this had been part of his initial attraction to Miriam Brodsky: her freshness. She was, after all, an heiress to cleanliness. David wanted the produce to look as he had felt as a boy in his grandmother's pink, shiny, shellacked beauty shop, where all the ladies brought him peppermints and shook their tits at him, and where Inez loved him in a manner that no other woman ever would or could again: with a smothering, all-over love that claimed him as it liberated him. Soon David began moving his version of science from his basement-cum-laboratory to his actual garden.

Of course, David Bloom knew that Essoil could not be consumed. But, still, he wanted to grow a perfect crop: the roundest, reddest tomatoes, the largest, firmest pumpkins, floating hydrangea as light and lovely as flakes of snow, or chrysanthemums as red and shiny as Dorothy's slippers. And so he separated the little garden into two sections—one side with produce that could be eaten and the other portion simply for admiring. The comparison was shocking. Day after day, David would look at his perfect crop with longing as he went to pick the herbs for a vinaigrette or a flower for a centerpiece from his more tired and sad-looking section of his garden. Actors, he'd think, admiring a perfect, round, red globe. Bravo!

One afternoon, a little over two years and two entire growing seasons in their new home, Miriam wandered into the garden, where her husband was planting his just-purchased daffodil and tulip bulbs. "Let's have Thanksgiving here this year," she said.

He made no response.

"Are you listening?" she said.

David's back rose before her, a question mark she watched transform into an exclamation point. "I hear you, Miriam," he said. "Just who would we invite exactly?"

He knew precisely what her response would be, and he positively dreaded the idea of their parents together. His parents and hers simply didn't work. East and west, oil and vinegar, no matter how you sliced it, they simply were not cut from the same cloth. Miriam's sister was in Massachusetts, and she wouldn't come down with her dull husband and two kids just for a night of eating. And David would rather kill himself, truly, than invite Dulcy, who had become an elitist of the worst kind ever since she set foot on the Abbot Academy campus her freshman year. Smith had positively done her in, and David could just imagine her with Sarah, glaring over their martinis at the Brodskys. For God's sake tell them to quiet down, Dulcy would whisper to Sarah. I like my Jews WASPy, she'd laugh into her mother.

"Why, we'd invite our families, of course, David." Miriam knew it could be a disaster—she'd heard more than enough from her mother about their dreadful week together at the lake house—but she still felt it was something she should do.

"Do you really think that's wise?" he asked her, now standing completely straight, sweat pouring from his face.

"You look earthy, don't you?" Miriam went sashaying up to her husband. She loved the natural appearance of him when he was not tidy and clean, dressed in those Brooks Brothers suits he wore to work. She wished then that she could smell him, an essence not covered by soap and shampoo, one that he did not share with the world, that only she would recognize.

"I don't want to do Thanksgiving," he said. "Sounds like a whole lot of trouble for very little payoff." What he wanted to say was: This will be a catastrophe.

Miriam kicked the ground, and a small tuft of young grass flew up and then landed with a light thud. She watched David cringe at the sight of it. "Are you sure?" she asked him.

"Positive." He bent down to attend to his planting, and she was again confronted by her husband's back.

Miriam crossed her arms and stomped a foot, unable to sway him with her feminine wiles.

"Well, it's too late anyway. I've already invited my parents."

Slowly David again rose from the ground and turned to face his wife. "Well, thank you for consulting me."

"I knew you would say no," she said. "Why do we have this beautiful house, the one *you* wanted, by the way, if we're not going to share it with our family?"

"Why would you invite them if you knew I would say no?" David asked.

Miriam shrugged. "Do you want to invite your parents then?" She raised one side of her mouth into a smirk. Another effect of her rhinoplasty was that only one side of her mouth really worked—in fact, only one side of her entire face was completely functional. She could wink only to the left, raise the left nostril, and now smirk with the left side of her mouth. It could never be proved—Esther would not hear of any such nonsense—but Miriam had always wondered if that doctor hadn't snipped some muscle that connected the whole right side. Somehow that side of her face was disconnected, and, in addition to her poor motor skills, somewhere behind her face floated two loose ends.

"Well, that would only be right now, wouldn't it?" He forced a smile.

"I have an idea," she said, knowing her husband was angry with her. "Let's invite Frances and Vladimir as well. They don't have kids, they're fun, they're sweet, they're in New York, it will be a nice way to avoid the whole family dynamic."

David had to hand it to Miriam. The lady had a way, didn't she? How did she not only get what she wanted but convince him that she was right and there was nothing for which to apologize? But she *was* right. It would be far more festive with the Zworykins. "Okay, Miriam," he said. "Let's do it."

Slowly a smile made its way over David's face as he pictured his wife coming out of the steaming kitchen, a huge hump of a golden bird surrounded by apples and carrots and onions, and this made him proud of her. He would use his own squash for the occasion, the rosemary he'd been coaxing into a bush since they'd moved in. He pictured himself shaking martinis, and, after passing them around the room—the smallest for his mother, or maybe, he decided, he wouldn't give her one at all—he'd lean against the mantel and take in the scintillating conversation. When his wife came in sniffling over the heaped platter, her cheeks rosy from the steam, David would be pleased to have had the evening, contented with the company, and so proud that Miriam had chosen him to accompany her in the world.

As luck would have it, everyone agreed to come. And David and Miriam prepared for over a week.

"It's our first big holiday in our new home," she told her husband when he berated her for all her list making. "I want it to go just perfectly."

David shook his head. Even if the bird sat in brine for a fucking month, the dining room table laid with the longest linen runner in the land, lighted candles on every smooth surface in the whole damn house, there was no way in hell it was going to go smoothly. "No matter what we do, it's not going to go perfectly, Miriam."

"Fine, David," she said. "If that's the case, at least let's have all our ducks in a row. In other words, does it hurt to be prepared?" She placed one more votive on the coffee table and tilted her head to see her handiwork. Now she pushed the votive two inches to the left and stepped back, crossing her arms.

He looked at her in disbelief. "I know what having all our ducks in a row means, thank you," he said.

But once again, she did have a point. And so David, who had never so much as dipped a mop into a pail or dragged a broom over a wooden floorboard, helped to clean up the place. He washed the counters and the downstairs bathroom with Essoil. He found that he enjoyed vacuuming—the constant noise of it blocked out the world, and carrying the awkward contraption from room to room, sucking up the dust and balls of hair, was also rather thrilling.

As he cleaned, Miriam bustled around the kitchen. She whisked together a vinaigrette with rosemary she'd picked from the garden herself. She put aside ten hearty sprigs to tuck beneath the skin of the turkey and then made the cranberry sauce from scratch. Stirring the fresh cranberries in the boiling water, she loved to listen to them burst open with a snap, which somehow compensated for her inability to smell them. Just like popping pimples, she thought, exhilarated. She could sit in front of the mirror for hours, pinching her skin and watching those little white teardrops emerge from her pores. Sometimes she would crawl into bed, her face splotched red and covered with the imprints of her fingernails. Who the hell bit you? David would ask, examining her temporarily ravaged face. Miriam would swat him away and hide beneath the bedspread.

Thanksgiving Day, she got out her mini pumpernickels and ryes, and finished preparing the salmon mousse. No party, Esther had always said as she stirred the mousse and prepared to pour it into the mold, is really complete without one. This one was Esther's recipe, and now Miriam readied herself to release the gelled salmon from the copper mold. She ran a knife along the edges of the fish-shaped cast and then, after sliding a plate beneath it, flipped it over. After knocking on the mold with the knife—not too hard, Esther constantly warned, you'll destroy it— Miriam carefully lifted it off. This was always the moment of revelation she happily anticipated. This time, however, this one very important time, the lifting of the mold revealed the shape of the fish to be missing a large chunk of tail and an eye, which had been gorged from its socket.

Not enough gelatin, Miriam said to herself, trying to remain calm as she attempted to patch up the fish. Scooping what had remained in the mold, she looked to fill in the eye and then will the tail into being with a knife as if she were grafting skin. But when she was done, the grafted salmon was a different consistency than the rest of the body. Somehow Miriam managed to stop herself from running upstairs and throwing herself on her bed to weep.

She placed a pitted black olive in the gorged eye socket, and that was all right. It looks kind of cute, Miriam thought, tilting her head. "Don't you?" she said to the salmon mousse. As for the tail, she had thought she'd fixed it with some swirls of her own making until David came in, beaded with water. He took one look at the mousse and said, "What happened to that poor old fish?"

The stress of the whole day became more than Miriam could bear, and she burst into tears and ran upstairs. She flung her novels, dictionaries, and papers off the bed and threw herself facedown on the spread. She wept for what felt like her whole life: for her mother's migraines, that low voice out of the darkness that never let her make any noise, the voice that always sent her away; her father's sad, fallen face, his scratched-up leather valise she'd forever think he carried; the way she would always have to fight her husband, the way he would never just smile at her and tell her, Okay, my love, as her father always had. And she cried for the horrible things her mother-in-law had said at her wedding, her wedding, of which, in the two years since, she could not even remember one moment of but was happy for the way she'd been allowed to forget it because remembering it would make her even more miserable. That would have saddened her father, Miriam knew, that he had worked so hard for a wedding she could not remember, though the fact that Irving Berlin had shown up, on account of his association with Seymour, would be constant cause for celebration. As she cried, harder now, Miriam thought of that crippled, eyeless salmon, how it had looked up at her as if to ask, How could you have taken this from me? My tail! How will I ever get upstream to spawn without it?

Miriam could hear her husband call up to her from below. "Everything okay?" he asked.

She pictured him, both hands on the smooth wooden banister, looking up the empty stairwell. But she was not there, she was here, in the bedroom. Who walks across the threshold in her wedding dress alone? thought Miriam. I do, she thought. If David did not come up to check on her by the time she counted to ten, she would know for certain that he would never care for her in the way she needed.

Twenty minutes later, a hiccupping, red-faced Miriam Bloom shakily made her way down the stairs and wandered into the kitchen, where David was running his index finger through the salmon.

"What's wrong, Miri?" He smiled at her. "Don't get so upset—it's just Thanksgiving. The holidays are always like this."

The holidays. He spoke as if they were a couple of goyim stirring mulled wine, trimming a tree, and hanging mistletoe and felt stockings. Watching him poke her salmon, she couldn't stop herself from shuddering. "What are you doing?" she asked, her anger bringing her out of her sadness.

"It's good," David said.

Miriam shook her head and went over to the fish. Fortunately, he had taken only from the already damaged tail. "Really?" she asked, knowing that she had to rely on him for the tasting.

"Well done," he said.

"Please." Miriam put her hand up. "Please, David," she said, "don't eat any more before the guests arrive, okay?"

"You mean our parents," he said, getting the Brie and Jarlsberg out of the fridge.

"And Frances and Vladimir," she said, as if this validated all her concerns.

Miriam looked at David as he turned away from the refrigerator, a cheese in each hand. Didn't he see her? she wondered. If she'd so much as stubbed her toe, her father would have come running for her. It seemed he had come from anywhere when she was hurt or needing. Sugar, he'd tell her. Here I am. Why had she thought it would be this way with all men? Miriam was too old to be reduced to liquid from a stubbed toe, yet still she felt often like a vulnerable little girl. Why couldn't her husband see this? See her deconstructed and unmasked.

"Not one more thing, David," she said sternly. "There really won't be enough. Okay?" she asked. "Are you listening?"

By two o'clock everyone was seated in the living room and well into the hors d'oeuvres. Miriam smiled as she bent toward Frances to offer her some salmon mousse garnished with the fresh dill, a long and lovely sprig of bright green cross-hatching she had picked from David's garden along with some daisies, while he vacuumed. In one swift move, Frances took the eye, olive and all, and plopped the large amount on a square of black bread.

Inadvertently, Miriam sucked in her breath.

Frances laughed and put the whole thing in her mouth, looking sideways at Vladimir, who she knew hated it when she ate this way. Never enough, he'd tell her. Like a camp survivor, he had said once, and she had slapped him. As she heaped on the salmon, Frances thought of that chopped liver swan she'd swiped on the neck all those years ago, on the day Solomon became the Terrier. Terrier. Still she missed him, though when he died, two months before he was to be released from prison, Frances hadn't had contact with him for years. She missed him far more than she missed her sister, though she did often wonder where Pauline had gone and what had become of her adorable nephew, Wesley. But she willed herself not to think of such things. Pauline was all dead and buried to her now. Frances looked over at Joseph and smiled. Still she remembered him as a young man who pressed a nickel in her hand to rent the oven from the baker on South Fifth Street.

As Miriam bent toward Vladimir with her platter in one hand, napkins stamped with her initials—MBB—in the other, he shook his head. "None for me, my dear," he said, looking squarely at Frances.

Joseph laughed. "It's okay, Vlad." He winked at Frances. "The ladies love it when Frances gets bigger. Eat up, Franny!" It was true, there was always a spike in sales when Frances was seen as a little on the plump side. Women related to her and, when she was at her heaviest moments, they must have felt a little bit above her. Like so many things that had to do with the popularity of Essoil, how this translated into sales was puzzling to Joseph.

Esther giggled and moved closer to her husband. She put her hand high on his thigh.

Just then, Sarah got up and wandered to the mantel, where David stood watching the guests move about the living room. "A martini for your mother, darling?" she asked him. She looked down at her silk blouse and brushed away invisible crumbs from her breast. She twisted her scarf so that the knot was at the side of her throat. David imagined that she would untie it and that her head would fall off.

"It's a little early, don't you think?" He looked at his watch. He had purposely put out spiked cider and red wine, which he knew his mother wouldn't drink. Esther, Joseph, and Frances drank seltzer, and Vladimir sipped slowly at his Chianti.

Sarah glared at her son and then shrugged as she pitched a handful of cashews from the crystal finger bowls on the mantel into her mouth. "How about a martini, darling?" she said, as if she had not asked before.

"Mom!" David whispered.

Sarah looked at him blankly. "I need a pillow," she said. She turned toward Seymour. "Where's my pillow?"

"Son." Seymour stood up quickly to preempt his wife.

Jesus Christ, thought David. When did he start calling me this?

"Son, the place looks terrific." He held his glass of cider in the air. "A toast," he said. "To David and Miriam. May they have many more happy memories in this lovely home."

David couldn't even crack a smile. He could not tolerate the way his father pretended that he had always been the man with a hand on

David's shoulder, guiding him through the world. Because he had not. He most certainly had not.

Sarah had wandered into the other room and sat sulking at the dining room table, set with full service for eight. The Wedgwood china, rimmed in silver, and the Orrefors water and wineglasses shone even through the dim, filtered light.

Esther nudged Joseph, as if to say, What will she do now? but Joseph steeled himself against his wife.

"Hear, hear," he said, holding up his seltzer.

They all sipped their drinks. Sarah fingered the snapdragon and statice, the last of the blooming flowers, which David had cut this morning for a centerpiece.

Joseph could see Sarah through the archway. Had it been two years since they had stayed together at the lake? What a week that had been, he thought now. Esther had been a crazy person, sneaking around the guesthouse like a common thief and reporting on the terrible state of it, strewn with clothes and curlers, the stench of stale liquor. He remembered Sarah's startled face when she looked up at Esther from the flower beds. And he had felt so sorry for Sarah, shaking her way up on water skis that afternoon Seymour had nearly killed her.

"So," Esther began. She had told Miriam she would be bringing up conversation topics. What should we discuss? her mother had asked. As "Dear Maggie" said, she had told Miriam, it is always nice to start the conversation with something cultural, something that everyone can talk about on an equal playing field. Theater isn't really appropriate, do you think? They're all such snobs anyway, she told her. "Has anyone read any good books lately?" Esther asked the room cheerfully.

Vladimir exhaled, and Frances patted his leg, knowing her husband was relieved Esther had not brought up anything about television. Everywhere they went—parties, launch events, restaurants—people always accosted her husband about television once they realized who he was. What's your favorite program? they'd ask him brightly. For how many years had people asked him what he thought of the previous night's guest on *Arthur Godfrey*? What did you think of last night's *Hawaiian Eye*? *Rawhide*?

Frances was always terrified it would come out that Vladimir never watched television. Sarnoff had told him time and again, Do not say such a thing in public, Vladimir, not to anyone. Can you imagine the backlash? Who would have thought that the very person who invented television never watched it? Vladimir hated television. They—the people of the world, the networks, the powers that be, his own wife—had ruined his baby, and he didn't want to be a part of it. Had he had children, he told Frances over and over again, he never would have let them watch it.

Frances twitched slightly at the thought of children. She had never gotten over the fact that she and Vladimir had not made something together, miraculous proof of them, memory of them, the very future of them.

"Has anyone read that boy Philip Roth?" Frances asked.

Esther nodded and pointed a finger as if to mark her place in the conversation while she raced to finish chewing. Miriam looked skyward. She had already heard it all: Esther had reported an entire evening of the book discussion at the synagogue.

"Yes," she said. "I certainly have. What do you think?"

Miriam set the salmon down on the coffee table and sat back on the couch in between her parents. Books. No one would have read what she'd been reading—the latest had been Augusto Monterroso and Juan Goytisolo—and this frustrated her, the gulf between her parents and herself. Then it struck Miriam, here was the man who had invented television. And here, next to her, was her father, who had invented the first two-in-one cleaning product ever. Miriam envied the time when they were coming up in the world—it seemed to her one could have done anything then. Yes, it had been hard, but the possibilities! She looked over at David. What was there left to invent? What would David do that his own father had not done?

Nothing, Miriam thought. What was the point? She couldn't even make a proper salmon mousse. And if she did get it right, just once, she couldn't even taste the damn thing. And here she spent her life translating, misrepresenting other people's words in her haste, she thought now. There was nothing else to be done, she thought.

"I think it's terrific," Frances said. "He's a fabulous writer, and he deserved that big fancy award."

Esther wriggled toward the edge of the couch. "Well, I think it's preposterous," she said. "Why read such a book by someone who, forget he's a Jew, but someone who portrays any people in that sort of negative light? It's downright insulting."

"Esther, please," Frances said. "How can you say such a narrow-minded thing? I think—"

Esther sat upright and looked side to side abruptly. "Narrow-minded?" she interrupted Frances. "Narrow-minded?"

Frances ignored her. "'Dear Maggie' loves the book." She gave Esther a knowing nod. "What do you think of that?" That wasn't entirely true—Maggie had merely responded to a comment a reader made about the downfall of literature today by saying that, though old values might be lost, perhaps this was not so terrible a thing.

Joseph cleared his throat and took a sip of seltzer.

"I think 'Dear Maggie' should stick to etiquette is what I think," Esther said. "And I think it a bit strange of you to think it's so fantastic for American Jews, after all we've been through, to be presented in such a disgusting way. Why else do you think the rest of America has embraced it so? That Roth sure gave them something to think about, didn't he?"

Frances waved her hand in a dismissive gesture.

"Phooey, Esther," she said. "We haven't been through anything. We were here, after all."

Joseph cleared his throat.

"Meaning what?" Esther said.

"What did you do, what did any of us do, when all those people were dying in Europe?" Frances asked the room.

"We didn't know," Esther said. She looked nervously over at her husband. "We just didn't *know,* Frances."

"We knew. We just pretended not to," Frances said.

"When zhey sent that ship back from Cuba, I knew," Joseph said. "And zhat night zhey looted all the stores. Zhe night that boy shot that German in Paris. I knew then too."

"I remember," Esther said.

"Yes," Vladimir said. "Me too. But I knew long before that."

Seymour looked into the dining room, where Sarah sat, oblivious to them all. "We knew, we didn't know. It doesn't make a difference now. We all know how it ended up," he said.

"And for your information, Frances," said Esther, "once it came to light"—she nodded in Seymour's direction—"I started a very important fund."

"I'm sure your money was extremely useful," Frances said.

"So," David said, moving away from the mantel.

Esther crossed her arms and slammed back into the couch. "Well, you find my money useful. You don't seem to have a problem taking my husband's, now do you?" she said to Frances under her breath.

Joseph grabbed her leg. "Enough," he hissed.

"Oh, bloody hell," Sarah said from the dining room. "Bloody fucking hell." She stood up and opened the doors that led out onto the deck. They all watched her head out the door and sit on the wrought-iron patio chair that David had shipped in from Czechoslovakia.

I refuse to follow her, Miriam thought, instead bouncing up and heading around again with the salmon mousse. This time, she was pleased to note, everyone in the living room tried it. Esther peered over her rye bread as she munched, signaling that it was not as good as hers but that it would pass muster nonetheless.

"Who needs a refill?" David asked, holding a bottle of wine and a bottle of seltzer. He was grateful his mother was not there to plead for a drink.

Miriam felt a wave of nausea as she lifted the cheesecloth from the half-cooked turkey to baste it. What is that? she thought, gripping her belly and looking from side to side as if she'd heard a sound.

As he leaned to pick up the demolished cheese tray, David also felt his stomach rising in his throat. How much have I drunk? he thought. They'd been seated for only an hour or so. He couldn't have had too much. David looked over at his father and saw a grimace on Seymour's willfully smiling face. Then he saw Frances bend toward the floor.

"I'm not well," she said.

Vladimir rolled his eyes. "Maybe you shouldn't have eaten so much," he said. "How many times do I have to tell you, Fran?" He shook his head. "Like an animal."

"No, really." Frances stood up. "Where's the bathroom?"

"There's one around the corner there." David pointed toward the guest bathroom.

"I need one too!" Esther said suddenly. "I'm going to be sick!"

David's stomach roiled, a million butterflies flapping their pow-dered wings. And then a cramp bit into his side. "Upstairs and to the left," he said. He dreaded the thought of his mother-in-law in his bath-room. He imagined her picking up and examining a pubic hair.

Both women stood up and ran, Frances waddling around the cor-ner and Esther hitting the stairs.

Miriam came out of the kitchen, not, as David had once fantasized, with the proud look of a woman who had cooked the perfect bird but with the wounded face of a little girl sent home by the school nurse. "I don't feel good, David," she said. Her face was a pallid shade of gray.

"Me either," he said. "What's going on?"

The sound of retching came from the bathrooms, one quite close, the other more distant, as if an echo of the first.

Vladimir, Seymour, and Joseph all stood at the same time and, knocking into one another, ran toward the deck, where they leaned over the railing and vomited.

"Do you think it was the fish?" Miriam asked her husband.

"Maybe," he said. "Was it sitting out long?" He grabbed his stomach as if this would keep what he'd eaten inside.

"Just while I went to the garden for the dill and rosemary. Other than that, it was in the fridge." Miriam started down the basement steps, headed for the only other bathroom in the house. She knew she should have picked the place with three proper bathrooms. But David had, of course, wanted the one with the biggest outdoor space.

Her husband followed her. "You picked the herbs?" he said.

They swung open the bathroom door. Miriam knelt over the toilet, and David scooted her to the side and knelt down next to her. In syn-chronicity, the couple heaved over the bowl.

After the first round was over, both sat back against the cinder-block wall and leaned their heads against the cold cement. Miriam wiped her mouth with the back of her hand.

"The dill," David said. "I told you *I'd* get everything from the gar-den. Where did you get it?"

"Well, you weren't available," Miriam said. She had screamed for him to pick the herbs right away, but the noise of the vacuum had won out. Now she wanted to wring her husband's neck. But the dill had been the most beautiful she had ever seen. "It was amazing," Miriam said, her body moving against the nausea that was coming over her again. "The dill was as large as ferns almost. And so very green." She felt now that she was in a sort of dream state. She imagined she was in a field of dill, a setting for a beautiful herbal fairy tale. She pictured herself with long blond hair, like Betsy Randolph's, flying out behind her as she ran across the field of giant dill. Toward whom? Then she moved to the toilet, and, placing both hands on the edges of the bowl, she vomited again.

David reached over and held Miriam's hair back with one hand. It was a gesture that, even in the middle of throwing up, made her smile and remember those times when as a child she was sick and her mother sat on the edge of her bed and took care of her. Miriam thought of Esther now in the bathroom off her bedroom, pitched over the toilet that had not been recently cleaned, and she burst into tears.

Things were not going at all as she'd planned.

"Miriam." David let go of her hair and knocked his head against the wall a couple of times until he felt a dull, numbing pain. "You took the wrong dill."

Her head rose from the toilet. She wiped her mouth with the back of her hand and turned to face her husband.

"Yes, Miriam. The wrong dill. The one doused in Essoil. You poisoned the whole family."

Like a cat readying to pounce, Miriam rose slowly from her crouched position. "*I* poisoned the whole family," she said.

David ran over to the bowl. "It sure seems like it," he said, his head still over the toilet.

"Me," she said. For a fleeting moment she thought of her ruined meal, each slaved-over dish, that blasted turkey she had worried about for days, the twice-baked potatoes, the salad dressing, all tainted by David's herbs, by her father's cleanser. "*I* poisoned us. You had nothing to do with it."

David could see where this was going. "Well, we're poisoned in any case," he said. "Whoever did it."

"You've got to be kidding me," Miriam said, becoming even more furious at her husband. But instead of pausing to articulate this further, she ran upstairs to check on the rest of the house. On the first floor, she heard Frances breathing heavily in the bathroom and continued up to her bedroom.

"Mommy?" The room was strewn with the books she'd thrown from the bed earlier. She ran into the bathroom. "Are you okay?"

Esther lay in a fetal position on the tiled floor. Miriam bent down beside her and took her hand. For a brief moment she imagined that Esther was her baby and that she had to lift her up and make her feel better as Esther had once done for her. She thought of that time in school a million years before, when the class had been learning about the concept of reincarnation. The teacher had asked what each would like to come back as. Miriam, not pausing a moment, had screamed out that she would like to come back as Esther's mother.

She put Esther's head on her lap. "Are you okay, Mommy?" she asked, stroking her mother's hair, stiff with hair spray.

For a moment, mother and daughter stayed this way, peaceful but for the sounds of the running water from the last time Esther had flushed the toilet. Esther rose slowly from her daughter's grip and looked into her eyes. She reached out and touched Miriam's damp cheek. "You are a terrible cook, Miriam." She laughed. "My Lord, sweetheart, when will you ever learn?"

David dragged himself up from the basement to find out what had become of everyone else and was drawn outside, where Vladimir, Joseph, and Seymour were curved over the balcony as if they were on stage taking bows. Seeing his father bent over that way, David had a strange and fleeting urge to spank him, to hold him over the balcony and just smack him until his ass was as red as his face looked right now. Then the urge was gone, and, were anyone to ask David had he ever had such a violent and perverse thought, he would have denied it and believed wholeheartedly in his denial.

The three turned to look at David, who had pulled up a chair and sat down behind them. He paused a moment, shocked by who these men were in history; the history of the country would be different without them. And now here they were before him, three aging men who had just spent the past half hour throwing up into his calla lilies.

"It was the dill," David said. "My dill. I had been doing some experiments with pesticides and, actually, with your Essoil, Joseph. Turns out, Essoil is a terrific but clearly inedible pesticide. Basically"—he rubbed his forehead—"we've been poisoned by the Essoil." Feeling slightly sadistic, he wondered if he could manage to make his father-in-law culpable.

Joseph looked utterly stunned. "My God," he said. "Surely you know that zhis is not for the foods?" he said.

"Yes, I know," David said. "I never intended for us to eat the food with the Essoil. It was an experiment gone wrong," he said. "I'm sorry." He looked down and debated telling them that it had been Miriam who had picked the wrong herbs. That it is Miriam who simply never listens, never, always has to do things when and where she wants them, so impatient. But David kept these thoughts to himself for now.

That was when they heard the giggling below.

Slowly the men turned to look at where the laughter was coming from.

Sarah.

David got up and leaned out toward the girlish sound coming from his mother, a sound he had not before heard from her. How could she be laughing? He realized then that she had been spared the salmon as she sat sulking in the dining room.

Below, Sarah was completely naked but for the light blue scarf that had been looped around her neck but was now tied around her wrist. Her clothes made a little path behind her, and she waved the scarf, reciting Shakespeare:

> *Things base and vile, holding no quantity,*
> *Love can transpose to form and dignity. Love looks not with the eyes,*
> *   but with the mind,*
> *And therefore is winged Cupid painted blind.*

Sarah danced over the lily bulbs David had just planted and crashed into the new shrubs and chrysanthemums he'd cut down the previous weekend.

"*A Midsummer Night's Dream,*" Joseph said.

Seymour looked over at him, for a moment stunned more by his knowledge of the reference than by the image of his wife dancing naked below.

David turned away from the sight of his mother's nakedness.

"Come down, boys," Sarah said. "It's so lovely in the garden." She waved her arms wildly above her head, and the scarf trailed behind gracefully.

"Sarah," Seymour called down to his wife. "Please, dear, put your clothes on, you'll catch cold!"

Vladimir cleared his throat.

Sarah laughed at him from below. "I'm free!" she screamed.

"Mom," David whispered.

Seymour put his hand on his son's shoulder. "She's been getting worse," he said.

Oh, really, David thought, shrugging his father's hand away. He watched Seymour head down the stairs and into the garden, an outstretched hand reaching toward his wife.

CHAPTER 19

Sundowning:
Sarah Bloom, 1960

PERHAPS, MANY DOCTORS SAID, Sarah Bloom had killed off too many of her brain cells with that terrible drinking and for this reason was confused about the difference between a potted plant and a teacup. Or perhaps she suffered from Alzheimer's, a disease nearly impossible to diagnose while the patient is still living, Seymour was told when he demanded an accurate assessment of why his wife was losing her memory at a terrifyingly rapid pace.

Either way, all that dancing in the basement had certainly taken a toll. Whatever the cause, Sarah's state worsened before Seymour's eyes. In a matter of months he watched her go from forgetting the teakettle on the stove, a small and forgivable infraction, to stacking his cleaned shirts on the top shelf of the refrigerator, to the horrible scene when she had shrieked naked through their son's garden on Thanksgiving.

Something had to change. Five months later, inside the Upper East Side brownstone, Seymour taped yellow slips of torn paper to most of the household objects. The one on the stove said "stove," the one on the bureau said "bureau." Their living room opened onto a deck, and when the lightest breeze blew off the East River, the bits of paper fluttered like insect wings in flight. The doctor had said that this labeling would help Sarah. Trigger, said the doctor, the same one who had looked Sarah square in the eye and, as if she were not even there, told Seymour that his wife's state could be her own fault. Labeling will trigger her memory, the doctor had told them. This term had led Seymour to think not of a series of recollections, accumulated images his wife must somewhere still hold, but of a gun, always a gun, the barrel of it switching in his mind's eye from his wife's temple to his own and back to hers again.

By the time the crowds gathered to watch the ball drop in Times Square, ringing in 1960, Sarah had stopped doing almost everything but watching television. *The Price Is Right, I've Got a Secret, What's My Line?* The hum was always present, and Sarah sat before it silently. At first Seymour could not understand why she watched game shows, vapid programs she would not have tolerated for a moment only the previous year. But listening to the ding of a contestant getting an answer correct, the abrasive sound of clapping from the audience, he realized that these programs contained no narrative—there was nothing about them to remember. And though the viewer was held briefly in suspense—What would the secret *be*? Would he get three in a row?— it was a fleeting emptiness. In seconds, the answer would be presented, and what Seymour came to realize was that Sarah's anxiety would be momentarily alleviated, until the next question was posed.

Seymour often thought if he could just press his memory down deep inside him—into his stomach, his intestines—his recollections, like his wife's, would simply not exist. Was her forgetting willful? Had their life together been so horrible? Seymour could not help but be reminded how on any number of nights they had been forced to leave a party early and he would say to her, as her martini glass tipped sideways, Sarah, can't we have fun tonight?

Her face had mocked him. Fun? She'd laughed at him. How many times had she *laughed* at him? Still he saw her mouth opening as if to swallow him up.

At the end of the night Seymour would have to help Sarah into the car so that she would not fall or catch her dress, and he saw the way the other partygoers, in their tuxedos and long, sparkling gowns, would look out at them with pity. This never ceased to make Seymour think about the long days before he'd met Solomon, how he'd dragged those heavy encyclopedias all over the five boroughs and beyond. One day, he'd known even then, that burden would be lifted.

Looking over at his wife, who stared blankly at the television, Sey-

mour felt a pang of sadness that nearly split him open. What, he wondered, would spill out? He imagined images from his past replacing
blood and water and electrolytes, and, in a kind of leaching, he fantasized that he too would be emptied of the past, nothing left behind him.
No guilt. No memory of Sarah before she turned into a bitter woman.
For this he would forgo the memories of becoming: the feeling of walking down Forty-second Street on his way to a show. My show, he'd
think, not so much with an inflated ego but with the feeling that what
he and the audience were about to experience—the glorious escape of
the theater—was something he was helping them to feel. No, he could
not help his wife, or even his children, but he could bring theater and
music to people who would be changed by it. As he was.

Sarah was his charge now. Only Seymour held the memory of how
they had skated on the Duck Pond before the war, before the children.
Would they have done it again, knowing what was to come? Sometimes
Seymour imagined their lives together as two hopelessly misfired
synapses. And sometimes he allowed himself to feel envious that Sarah
had always been able to escape everything, jealous that she was allowed
to forget what great disappointments they had been to each other and
their children.

The straw that broke it came in April 1960, when Sarah tried to
crawl into the oven, set at 450 degrees.

"What are you doing?" Seymour asked as he watched her shove herself in.

"Trying to get warm." Her voice was an echo inside the stove.

He ran over to turn it off and pull her out. What if he had not been
there?

"She's become a danger to herself and to this household," Seymour
told his son. He had phoned him at home so no one at work would
hear him speak of it.

David could not bear to think of his mother like this.

"Hmm-hm," he said. But was this his father's fault? Had his father
ever tried to stop her drinking? David couldn't think of a time he had.

"Really, son, she is going to hurt herself."

David wanted to bash the telephone against the wall over and over
again. He wanted to rail against his father, but instead he said, "I see,"
between clenched teeth.

"We're going to have to find a home," Seymour said. "She needs help."

David let out a laugh. He couldn't help himself. *Now* she needs help. And all those years his mother had wasted her life, what had she needed then? Now that Seymour was left alone with her, he wanted to send her away.

At that moment Seymour was exhausted. He could hear the tone in David's voice, and he was too tired for it. Sometimes his son's attitude completely eluded him—Seymour had worked hard in this life to give his son what he himself had never had. This was not the time for David and his rebellion. What a selfish, useless boy, Seymour thought. He works four days a week at a job I handed to him on a fucking silver platter. He hates me so much, why doesn't he go try his hand on Wall Street then? Why doesn't he go to law school? When would David become a man? Seymour had been forced to be a man when he was twelve years old and had to look after his little brother while Inez worked. His mother. Still he could not bear to see his own mother in Sarah's condition. Inez was old now, but no crazier than she had been when he was growing up. It would have been horrible for him to have to see what David and Dulcy were witnessing in their mother. And yet, it was not easy for him either. When, Seymour wondered silently, would his son reach over and place a firm hand on his shoulder, offer him the support he needed as well? "You can either help or not," he snapped. "You decide," he said and hung up the phone.

At David's suggestion, Seymour had tried to get a nurse, but the doctor told him that, at least for a while, Sarah would need to be closely monitored where hospital facilities were available.

"Where there is no alcohol," the doctor said pointedly.

When he said this, Seymour flinched. It had been selfish, he knew now, to have alcohol shipped especially for her. Back then, he'd had no idea what would happen. Seymour had simply thought he was saving them both some trouble: Sarah from the covert way she sneaked around the house stealing Mob liquor, and he, well, from the prospect of being killed for the indiscreet way she watered the whiskey down. Now Seymour saw he had taken the easy route when it came to his wife, and now, now, he saw that he was paying the price.

"There is no liquor in our house," Seymour said.

The doctor cocked his head at him. "It's for the best," he said.

"Of course," Seymour told the doctor. "Thank you," he said, on the verge of weeping.

Sarah Bloom, barely sixty years old, watched television in the den as David helped Seymour get some of her things together.

"She's not dead," Seymour said to his son coldly, as David aggressively ripped through his mother's closet. "She'll be coming back soon."

But would she want to come back as she had been? David thought. He remembered that day they had first seen Frances Gold on television, the day Sarah had been thrown into an inconsolable rage. In what David now recalled as a brief moment of lucidity, his mother had stilled him with her gaze and asked him never to let her lose her mind.

David grunted and threw clothes for all seasons onto the bed. Not dead, he thought, merely hovering. Haunting. As he heard the clapping of game show contestants, he couldn't help but wonder silently if the war between him and his mother—a war that had everything to do with how much he had already loved and lost her—was finished. He would give almost anything to have his mother's hands shaking over the paper as she read "Dear Maggie," making one vicious comment after another. Who is this Maggie telling me that an unhappy wife's dignity demands she never show her disapproval of her husband? Clearly, she was never married to your father, Sarah would say, laughing to her son.

Who had won? David opened the upright desk in the bedroom, where he had seen his mother write on so many dreary afternoons. He'd watch her from the hallway as she wept and threw balls of paper behind her. Sometimes when he came in, his mother's head was propped on her elbows as she stared blankly at the bottles of ink and paper, the letter opener gleaming from its leather case. I hate your father, she'd tell her son from this pose. Hate him.

For all her hatred, she had certainly kept a good deal of Seymour saved in that small space. Upon unhooking the writing table, David found his father's embroidered linen handkerchiefs scented with cigar smoke and balled from use, his matchboxes, stacks of *Playbills*, a pair of shattered spectacles. David contemplated calling Seymour over to show him, but what would it lead to? Whatever it was, David was not up for it right now.

Stacks of letters filled the built-in cubbies, several piles sticking out and tied with fading ribbons. Was he finally gaining access? David could not resist. He slid one out of a pile:

June 1931

Sarah,

   Just suffer through it. It is our lot, dear, to be both over and underused at the exact same time. If you must, then why not get a little tight in the daytime and do a bit of dancing? The way I see it, life passes us by in either case.

Let's go to the Plaza,
Celia

David pulled another out from the stack:

April 1932

Dear Maggie:

   I remember dressing up in my mother's clothes in that musky attic, and now here I am a grown woman. When I get all gussied up some days—especially when I wear my new summer silk dress with the blue sash, I feel like I've become my mother, am looking out from her perspective: Did the world seem as small to her as it does to me?

"What are you doing?" Sarah stood behind David as he began to read a letter from his father.

"Nothing," he said, throwing down the page and turning in the chair toward his mother. "Just getting you ready to go, Mom." David tried to regain his composure. Who was the girl in this letter, and how had she turned into the woman who stood behind him, whom he was helping to send away?

She grabbed the chair from behind and tried to shake it. "Stop looking at me!" Sarah screamed. The chair, heavy with David's weight, didn't budge. "Stop it right now!" she said.

David turned and hooked his arm over the back of the chair. "I'm sorry, Mom," he said, rising from the desk. Did she remember these letters? He imagined his mother at this desk on all those nights he came in to kiss her good night before Mary read to him and put him to sleep. Did she return to her letter and mention her only son? "Dear Celia," David imagined she wrote to her old friend, "Adorable David has just come in to kiss me good night, and this makes me so happy."

Of course David knew this was not the case. Now, looking at Sarah, her eyes spilling with outraged tears, he thought that though she could not always remember that a mirror was a mirror, perhaps her memory reached further back. Would that be to his childhood or to hers? He tried to think of his mother as a young girl but could remember only the pictures he had seen of her, a head of blond curls on a sad, stoic face.

David lifted the writing table, still strewn with letters, and clicked it shut. "Okay?" he said.

Sarah ran her hands over her salmon-colored blouse, and the fleshiness of the color mixed with the cold shininess of the fabric struck David as morbidly depressing.

She nodded her head succinctly. "That's better," she said and headed back to the television in the den.

The director had quit, the lead and her understudy were fighting, and the set was falling apart on David's rehearsals for *Greenwillow,* and so Seymour and Dulcy brought Sarah to the Longevity Center in Connecticut without David. He was not particularly upset by this. The prospect of "committing" her, which was how he had taken to referring to it, was overwhelming. He imagined his mother would fight the whole way, kicking and screaming, arms gripping the side of the car, refusing to get out, and David couldn't bear to watch.

So when David and Miriam finally went to visit her after her first few weeks, they were expecting to find Sarah in an even worse state than before.

"I'm sure she's an absolute wreck," he said, turning off the Merritt. Seymour and Dulcy both had reported that everything had gone "smoothly," but David hadn't believed them.

Miriam looked out the window. Perhaps it would be nicer to live up here, she thought. In the country. Though the landscape did not resemble it, she remembered Costa Rica, the feel of the earth beneath her feet as she walked through the forest with Enrique. Now Miriam imagined waking to birds singing in an effort to avoid thinking of the afternoon that lay ahead of her. She had dreaded this day since she'd found out the week before that David wished her to accompany him on this visit. Somehow she'd always imagined he would like to go alone, and now Miriam knew she would be called upon to muster sympathy. For both of them, she thought, and yet, as David parked the car and dramatically knocked his head on the wheel, she didn't have the sympathy she knew a good wife should have for her husband and her mother-in-law.

For whom she lacked it, David or Sarah, she couldn't tell. Ever since the wedding, she had barely tolerated her mother-in-law. And since this last Thanksgiving, she hadn't been too fond of her husband either. For six months she had harbored this resentment. Everything she did was informed by the fact that, yes, she had picked the dill and the rosemary, but David had been the one actually to poison them. And she felt the way he had done so with Essoil was some sort of psychological meanness: When it came down to it, no matter whether they had eaten it that day or on another day, David had wanted to hurt her father. It had devastated Joseph that what he had spent his whole adult life working toward had ended up practically killing everyone close to him. He had not seen a bit of the humor in it. Esther, by contrast, could see it vividly. After she had vomited so much that bile came up, bright and shiny as neon, she and Miriam had lain on the bed together, completely spent. They had lain there looking up at the ceiling, which, Miriam was chagrined to note, needed painting, and Esther had started to laugh. Joseph had wandered upstairs deliriously and been furious at the sight of his wife rolling around on the bed with Miriam, laughing so hard tears streamed down her face.

"Killed by dill!" she had screamed.

"I fail to see zhe humor in this, Esther."

"Oh, Joe," Esther had said, sitting up and wiping her eyes. "We're all fine. We lived. Lighten up, sweetie."

He'd headed back downstairs.

They were all changed by that sad afternoon, Miriam thought, as she looked at the ranch-style institution her mother-in-law now lived in. And David had not so much as apologized. He'd only moped about the house and garden, more irritated that he would no longer be able to practice his science on the precious produce than contrite for what his produce had done to them. From the bedroom Miriam had watched him fingering his stupid string beans, streetlights clicking on, mothers from the neighborhood calling their children home for dinner, and she had wanted to jump from her window and stomp on the whole garden. She imagined autumn squashes bursting, the buds of late fall flowers snapping from their delicate stems.

And yet she missed David's gardening, the way he would come upstairs smelling of earth and growing things. She hadn't even minded him dirtying her Egyptian cotton sheets with the loose soil. After Thanksgiving, their lovemaking had lessened and grown more mechanical. But on the nights Miriam managed to release her anger from her body—this happened most often after she had come home from one of David and Seymour's shows and had lived in a parallel world for only a few hours—the primitive quality of their sex returned. But now it was best when they reached for each other in the middle of the night. Awakened by a reversing truck or the house settling, the two would turn to each other without any of the trappings of the dailiness that had come between them. In these moments they were themselves and also more than themselves, and they made love in the sad and lovely way saved for two people who have seen the failings of each other and have stayed together despite them.

"Well, come on, David," Miriam said now, as she watched her husband grip the steering wheel. She knew she should reach out and touch him in some way, and knowing this made it even harder to do so. "Let's just get this whole thing over with," she said, opening her door, her feet hitting the pavement hard.

"Sarah Bloom," David requested at the first nurses' station of the Longevity Center. He tried not to take in the long, shining hallways and the occasional screams that echoed through them. How could this have happened? Were his mother to become aware of anything, David thought, she would absolutely die to see herself living this way. He saw now that his mother's life had not been what she imagined. But why not? Because it could have been. There were dances and balls and open-ing nights. There was the symphony and two children who adored her. There was Madison Avenue. What else could his mother have wanted?

Sarah seemed to appear out of nowhere, waltzing out of her room with an enormous smile plastered on her made-up face.

"Mom," David said, surprised. His mother had never worn much makeup, and now she had big streaks of rouge on each cheek, dark lined eyes, and purple eye shadow up to her eyebrows.

She embraced them both warmly.

David stepped back. At first he thought she had an open wound across her forehead, as if his mother had had a lobotomy that he had not been told about, but then he saw the headband stitched with red sequins. She wore a straight-cut gunnysack with spaghetti straps, fringed at the hem.

"Welcome," Sarah said, curtsying. "How wonderful to see you both," she said. She pulled them toward the common room.

There another woman, also dressed for flappier days, joined them. The two beamed at each other.

"Where have you *been*?" Sarah asked.

"Movement," the woman said. "I thought you were coming. And who are these?"

"How rude of me! Hazel, this is . . ." Sarah turned to look at David. A vacant look passed over her face, and she tilted her head as if to search for his identity.

"Your son," David said.

"And your daughter-in-law," said Miriam, nudging David.

"My son!" Sarah beamed.

"Lovely to make your acquaintance!" Hazel reached out and vigor-ously shook David's and then Miriam's hand.

Hazel took Sarah's hand and, tugging her near, kissed her on the cheek. Her red lips moved into a smile as they got close to Sarah's face.

"Shall we walk?" Sarah said, blushing.

"Why not?" David said. "Would you like to show me your room?" he asked her.

Sarah shrugged. "I suppose," she said.

"Perhaps we could talk alone, Ma," he said, looking toward Hazel and then Miriam. "Miriam will keep Hazel company awhile."

Miriam glared at David. "Of course," she said to Hazel. Why, she thought to herself, had she come here? To babysit?

"I could show you where we'll be putting on our play!" said Hazel.

"That would be lovely." Miriam smiled genuinely toward her mother-in-law's new friend.

"A play?" David asked them both.

"We're doing *Gigi*!" said Sarah. "I'm to play the lead, of course," she said. "The night they invented champagne," Sarah began to sing, bobbing her head back and forth in rhythm.

"Sarah is a fabulous actress." Hazel looked toward her friend with admiration. "We're very lucky to have her here in time for our production."

"You are," Sarah said. "Quite lucky."

"*Gigi* is a young girl," David said. "She's eighteen years old, tops." He couldn't help but think of the irony of the lovely charm song between the older couple, "I Remember It Well."

Sarah and Hazel looked questioningly at David. "I'm fabulous in it," Sarah said. "Just terrific."

"She is," piped in her friend. She put her chin on Sarah's shoulder. "Truly."

Sarah smiled and patted her head. "Do you remember college, Hazey? My Lord!"

"I don't think I went to college," Hazel said.

Sarah whipped her head around, bumping Hazel from her shoulder. "Why, you most *certainly* went to college. You went to Smith! Don't you remember *Smith*?"

Hazel turned this thought over for a moment. "Fine." She shrugged. "Smith."

"That's right!" Sarah said. "Of all *things*, Hazel!" she said.

"So let's go see your room then." David began to walk away from them.

"It's this way," Sarah said. "Follow me."

Sarah's room was a cross between a college dorm room and a hospital room. David could see out onto the parking lot, his little yellow Renault Dauphine shining in the sunlight. Then he turned to look at the pictures pasted on the wall above his mother's bed. He leaned in closer: magazine photos of movie stars combined with advertisements. Marilyn Monroe's unmistakable body attached to the head of a monkey. Elizabeth Taylor's face atop the body of a wingless bird.

David stepped back. He had been told not to question her, because this could be frustrating for both of them, so he resisted the urge to ask his mother exactly what all this was about. He sat down on the twin hospital bed that was cranked so the head rose above the feet section. He patted the space next to him.

"Sit down, Mom," he said. His heart beat wildly.

Sarah sat down and smiled at her son. Her teeth were stained with bits of bright red lipstick, and when he looked down to turn away from the obscenity of his mother's mouth, he saw the sequins on her dress, some bent, casting tiny frowning shadows. Many of the beads had come loose, and several of the ones that remained were cracked or chipped. The fabric beneath, David noticed, was fading to yellow. Sarah used to walk down the stairs in her flawless gowns, the diaphanous fabric rising and falling as she took each step. Little black clouds, David had thought as he had watched the hem of his mother's dress.

"Mom," he said now. He knew what he was about to do was questionable, but he also knew there was no alternative. He would honor what his mother had asked him all those years ago.

"Yes, dear." She looked around the room. "Do you like my new place?" Sarah scratched at the skin beneath her headband.

David looked up to see what he knew was Rita Hayworth's body—he would recognize that anywhere—attached to an ad for toothpaste. Beneath this, he noticed, was a torn advertisement for Essoil. "The future" was all that he could make out, and, from the place where the woman would be holding the bottle, her arm and hand were torn loose, leaving only the very tips of her fingers.

"It's very nice," he said.

"Thank you," Sarah said as she happily settled back on the bed.

"Let's talk," David said.

"Sure," she said.

"Are you happy, Mom?"

"Sure," she said.

David shook his head. "Really?"

Sarah shrugged.

"Because you know you're not going to get better," he said.

Sarah blinked at her son and smoothed down her dress. The sequins snapped and ruffled beneath her touch.

"This is it. You're only going to get worse," he said. "You're going to stop remembering everything." He held up the plastic glass of water on the nightstand. His hand shook. "What is this?" he asked her, his voice trembling.

"A cup," his mother said. Her eyes darted from side to side with fear, and then she nodded her head, relieved. "It's a blue cup, dear." She nodded definitively.

"Yes, it is, Mother. But one day, maybe tomorrow, maybe next year, you won't know it. You will be stuck here forever," David told his mother. Some people, the doctor had said, are incurable. Some people! When had his mother become some people? David knew he was beginning to get hysterical. "You will never come home," he said.

Sarah looked down at her lap. "I like it here," she said quietly. Her quietness nearly cut David Bloom in half. In his youth it had been her cruelty that had wounded him, but now he imagined his body sliced up and hung on the wall by his mother's sad voice.

Sarah rocked back and forth on the bed, her arms crossed.

What, he wondered now, was she thinking? Was it of him? Because right now, all he could remember was the way he had once adored her. "There's no business like show business . . ." David and his mother had once sung Irving Berlin together. "Like no business I know." For some reason they had been singing outside the brownstone when it had started to rain. The two of them had hopped over the puddles beginning to form in the cracked slopes of the sidewalk: "Nowhere could you get that happy feeling, when you are stealing that extra bow . . ." Sarah had stared out at the river, the lights of Queens shining in the distance. Thank you, she had screamed across the river, curtsying. She blew kisses into the night, and David took a bow.

This was unbearable. His mother was far too young to have this happen to her. He was far too young, for Christ's sake. Sarah had robbed him of a safe and happy childhood, and now, when he had finally escaped her, she was robbing him again of a secure adulthood. Of the prospect of a happy future with happy children of his own.

Would there be happy children? When he had run into Miriam on the street in Manhattan, an image of her walking behind a child, holding the outstretched hands by the thumbs, had socked him in the stomach.

"Look, Mom," he said. He searched her eyes and grabbed her wrist. "What I'm saying is, I can help you." He paused.

"Wonderful," she said.

"No, *help* you," he said again, tugging her wrist. He knew this was the right thing, what his mother, or the woman his mother had once been, would want him to do. "I can get you pills, Mom. If you want to make this all go away."

"This?" she asked him, pointing to the cup that David had placed back on the nightstand.

"No, *this.*" He brought out his arm to show the room. "The sickness." Inadvertently, David pointed at his mother's heart.

"Why on earth would I want to do that?" she asked.

David looked at her.

"I'm to be Gigi." A hand fluttered up to her neck.

"Gigi," David said.

"I was thinking, you know"—she leaned conspiratorially in to her son—"we could do the show together."

"Really?" David said, straightening. "You'd like that?"

"Sure!" Sarah swatted him on the shoulder. "What fun. You could play Gaston."

"Gaston. Your suitor?"

Sarah nodded.

"Your protector."

"You know my husband has connections," she said. "I could certainly get you an audition."

David had to laugh at himself. How many years ago had she forbade his acting? "Sure, Mom," he said. "Or perhaps you could just get me great seats."

"That's a cinch," she said, snapping her fingers.

"Forget it," he said.

Concern flickered over Sarah's face, and, for a moment, her eyes moved back and forth as if she were searching for textual evidence. "The tickets?"

"Everything." Where had she gone? David wondered. And how far back did she go? He prayed that she would forget this conversation the way she had forgotten all the disappointment, the heartbreak. He wished he could forget that too.

He had thought this would be what she wanted. Or was giving his mother an overdose of pills more what he wanted? Maybe this was unbearable to him, not to her.

At that moment, Miriam appeared out of nowhere in the threshold.

"Oh!" David said. "You surprised us."

His wife kicked at the floor, and her Ked squeaked against the bright tile. "Hazel had to go with the nurse somewhere," she said. "I'm sorry to interrupt." Miriam looked straight at David.

Through me, he thought. She sees, he thought, but what he knew was, she heard.

David got up from the bed and held his hand out to help Sarah. He took a deep breath. "Ready, Mom?" he asked brightly.

She nodded slowly. Afternoon light streamed in through the windows, illuminating the glossy eggshell white walls that crawled with rows of tiny fingerprints. Hers? David thought. Those of someone else who had been trapped in here before? The shiny magazine pictures were suffused with light, and it was impossible to make out from where he stood what was on their surfaces.

Outside the sky was turning to yellow and orange and blue-purple, and Sarah began to cry.

"What's wrong, Sarah?" Miriam went toward her mother-in-law and knelt down before her.

David craned his head out of the room. "Nurse!" he called.

"It's okay." Miriam looked with a cold, meaningful stare toward her husband.

Orange light poured into the hallway, and David saw another woman alone, turned toward the wall, sobbing in a corner.

"Nurse!" he said in a growing panic.

A nurse walked toward him, registering his stunned expression. For a brief moment, her hard, medicinal look turned soft. "It's the sundowning," she said.

"What?" David asked.

"Don't worry," she said. "It's just the time of day. The quality of light. At sundown, everyone seems to remember, even the worst ones."

He looked over at Sarah being comforted by Miriam, and relief washed over him. Sarah crying was a familiar image, and for a brief moment he imagined that she was back to herself, that this awful scene had never passed between them. David remembered many things about his mother: her elegance, the way her silk robes flew out behind her as she raced around the house. The way she would hear only a few bars of a symphony and instantly be able to identify it. Brahms, Number 3, in F, she'd say, always pointing.

"I'm to be the star," she said now. "Gigi! Everyone has always told me I have star quality."

"I know, Mom," David said from across the room. "You always have."

"You did too," she said. She looked up at her son. "You did, you know."

David couldn't look at his mother or Miriam.

"And what have you done with it?" she asked. "It's all been wasted."

Sarah stood up. Her dress crinkled loudly. "May I have this dance?" she asked, sniffling.

"No, Mom," he said, looking straight ahead. "Sit down."

"Come on," Sarah said, dipping her head and curtsying.

David paused for a moment, and then walked toward his mother. He took her hand to help her stand.

"They asked me how I knew my true love was true. I of course replied, something here inside cannot be denied," Sarah sang softly. She moved closer, placed her head on her son's chest, and rocked slowly from side to side.

David stiffened and looked over at Miriam, still seated on the bed. Seeing his wife's tearstained face in the early evening light somehow made him soften, his shoulders relaxing, his fingers and wrists loosening. Everything was serious. He put his hand at the small of his mother's back and felt the hard, bent sequins scrape his palms.

"When your heart's on fire, you must realize, smoke gets in your eyes," Sarah sang.

David could feel the vibration of his mother's voice through his rib cage, and he could smell her hair spray and heavy perfume, a scent he didn't recognize. He watched the motes of dust float in and out of the soft bands of light still coming in through the windows as he placed his chin on his mother's head and guided her slowly around the room.

CHAPTER 20

Selling: Essoil, 1960

JOSEPH AND ESTHER SAT in the study, desks facing each other in a permanent kiss, as they went over bills. Joseph ran the business of Essoil, but Esther had always been in charge of the domestic empire. Her feet tapped the Bean braided rug as she shuffled through the gas, the oil, the phone and electric.

Esther sighed. "What is it, Joe?" she asked him. "You look tired."

Joseph slid his glasses down his nose and looked at his wife. "I zhink we should sell, Es," he said. He scratched his chin and looked out the window, to the peaceful suburban street, high on a hill overlooking Casco Bay. The view had been what sold him on the place. As soon as the real estate agent had taken him onto the back deck and held her hand out to the water, he had remembered the evening he watched the sun go down with Esther all those years before. He never remembered crashing into that tree, only watching the sun set over the water, a crescent moon rising behind them. There was a tremendous silence to his life here. If he chose to, Joseph could go months without speaking to his neighbors. How unlike the crowded stoops of Brooklyn, where, even in the dead of winter, everyone was on top of one another, and rumors passed between households quick as boys snatching baseball cards and bubble gum from the candy store.

Many of the conversations between Joseph and Esther began with talk of selling the company. They had started contemplating it back when they still lived in Boston. Procter & Gamble had been hounding Joseph for years. Had they forgotten how they had berated him to sell

sell, sell in those days he was on the road, his cold finger on the soft, creased map, tracing a route they'd insisted he take? He had been a disappointing salesman, fortunately, he now thought.

Esther had always encouraged the offers, believing it was the cleanser itself that was keeping her so far from Maine. I want to go home, she would tell Joseph when she was waxing the dining room table or chopping meat and carrots and potatoes and onions for the pressure cooker.

It always made him feel that their life together had been only a short vacation.

And so Joseph, who liked to be involved in all aspects of the business, had miraculously hired managers and agreed to move north without selling the company.

It wasn't until the year after the disaster at Miriam and David's that Joseph finally decided to sell.

"Really?" Esther asked now. She put down her stamps, rolled up in a sterling silver dispenser that had been her father's.

"All zhe time, I'm thinking about that day, what zhe cleanser did to us all." Joseph rubbed his shiny forehead. "I can't believe it," he said. "In a way, it started vith Miriam nearly killing herself from zhe chemicals. Maybe it's a sign to end with her nearly killing us all from Essoil."

Esther nodded. Joseph knew it thrilled her when he talked about his emotions, and he knew she was trying to remain still, as if her making any false moves would cause him to retreat into the language of business he used all too often.

"And it would be nice to have more time for walking," he said.

Since they had come to Maine to live permanently, Joseph had begun taking long walks alone in the forest. He spent hours identifying the local flora and fauna: This is from a maple, he'd tell Esther, twirling a crimson leaf for her upon his return home from Mackworth Island, a tiny, carless island ten minutes from their house that was home to the Governor Baxter School for the Deaf. The parking lot at the school was as far as cars could go, and often Joseph parked in the lot and walked the mile-long path that circled the island, looking out over the bay and spotting his house. Sometimes he would walk there with Miriam or Gloria when they visited. See? he'd tell his daughters. Our house, he'd say, always amazed at seeing it from this faraway perspective, wondering what Esther was doing in there without him.

Sometimes, as Joseph walked the main trail, he would see large groups of young people gesturing to one another as they tramped through the woods, silent but for the eager stomping over moss and fallen pine needles. What if no one could hear my voice? he would think as he walked over the fallen pine needles and down to the rocky shore. A world without language struck him as a pure world. It seemed terrible that who we are on the inside could never exactly match the outside. Is that what he had been trying to do all these years, make everything match up?

"Perhaps I vill learn another language," Joseph told Esther.

She laughed. "Let's worry about learning English first," she said.

"I know English!" Joseph straightened in his chair.

"Of course you do, Joe," Esther said. She reached over her desk to touch his hand. "I was only joking. Let's learn Japanese together." She laughed again. "Or even Italian."

"Ve could, you know," Joseph said. "Ve could do anything ve vant."

"So sell, Joe," Esther said. "I'm terribly busy—I've got the temple, the hospital, the museum fund-raisers—but it sure would be nice to have you around all the time."

Esther was so agreeable to the idea that Joseph looked up from his inventory papers to see whether this was in fact the same woman who had screamed to him to "put in the storm windows already, Joe, it's getting cold," just that morning.

"I zhink it's time," he said, remembering the day he had pulled his limp daughter from the bath of chemicals. And how that night he had felt it, in his gut, known that he had made something no one had made before. But he'd had no idea what it would bring him. "I really zhink it's time," he said.

Joseph took an offer from Procter & Gamble that was surprisingly less lucrative than it had been when they'd begun bidding years earlier. Now, what did he care? They were just fine. And so were their children.

There were so many products now, from Mr. Clean, with its label of that bald man's goyisha face—who would buy from a face like that? Esther asked Joseph every time she returned from the supermarket— to Pine-Sol. Even the disinfectant spray Lysol had an all-purpose cleanser. Though Joseph had been the pioneer, it didn't much matter anymore. Had he sold earlier, perhaps they would have made many millions. Now cleansers came in lotions and sprays and creams. They had so many scents to choose from it was dizzying, thought Joseph. Procter & Gamble bought Essoil more for what it had once been than for what it now was.

But it was plenty as far as Joseph was concerned, and the irony of having come so far was not lost on him. He hated to admit it, but the offer was far more than he'd ever imagined he was worth. And when Joseph and his team of lawyers went to make the deal and sign all the paperwork, he couldn't help but think how much the nature of selling had changed. All those years schlepping bottles from town to town, driving and driving—even now he couldn't bear Route 9—getting down on his knees and scrubbing. Now he said, Yes, I'll take the offer, and simply touched the firm brim of his hat. He had the men draw up the papers and deliver them to him, and simply signed his name: *Joseph Brodsky*. A lot easier than the scrubbing. Joseph Brodsky. When his lawyers bowed to him and gathered the papers together, stamping them here, notarizing them there, Joseph couldn't help but think what his name had come to be worth. He thought of that man he'd met on the road all those years ago: Young man, get off the road before the sand settles permanently in your shoes, he'd said. Joseph had been able to leave before the sand had turned to stone and pinned him to the road.

The hard part was telling Frances Gold, who, the executives at Procter & Gamble insisted, did not come with the deal.

"No way, no how," the attorney had said when Joseph had merely attempted to discuss her current contract. "It's a deal breaker."

Frances did have a fairly lucrative contract they would pay out, but her career as the spokeswoman for Essoil was officially terminated.

Joseph contemplated going down to New York to tell her the news in person. It is the right thing to do, he thought as he stood in the bathroom, staring into the mirror. Better than she should get a letter from a lawyer, the way he had when Solomon died. Solomon Brodsky has expired, the letter had said. At least this was what he remembered. What had it mattered, really? All Joseph had felt was a strange sensation of being frozen in time. No one could forgive anyone now; his anger was petrified. As was Solomon's wickedness. No one can come up from behind and say, Hey, Joey, where ya been all these years? just as Joseph always secretly imagined that one day Solomon would do.

Joseph practiced what he'd tell her: Frances, he started. As he looked into the mirror to make sure his face revealed his genuine sympathy, he realized that what it revealed was bewilderment. His shiny scalp and small eyes, eyelids beginning to droop, his creased forehead, all made Joseph look baffled. He scrunched up his eyebrows to look more serious, but this only made him look as if he were acting stern.

Acting, Joseph thought, raising his head toward the mirror.

Though he had fired people before, he had never had to tell someone he had known for fifty years that she was no longer of use. She had been the face of Essoil. He looked at himself. Or had the face been his face?

His face. He *had* been baffled and bewildered. Coming to this country had been baffling. Living through a childhood in Brooklyn, the way his brother got away, that too had baffled Joseph. He had been baffled that Esther had finally let herself choose him, baffled by his two beautiful girls, the way his company rose in the world. How can your face express what you don't feel? he wondered now. Things do match up in the end, he thought.

Joseph thought of Mr. Clean. An American giant, that one. It was going to have to happen anyway, Joseph knew. Frances would not have been able to sell Essoil much longer, as she was of the age when her children, had she had them, would have been grown and the cleaning should have been done by someone else. The image of Frances cleaning, Joseph thought now, would surely depress anyone.

"Frances," he said out loud, "you have been integral to making Essoil vhat it is today."

He shook his head. Such language. He imagined again that he would simply sign what he had to tell his old friend, the way the deaf people on the island did: You have been a jewel and I have loved you but it is over now. How, he wondered, would he say this with these chapped, thick hands? Joseph looked down at his hands and turned them over and over.

Hearing her husband speak, Esther came out of the bedroom. She padded along the hallway and peered into the open bathroom. Joseph held a hand over his heart.

"You okay?" she asked.

Joseph nodded. He saw his father in his face, Herbert Brodsky's sinking eyes. As a boy, Joseph had thought it was disappointment that made his father look that way. Like a flounder, he had thought. Now, he realized, disappointment or success, it is simply living that does that to a face.

"Sure, Esther," he said, walking out of the bathroom to join his wife in the hallway. "Just fine," he said, placing his arm around her.

Turned out, the drama of losing her Essoil contract was completely lost on Frances.

"Okeydokey," she said when Joseph, who couldn't bear to have her watch his face, called her one December evening.

"You're not so upset?" Joseph looked out the window onto the street. Snow was piling up in heaps, and streetlights illuminated the falling snow and the bowing, leafless branches

"Joseph, darling," Frances said. "I can't believe this lasted half as long as it has."

Joseph had been more than generous with her, but in the back of her mind she'd always wondered whether those commercials prevented her from doing other things. Or would those other parts—in the movies, plays, television—have eluded her anyway? Even a part as a character actress was hard to find. "I still can't believe you chose me," she said.

"Of course I chose you," said Joseph.

But how could one tell what was a hindrance and what was the best thing that could have happened to her? Frances was always grateful that the advertisements had made her just a little famous. Still, a day didn't go by when at the very least, someone squinted at her, trying to place her face.

"It's fine," she said.

"Oh." Joseph rubbed his head. "Goot!"

Every time she spoke to him, or when he occasionally stopped by on the set to watch the production, Frances was filled with adoration and flooded with the memories of the women on her block clucking at one another with thick, cruel tongues, the sound of weeping, the sound of a broom sweeping over pavement, the smell of cabbage, the smell of saliva and peppermint, burning yahrtzeits, her father's soothing voice, the quiet of Saturdays.

"I will see you soon, Joe," she said.

"Okay," he said.

"You can hang up then." Frances laughed. A similar thing had happened after Thanksgiving at Miriam and David's. Joseph had called a thousand times to apologize. Once she'd heard what happened, Frances had first found it hysterical and then slightly ominous. A bad omen? Perhaps. Or perhaps it foreboded her loss of the Essoil contract.

"Okay!" he said. "Good-bye, Frances."

"Good-bye, Joe," she said, putting down the receiver.

Vladimir sat at his desk, and Frances came up behind him and locked her arms around his neck. "Vlad?"

He reached up to touch her wrists with the tips of his fingers. "Hmmm?" he said.

"Joseph sold Essoil," she whispered in his ear.

Vladimir turned toward her with a grin on his face. "Yes?" he said.

"And I've lost the contract." She kissed his nose.

"Really," he said, looking up at his wife. When Vladimir found out that he had been poisoned by Essoil-soaked herbs, he had not been amused. That stuff is evil, he had told Frances. Pure evil. He had made a production of taking the bottle from the broom closet and pouring it out in the bathroom sink. Frances had stood watching him, hands on her hips, shaking her head. Vladimir, she'd said. Sweetheart. You know we have four cases in the laundry room. You know, she'd said, that Gladys won't clean with anything else.

"Yup," she said now. "All gone."

Vladimir took Frances in his arms. "That's great news," he said and buried his face in his wife's chest.

"You know what I think?" She tilted her head and ran her fingers through the thick hair on her husband's chest.

"What do you think?" he asked.

"I think we should move out to California."

Vladimir lifted his head and looked at his wife.

"What?" Frances said. "We should!"

"Not again with the California!" he said.

"And why not?" she asked, leaning back. There had always been work and work and more work. But that had changed—Vladimir had done enough work, and now he could decide for himself what he did. The image of a wide street lined with palm trees rose up in her imagination. Frances imagined being brought to a table at the Brown Derby next to Lana Turner or Judy Garland. "Can't you see us driving down sunny streets and turning toward the ocean?" she asked her husband.

"I never could picture it," he said. "Could that person in the convertible zipping down the street so grandly be me? It doesn't really seem possible."

"Why not?" she said. "It would be a nice life."

"Why not?" Vladimir shrugged. "Anything's possible."

A smile spread across Frances's face, and the single hair on her chin, which she saved for plucking right before beginning production on a commercial, trembled with happiness. She had expected Vladimir to say no once again. "Well!" she said.

Frances imagined herself on the Paramount lot, walking past sets, some being wheeled away before her eyes. People scurried by on their way to meetings and shoots. She saw the mountains in the distance, covered in a sheer layer of light haze, a waiting promise. We'll take the train! she thought now, imagining herself next to Vladimir, her head leaning against the window, the whole country whirring by. Lightning over open fields, deep, ridged canyons, mountains ringed with smoke, images she had seen only in the movies. The movies. All the different people of this country bending to lift their bags as they got on and off the train. We're going all the way west, she'd tell whomever sat across from them. All the way to the Pacific Ocean. They'd invite their new friends to join them in the dining car. We're going to Hollywood! they'd tell them when the waiter lifted the silver lid to reveal the platter of roast beef and pudding. And then the baked Alaska, the flame flickering with the swaying rhythm of the train.

"Maybe," Vladimir said, "it would get you out of everyone else's living room. Perhaps."

"I'll get packed right away!" Francis jumped up. "I'm calling my agent this minute," she said.

"I could have a little studio in the hills, looking out at the sea," he said. "Invent something useful again. Go back to researching, but for a good cause. Teach even. Perhaps it would be a nice life." He looked at Frances. "But the movies?" He pinched her waist. "I love this," he said. "Also this." Vladimir touched her nose. "A face I can laugh with," he said. "And you wear your charm like some women wear furs."

"Yes?" she teased.

"I hope there are still parts to play," he said. "In the movies."

"Of course there are, Vladi," she said.

"I want nothing more than your happiness, Frances," he said, "but let's face it, darling, you're not getting any younger."

"True," she said. "True."

"What parts will you play?" Vladimir asked.

Frances smiled at her husband. "I'm not worried."

"Really, Fran?"

"Really," she said. "I am a *character* actress."

"You certainly are." Vladimir tapped her on the behind.

Frances was already having a mental conversation with her agent. She was picturing herself in a flowered dress and a straw hat, with sandals the color of her tanned skin. She was looking out to sea. A school of dolphins were far in the distance, and she could see them when she shielded her eyes from the bright sun, their fins arcing against the horizon.

The movies, she thought. A chance to be a mother. Don't fill up on sweets, she warns in a little kitchen with a checkered tablecloth. Two smiling faces dotted with freckles look up at her. Frances puts an arm on the back of each chair and kisses their noses. Take three, Mrs. Gold. Already the director was calling to her as Frances turned to leave Vladimir's studio.

CHAPTER 21

Skin: The Ensemble, 1962

THREE MONTHS AFTER signing Essoil away, Joseph Brodsky was sitting on the back balcony watching the tide come in when he felt a pain in his chest. Esther came out with a liverwurst sandwich only to see her husband looking blankly out at the bay.

"Joe?" she asked tentatively. "Are you okay?"

"I'm not feeling so vell." He scrunched up his nose. When they'd first moved to this house, he would stand out on the balcony all afternoon to watch the Sunfish moving along the water. The first time he saw them, bright-colored sails heading into the sun, he had screamed inside. Look, Es. Sailboats small enough for one person!

Now Esther put her hand on his shoulder. "Why don't you eat something?" she said, handing him half the sandwich. "Rye bread." When he refused, Esther grew concerned.

"What?" she said.

"I just don't feel like myself," he told her.

Not fifteen minutes later, Joseph was bundled up against the spring cold and taken to the Portland hospital.

Miriam was not prepared for the news that her father was to have surgery when her mother called to tell her.

"It's just exploratory," Esther said. "The doctor said it's a matter of fortification."

"Exploring what?" Miriam asked. "Fortifying who?"

"His heart," Esther said. "Dr. Benton said there's really nothing to worry about."

Miriam rolled her eyes. Getting her mother to question anything any doctor told her, especially if he was handsome—forget it if he had the clear blue eyes that Dr. Benton had—was nearly impossible. "Maybe he should go to Boston," Miriam said. "There's better care there."

"There is no one better than Dr. Benton," Esther said. "We have a very fine hospital here, Miriam. And anyway, this is only exploratory."

"I'll be there tomorrow," Miriam said, hanging up before her mother could tell her that it wouldn't be necessary and that perhaps her energy would be better spent with a few turns around the house with a vacuum. Or taking some of those lovely French cooking classes like Esther's friend Myrtle was taking up at the Y. It wouldn't hurt you, Esther always told her, to learn how to make a proper savory soufflé.

Esther and Miriam went to the hospital the next night to visit Joseph. Esther pleaded with her daughter not to make a fuss.

"You'll just make everyone more nervous than is necessary," she said in the car on the way over. "Gloria listened to reason and stayed home with her children. There's really no sense in all this. Now just go in and kiss him good night. Quick, quick. Don't make a production. Please, Miriam, no drama."

So, Miriam had a brief visit with her father. She told Joseph about work, the United Nations conference where she was to be the head translator, David's upcoming production of *All American,* the new mahogany cabinet that they had gotten for all their wedding china. "We can finally unpack," she told him.

"Good night, sugar," Joseph said when she got up to leave.

Lying in that hospital bed in his white gown, her father looked so small.

And Joseph felt small, dwarfed by the world, and by his place in it. He had always felt this way, really. He remembered how he had made everyone wear surgical masks when Miriam was born. He had been so terrified that the world would hurt her.

Now he saw his daughter in that single moment as all the ages she had ever been: a loaf of bread in his trembling arms, a pudgy girl on roller skates, a young woman turning the tassel of her graduation cap, the veiled bride he had walked down the aisle and handed over to David Bloom.

"It will be fine," he told his daughter, patting her hand.

The skin on Joseph's hands, still chapped, had grown looser with age, and Miriam resisted mentally skinning her father, peeling back his slack flesh to see beneath to muscle and blood and bone, his very structure. What was her father made of? As he touched her hand, she remembered something that she had not thought about since she was a girl but that now seemed never to have left her imagination for a moment. It was a night she had gone to kiss her father good night. She had walked into their bedroom and seen Joseph distractedly picking at his hands, peeling the rough skin from the insides of his palms. Miriam had watched as he picked at his raw fingers and placed the bits of skin in a tiny silver bowl. The next day, when he was at work, she went to her father's bed and looked into the smooth silver bowl on his night table. The skin was still there, dry and crisp, yellow and semitransparent, and Miriam dropped some of the pieces into her smooth, open palm.

Now she shook away the memory of holding these bits and pieces of her father's hands.

"Good night, Daddy," she said, rising from the chair by her father's bed. She kissed his cheek and left the room.

Esther went in to talk to Joseph, and Miriam waited for her in the hallway.

His wife told him, "Joe, don't you leave me alone in this world."

"I won't, Es," he said. "Don't you vorry."

"Well, all right then," she said. There was a pause—a kiss? the touch of hands? Miriam wondered—and then Esther clicked out of the room.

No one knew that Joseph Brodsky's heart was breaking, that the next morning, when the surgeon cracked him open, his aorta would disintegrate in his hands.

"How could that *be*?" Esther said. Miriam came out of the guest bedroom upon hearing her mother on the phone. "But it was only *exploratory.*" Esther's hand covered her mouth. "I see," she said. "Thank you, Dr. Benton," she said.

You always know, don't you? thought Miriam. Unless you don't.

She watched her mother, in her pink and black Pucci housecoat that zipped up the front, straighten and place her hands on the kitchen table.

"Mom," Miriam said. She knelt down beside her mother, a hand on her shoulder. The nylon of her robe felt cold to her touch.

Esther nodded. "Call your sister," she said.

"Okay," Miriam said. "Of course." She didn't move.

Esther looked around the kitchen. "This place is such a mess," she said. She put her head in her hands.

"It really isn't," Miriam said. "But I'll call Melinda to come in and clean tomorrow if you want," she said.

Esther got up slowly and went to the broom closet. She took out the mop and the bucket and the bottle of Essoil. "No," she said. "I'd rather do it myself."

Miriam stood up. "Let me help you, Mom," she said. She took the bottle from her mother, who gripped it tightly with two hands. She unscrewed the top and put her nose over the opening.

For the first time in fifteen years, Miriam could smell. One whiff: her father, freshness, everything clean and good and lovely, her entire childhood.

"Mom, smell," she said, holding out the open bottle. Miriam willed herself not to cry, so worried was she that it would stop her ability to smell.

Esther shook her head. "No," she said. She took a balled-up tissue from under the sleeve of her housecoat and blew her nose. "I'm going to bed," she said and turned to leave the room.

While she waited for her sister and her husband to come and help with the arrangements, Miriam, in her nightgown and bare feet, cleaned. She could hear her mother weeping through the closed door of her bedroom as she mopped all the tile and Formica floors, and washed every counter and mirror and bath in her parents' house. With each dip of the mop, every wringing out of the rag, Miriam remembered her father's long nose, the way he hung his hat before walking in the door, his shiny bald head, his sweet laugh, his voice, the way it felt to walk away from him, to dance with him, to put her hand in her pocket instead of to hold his hand, the way he held his head while shaving, the way he opened his valise, the way he pushed her on the swing, high, higher, highest, the fireflies he helped her capture and then set free, the way he piled leaves around her so he could pretend she had disappeared. The afternoon was a gift from her father, Miriam knew. For her only. And inhaling grandly in the kitchen when all her cleaning was finished, she was overwhelmed with the grief of being met with what followed: nothing. By the time she had capped the bottle and placed it back in the pantry, her ability to smell had disappeared.

That night, Miriam had a dream. In it, she was a little girl holding a red balloon in her tight, clammy fist. Joseph stood next to her, walking with her from booth to booth at an old-time fair, his hands on her back as he guided her through the crowd toward the Ferris wheel. The balloon slowly began to slip out of her fingers, and Miriam tried to hang on to it. When she turned to tell her father that she couldn't hold on anymore, he started to disappear before her eyes. There goes Gloria's balloon, Miriam told herself in the dream as she watched her father slip away, a genie emerging from a bottle, spiraling high above her head and into the atmosphere.

Off to the moon. Esther came up from behind and grabbed hold of the balloon. It's time for a new permanent wave, young lady, she declared.

At the cemetery in Portland, a cantor sang and Esther pulled on Miriam's sleeve. She whispered into her hair, "He was in the camps." The cantor's voice sounded to Miriam as if it were breaking.

As he threw the dirt, David tried to picture the coffin the way it had been at the service, Joseph prone below the bema, inside a casket draped in a dark cloth, a white Star of David shining from the fabric. Now there was the terrible thud of gravel hitting wood.

Then Frances Gold.

Then Seymour Bloom.

Then Vladimir Zworykin.

Then Gloria and her husband together.

Then Miriam, a trembling little girl with a shovelful of dirt.

Miriam nudged her mother toward the coffin, but Esther wouldn't budge. "Not a chance," she said.

Miriam did stop a moment to wonder how her father would have taken it. Covered in dirt. By his own family.

She fingered the ripped ribbon the rabbi had given her to wear at the funeral, like the ones he had given them all. She stuck two fingers in her mouth.

"Such a dirty habit!" Esther slapped her daughter's hand from her mouth. "Pull yourself together!" she said. "People are watching us."

Were prayer and memory the same? As Reb Skye, the rabbi Esther had wanted so desperately for Miriam's wedding, said Yizkor, Miriam looked over at her mother, and there was Joseph in the threshold of Janie Silvers's door at nightfall, his hat in his hands.

As the driver helped Esther out of the limousine, Miriam watched her pause a moment in the circular driveway.

What would her father have said? All these years and not once had he been driven in a limousine. Even the few times he'd needed a driver to take him from Portland back to Boston when his own car was in the shop, he'd insisted on a town car. Nozhing fancy, he had told his secretary. As Miriam walked into her parents' house, she went to look in the den—two leather La-Z-Boys facing the television—so she could tell him all about looking out the darkened windows as she, her sister, and her mother rode through town like royalty without him.

Miriam had told her mother that people would bring food, but Esther had insisted on a caterer. When they got to the house, the tuna, egg, and whitefish salad were laid out in her smooth Steuben crystal bowls, the bagels and nova arranged on a silver platter.

"The kugel isn't browned enough," Esther said the moment she saw it cut into small squares and stacked like bricks on her Lenox plate.

For the shiva, Miriam and Gloria stood flanking their seated mother like two soldiers. Esther kept on her dark glasses as a whir of people came and went. Miriam nodded thank you as the mourners leaned down to her mother's arm or the hem of her navy blue suit skirt, kissed her cheek or patted her shoulder.

"Did you have the chance to say good-bye?" Nelly Barowsky, whose husband had practiced law with Esther's father, asked.

Miriam looked down at her mother. She pictured the surgeon's hands reaching over themselves to stop the blood.

"I did," Esther said. She touched her dark glasses.

Miriam gripped her shoulder and searched the room for David. When she spotted him, for the first time in what seemed like years, her stomach jumped and fluttered just as it had in college. Still he is as beautiful as Orson Welles, she thought as she nodded her head to the mourner. I have a little secret, Miriam thought, catching her husband's eye across the room. Willing herself not to think of the man who grew poisonous herbs, the same man who sat beside his mother and offered to help her die, Miriam rubbed her belly. The memory of her wedding, of looking across that crowded room and seeing her husband, a stranger, was beginning to fade. Her marriage felt unexpectedly different: something precious, something breakable that she suddenly wanted to keep pristine. How much damage had been wrought, Miriam couldn't tell, but she imagined tiny hairline fractures, hardly noticeable if, from now on, they were careful. She looked down at her mother, whose eyes were closed tightly beneath her sunglasses, and knew that Esther was hoping to hell that no one spilled on her cream-colored carpet.

Seymour Bloom leaned in to kiss Miriam and Gloria, and then Esther. Still she had that smell he remembered: pressed face powder and lavender, hair spray, lipstick. "Esther," he said. "I'm so sorry."

She nodded slowly.

"Sarah sends her love," he said.

Seymour had thought to bring Sarah and then quickly decided against it. Though he never knew what to expect from his wife, he knew he could count on her to make a spectacle. Just last month he had taken her out for lunch and a walk, and she had insisted on wearing her brassiere over her shirt. The bra had been yellowing, as if it were burned along the edges with an iron held down too long, he remembered now. Fading. She's fading away, thought Seymour. Then Sarah misplaced her handbag and wept into her corn chowder until the waiter came and took it away. It had infuriated Seymour how he just took the tiny bowl of soup without even asking.

It wasn't her fault. But bringing Sarah would not have been right,

Seymour had reassured himself as he'd passed the exit to the Longevity Center, driving up to Portland.

"How is she doing in there?" Esther asked.

Seymour nodded. "She's well," he said, standing. "We're just so sorry about Joseph." He wiped his eyes.

He had been stunned by the news. When David had called to tell him, he'd instantly imagined Joseph tooling around in that crappy little motorboat like he was the cat's meow. The good life is so damn short, Seymour thought. One moment you're working to make a better life for yourself, for your children, work morning, noon, night, and then boom, you're dead before you can relax and enjoy it.

Seymour patted Esther's knee and kissed her cheek again. He went out on the stone balcony that overlooked Casco Bay. A boat silhouetted against the setting sun tipped its sail toward the water on its way into shore.

The tide was out, Seymour could tell. The B & M baked bean factory lighted up as he looked across the water. He smiled to think of Joseph here, standing where he now stood looking out at the water and the lights. He remembered the day they went waterskiing together. That was just five years ago, but now it seemed a lifetime.

Seymour saw Sarah, the sun high and blinding in the sky, as she sank down into the water.

He shook his head at the image of her disappearing. What was she doing right now? he wondered. Seymour's memory of Sarah had changed—somehow she had become young again, her pale skin rosy with cold, the steam from their shared hot chocolate warming them. Seymour's singular memory of Sarah's bright, ebullient youth allowed him to miss her, sometimes desperately, in a way he had never thought possible. Inez, still tooling around in that Brooklyn apartment drinking Pernod and peering through her peephole at all the men who continued to visit Mae West, told her son to forget about his wife. Pretend she is dead, Inez had told him when he'd briefly let his mother in on his troubled emotions. Believe me, it is easier with the living this way, she had said. Seymour wondered had his mother, upon coming to this country all alone, willed herself to forget the Friday trips through the Marais to the fromagerie, running to get home before sunset, her mother waiting with stern hands on large hips?

Seymour remembered the fortune-teller at Coney Island. He and Sarah had stumbled into her tent, dimly lit and thick with the scent of incense. Foreign tapestries sewn with tiny mirrors were thrown over naked lightbulbs, and Seymour could see bits of his own reflection as the gypsy looked at Sarah's hand. A long line that is hardly visible, she'd said, tracing her finger all the way to Sarah's wrist, lingering there until Sarah jerked her hand away. Sarah had laughed and pulled him onto the boardwalk, where they had stood, breathless beneath the stars, couples walking toward them eating funnel cakes and fried oysters, holding hands, the Ferris wheel lighted and spinning in the distance, young girls kicking their feet high in the air.

Across the living room, Vladimir sat with a red-eyed, puffy-faced Frances on the couch.

"But you love whitefish, Franny!" he said, trying to shove a forkful into her mouth.

Frances clamped her mouth shut and pushed the fork away. "Stop, Vladimir," she said. "It's not helping."

"California!" he said in her ear. "Hollywood! Palm trees!"

Frances shook her head. "Stop it," she said.

She had not felt this way since the day her father died. All morning she had lain with a cold compress on her head, trying to make that terrible all-over feeling go away. It stayed and stayed. Joseph was gone, yes, but everything else was gone now too. Frances knew she was being selfish, but she couldn't help but think how her childhood had finally been wrested from her. Who else would ever remember Portia Ginsburg's goiter? It always shook when she yelled, and all the kids thought it would explode. What was inside it? they asked one another. Still she had no idea, and now she knew it was a memory that soon would disappear.

Frances heard the guests entering the house, whispering, shucking off wraps as if this were a party. It seemed festive, people coming in with food, bringing with them the smell of falling leaves and that crisp air that always made her sad. Time passing. The smell of the graveyard, she thought instinctively. Please tell me Esther put out the Downys and a pitcher of water so that people could wash their hands from the grave. Frances looked up from the sunken living room toward the front door, where she peered at the hands of the woman and young man entering to check for any signs of recent washing.

Both sets of hands dry as chalk, as far as Frances could tell. She flopped back into the couch and watched the guest hand the caterer a casserole dish. Frances looked up at the woman removing the pins from her enormous hat and handing each one to the longhaired, bearded young man, who grasped a shopping bag. The woman took off her hat and shook her long brown hair free.

"Pauline!" Frances whispered, breathing. Pauline.

Vladimir looked up from his forkful of whitefish salad.

Frances sat up straight and watched her sister hand her coat off and scan the room.

Immediately Frances was the girl waiting for her sister to come pay her respects to their father.

Without hesitation, she ran across the room to her sister and threw her arms around her. "Pauline!" she said, sobbing.

If Pauline was shocked or alarmed by the display, she made no show of it as she hugged her younger sister close. "Franny," she said quietly. The two women rocked back and forth for a moment. "Look at you!" Pauline said, cupping Frances's face in her hands. "I know you from the television!"

They both laughed, and Frances sniffed and wiped her runny nose with the back of her shirt cuff. She hugged Pauline again.

"You were going to be the movie star!" Frances said. "Where have you been, Pauline?" she whispered.

Pauline cleared her throat and pulled back from her sister. "Remember Wesley?" she asked.

"Oh my goodness!" Frances looked at the young man with wild hair and an unkempt beard. She had sat with him, a two-year-old racing over and around her as she begged Solomon to invest in the Kinescope. That was the last time she'd seen her nephew. Vladimir's television had already grown as old as this young man. "Look at you!" she said, crying again, and going to hug him. "A beatnik!" she said. Frances had never met one before. "You don't remember me, do you?"

"No," Wesley said sheepishly. He brushed the hair out of his eyes with his mother's hat pin.

"Of course not," she said. "Why would you?" She looked down at her toes.

"I've heard a lot about you, though," Wesley said.

"We live in Boston," Pauline said hurriedly.

"Really? Is that where you've been all this time? Just Boston?"

"Yes," she said. "All these years."

"So close by," Frances said softly. "I imagined you far, far away, in some place terribly exotic, like Tangiers or Bombay." Frances had pictured her sister in a long silk caftan and heaps of jewelry, walking through a crowded marketplace.

Pauline laughed. "Hardly," she said. She looked at her son. "It's been complicated."

Frances's face clouded, and she crossed her arms over her stomach. "For us all," she said. She looked at her sister. She had thought she would never see her again. Remember everything? she'd wanted to ask her just then. "I wish I'd known," she said.

"Well . . . ," Pauline began. "In a way, we've been in hiding."

Frances nodded. How was it, after all these years of rage and then indifference and then, on some days, forgetting even, that it had all drained from her? Right now, she felt she could forgive everything.

Vladimir came up behind her and took his wife's hand. Pauline looked over at him.

"This is my husband," Frances said. "Vladimir. Remember him?"

Pauline shook his hand. "My goodness," she said. "I never thought I'd see you again! Not in this country."

"I've heard so much about you," Vladimir said. "We had no idea where you were."

Pauline looked down. "I've been nearby," she said.

Wesley shifted the bag and held out his hand. "So nice to meet you," he said.

"Vladimir invented television, you know," Frances said out of nowhere.

"Frances," Vladimir said.

"I know," Pauline said. "That's really incredible."

Frances sighed, remembering why they were all there just now.

"I brought this for Joe's wife," Pauline said, taking the shopping bag carefully from her son. "But I'm not sure I should give it to her. Really, I meant to give it to Joseph for so many years." She shook her head. "I always planned to give it to him, and now, well, now I can't."

Frances took the bag. "What is it?" she asked tentatively.

Vladimir leaned in behind her and then stepped back.

Wesley put his long hair behind his ear. "It's my father's tallis," he said.

Frances lifted the garment. It felt cold from the outside air, but for a moment she thought it was wet.

Pauline shook her head. "Can you believe we were married beneath this?"

"You were?"

Pauline shook her head. "Solomon insisted on it. It was his father's."

Frances covered her mouth. "It's in a Bonwit's bag, Pauline!"

"Well, I don't know what I'm supposed to carry it in!"

Frances shook her head. She smoothed out the tangled fringes and then put the shawl back in the shopping bag.

"You know Solomon died almost ten years ago?" Pauline said. She reached for Wesley's hand.

"Yes, I know," Frances said, her anger and resolve to separate herself from her sister slowly returning. "I heard." Pauline couldn't have sent a note to tell her, "Hello? I'm alive. I live in Boston . . ."? "Solomon and I wrote to each other several times," Frances said. "He never let me visit, though. Not once. That day in court was the last time I saw him." She had read that he had died in prison, of natural causes. But her sister had never let her know.

"Me too," Pauline said. "Well, I never did visit him." She sniffed loudly. "They don't bury you in your tallis in prison. And I'm sure he'd made no arrangements for such a thing. You know Solomon," she said. "But at the bottom of it all, he was a religious man. Wouldn't be caught dead in shul, but sometimes, on high holidays, I saw him wear this, davening in that damn library he loved so much, with all those old leather books."

Frances nodded and pictured the short, squat Terrier somehow managing to bend toward God, who, Solomon believed until the day he died, saw everything. Everything. Old leather books. Frances had to laugh at her sister, still pretending.

Vladimir reached out to take the package.

"He did a lot of horrible things, I know, but . . . Really, I should have given this to Joe a long time ago," Pauline said. "But I couldn't."

"And to think you lived in the same town as Joseph," Frances said. "I'll take it. It will only upset Esther right now."

Pauline nodded.

"So tell me, Pauline. What have you been doing?"

Pauline took her sister's hand. "When I tell you," she said, "you will be very surprised."

"Really," Frances said flatly. I am going to Hollywood, she thought to herself, a mantra. There will be sunny sidewalks pasted with silver stars, long sunsets in Malibu, a balcony that hangs over a beach, a cliff, a terrace facing away from here. Good night, sweet darling, I'll say in the movies, as I lean down to kiss my daughter good night.

"I had to become someone else. I just had to," Pauline said.

"What about before Solomon went to prison? You had to leave us behind then?" Frances's throat tightened as it had already so many times today. Her goodwill toward her sister had dissipated.

"That was different," Pauline said. "You all hated me after I went off with Sol."

"I was sixteen, Pauline. I didn't hate you."

Pauline was quiet.

"Sixteen," Frances said again. "I hated you when I turned seventeen."

Frances smiled at Wesley, the way she had done over thirty years ago when she had marched by her sister without even saying hello. Just then, she realized she did not want to know where her sister had been for the last twenty-nine years. Or more, she did not want to know her sister. "It's so nice to see you again," she said to her nephew.

Frances took Vladimir's hand and led him down the hallway and into the den, leaving Wesley and Pauline in the foyer alone, looking out onto a house of mourning.

The night of the funeral, after they all had sat and leaned their heads toward the rabbi, saying Kaddish, and after they had eaten more cakes and cookies and tuna salad than they could possibly bear, Miriam pulled David aside.

"Let's take a drive," she said.

Miriam imagined driving to Sebago Lake, to the house she had gone to each summer since she was a girl. She imagined pulling the *MiriGlo* from the shed where it was stored for the season and, with all her strength, dragging it off its wooden stilts, over the yard, and into the soft water. She wanted to drive the boat out into the lake and lie beneath the stars tonight, feel the soft ripple of the water swish against the boat.

"Whatever you want to do," David said.

Sebago was too far. Miriam led David to the garage and pulled down a flashlight as big as a drainpipe from a metal shelf in the garage. They got into Joseph's Oldsmobile—her father's smell of leather, perspiration, and Essoil caught David by surprise, but he thought better of telling Miriam, who he knew couldn't smell a thing—and Miriam pulled the car out of the driveway, down to Baxter Boulevard, and over the wooden bridge to Mackworth Island, which her father had talked so much about when he first moved to Portland. The few times she'd come to visit, Miriam would always walk with him along the rocky shore. This is a bay, Joseph would say. Salt water. An estuary, he'd tell her proudly.

We should have visited more often, she thought.

"Where are we going?" David asked.

The old wooden slats of the bridge creaked beneath the car, and Miriam opened the windows. Salt air spilled in. Lights and water flanked both sides of the car.

"Mackworth," she said. It was the next best thing.

Miriam liked the place best in the rain, the sky overcast as she and Joseph made their way along the seaweed- and barnacle-covered rocks, the water a deep green against the light gray sky. It would be nearly empty, but for a woman shelling in a yellow slicker, a bearded man and his Irish setter, the dog's shining red coat flashing in and out of the trees along the trail above the shore. Seagulls would swoop down, calling to one another, and Miriam always felt like a young girl again, walking toward the cotton candy stand at Old Orchard.

When they got to the lot, the gate was closed, so they pulled up as far as they could and parked. Miriam hesitated.

"It's pretty dark out, Miri," David said. "Do you think we should go in?"

"I want to," she said.

They slid under the barrier.

Sweeping the light over the ground, Miriam and David tried to find a path down to the water's edge. Miriam couldn't locate one, but, noticing the trail that wound above the shore, she led them along that, leaves rustling in the night wind.

When they found rocks leading to the shore, they scrambled down them until sand crunched under their sneakers. "Ouch," Miriam said, dropping the flashlight as she hit her shin on a rock.

David picked it up and scanned it over the sand and into the water, which made a gentle, lapping sound. The lighthouse beacon flashed, and the town rose and blinked across the black water.

They found a flat rock and sat down on it, wrapping their arms around their legs. David turned off the flashlight so that Miriam could not see him, and she put her head sideways on the table of her knees, closed her eyes. The salt air, the rippling water, darkness, surrounded them.

David pulled at Miriam's jacket from the back, and she lay down next to her husband, looking up at the sky—black—more black than the water, stars everywhere. She blinked from the brightness of them all. It was so unlike New York, where a gorgeous night in the city is a starless one, its beauty in the flash and blink of skyscraper lights skimming into fog, or in the liquid movement of headlights and taillights viewed from above.

Everything felt as if it was falling away.

Miriam put her hands in front of her and could see them only in the silhouette they made as they blocked out the lighted sky. She could see each of her fingers as she spread them apart above her head. And then she saw the outline of David's hands against the stars. She reached up to touch them, a peace offering: We make peace and now, please now, we grow up. It was the first time in so long she had not wanted to hurt him.

"I'm pregnant," she said.

David hooked his pinkie to hers, and Miriam turned toward him. She buried her head in his chest, and he could feel the warmth of her crying through his windbreaker.

After a moment, Miriam wiped her eyes and sat up. David turned on the flashlight, shining it along the water's surface. Miriam imagined he was looking across the bay to spot her parents' house. She imagined it bathed in starlight, her father walking up the front steps, opening the door, a rectangle of light, home.

Zhis is zhe driftvood. And here, a piece of sea glass, smoothed over by sand and vater. By time. You vant to hold it? Here. Hold it, Joseph had told her when they'd walked together here not so long ago. Her father had cupped a hand over Miriam's shoulder. Look quick. Your island, he'd said, his rough fingertips pressing lightly at his daughter's collarbone. *Goldene medina!* Golden country, he'd said, and Miriam had looked out across the water searching for that tiny flash of her parents' house.

"That's wonderful," David said.

Children. He imagined a little girl running toward him in a swirl of yellow leaves. She wore a red coat. She had huge eyes and pigtails.

"What would you have done if your mother said yes?" Miriam asked after a few moments of silence.

"Yes to what?"

"Would you have gotten her those pills, David?"

"I don't know," he said.

"So you would have killed your own mother?" Miriam rubbed her forehead.

"I'm not sure," David said. "But I might have helped her along if it had been what she'd wanted." He saw his mother in that torn, yellowed dress, walking toward him like Dickens's Miss Havisham in that horrible shining hallway, scrubbed with Essoil, he imagined, until it gleamed. "But the point is, I suppose, that she's happy now. Now she doesn't want to die."

"I think it's just awful," Miriam said. "I can't imagine ever doing such a thing." She remembered looking out the window on her wedding night: What will my life be *like*? she had thought. It was what she always thought, as if she was not now living.

"Well then, you didn't know her," he said. Was it awful? He would want his child to do the same for him. A child. They were going to be parents.

David and Miriam sat together, the water lapping quietly along the shore. After a few minutes, he stood and reached for his wife's hand, and she stood up, following him along the sand. When they finally felt their way back, David got in the driver's seat. As they were leaving, Miriam turned to see the school above the parking lot, two people silhouetted in a third-floor window, gesturing to each other in the soft orange light. Their hands moved quickly and delicately.

As they drove away, Miriam twisted in her seat to watch the island recede into the black sky and water, and then disappear.

Silently, they headed back to the house. Miriam remembered her father making room for her at the wheel. Go ahead, sugar, he had said to her. You drive for a vhile. She was thinking of the way she had put the boat into gear and it had lurched ahead, nosing the water and then tipping them all backward. Joseph had put his hands over his daughter's, and she remembered the tanned skin of his fingers as he guided her hands and the boat into first gear.

When they got back, most of the people were gone, and Miriam went straight into Esther's bedroom to kiss her good night.

Her mother was seated on the edge of her bed.

As Miriam switched on the vanity light, the naked lightbulbs, screwed into clouded crystal shells, illuminated photographs of Miriam and Gloria in all the stages of their lives, Gloria's two children, and a tiny picture of Esther and Joseph holding their hats and walking down the boardwalk at Coney Island, framed in gold.

"Are you okay, Mom?" she asked.

"Did I ever tell you about our honeymoon?"

"About the anti-Semitism?" Miriam asked. Her mother had told her the story close to a million times. Be sure they know who you are when you go, she always warned. Because when you get there, they'll let you know anyway.

"Well, yes, there was that, that was just awful, but that's not what I mean," Esther said. "I'm talking about how I went to the bathroom in the hall, all dressed up in my fancy-schmancy lingerie, and then I couldn't remember which room was ours. I tried every door down the hallway looking for our room."

Miriam laughed.

"You know, that's what I thought of when that doctor called," Esther said. "Isn't that strange? Me in my silly old nightie, scratching on every damn door looking for Joseph. That's the first thing I thought of when the doctor called to say he hadn't made it through." Esther leaned back and looked blankly at the ceiling.

Miriam lay next to her mother on the tiny twin bed. She brought her mother's hand to her chest and remembered a time she had lain with Esther on this bed, turning the pages of one of Esther's scrapbooks. Their legs had kicked in the air, and Esther had told her daughter, I had so many boyfriends. I was boy crazy, she'd said. Boy meshuge. Oh, I loved him, Esther had said of a photo of young man in a suit, his hair slicked back. And him. She pointed to a boy in a lifeguard's outfit, his nose and cheeks smeared with zinc oxide. When they had turned to a photograph of the man in a tweed hat on a cobbled city street, his eyes tiny points of dark light, quietly, she said, But he was the one. Her finger had poked his nose and then traced the line of Joseph's lapel.

"I'm pregnant, Mom," Miriam said suddenly.

Esther grabbed her hand away from Miriam's. And then she put it back.

"That's wonderful, Miri," she said. "It's too bad your father will never know. But I will say this: it's about time. We were all beginning to wonder."

"I don't know why I didn't tell him," Miriam said. A knot, a tight fist, a ball of bones and teeth and hair, a planet was growing inside Miriam, and she had known it now for weeks.

"Because you didn't know it was the last time you would talk to him, is why," Esther said.

Miriam leaned into her mother's shoulder, grateful that she had not said what she had meant. She had wished she had given her father more of a reason to get through as well.

"You know I will be a better grandmother than I have been a mother," Esther said. "It is the way it always goes, you know."

"You've been a good mom," Miriam said. She remembered driving into Naples for soft serve and to watch the water planes land. Esther had told her that she would never get in one of those planes, not a chance, but that Miriam would be going farther than these could ever take her. Just you wait, her mother had said, licking her cone. "You have," Miriam said.

Miriam thought of herself as a little girl watching television and wondering what her life would be like. *Women of the future will clean the moon with Essoil!* Now that future was upon her. A future that did not contain her father. She pictured herself leaning over a pram. She imagined tying a child's shoe.

Miriam closed her eyes and prayed for a boy. When she opened them, David was standing before her.

"How are you ladies doing?" he asked. He held the evening paper folded beneath his arm.

Miriam nodded.

"You'll never believe this," he said, handing the paper to Miriam. "'Dear Maggie' is about Joseph."

"'Dear Maggie'?" Esther tore the paper from Miriam. "I can't believe I didn't read it today."

"Well, she was here," David said.

"Here?" Miriam asked.

"Here!" he said.

Miriam and Esther tugged at the paper and then, placing it between them, looked on together:

Dear Reader:

When an editor approached me over twenty-five years ago in a dentist's office upon seeing an article I'd written on how women should prepare themselves financially for the deaths of their husbands, I had no idea what it would lead to. "Dear Maggie" began as women writing to one another, sharing intimate secrets under the cloak of anonymity. But this changed as the world changed.

Such dark times we have lived through.

It seemed important to have answers. To have order. And etiquette gives us both.

All these years of a manners column and I have completely forgotten mine. I will see my old friend laid out today. I grew up with him. I was married to his brother. We lived in the same town for two decades and I never once paid him a visit. I have not paid anyone a visit for over thirty years. Joseph Brodsky is no longer here to refuse my apology or to forgive me, but you, Reader, still are. I hope that you will.

When you discover who I am, I may no longer be of use to you. Will you

take such advice from someone like me? If that is the case, may I just say
that it has been a glorious twenty-nine years spent alone with you and your
letters. A lovely stint to be trusted to dispense my humble advice.

> *Sincerely,*
> *Maggie*

"I'll be damned," said Esther, throwing down the paper. "I'll be god-
damned."

"Wait," Miriam said. "I thought Daddy's brother died in the war."

"What war, Miriam?" Esther asked, sighing heavily. "What war
would that have been?"

Miriam was silent. "Well, who is it?" she asked.

"I suppose it's Frances's sister," Esther said. "In any case, the column
stinks now."

"It really does," Miriam said. "I don't care about when to wear short
gloves and when to wear long ones."

"I know you don't," Esther said. "But you should. *Anyway,* did you
see her?"

"I did," David said. "Gorgeous. Very well dressed, with that big hat
and the trumpet skirt. She was with her son. A real beatnik. They said
hello to you."

"I can't remember a thing," Esther said quietly. "'Dear Maggie.' You
just never know. Taking advice from a criminal—" She got up from
her bed in midsentence.

"She wasn't a criminal," Miriam said.

"No?" Esther asked her daughter. "Do you know who she was married to?"

"Now I do," Miriam said.

"Well, I hate to be the one to tell you, but your uncle was not a good
man. Joseph is probably turning and turning to hear me say it—and on
the day of his burial—well, but it is true. A real thug, that man."

David braced himself for the next comment.

"You know he did business with your father, don't you?" Esther said
to David.

"Hmm," he said. "Well—"

"But you know what's really criminal," she interrupted. "All these
years. A Jew from Brooklyn telling me how to behave like a lady. That's

criminal," she said. "You know once I wrote a letter to her, and she printed it." Esther stood up and looked into the vanity.

"Me too!" Miriam said. "I remember—"

"Will you look at my hair?" Esther patted it down. "The way I'm dressed, you'd think I was coming from a funeral."

Miriam left her mother's bedroom when she heard Frances scream from the living room.

"What?" she screamed. "Who?" she said as David held out the paper.

Frances leaned on Vladimir. "It's preposterous," she said. And she had fallen for it. Her sister was the better actress after all. Frances took her hand from her husband's shoulder. "How could she?"

"But what has she done really?" her husband asked. "I'm just wondering. It seemed she was a ghost and she needed to find a way to live as a ghost."

Hollywood, thought Frances. Sunset Boulevard. My face on an enormous screen. "But that's what I did," she said. "Don't you remember?" She pictured Etta's cruel, toothless smile, her right hand curled around a pen: the past. Frances thought of all those people lining up in Brooklyn to tell her their lies. Day after day, she took down their elaborate fantasies like dictation. Still she could hear the clinking, coins dropping into her mother's glass jar. Frances had hated the sound of money, and yet she had feared that one day she would wake up and no one would pay her for writing down his dreams. *Clink clink.* It was the only sound that made her mother smile.

"And you no longer do this," Vladimir said. "It's been over thirty years. Who cares?"

Frances crossed her arms. "Well, it was my idea," she said.

"Yes, it was," he answered.

"She steals everything," Frances said. She thought of her sister now, alone in an apartment, letters from loyal readers stacked to the moon. "What do you think will happen now?" she asked her husband. Would her sister be killed? Jailed? Or did anyone even remember the Terrier and all the gangsters who went down after him, a row of evil men, falling like dominoes? She recalled Tom Dewey's mustache growing and growing until it twisted into curlicues at the sides.

"My dear," Vladimir said, putting his arm around Frances and bringing her close. "Don't you think enough's enough? Everything has already happened."

David had to get back to *All American,* and Miriam was expected to attend that United Nations conference, so the couple left Portland two days after Joseph's funeral. Frances was horrified when she heard they would be going. There are still five more days of the shiva, she'd said. And you are the elder daughter! For her father, Frances had sat straight in silence, in a room of covered mirrors, the neighborhood clucking at her for a whole week. She had gone to minyan and not been counted. Frances did not want the mourning to end; it would mean that everything was over.

But Esther pooh-poohed Frances. "I'm not sitting here for seven days," she said. "I'll go mad. And I'll get even fatter than I was before Joe died." She thumped her burgeoning stomach.

Frances looked at Esther with wide, judging eyes and stomped off into the kitchen for some more of that delicious crumb cake, already half eaten, that Rita Shore had brought only yesterday.

Esther put her hand to the rim of the dark glasses she still wore in the house to receive visitors. "Does this mean she's staying for the next week?" she asked Miriam. "Jeesum Crow," she said, but she was smiling.

Frances and Esther came out front, arms crossed at their waists, to see Miriam and David drive away.

Miriam watched until her mother and Frances disappeared. They drove in silence. Towns whizzed by: Portland, Old Orchard, Kennebunkport, Kittery, then over the green bridge to Portsmouth. Then the now-familiar names that had replaced the landmarks of her childhood— Mamaroneck and Pelham—signs to towns, illuminated beneath the rising moon. The Indian names made Miriam think of the trading post with the big wooden Indian out in front of Levinsky's in Freeport, where Esther had bought Miriam and her sister moccasins with beads sewn in like rays of the sun.

Miriam turned toward her husband, catching a glimpse of his profile as she had her mother's all those years ago on the way to get her new nose—or more to lose the old one—in New York. Her mother's face had brought her comfort that day—she remembered that it had, because it had been so shocking to her. This is my mother, she'd thought, as if for the very first time. Now, as David stared straight ahead at the road, his contours somehow became her own. She had once looked at her mother and recognized herself. She looked at her husband and not only saw him but actually was him. The family you are born to and the family you choose, she thought to herself.

A crescent moon dangled in the sky as if on a wire. Manhattan was spread out before Miriam and David, winking in the distance. Joseph had always told her: Look at zhe lights, zhe lights! And the Empire State, he'd told her. Built just for you. Don't you vant to put the skyline in your little pocket, sugar? Here, he'd say, pretending to scoop it up and hand it to his daughter. She had wanted to keep it. She had wanted to put it in that time capsule at the World's Fair the day her father showed her television. What else had she wanted to keep? Now she wished for a tape of her father's voice, those dried bits of skin, his Irving Berlin scores. Miriam pictured her mother at the kitchen table, fingering the yellow tablecloth, alone. She looked at David again. A lock of his hair, his kiss, a black-eyed Susan, the Chanel gown he loved to watch her zip up the side. When had she not known him?

David watched the road ahead as they headed down the FDR, toward the turnoff to his parents' house. But now of course it was only his father. He could picture his mother tearing through her room, the black embroidered silk robe flying out behind her. His mother at the top of the stairs, singing. "They say that falling in love is wonderful. It's wonderful. So they say."

David looked over at Miriam, who now turned toward the window. Her hair was tied back in a black ribbon, and he could see the nape of her neck, as he had the first time he'd met her, in college. Miriam Brodsky. He wanted to preserve this image of her now, headlights flashing over her features, briefly illuminating her pale, turned face as a flashbulb does, forever, in that time capsule he had seen with his father at the World's Fair. That had been an astounding day, one of the few he'd spent alone with his father. This is hope, son, his father had told him. This is tomorrow. Now David reached for Miriam's hand and squeezed it, and she turned toward him, her face somehow a reflection of his own grief. He smiled at his wife and looked down at her stomach.

At that moment David wanted to write a letter to his child. Before she came into this world red-faced and screaming, he wanted to say something. Say everything. What would that be, and how would it ever be enough?

He looked ahead at the skyline. They had become adults suddenly, only just this moment. The city got closer and closer as they drove along the river, until Miriam and David were in it, surrounded by the uptown buildings and lighted windows, the honking taxis, streetlights.

What will I write? The Brooklyn Bridge hovered in the distance, strung with a million lights. David Bloom turned west, away from the river, toward the park, toward home. I want to be a good father, he thought. I hope that I won't disappoint you.

ACKNOWLEDGMENTS

There are too many people I am indebted to for helping me make this book. To name just a few:

Thank you to my husband, Pedro Barbeito, my soul mate in life and in work.

To my parents, Richard and Judith Gilmore, for never doubting, not in all these years, and to my sister and fellow traveler, Kate Gilmore.

To the late Adeline Seamon Barowsky, who unknowingly started me on my way.

To Stephanie Vaughn, Alison Lurie, Dan McCall, Lamar Herrin, Nina Revoyr, Jackie Dowdell, Drew Bennett, Cornell University, Adam Langer, Elissa Schappell, Kyle Smith, Emily Chenoweth, Daniel Slager, Patricia Barbeito, and Harcourt, for everyone's support. To John Fulbrook, Katie Monaghan, Susan Brown, and all the good people at Scribner.

And to the amazing Harriet Wasserman, my agent, and Alexis Gargagliano, my extraordinary editor. I am still astounded and so incredibly grateful that they believed.

Jennifer Gilmore's work has appeared in magazines, journals, and anthologies including *Alaska Quarterly Review, Allure, BookForum, CutBank, Nerve, Salon,* and *The Stranger.* She works in publishing and lives in Brooklyn, New York.